The Tainted Crown

VOLUME FOUR OF THE
HORSTBERG SAGA

Books by Elizabeth D. Michaels

Horstberg Saga
Behind the Mask (Volume One)
A Matter of Honor (Volume Two)
For Love and Country (Volume Three)
The Tainted Crown (Volume Four)
Through Castle Windows (Volume Five)

The Tainted Crown

VOLUME FOUR OF THE HORSTBERG SAGA

Bestselling author Anita Stansfield writing as

Elizabeth D. Michaels

WHITE
STAR
PRESS

This is a work of fiction, and the views expressed herein are the sole responsibility of the author. Likewise, certain characters, places, and incidents are the product of the author's imagination, and any resemblance to actual persons, living or dead, or actual events or locales, is entirely coincidental.

The Tainted Crown: Volume IV of the Horstberg Saga

Published by White Star Press
P.O. Box 353
American Fork, Utah 84003

Crown painting copyright © 2015 Anna C. Stansfield
Cover and interior design by Epub Masters

Print ISBN: 978-1-939203-60-1
Printed in the United States of America
Year of first printing: 2015

For Smith Jacob

Chapter One
RELATED BY BLOOD
Bavaria—1849

Erich du Woernig glanced in his bedroom mirror and haphazardly raked his fingers through his damp, dark red hair. He was glad for the way the loose curls always seemed to just fall into place, which disguised his need for a trim as much as his aversion to fussing over his own appearance. He glanced at the clock, grabbed his jacket, and hurried out of the room, down the stairs, across a corridor, and up a different set of stairs before he pushed open a door and entered the castle nursery, announcing himself with an exuberance that had become expected of him. More than half a dozen children came running, throwing themselves toward him all at once while he pretended to fall over from the onslaught. He tickled them while they tried to tickle him, and even though he wasn't ticklish, he pretended to be in some form of hysterical agony that made the children laugh and laugh.

Erich's sister, Maggie, who was mother to three of the children, shouted to be heard over the ruckus. "Enough! Get back to your breakfast!"

The children hesitated, not wanting to stop the fun, but Erich nudged them along, reminding them quietly to mind the rules.

"You know," Maggie said to him, "every time you decide to grace the nursery with your presence, it takes twenty minutes to settle them down." She feigned a glare of disgust, but Erich could see the humor sparkling in her eyes.

"They love it," he said. "And so do you."

She let out a childish squeal of laughter as he lifted her briefly off the floor and swung her around gently, taking care to remember that she was expecting a baby, even though the pregnancy was barely beginning. The children all turned to watch while Maggie playfully slapped his arm in some attempt to scold him, but she couldn't hold back more laughter, and the children laughed, too. Erich noticed the nanny watching them discreetly while she overtly fought to suppress laughter of her own. He winked at her and her laughter jumped out. Since she was twice his age, she knew he wasn't flirting with her.

"Now you've disrupted *everyone*," Maggie scolded and slapped his arm again.

"You're a vicious woman, MagdaLena," he said and walked past her to sit with the children on a chair that was far too small for him. They quieted down as he asked his niece, Hannah, about her music lessons; she always loved to talk about music. He then asked Hannah's brothers, Stefan and Gerhard, about their studies and hobbies. He made a point to remain abreast of each of the children's interests and progress in school. He felt a special closeness to Stefan, even though he was careful not to let on in a way that might spur any kind of difficult feelings between the children. He'd been drawn to Stefan since the day he was born, and as soon as the boy had been able to talk, it had become evident that he had much in common with Erich and they understood each other well.

After Erich had spoken to his niece and nephews, he spoke for a minute to each of the other children, all of whom had a parent working among the higher-ranking servants at the castle. Royalty and servants had always played and learned together at Castle Horstberg, and there was a long history of goodness that had come out of the bonds of friendship developed in this very room. There were nurseries elsewhere for younger children—the infants and toddlers—all equipped with competent and loving nannies who were carefully chosen, even though the parents were all involved with the children's care as much as possible. The children, presently enraptured by Erich's attention, would soon be having their school lessons with a tutor who would be arriving within the hour, and the day would be a mixture of playtime and education. He knew the routine well from his own childhood.

When he'd completed his visit and said elaborate farewells that made the children giggle, he paused near the door to have a more serious moment with his sister. "You look lovely, as always," he said. "How are you feeling?"

"I'm fine, thank you," she said.

"And how is that husband treating you?" he asked with mock concern. Since Han Heinrich was Erich's dearest friend and also worked as his highest advisor in all political matters, Erich felt sure he had the right to continually make fun of him if he chose to. "Do you need me to give him a bloody nose to keep him in line?"

Maggie laughed softly. "You know very well he treats me like a queen."

"As he should." Erich winked before he pressed a kiss to her cheek.

"If I'm late for breakfast—or miss it altogether—tell Mother and Father I've gone to see Dulsie and not to worry."

"Is she all right?" Maggie asked.

Erich sighed and looked down, knowing Dulsie would prefer that he avoid repeating any details of the challenges in her life that she had shared with him in confidence. And yet the royal family knew her far too well to not have some awareness and legitimate concern. He sought for an appropriate answer and looked back up at his sister. "She's had a bit of a setback, but I'm certain she'll be fine. I just want to check in on her, and make certain she knows I care."

"She could never doubt that," Maggie said with a sincere smile. "You've always been a good friend to her."

"As she has been to me." He gave Maggie another quick kiss. "I must go. Busy day and all that."

"It always is," Maggie said.

Erich hurried from the room. Even walking briskly and breaking into a run here and there, it still took him several minutes to get to the main door of the castle where he stepped out into the courtyard and breathed in the fresh air of a lovely morning. He crossed the courtyard with an unhurried run and slowed down as he came to the long, well-kept corridor between two rows of fine apartments where higher-ranking military officers and upper-class servants lived with their families. Erich had many friends and acquaintances among the residents of these apartments but none more dear to him than Dulsie Dukerk. She was the oldest child of the Captain of the Guard, and she had been a continual part of his life for as long as he could remember. Lance and Nadine Dukerk were like an uncle and aunt to Erich and his siblings. They had always been around, and it was impossible to imagine life without any member of the family. Dulsie had three younger brothers, although Erich only knew Jacob, the eldest of them, well enough to call him a friend. Still, he was more drawn to Dulsie. They had always been able to talk to each other about anything and everything, and he felt most comfortable with her. Given that he was the heir to Horstberg, and he couldn't go anywhere without everyone knowing who he was, his true friends were few and well chosen. And Dulsie was a choice young woman in every regard.

Erich knocked at the door and waited only a moment before a maid answered and gave him a familiar smile. She was quite accustomed to his frequent visits, and he was glad to see that she seemed to be getting over the typical awe that most people displayed toward him when they didn't know him well.

"How are you this morning, Didi?" he asked.

"I am well. And you?"

"Very well, thank you." He was glad to hear that she'd stopped calling him *Your Highness* every time she spoke to him.

"Miss Dulsie is in her sitting room," she reported. "You know the way."

"Yes, I do. Thank you." He headed up the stairs and down the hall, meeting Dulsie's mother as she came out of the door just as he was approaching it. She closed the door as if to let him know she didn't want Dulsie to overhear whatever she had to say.

"You heard me coming," he said to Nadine, trying to keep the mood light.

"I did," she replied with a smile. "The sound of your stride is unmistakable."

"Perhaps I shall have to disguise it to make your life more interesting." She let out a gentle laugh, but it didn't hide the severity in her eyes and he asked more quietly, "Is she all right?"

Nadine looked up at him with blatant concern in her countenance.

"Has the doctor seen her again?" he asked when she seemed hesitant to answer the first question.

"He has. It's always the same. There is nothing physical that ails her, even though her depression seems to bring with it physical ailments. He said the fatigue and aching in her muscles are real, and we should respect that, but . . ." She sighed deeply. "It's just so difficult to . . . understand." She met his eyes, her concern deepening. "Erich," she whispered, "you have always been so good to her; you know her better than anyone besides her father and me. You know the real reasons for her greatest struggles, even if she prefers not to talk about them. Still . . . maybe she *needs* to talk about them, but she . . . doesn't want to. Perhaps *you* can get her to admit to how deeply this has hurt her . . . and why. You promised her—and me—that you would never tell anyone the whole truth, but now I wonder if we were wrong to try and keep the matter so quiet. It seems everyone in the entire country knows the truth—except certain members of the royal family. How is that possible?"

"Because people say things behind our backs that they would never dare say to our faces," he said, trying not to sound as perturbed as he felt over the idea.

"That's right," Nadine said, "and Dulsie is finding that she is a victim of that very problem, and yet she is *not* a part of the royal family—and so the quandary keeps coming up and causing her grief."

Erich sighed. He understood the implications between her words, but he didn't know that he was any better equipped to help Dulsie than her parents. "I will do my best," he said. "You know I will."

"I know." She squeezed his hand. "You've always been so good to her. Without you, I fear . . ." She cleared her throat gently and Erich was glad she didn't finish the sentence. They both knew to what she referred; there was no need to say it.

Erich kissed Nadine on the brow and said, "I will make her smile if it kills me."

Nadine laughed softly and hurried to wipe a hand over each cheek where tears had fallen. "Thank you. You know where to find me if you need me."

"Yes," he said and opened the sitting room door while Nadine moved on toward the stairs.

Erich entered the room to find Dulsie sitting in a spacious chair near the window, her feet tucked up beneath her skirts. She was undoubtedly beautiful, with dark hair and pale skin—the latter mostly a result of her hardly ever going out into sunlight. But she'd always kept her beauty well hidden by always dressing in dark colors and unfashionable styles, as if she were living her life in some kind of mourning. And her striking eyes were most often turned down, avoiding the possibility that anyone might look into them and see the truth about who she really was. Her parents had raised her well, had taught her to rise above the truth that didn't have to define her. Yet somehow childhood taunts had merged into outward cruelty from others during her youth, and now she considered herself a spinster beyond all hope of finding any kind of real happiness in this life.

"Good morning," he said and closed the door, leaning against it. She glanced toward him and showed a hint of a smile, but she said nothing before looking back toward the window. "Let's run off and join a circus or something," he added, and her smile widened, appearing to do so against her will. "I'll be a clown, and you can train tigers, perhaps."

"I think I'd rather ride an elephant. And I could be its caretaker."

"You would need my help." Erich plopped himself down into a chair that was familiar to him. "An elephant would eat a great deal, and that means a great deal of cleaning up, too—if you know what I mean."

She smiled again. "Yes, I know what you mean."

"So, you would need my help," he said again.

Dulsie looked right at him and said, as if he didn't know, "You can't run away and be a clown or clean up after an elephant. You're the next Duke of Horstberg. You have to stay here forever."

"But you don't," he said more seriously, knowing they needed to acknowledge the heart of the problem. He'd decided long ago he would not avoid the things that troubled her, nor pretend they didn't exist. Even though she rarely commented or shared her own feelings, he refused to ignore the problem. He believed that was one of the biggest reasons they'd remained so close over the years. "Maybe you should leave here; go somewhere else . . . where no one knows. And you wouldn't have to join a circus."

"You say that as if you've never brought it up before."

"Perhaps it wasn't right before now; perhaps this is the time."

"The people I love are here," she said. "Where would I go?"

"I don't know, Dulsie. I just want to understand."

"You *do* understand. There's nothing to say that hasn't been said between us many times before."

"All right, then," he said with an exaggerated sigh, "you must marry me."

She actually laughed, but he suddenly didn't want to be anything but completely serious.

"Dulsie," he leaned forward and took her hand, "why not?"

"Erich," she said in a tone that implied he'd lost his mind, "you've asked me a hundred times at least, and you can ask me a hundred more; the answer will still be the same."

"But . . . this time I really mean it."

"You've meant it before, or so you said."

"I *did* mean it," he insisted, then smiled. "Well, at least once or twice." He tightened his hold on her hand, drawing her attention more fully to him. "But this time I *really* mean it. Marry me, Dulsie. We can make each other happy. You know we could. We are perfectly matched, and we're in a perfect position to solve each other's problems."

Dulsie withdrew her hand and looked away. "Is that reason enough to marry anyone? To solve each other's problems?"

"It could be," he said firmly. "We love each other."

"We do," she said with sincerity. "But not like that. It's never been that way between us, and we both know it."

"But maybe what we have is enough."

"And what?" She sounded mildly angry. "Allow the stigma and shame of my existence to taint *your* family and position? I would never do that to you!"

"I do *not* consider you to be any kind of stigma or shame," Erich said, angry himself. "I don't care what people think; nor should you."

"That's easy for you to say," she snapped. "You cannot possibly know what it's like, when people practically fall to their knees in worship at your very appearance. I can assure you it is quite the opposite with me. You've always been more than kind and gracious with me, Erich. But all of your public appearances with me on your arm have not changed the truth, nor the way people see me. I cannot be the Duchess of Horstberg—even if I wanted to, which I do *not!*"

"Should I be insulted?"

"No. And you shouldn't act surprised. It's not as if you didn't know that. I would bring a curse upon you if I were to hold that position."

"That's ridiculous and you know it!" Erich insisted. "And don't start the argument again about the blood in your veins, because you will never convince me that the worth of a person isn't determined more by the goodness in her heart than by anything else."

Dulsie looked out the window. "And once again we come to the same impasse."

Erich sighed loudly and leaned back in his chair. "What can I do for you, Dulsie? Tell me how I can help and I'll do it. Anything!"

She turned to look at him, her expression softening. "You're very good to me, Erich. If I knew the answer to that question, I would tell you. Because I believe you; I believe you *would* do anything for me. I also believe you need to have the good sense to remember who you are and what your obligations entail."

"I know that very well," he insisted. "I assure you my obligations are not being neglected, nor will they be tainted by our association."

"So you keep telling me."

"Dulsie . . . please."

"Forgive me," she said. "You know I take it out on you because you are kind enough to let me. I know you'll love me no matter what I say or how I say it."

"Yes, that's true. I just want you to be happy."

"And I just need some time."

"Time to what?" he demanded. "Another year or two spent in this room? Looking out the window while the world changes all around you?"

"I did what everyone has been urging me to do for years. I took a risk, I opened my heart, I engaged myself in new social habits and made new friends. And look where it got me." She glared at him as if it might be his fault. And maybe it was. He had certainly encouraged her to do those very things, and she had certainly ended up with a broken heart. "This room is safe," she added, and he sighed again.

After grueling minutes of silence, she said, "Enough about me. Tell me what you've been doing. Distract me."

Erich told her about the children and their antics, but there wasn't anything else to tell her that she didn't already know—since

he'd been there to visit the previous afternoon. He finally declared
that he needed to go; he knew there was business to be completed
before meetings that would take place this afternoon. He hoped
to get away in between to share lunch with Han at the pub. He
kissed her brow and squeezed her hand, then hurried from the
room, wishing that its stifling effect didn't always cling to him.
He felt fresh compassion for her family members who tried so
hard to help Dulsie with no success. He saw Nadine at the foot
of the stairs and wished he had something positive to say that
would ease the concern in her eyes.

"I asked her to marry me," he said with false brightness, "but
again she has refused."

Nadine *did* smile, but it faded quickly. "I dare say you *would*
marry her if she'd even consider it."

"Yes, I would, and I told her so."

"But I fear you would only have a depressed wife, and everything would only be worse."

"Perhaps. That doesn't mean my offer isn't sincere."

"I know." She gave him a motherly hug. "Thank you for your
visits. I'm very grateful."

He offered a wan smile. "If you think of anything I can do . . ."

"Of course. I know where to find you."

He left with a heaviness in his heart that he knew was small
compared to that in Dulsie's. Then he considered the time and
ran across the courtyard, into the castle, and to the dining room
where his family was just finishing breakfast.

"Ah," Cameron du Woernig said wryly, "how nice to actually
see my son at breakfast."

Erich sat at his usual place. "You work with me far too many
hours of the day. I'm certain my being late for breakfast will not
cause you too much grief."

"You were visiting Dulsie," Abbi du Woernig said. His mother
had obviously been told that he was, since she was commenting
rather than asking. And he knew what was coming next. "How
is she?"

"The same," was all Erich offered, and he was glad when Han changed the subject and lightened the mood. His best friend turned brother-in-law was gifted at keeping the struggles of life in perspective with his optimism and humor, and Erich was especially grateful for it now. He also felt grateful for the family that surrounded him. He was glad to permanently be residing with his parents, as well as with Maggie and Han and their growing family. Han's father, Georg, also lived in the castle and shared meals with the family since he'd lost his wife some years earlier. Georg had always been like part of the family, so having him around all the time felt completely natural. And because he was the duke's highest advisor, Erich worked with him as well, and he had a deep respect for Georg's wisdom and intellect, as well as his unending kindness.

Erich was glad for trivial conversation at the breakfast table, and the others hovered there even though they had finished eating. He liked mornings when there were no urgent meetings to get to, even though there was always plenty of work to be done. But the pleasant atmosphere in the room fragmented when Maggie said, "I've been especially worried about Dulsie since Klara told me the most astonishing thing about her. If the servants are saying such things—and believing them—it's no wonder she doesn't want to come out of her room."

Erich tried to ignore the sudden tension in the room and cleared his throat. "Be careful, little sister," he said. "Don't give too much credence to gossip from your lady's maid."

"Klara has been with me since I was a child," Maggie said, "and she is not one to pay attention to idle gossip. She would not have told me if she didn't believe it had some validity."

Erich wondered why Maggie hadn't brought this up when they'd crossed paths earlier in the nursery, but with the children in the room, it likely wouldn't have been a good idea. He preferred that she not bring it up at all, but it was evident she intended to. He strongly suspected what she was going to say, and wished that she wouldn't. But perhaps, as Nadine had said, it would be better if the royal family knew and talked about all of the things that were said about them behind their backs.

"Although," Maggie said, "I can hardly believe it's true. How can we have grown up with her and not have known such a thing?"

Erich noticed the way his parents and Georg became solemnly alert, as if they all knew exactly what Maggie was talking about. *Did they?* he wondered, feeling as incredulous as Maggie. *Could they all have known all this time, and it has never been discussed?*

"I don't consider anything said among us here to be gossip," Maggie continued, "because we're not like that; we're family. But I have to say it. I have to know if it's true."

"So say it," Han said, encouraging his wife, even though he clearly had no idea what she was talking about.

"Well," Maggie seemed hesitant, and almost looked as if she might cry, "Klara said that Dulsie is not Captain Dukerk's daughter by blood, that he married Nadine when Dulsie was a child, and she is one of Nikolaus du Woernig's many illegitimate children."

Han gasped and his eyes went wide. No one else spoke or moved. Maggie looked around at the lack of response from everyone but her husband and declared the obvious. "You knew! You all knew!"

"*I* didn't know!" Han looked at his father. "Is that true?"

"I'm afraid it is," Georg said. "I'm genuinely surprised you didn't know," he added, looking at Han, then at Maggie.

Her quick glance at Erich made it clear that he'd already known, and Maggie jumped on verbalizing the reasons for that. "You knew, as well," she said directly to Erich. "You've been her friend all these years, and you knew."

"Yes, I knew," Erich said. "And you can't be surprised that I would keep such information in confidence."

"No, of course not," Maggie said. "I would never want or expect you to repeat such a thing, but . . . if the servants are talking about it, then . . ."

"The whole country knows," Abbi stated. "That's the nature of being royalty, isn't it? We're always the last to know that everyone knows everything. So we just have to assume that they do."

"I can't believe it," Maggie said and she *did* start to cry. She looked at her father. "She's our cousin, then."

"Yes," Cameron said, but he had an expression that was typical whenever the abhorrent behavior of his deceased brother came up.

"Every bit as much as Nik Koenig," Maggie added, and the hatred she felt for Nikolaus du Woernig's son was evident in her tone. But they all felt that way; he had caused a great deal of grief for all of them. Of course, Nik was a legitimate child to the late Nikolaus du Woernig, even if no one had known of his existence until he'd reached adulthood. But he had proven to be a deplorable person with selfish and destructive motives, much as his father had been. And no one sitting in the room wanted to even acknowledge his existence. But Maggie had stated a fact that had to be addressed, and the temperature in the room had suddenly become colder.

"Yes," Cameron said again, his voice husky with barely suppressed anger.

Erich cleared his throat and drew together the strength to say what he knew needed to be said. Now that the subject had been opened, he preferred to offer some clarity to the situation as opposed to allowing his sister and her husband remain blind to the whole picture. "You must understand," he began quietly, "that Dulsie has a sensitive personality. And people have known the truth since she was a child." He repeated what he'd said earlier to Nadine. "The reality is that people say things behind our backs that they would never dare say to our faces, which means we often don't know what's being said. So, while we might be oblivious to the impact of her paternity, she has suffered greatly for it. Even though I believe she is much stronger than she thinks she is, I can't blame her a bit for not wanting to go out into the world and subject herself to that."

"Nor can I!" Maggie said vehemently and wiped her tears. "I just . . . wish I had known. Perhaps I could have . . . I don't know . . . helped, somehow."

"And perhaps there is simply nothing anyone can do," Abbi said. "We've always loved her as part of the family, and—"

"And she is *literally* a part of the family," Han pointed out.

"Yes," Cameron said again, exchanging a glance with Abbi that seemed to hold some hidden meaning. But Erich felt certain he didn't want to know whatever else he might not know.

"Is that the reason?" Maggie asked Erich, looking directly at him.

"The reason for what?"

"Is that the reason this recent courtship ended so abruptly for Dulsie? Does it have something to do with this?"

Erich heaved a ragged sigh. "Yes," he said and looked down. "It was all going very well with this young man, until his parents got wind of the gossip. When they learned it was *not* gossip but actually true, they did not want their son to see Dulsie any further. Even though he protested, she did not want to be associated with a family who could not set the issue aside and accept her on her own merits. And I don't blame her. Who would want to always have that hanging over them? How could she marry into a family with such an attitude in place?"

"I agree," Abbi said. "As difficult as it is to see her alone, at least she is loved without condition among family and friends. I hope she can find someone who can see past all this nonsense that has nothing to do with her, but we simply have no control over the matter." Abbi then looked directly at Maggie and said, "You must be careful not to behave differently toward Dulsie now that you know. She is sharp and she will sense it. Just be kind and gracious to her as you have always been."

"I can assure you that she doesn't want to talk about it," Erich added. "And she doesn't want attention drawn to the matter. Let's just . . . leave it that."

Maggie nodded and wiped more tears. She was always more

prone to crying when she was pregnant, but it was obvious that her compassion for Dulsie went deep. "I can't believe you all knew," she said again, glancing toward her parents.

"Of course we knew," Cameron said, looking mostly at her. "Nadine had believed—like many other women—that she was married to Nikolaus. He sent her away when she got pregnant, and quickly stopped sending her any financial support. He'd abandoned her long before he died. She finally came here in desperation with her young daughter, and we did our best to help her. Lance fell in love with Nadine—and with Dulsie. He's the only real father she's ever known, and the only one that matters. And that is all that any of us needs to know. Enough said."

Cameron rose abruptly to his feet as if to declare an end to the conversation. The other men did the same, and Erich joined them, not feeling much appetite. A few minutes later they were settled in the office, focusing on the business at hand, but his own thoughts were drawn frequently toward his concern for Dulsie. Would she truly remain a spinster and find nothing in her life beyond what she had now? And he wondered if he too would forever remain single, unable to find a woman who could fill his heart and take on all that was required to stand at his side. A part of him believed that he and Dulsie were truly well matched. But he also couldn't deny her reasons for being opposed to the union. He longed to find the kind of love he knew his parents shared. But he'd been feeling that way for years, and he wondered if it would ever be.

Kathe Lokberg vehemently kneaded the bread dough against the surface of the table, occasionally glancing out the window for any sign of her brother's arrival. Theodor worked on the other side of the valley, and occasionally he took his son, Karl, to stay with him there for a few days at a time. Little Karl lived here in the family home with Kathe and her father—who was also named Karl—since Theodor's wife had died while bringing Little Karl into the world. Kathe knew it was good for the child to be with his father as much as possible, but she missed him when he was gone, and she knew they should have arrived by now.

Her thoughts wandered through sporadic memories while she got the bread into the oven and worked to clean up the mess. She was taking out the freshly baked bread when she saw her brother's horse coming up the long drive, and a minute later Karl burst through the side door of the house, his father right behind him.

"We're back!" Karl shouted and ran toward her.

Kathe wiped her hands on her apron and bent down to hug Karl tightly. "Did you have a good time?" she asked.

He beamed and nodded, announcing, "I'm going to go tell Grandpapa what we did."

After Little Karl had gone back outside in search of his grandfather, Kathe frowned toward her brother. "He'll be spoiled rotten if you keep taking him up there so often."

"The princess's children are well disciplined, I can assure you," Theodor said. "With the way you talk about them, you'd think I was exposing him to leprosy or something."

She scowled and turned back to her work.

"What are you making?" he asked, lifting the lid off a pot to take a deep whiff.

"Stuffed cabbage," she announced. "Get out of there. If I find any evidence that you've been sneaking food before lunch is ready, I'll have you scrubbing floors."

Theodor laughed. "Ooh, you get sassier every day."

"I'm competent. Isn't that what you always tell me? And be glad I am, or you would be in a fix."

"I'm grateful for all that you do for Karl," Theodor said, putting a gentle hand on his sister's arm. "I know I don't say it often, but your sacrifices haven't gone unnoticed."

Kathe smiled. "I love Little Karl. It's no sacrifice."

"I know you do, Kathe. But you have your own life to live. You need to get out more. Do you have any friends?"

She turned away from him defensively. "None worth mentioning. I enjoy what I'm doing with my life."

"Cooking? Cleaning?"

"I spend a lot of my time in the garden."

"Yes, and it's lovely. But there is more to life than that."

Kathe ignored him and moved the pot off the stove, well aware that he knew she wouldn't send him away hungry. "I assume you have to hurry and eat so that you can get back."

"Actually . . . there is nothing important going on for His Highness today; at least not anything that requires a change of clothes. Therefore, I have the rest of the day off."

"How delightful!" Kathe said, and together they set the table for lunch before Theodor went out to their father's workshop behind the house to get him and Little Karl. Kathe enjoyed having Theodor there throughout the remainder of the day, and she was relieved that he didn't bring up anything more about her lack of social exposure. She genuinely didn't care about that at this point in her life, but she wasn't certain how to convince her brother.

The following day, Kathe walked the short distance into town, hoping to get to the butcher's before his best cuts were gone. She would then enjoy looking over the produce and other items set out by the many vendors. Since it was market day, there was always the best quality and variety available.

She left Little Karl in the care of his grandfather and put a basket over her arm in which she would carry her purchases. While she walked at a leisurely pace and enjoyed the pleasant weather, her mind wandered to Theodor's reasons for concern on her behalf. She'd been unable to push it out of her mind as she had in the past, and she wondered if she *did* need a change in her life. At times she nearly felt as if she were Little Karl's mother. But now that he was getting older, he depended on her less and less, and admittedly she felt lonely when he wasn't there. Was that the reason she resented the time he spent at Castle Horstberg? Or did she fear he might actually grow so accustomed to being in the company of royal snobbery that he wouldn't want anything to do with her?

Kathe had never felt any interest in having a social life. She had plenty of years ahead to be concerned about such things. Right now, she was happy to just stay at home and do the things she was comfortable doing. Her father had suggested once that she was afraid to get out in the world, perhaps because of the losses she'd experienced in her life. Maybe that was true. But Kathe didn't care whether or not it was. She was happy and content, and she wanted to be there for Little Karl as long as he needed her.

Kathe wandered idly through the congested market square, lost in her thoughts. She heard some commotion behind her and turned to see two well-dressed men riding slowly through the crowd on horseback. By the way people eased back in awe, she felt certain they had to be members of the royal family, though she couldn't be certain since she wouldn't have known any of them on sight. She could see no resemblance between the two men. They were both equally tall, but their coloring and appearance had no similarities. Kathe paused curiously, trying to comprehend her brother working for these people. She was surprised at the way they interacted amiably with the commoners when she had expected them to just ride through with their noses in the air. She noted that one of the men had curly red hair, unlike anything she'd ever seen before. She recalled that Theodor had told her the du Woernigs had all inherited red hair from the duchess. This surely had to be Erich du Woernig, the heir to the Duke of Horstberg. The duke and duchess only had one son.

Though she remained at a distance, Kathe observed him more closely, trying to imagine her brother being his personal assistant each and every day. Then she recalled that she had seen Prince Erich briefly around the time of Leisl's death, though she'd been far too caught up in her own grief to give the encounter much thought.

Theodor always spoke of Erich as if he'd somehow descended from heaven or something, but he looked awfully ordinary to Kathe;

perhaps far more ordinary than she'd ever imagined. Though she'd never admit it to Theodor, she couldn't deny her intrigue for the prince as she heard him laugh over something an elderly woman said to him. She watched as he bent low in the saddle and pressed the woman's hand briefly to his lips. He smiled, and Kathe became unexpectedly seized by a rush of butterflies. He was adorable. The curly hair and dimpled cheeks nearly made him look like an overgrown little boy. Yet as he straightened in his saddle and eased his mount slowly forward, she was struck with his stature, his majesty, his regal demeanor.

Unnerved by her reaction and the way it contradicted everything she'd believed about this man, Kathe forced her attention away. Her eye was drawn to a young child riding his own horse between the prince and his companion. From his size, Kathe guessed him to be near Little Karl's age, yet his stance and manner constituted someone much older. It was almost incongruous the way he rode the massive stallion with perfect ease. While Prince Erich seemed like a child in a man's body, this boy seemed the opposite. The dignity and presence about him was that of a grown man. His wavy rust-colored hair made it evident he had du Woernig blood. Surely he had to be the young prince born the same year as Little Karl. Seeing him like this, it was difficult for Kathe to imagine the boys playing together at the castle. Kathe felt certain now that the other man riding with them was this child's father, who held some important position worthy of being married to the Princess MagdaLena.

In the few minutes Kathe observed them as they rode past, apparently to some important destination, she couldn't deny feeling something change inside her. Through the course of completing her errands, and all the way home, she wondered about the family her brother worked for, when she'd hardly given them a second thought before. Perhaps it was just seeing them that made them feel real. That night as Kathe prepared for bed, she felt unnerved to find her thoughts still preoccupied with Prince Erich and his young nephew. She gazed out the corner window of her bedroom toward where Castle Horstberg sat at the far side of the valley, and tried to comprehend these people eating and sleeping just like everybody else. Recalling a vivid picture of Erich du Woernig smiling at the old woman, a fresh rush of butterflies seized her. Had she gone mad?

For several days, Kathe found herself fantasizing about Prince Erich of Horstberg. While her mind wandered, she began to question whether or not she was truly content—or if this fear her father had suggested was more real than she wanted to admit. Figuring there was little to be done about it either way, she indulged in her fantasies, certain that every young woman in Horstberg must have had similar thoughts concerning the prince. Knowing she would likely never cross his path, she considered thoughts of him a harmless pastime. But eventually her fantasies became tedious, and she convinced herself that even *if* a prince ever took a second glance at her, he was likely too arrogant and stuffy to make *any* woman happy.

Erich continued to visit Dulsie every morning before starting his typically busy day. He grew increasingly concerned by her darkening mood, until he felt compelled to request some time with both of her parents to privately discuss the matter. Captain Dukerk could be an imposing man, and Erich had certainly seen him in his role as the Captain of the Guard over the years. But just like Erich's own father, Lance Dukerk could set aside his position and be a man, a friend, a husband, and a father. And Erich had witnessed that transformation as well throughout the course of his life. When he sat down with Lance and Nadine in one of the castle parlors, they felt as they often had, more like an aunt and uncle to him, and he knew he could have this conversation with them.

As he had learned to do by working with good and powerful men for many years, he got straight to the point. "I'm growing increasingly concerned about Dulsie, and I'm certain you both must be feeling the same."

"We certainly are," Lance took hold of his wife's hand. "But we feel helpless."

"As we know you do," Nadine said.

"No one knows her struggles more than the three of us sitting here," Lance added, "but we know she opens up to you more than she does to her parents."

"Perhaps," Erich said, not wanting to discredit what very good parents they were to Dulsie. "I keep having a feeling in regard to her that I've tried to push away, but I can't do it any longer. No one knows but us how close we came to losing her when . . ." Erich hesitated to bring up the horrible time when Dulsie had tried to take her own life. His usual visit had saved her—quite literally, when he had found her bleeding profusely. With the help of her parents and a trusted servant, they had been able to stop the bleeding and see her cared for without anyone else knowing. And Erich had to admit now, "I look back and realize that I had felt uneasy for a long time before that terrible day. I can't ignore my feelings now." He noted how Lance and Nadine eased closer together and tightened their grip on each other's hands. "Forgive me if this sounds abrupt, but I really believe she needs to leave Horstberg. It nags at me and I feel conflicted; that's why I haven't brought it up. Her family and closest friends are here, I know. And I know how difficult it would be for you to have her live elsewhere, but . . ."

"But we want her to live," Lance said.

"And not just remain alive," Nadine said with the arrival of tears, "but to have joy in her life."

Lance sighed. "I believe we've both felt the same but haven't wanted to admit it." He and his wife shared a long gaze before looking back to Erich. "Perhaps we needed you to help us make that decision."

Erich felt encouraged by the validation of his ongoing feelings over the matter and went on. "I would miss her dreadfully, as I know you would. But we all want to see her do much better than she is now. I just feel in my gut that she will never be free of what haunts her as long as she remains in Horstberg. For her, the taint exists in *this* country. Elsewhere, it wouldn't matter." He took a deep breath and continued. "I understand Didi has family less than an hour's drive from here that she visits somewhat regularly."

"That's right," Lance's eyes widened slightly.

"Didi is close to Dulsie; she knows everything but cares for her with sincere affection."

"Yes," Nadine said, a mild lilt of hope in her voice as she was apparently picking up on where his idea might be going.

"I suggest that you could possibly arrange for Dulsie and Didi to go live there. I know you have ample resources to get them a home of their own. Let Didi care for her as she does now, as a lady's maid and companion. They can live close to Didi's family but not with them, thus not causing a burden, but they would have support. Didi has mentioned that she herself has more than one male admirer there, and I've seen how her eyes light up when she speaks of such things. She came here looking for work, but I sense she would rather live there. It's not so far that you couldn't see Dulsie regularly, and letters can certainly be sent back and forth often. Perhaps it's the answer. Whether Dulsie remains single or finds someone to settle down with, she can do so in a country where she is not forever tainted with the curse of du Woernig blood."

Erich noticed Lance flinching slightly and feared that his comment had sounded insensitive to Dulsie's plight, but that was the truth of it. And for all that Erich was a legitimate heir and his challenges were entirely different from Dulsie's, he still felt sometimes that it was more a curse than a blessing to be a du Woernig. He loved his family, but he often wished they could be farmers or shopkeepers. It would certainly make life a whole lot less complicated.

There was silence while Erich's words seemed to settle. Nadine finally spoke, "I think it's a brilliant idea, Erich. I'm ashamed that I never thought of it myself. Perhaps I'm too close to the problem to see what now seems obvious." She turned to her husband and asked, "What do you think?"

"I think it's perfect," he said, but with a crack in his voice to indicate that he would sorely miss his daughter. Erich's heart warmed with poignancy and admiration to see how literally Lance had taken on the role of Dulsie's father, and how much he loved her. He thought of the irony of Nik Koenig technically being his cousin, and how much he loathed the man. While Erich respected the sharing of blood, he couldn't deny that family was so much more than that. He could never consider Nik Koenig as family, but he felt that being family well described these good people who had so much love in their hearts.

Lance cleared his throat and composed himself before looking Erich in the eye and saying, "Thank you, son." Erich loved it when Lance referred to him that way; Georg often did the same, and he was honored that these great men would consider him to be like their own son. They had both said as much many times, and for him, the feeling of family was mutual. "I think we should speak with Didi and Dulsie about it right away and not hesitate. I can take a day or two off work and see to arrangements."

"I completely agree," Nadine said, even though her tears made it evident this was a quandary with no ideal solution and she would miss her daughter terribly. She summed it up when she added, "I just need to know that she is happy and that she feels safe."

She sniffled. "I know what it's like to not feel safe, and I don't want that for her. Perhaps we have been selfish in trying to keep her close to us."

"You can't look at it that way," Erich said. "We've all believed that keeping her close *would* keep her safe. But perhaps it's time for a new season in her life."

"I'm certain you're right," Lance said. "Thank you . . . for all you've done for her."

Erich assured them that his friendship with Dulsie had never been any sacrifice for him, and that he would certainly keep in touch with her whether or not she decided to leave the country. He prayed that she would go. In his heart he knew this was best.

He visited with Dulsie's parents for another hour as they talked through many facets of what they felt was best, and they all hoped that Dulsie would be in agreement. They felt that it was best for her parents to propose the plan to her, although they would be honest about having spoken with Erich about it. They promised to let him know if he could do anything.

Erich felt some relief in having shared his feelings with Lance and Nadine. He visited with Dulsie the next morning and found her torn over whether or not to leave, but leaning toward making the change, believing it was a good idea. Didi was all in favor of it. She loved working for the Dukerk family and was especially fond of Dulsie, but she admitted to missing her own family. The idea of being closer to them was thrilling for her.

The following day Erich found Dulsie packing her things and in good spirits. Lance and Nadine had gone with Didi to her home country to see to some arrangements, and they had returned with news that a small home had been purchased, two servants hired to watch after the women, and all other arrangements had been made.

Two days later, Erich was in the courtyard when the last of Dulsie's things were loaded onto the waiting carriage. He'd shared a long talk with Dulsie the previous evening, so they'd already given the bulk of their goodbyes. But he needed to be here to see her off. They'd already promised to write letters regularly, and to visit when possible. Although they both knew that her returning to Horstberg would always be difficult, and his life was so busy and complicated that getting away to see her wouldn't happen very often.

When Erich saw Dulsie approaching with Didi and her parents, he was overcome by an unexpected surge of emotion, and he had to consciously will himself to hold back a hot rush of tears. He knew in his heart that this was best, but they had shared a long and meaningful friendship since they were children, and he knew that nothing would ever be the same between them. He had an urge to beg her to stay and marry him, and to promise that he would imprison anyone who spoke ill against her, but he knew in his deepest self that it wasn't right for either of them, as much as he might want it in that moment.

"I thought we'd already said goodbye," Dulsie took the hand he reached out toward her. The others discreetly kept their distance to allow Erich and Dulsie some privacy.

"You know I couldn't let you leave without being here to see you off," he said, proud of himself for the steadiness in his own voice.

He saw the glimmer of tears in her eyes and a hint in her expression that she almost wished he *hadn't* been here now, if only so they could avoid this moment laden with emotions that felt unbearable.

She surprised him when she threw her arms around him in a tight hug. "You know how I love you, Erich. You're the best friend I've ever had. But it's time for both of us to move on."

"I know," he said, his voice now trembling. "And you know the feeling is mutual."

Dulsie drew back with courage in her eyes and a forced smile. "So, let's just say goodbye and get it over with. I will write to you as soon as I'm settled, and I'll expect a letter back right away. Promise me."

"Of course." He felt stray tears escape his eyes as she kissed his cheek. He kissed hers in return and found it wet.

Erich turned to help her into the waiting carriage, squeezing her hand tightly. He hurried to wipe his tears away before he nodded toward Didi and said, "Take good care of her."

"I will, Your Highness," she said with a nod in return. "I promise."

Erich stood in the courtyard and watched the carriage roll away. Considering how difficult Dulsie's life had been, Erich could only believe that this was a good thing. He drew in a long sigh and forced himself to hurry to his father's office and begin his work for the day, all the while carrying a prayer for Dulsie in his heart.

Within just a few weeks, Dulsie's letters began to get brighter. She was settling in, loving her home, her neighbors, her new surroundings. Didi's family was colorful and kind and welcoming, and all was well. Erich loved the details she shared with him, and he wrote back with nothing new to tell her, but with support and encouragement for the new life she was beginning. He only wished his heart would stop aching over the lack of change in his own life. And he wondered if he would ever find the happiness that he wanted to believe was out there somewhere for him.

Kathe noticed over a number of weeks that Theodor had begun bringing gentlemen friends home with him for Sunday dinner. After it happened the third time, Kathe began to realize he was deeming himself personally responsible for putting some romance into her life. They fought over it more than once, but when her father sat down and had a long talk with her, she agreed to give a particular gentleman a chance. It quickly came to nothing, as did her next several attempts to be gracious and interested in a man.

When Theodor came to visit the day after she had ended yet another potential relationship, she was shocked to hear him say, "Perhaps you should marry the prince. I think the two of you are well suited."

Certain he was teasing, she countered, "If you're trying to say that we're both arrogant and impertinent, I would have to say that is one of the most unkind things you've ever said to me."

Kathe was even more shocked by his genuine surprise. "The prince is neither arrogant *nor* impertinent."

"But I am?"

"You said it, not me," Theodor insisted, and Kathe made a huffing sound and turned her back to him. He chuckled and she felt certain his suggestion about matching her up with the prince was entirely in jest. It had to be! He'd teased her about the possibility in the past, when she'd been far too young to be considering marriage. Even though it hadn't come up for years, he surely had to be joking.

Kathe felt increasingly irritated when Theodor persisted with his new game of teasing her about marrying the prince. She almost wondered at first if he had read her mind even though she'd tried very hard not to think about Erich du Woernig. But Theodor seemed to believe her when she insisted that she wanted nothing to do with royalty and if he brought any of them anywhere near her, she promised to embarrass him.

Every time Kathe saw her brother, he told her that if she didn't stop being so sassy, she would end up an old maid. Kathe told him she didn't care, but in her heart she could no longer deny the truth. She was lonely. And while she was convinced that the most eligible bachelor in Horstberg was not the man for her, she began to wonder where exactly she might encounter the right man.

Chapter Two
THE VALET'S SISTER

Erich drifted to sleep after a typically exhausting day of meetings spent arguing with dignitaries from bordering countries, followed by socials where they interacted as if they were the best of friends. He had a vague awareness that he was dreaming as he found himself wandering through long castle hallways that felt eerily silent and empty. His most prominent feeling was that he needed to find Dulsie, but even in the dream he recognized that he knew Dulsie was safer than anyone else and he envied her being able to leave. He continued wandering the castle halls, aware now that he was searching for members of his family, but he couldn't find any of them. He began to feel panicked. Something was wrong. Then he turned a corner and came face-to-face with Nikolaus Koenig, a specter come back to haunt him from his past. Erich knew that his own life was in danger from Nik's presence, and he still felt a distinct panic over the absence of his loved ones. With no warning, Nik pointed a pistol at Erich and pulled the trigger without hesitation. Erich was thrown backward by the force of the shot and came awake gasping, as if he were truly on the brink of death.

It took minutes for Erich to steady his breathing, and nearly an hour for his heart to return to its normal beat. But morning came and Erich could not convince himself that what he'd dreamed was not some kind of premonition that refused to be left unacknowledged. Nik Koenig had not done anything for years that had implied any threat to Erich or his family members, but a sickness smoldering in Erich led him to believe that their peaceful reprieve was coming to an end. Still, what could he do about it? He considered telling someone about his dream, but he couldn't see any positive outcome to that. It would only upset others, and he preferred to keep it to himself.

Forcing thoughts of the dream away with distractions of daily life, Erich prayed that he would not have any more such nightmares, and that perhaps it was indeed only a dream. Within a few days he could almost go an hour without recalling the dream and its eeriness, and he chose to let those around him only see the lesser but still taxing issues in his life—most especially the fact that he was still single and perhaps doomed to stay that way.

"I heard that people are gossiping about me," Erich declared wryly as Theodor helped him into his coat. Han relaxed and looked through a newspaper nearby, and Stefan sat alongside his father, reading from a picture book.

"Is this meant to be surprising?" Han asked and turned the page.

Erich chuckled and went on. "Dulsie wrote and told me that her mother had been told by their maid, who had heard it from one of the kitchen maids in the castle, who got the news from the miller who delivers grain to the kitchen, who had heard it from his daughter, who is friends with the tailor's son, who—"

"We get the idea." Han tipped down his paper to scowl at Erich, who laughed, which made Theodor laugh as well. Han furrowed his brow and added, "And Dulsie, who lives in another country, is telling *you* about local gossip."

"That's how it works," Erich said.

"How is Dulsie, by the way?" Han asked, going back to his reading.

"Very well, I'm happy to say," Erich said, so glad to be able to say that and mean it. Knowing that she was doing well greatly compensated for her absence. In a way, their friendship had become better through their exchange of letters than it had been in many years, mostly because she was happy and felt emotionally safe.

"What exactly is this gossip that you heard?" Theodor asked as he meticulously brushed any trace of lint from Erich's shoulders.

Erich changed his voice to mimic a woman gossiping. "Prince Erich is now in his thirties and his sister is expecting her fourth child." He changed his tone to imitate a different voice. "What do you suppose is wrong with the boy that he can't settle down and have an heir?" He changed his tone again. "Do you suppose he doesn't take his responsibilities seriously? Do you suppose Horstberg will survive his frivolousness?"

"As my wife would say," Han muttered without moving the newspaper, "it's all a lot of baggage. Let them talk. You'll find someone."

"Not if you don't start looking," Theodor said, and Erich glared at him. "Sir," he added quickly and with a smirk.

"I gave up on it long ago," Erich said. "I had enough of it years back—being paraded around in front of women. If the dear Lord wishes for me to marry, He's going to have to send the right woman my way."

"Do you suppose the Baron Von Bindorf has the right woman for you?" Han asked, setting the paper aside.

Erich snorted a noise of disgust. "That family has been trying to pawn one of their daughters on *this* family for decades. And there is a reason we are barely on speaking terms with them. I will die a bachelor before I would marry one of those wretched girls. They are too much like their father."

"They're very beautiful."

"And that's all," Erich said. "I wouldn't trust them with my laundry."

"I think I liked it better when we were *not* on speaking terms with them," Han said with exaggerated dismay. "But international relations must be attended to."

"Papa?" Stefan asked, leaning against his father's chair, his demeanor bored.

"Yes, son."

"Will Uncle Erich ever be ready to go? Grandpapa is waiting for us. And I'm—"

"Hungry," Han laughed. "Yes, I know."

The child grinned sheepishly, and Theodor said directly to him, "I'll have him fixed up in just another minute."

"Theodor?" Stefan asked methodically.

"Yes?"

"Will you bring Karl to the castle with you tomorrow? Papa said it would be all right."

"I think Karl would be delighted. It's been some time since the two of you have had a chance to play, hasn't it."

"I have a new horse he can ride," Stefan said proudly. "Uncle Erich?"

"Yes?"

"Can Karl and I go riding with you tomorrow?"

"I can think of nothing more delightful," Erich said.

"I can," Theodor inserted.

"Oh, no," Han said, "here we go again."

"Let's have it," Erich said with light sarcasm.

"Have what?" Theodor asked innocently, but his expression betrayed humor.

"Come on," Han said. "Get it over with. Tell him he should meet your sister. They'd be perfect for each other and all that stuff. Then he can give you his regal speech about women that he's already given once today." Han stood up and took young Stefan by the hand. "If you're going to start that, I'm leaving."

"Are we going to the banquet now?" Stefan asked as his father led him from the room. Erich found it quaint that Stefan preferred to attend a banquet with visiting dignitaries as opposed to playing outside with the other children, all of whom loathed the idea of a formal banquet.

"We most certainly are," Han said and left Erich alone to pull on his boots.

"You could at least consider it," Theodor said in a teasing tone.

"I'd consider almost anything to stop your nagging." Erich chuckled. "By the way, just how old is this sister of yours now?"

"Twenty-one," he stated.

Erich stopped for a moment, genuinely surprised. "I was still imagining a child." He laughed. "Is she pretty?"

"Beautiful," Theodor said.

"Now, why should I believe that *you* would have a beautiful sister?" Erich asked.

"You don't have to take my word for it," Theodor said with a laugh. "Come to dinner and decide for yourself."

"I'll think about it," Erich said, rushing toward the door. "Like I told you, I'd do nearly anything to stop your nagging."

A week later, Erich finally consented to meet Theodor Lokberg's sister, but he made him swear not to tell Han or he'd never live it down. He reminded Theodor that he was determined to follow his parents' example. He would marry for love, first and foremost, but she also needed to be capable of holding the position of the next Duchess of Horstberg. He wasn't necessarily optimistic about finding a woman who could fulfill his expectations—whether it was Theodor Lokberg's sister or anyone else.

As Erich contemplated the situation privately, he felt certain this would come to nothing. He couldn't count the times he'd endured dinner with people who had believed that a daughter or sister or friend would surely win his heart. As of yet, no woman had even turned his head. And Theodor Lokberg was a stout, balding man, whose charm was in his personality. He was faithful as a valet and he'd become a good friend, but Erich could hardly comprehend him having a sister who might catch his attention. Not that Erich was concerned entirely with a woman's appearance, but it didn't hurt. All he remembered of Theodor's sister was a gangling girl with stringy hair. Nevertheless, Erich consented to go to Theodor's home in the valley for dinner, if only to get it over with. He'd heard about this sister since she was twelve.

Kathe was furious. "How could you?"

"It's just dinner," Theodor retorted.

"You will not make me believe you invited him to dinner so the two of you could have a friendly chat. You've been teasing me for years about marrying him, and I won't be pushed on some stodgy prince just for the sake of your pride."

"My pride?"

"Yes, your pride. You'd love to have your sister marry into that family. It would be so . . . *prestigious* for you."

"I want nothing but what is best for you. You are the most stubborn little—"

"I learned it from you."

"Erich du Woernig is a nice man. Prince or not, he's just a man. I know him. I know you. I think you'd like each other. Having dinner with him is not going to kill you. After tonight I will do or say nothing more. If fate doesn't take over, fine."

Kathe looked at him sharply to see if he meant it. "Do you promise?"

"Of course," he chuckled. "I only want the best for you, Kathe. You know that."

"But what on earth will I prepare for dinner? I don't know what to feed a prince. And what will I wear? This is insane."

"Believe it or not," he said, "pomp and grandeur mean little to him. Except for certain formal occasions, he rarely dresses differently than any other man, and no matter what you cook, it will be appreciated. You are a marvelous cook."

"You're flattering me." But she couldn't help smiling.

Theodor pointed a finger at her. "And don't you dare embarrass me, little sister, or you'll never hear the end of it."

"I can't make any promises, but I'll certainly *try* not to embarrass you."

"Good enough." Theodor put his arm around her and laughed.

Once Theodor had given her the bad news and hurried back to work, Kathe sat alone in the kitchen for nearly an hour, trying to figure out something worthy of feeding to a prince. While she planned and prepared for their royal visitor, she couldn't help recalling the one time she'd seen him in the market square—and the effect he'd had on her. She reminded herself that he was a prince, and surely every young woman in Horstberg had fantasies about catching his attention. She felt unnerved by her emotional involvement in this escapade—even though she would never admit to it aloud. And while she wished at moments that Theodor had not put her up to this, she couldn't help feeling some anticipation.

In spite of frequent bursts of butterflies somewhere in her middle, Kathe was pleased to have everything under control ten minutes before Erich du Woernig was due to arrive. Her father and Theodor were in the parlor visiting. Little Karl had been threatened into behaving himself. The table was set. Dinner was all but ready to put out. And Kathe felt as presentable as she would get. An hour later their guest still hadn't come.

"This is ridiculous," Kathe insisted. "Come along, Karl." She took the boy's hand. "We're going to eat. I'm not holding dinner another minute—prince or not."

"This isn't like him," Theodor said, following Kathe to the dining room. "He's dependable, I tell you. Something important must have come up."

"Obviously," Kathe retorted, dishing up a plate for Little Karl while her father helped himself and silently observed. "He's probably too arrogant to *really* want to have dinner with people like us. I hope he chokes on whatever he *does* eat for dinner."

"From what I've seen," their father interjected, "young Erich is a good man. I'm certain he'll come."

Kathe made a disagreeable noise and sat down to eat. A minute later there was a knock at the door. Theodor went to answer it while Kathe attempted to calm herself and see that everything was in order. But he returned with only a message, which he read aloud.

"*'Erich sends his regrets. It couldn't be helped. He'll talk to you in the morning.'* It's signed by Han. That's his brother-in-law," he explained.

Kathe gave her brother a look that said, *I told you so,* and they ate in miserable silence.

The following morning, Theodor went to Erich's room early. There were no appointments to be met, but he felt impatient to know what had been so important as to put him in the embarrassing position he'd endured last night with his sister. He entered quietly because it appeared that Erich was still sleeping, but he'd barely closed the door when Erich's voice startled him. "Don't tell me it's morning already."

"It's early yet," Theodor said, unable to help the terse tone. "There's no good reason to get up."

"Then what are *you* doing here?" Erich snarled. He was obviously in a foul mood. While Theodor was contemplating an answer, he added, "You're probably here to beat the devil out of me for missing dinner last night."

"Since you mentioned it," Theodor said, "you certainly put me in the doghouse with my sister."

"Ooh," Erich said, "she must be spunky."

"Quite."

Nothing more was said while Theodor pulled back the drapes and straightened up the room. But he was taken off guard to find blood in the basin, an open jar of salve, some gauze bandaging, and several bloodied rags.

"Good heavens, what did you do to yourself?" Theodor asked.

"I was trying to forget about it," Erich said. "And now you had to bring it up again. Damn thing kept me awake all night, although it doesn't hurt quite as badly as being shot."

Erich explained the whole thing to Theodor while the valet helped him replace the bandage around his hand. Then Erich went back to bed and managed to sleep for a couple of hours, while Theodor did some mending and polished Erich's boots. It was midday before Erich finally got out of bed and got cleaned up, in spite of Theodor's protests.

"Maybe you should just rest."

"I have one thing to take care of," Erich said and left the room.

Once Erich got outside, he felt better. Most of the pain in his hand had subsided, and what little sleep he'd gotten was holding him so far. He just hoped he could get Theodor out of the doghouse.

Kathe looked up from her weeding when she heard a horse coming down the long drive. The animal halted between the garden and the stable, and she shifted her position to see who it might be. She nearly cursed her heart for the way it quickened when the high sun glanced off a head of red curls as the rider dismounted and tethered the horse. He glanced around casually, and she quickly turned back to her work before he saw her.

"Hello," he said.

Kathe barely glanced toward him for a second, only long enough to see that he was dressed in a casual white shirt and dark slender breeches. He wore an average looking waistcoat that was left unbuttoned.

"Hello," she said, focusing intently on her work. "May I help you?" she asked, wondering what on earth he would be doing *here*.

"I'm looking for Kathe Lokberg," he said, taking a step toward her.

"That's me," she replied without turning.

Erich couldn't deny the intrigue that filtered through him as he absorbed the silky, dark braid hanging down her slender back.

He watched her as she lithely came to her feet and brushed the dirt from her calico dress. She finally turned toward him and pulled off her straw hat, saying in a fluid voice, "And you are?"

"Erich du Woernig." Their eyes met and any further introduction stuck in his throat and left him breathless as he absorbed this dark-haired beauty. Surely this wasn't Theodor Lokberg's sister.

Kathe nodded toward him. *This is no prince,* she thought. He dressed and behaved far too normally. "It's a pleasure to meet you, Mr. du Woernig," she said, not wanting to give him the satisfaction of believing she had known who he was.

Erich chuckled, and she noticed the deep dimples in his cheeks and a prominent sparkle in his eyes. "Is something funny?" she asked.

"No one calls me Mr. du Woernig."

"I'm sorry," she retorted tersely. "You must forgive my ignorance. I'm not well versed in royal etiquette."

"Don't apologize. It's actually quite refreshing."

Their eyes met again, and Erich wondered if this was how his father had felt when he'd first seen Abbi Albrecht.

"It is I who must apologize," he said, pushing his waistcoat aside to hook a thumb behind one of the straps of his leather braces. "You must forgive me for not making it to supper yesterday evening. Theodor tells me the meal was fabulous, and I have to assume he was telling me the truth."

"Why is that?"

"He told me his sister is beautiful. He was obviously right."

While Kathe was trying to think how to respond to such an overt compliment, she noticed his other hand was bandaged around the palm. "What happened?" she nodded toward it, grateful for an avenue to change the subject.

"Oh," he chuckled, seeming embarrassed by her attention to it, "actually, that's why I didn't make it last night. I was in such a hurry to finish what I was doing and meet our appointment, I fear I wasn't paying attention. A bottle broke in my hand."

"It's bleeding," she said, noting the deep red stain on the bandage.

He glanced at it as if he hadn't noticed. "I guess holding the reins got it started it again, but—"

"Come inside and I'll fix it for you."

"Oh, that's not necessary. I just—"

"Are you too proud to take some help from a common woman, or—"

"No, of course not." He couldn't help sounding defensive.

"Then come inside and let me get you a fresh bandage. If you have an appointment or something, you'll—"

"Oh, no. I'm not in a hurry. I just don't want to bother you with—"

"Good," she said and started toward the house. He had little choice but to follow.

Kathe ignored the quickened pace of her heart as she held the door open and motioned this man—a prince—into her home. She closed the door and ushered him toward the kitchen. "Have a seat." She indicated a chair next to the big work table. "I'll be right back."

Erich quickly took in his surroundings and felt a coziness that he couldn't quite define. He'd not been inside this house since Theodor's wife had passed away at the time Karl had been born.

When Kathe Lokberg walked back into the room, his blood quickened. He observed her closely, trying to discern the reason. Was it just her simple beauty, or something more? She washed her hands at a water pump, then got some things down from a high shelf. Sitting across the corner of the table, she took his hand. Something came alive in him at her touch. He felt as if he could look at her forever as she carefully unwound the bloodied bandage.

"Merciful heaven," she said when his palm came into view. "What on earth did you do?" The bleeding gash was surrounded by blistered burns.

"That bottle I told you about . . . it had a chemical in it that doesn't react well to human skin."

"So, I see," Kathe said. "Did you have a doctor look at this?"

"Oh, that's not necessary. He's a busy man."

She glanced at him before dabbing disinfectant onto his hand. He took a sharp breath, and she looked up to gauge his reaction, certain he was hurting far more than he was letting on. She smiled from the subtle wrinkle at the top of his nose.

"You don't seem like a duke," she said, turning her attention back to his hand.

"I'm not," he replied. "My father is the duke."

"And you are his heir, are you not?"

"Yes."

"Then you're as good as a duke."

"I hope my father lives a long time."

"I hear he's a good man," she said, and the statement warmed him.

"The best," Erich admitted readily. "His shoes will be difficult to fill."

Kathe folded a clean piece of gauze into a thick pad and pressed it over the cut, holding it there firmly.

"You're very capable, Miss Lokberg."

"Thank you," she said, then wondered what to call him. "If you're not the duke, what are you exactly?"

"Just a prince," he said nonchalantly.

Kathe laughed softly.

"Was that funny?" he asked almost indignantly.

"It's the most incongruous statement I've ever heard. *Just a prince*. It's like saying a tornado is just a breeze." Kathe chuckled again, but when she met his eyes, there was no trace of amusement there. "Did I offend you?" she asked.

"No," he replied with no hint of malice. "I'm quite accustomed to people regarding me with all degrees of deference. But it's difficult to make people understand that while I consider my position an honor and I don't take it lightly, it is also a great burden at times. Having a country on your shoulders is not often a pleasant experience—quite humbling, in truth."

Kathe was stunned into silence. She became somehow lost in his eyes. Reminding herself not to gape, she turned her attention to his hand, briefly lifting the gauze away. When blood oozed from the wound, she quickly put pressure on it again.

"As you can see," he added with a subtle smile, "I bleed red, just like any other man."

"Forgive me. It's just that Theodor talks about you as if you were some kind of god or something. I just expected you to be more . . . dare I say, arrogant?"

His smile deepened. "Maybe I am. You only met me a few minutes ago, Miss Lokberg. You know absolutely nothing about me."

"On the contrary. I know you don't miss appointments without good cause, or without personally making amends. And you don't send for a doctor when you probably should, while I expected you might have one on hand to minister to every mosquito bite."

Erich chuckled.

"You're laughing at me again, sir."

"It's just that you certainly have a high opinion of royalty," he said with gentle sarcasm. "Although, I confess to knowing some people who would not disappoint your assumptions."

"Really? Do tell."

"They don't rule *this* country, thankfully, but I have to work with them on occasion, nevertheless."

Kathe smiled, and Erich felt a giddy lurch somewhere deep inside. *She was incredible.* Following her candid example, he said, "You're not what I expected, either."

"How is that?" she asked, peeking beneath the gauze to be assured that he was still bleeding.

"It's like I told Theodor, why should I believe that somebody like him would have a clever, beautiful sister?"

Kathe looked up in surprise, then she felt herself turn warm from the smile in his eyes.

"Theodor is very sweet," she said in his defense, "most of the time, anyway."

"Yes." Erich chuckled. "He's a good man—and he does good work," he added emphatically. "I would be lost without him."

"He enjoys his work very much," she said. "Though, actually, I don't see him often. You keep him busy."

"Yes, I suppose I do. I understand it's you who has mostly raised Karl. I've often wondered what Theodor would have ever done without you. Losing Leisl was very difficult for him."

Again Kathe had to remind herself this was Erich du Woernig. While she'd imagined him ordering his servants about with little interest in their personal lives, he was well aware of Theodor's circumstances. He even knew the name of a woman who had been dead several years.

"Yes," she agreed, "it's been difficult for all of us. But Karl is a good boy. I've enjoyed helping with him, though I must confess, my father has done the majority of the *raising*. I mostly just keep him fed and out of trouble."

"Which is no small thing."

Kathe ignored the compliment and gently lifted the gauze from his hand to see that the bleeding had mostly stopped.

"That's better," she said, and Erich concentrated on her face as she gently dabbed a sticky salve over the burns on his hand. "Does it hurt much?" she asked.

"Not nearly as much as it did last night," he admitted. "I confess that I hardly slept."

"I can well imagine." She grimaced slightly at the thought. "It may get worse before it gets better when those blisters open up."

"Oh, that gives me something to look forward to," he said with light sarcasm.

Kathe chuckled softly and put a clean gauze pad over the cut before she wrapped gauze carefully around his hand to cover the entire wound and keep it in place. She split the ends and tied them, announcing triumphantly, "There. All fixed."

"Thank you," he said, wondering if he should get up and leave now. He certainly didn't want to.

"You're most welcome," she replied.

Erich took hold of her fingers with his good hand and deftly pressed his lips to her hand. "You are an angel of mercy, Miss Lokberg. It's too bad I didn't find you years ago."

Kathe wondered by the look in his eyes if he was implying a deeper meaning, but she willed her heart to stay calm and convinced herself that he was just being gracious. Diplomacy was no doubt one of the skills he'd acquired through his upbringing.

"And why is that?" she asked.

"There have been many times in my life when your expertise would have been greatly appreciated, if not your bedside manner."

"Do you commonly require medical attention?" She stood to return the medical supplies to a high shelf.

"Only in cases of gunshot wounds, coma, or temporary paralysis," he stated as if he were discussing the weather.

Kathe turned to look at him dubiously. "Surely you're joking."

He laughed as she returned to her chair, but for a moment Kathe saw something vulnerable, almost shy, about him. "Surely you don't want to hear the horror stories of my life, Miss Lokberg. They are quite tedious, I can assure you."

"But you've aroused my curiosity now."

"Perhaps another time."

She tingled from the thought of actually seeing him again. "Perhaps it would give us something to talk about when you come to supper this evening; unless you're busy, of course."

Erich smiled. "Oh, I'm not busy, but you mustn't feel obligated to—"

"I cook supper *every* evening. Feeding one more mouth shouldn't be a problem. Although I can't promise it will be quite as fancy as it was yesterday. I cooked a meal fit for a prince."

"And why did you do that?" he asked impishly.

"My brother told me to expect one."

Erich sighed. "I'm truly sorry about that. I—"

"It's all right," she interrupted. "I understand, really." She smiled. "Are you hungry?"

"What, now?"

"It is well past noon," she reported. "I was going to heat up what was left over. Why don't you join me?"

Kathe nearly expected him to refuse, or at least stammer apologies and excuse himself. But he smiled and simply said, "I'd love to."

Kathe stood up and began pulling items from the icebox. "I'm afraid it's just the two of us. My father took Little Karl fishing for the day. I hope you don't find my company too tedious."

"No chance of that," he said, and she tried to suppress the way her heart reacted. While she noisily dug out the necessary pans, Kathe reminded herself once again that he was a prince. Surely every woman in Horstberg felt intrigued and awed in his presence. And surely he would have no interest in a woman so common.

"Do you want some help?" he asked, coming to his feet.

"Do you *do* that?" she retorted, wishing it hadn't sounded so astonished.

Erich chuckled and proceeded to light the stove without her permission. "There," he said, holding his good hand a few inches above it to test the heat, "that ought to be about right for heating up a meal fit for a prince."

"Thank you." She forced herself to look anywhere but at him.

Feeling suddenly nervous, she was relieved when he said, "If I'm staying a while, I think I'll see that my horse is comfortable; if you will excuse me."

"Of course. The stable is open. Make yourself at home."

By the time Erich returned, Kathe had set dishes out in the dining room and prepared a pitcher of fresh lemonade, and the food was hot enough to put onto serving plates. She returned from taking a tray into the dining room to find him washing his hands at the water pump in the kitchen, taking care to avoid getting the bandage wet.

"It smells wonderful," he said.

Kathe only smiled and picked up the last of it. "If you'll come this way, Your Highness, lunch is served."

Erich smirked and followed her through the door. He gave in to the urge of watching her as she walked, and couldn't recall ever taking such an interest in the sway of a woman's skirts. He marveled at her efficiency as she lit candles on the table, poured out lemonade, and motioned for him to be seated.

"After you," he said, gracefully helping her with her chair.

He sat down across from her, and she said, "We must bless it."

Erich nodded, then listened as she offered a brief but sincere blessing on the food. She reminded him of his mother. They proceeded to eat mostly in silence until he said, "Did it taste this good the first time?"

"Better."

"An accident has never caused me such grief." He smirked.

"Not even the temporary paralysis?" she asked, certain he'd been teasing her about that.

"No, not even that."

"Dare I ask what you were doing with a bottle of some chemical potent enough to do *that* to your hand?"

"I'm a chemist."

"I thought you were a prince."

"Being a prince is my job," he stated with an impish sparkle in his eyes that she realized was common. "Chemistry is my hobby."

"I see," she said, then probed him with questions about it. His enthusiasm about chemistry made his enjoyment evident. Kathe had to admit as she listened to him that her intrigue was settling into something deeper. He was everything she hadn't expected, and she actually liked him. She wondered if he always smiled so much, which gave her ample opportunity to observe the dimples that appeared in his cheeks when he did. More than once he tucked his hair behind his ear with his fingers, or quickly pushed a hand through it. The loose curls of deep red added to a boyish appeal that was starkly contrasted by his overall virility. She could have watched him forever.

"So," she said after a brief lull of silence, "tell me about this coma and . . . whatever else it was you suffered from."

"Gunshot."

"Yes, of course." She smiled. "Gunshot."

"You're determined to have me start bragging about my battle wounds and make a fool of myself, aren't you."

"*Battle* wounds?" she questioned.

"Well, not literally." He leaned toward her and added, "Enough about me. Tell me about *you*, Miss Lokberg."

"There's little to tell. I'm a very common woman."

"By whose standards?" he asked, showing those dimples again.

"This is where I live. This is what I do."

"You're a marvelous cook. And you have a beautiful garden. Theodor told me that you love your garden."

"Yes," she smiled timidly, "I confess that I love my garden."

Kathe was in awe of the endless string of questions he asked that kept her talking about her garden and the trivial aspects of her life. They finished their meal and sat for a long while at the table while she marveled at the genuine interest in his eyes. She reminded herself that she was nothing more than a temporary pastime for a very busy, very prestigious man, but she made up her mind to enjoy his attention while it lasted, and not concern herself with tomorrow.

When silence finally fell, Kathe resisted the urge to just stare at him and rose abruptly from the table. "Oh, look at the time. I'm certain you have important things to be doing that—"

"Actually," he interrupted with apology, "I do have a few things I need to attend to. But I have an appointment this evening that I certainly don't want to miss—if you think you can tolerate any more of my company in one day."

Kathe smiled. "Shall we say seven o'clock?"

"I'll be here. I promise."

Kathe walked Erich to the door where he thanked her twice and told her how delicious the meal had been. When he finally left, she closed the door and leaned against it for several minutes, just trying to make sense of what she was feeling. Recalling that he would return in a matter of hours, she stifled a whoop of excitement and hurried to put things in order.

Erich hurried to the office and found his father there alone. Cameron glanced at the clock. "That was an awfully long errand."

Erich sat down and put his feet up on another chair. "Did you miss me?"

"No, but I was hoping to pawn some of this paperwork off on you. Where have you been, anyway?"

Erich grinned and leaned back. "I was having lunch with a woman."

Cameron pushed his glasses down on his nose and looked at Erich over the top of them. "My ears must be going bad. I'd swear you just said you had lunch with a woman."

Erich laughed and leaned forward. "Let me repeat myself, Father. I had lunch with a woman."

Cameron took off his glasses and tossed them on the desk. "Is she pretty?"

"Almost as beautiful as my mother," he said, lifting his brows quickly.

"Wow," Cameron leaned back and smiled, "she must be incredible."

"She is, and I'm having dinner with her this evening, too."

"Wow," Cameron repeated with a chuckle. "It must be serious."

Erich's expression sobered as he asked, "Do you believe in love at first sight?"

Cameron tucked his hair behind his ear with his finger and chuckled warmly. "You know, I spent weeks trying to convince myself that what I felt for your mother was nothing more than some primeval male thing because I'd been alone for so long before I found her. But one day I just had to admit that I loved her. And I realized I'd loved her the minute I saw her. How do you explain what happens when two people look at each other and they just *know* their lives will never be the same?"

Erich didn't understand why a sudden rush of emotion burned into his eyes. He looked down and managed to blink it back before his father noticed. But as his mind conjured up a clear image of Kathe Lokberg, the emotion inside him intensified.

"I don't know," Erich said, still looking at the floor, "how do you explain it?"

"If I knew," Cameron chuckled, "I wouldn't have asked you. You're the chemist. How do you explain the way some mixtures do nothing while others become volatile?"

"Good analogy. I didn't realize you were such a deep thinker."

"Actually," Cameron admitted, "Georg mentioned it once."

"Well, tell him I said it was a good analogy."

"Where you going?" Cameron asked as Erich stood and moved toward the door.

"I've got to get ready for dinner."

"It's early yet."

"Early? I'm in my thirties, for crying out loud."

Cameron shook his head and laughed.

"Face it, Father," he said, "I'd be useless to you today. I'm afraid you're going to have to manage."

"Get out of here," Cameron said in mock anger. "But don't wait too long to bring her to meet us."

Erich smirked playfully and hurried upstairs. Coming to the top, he stopped suddenly as the long hallway came into view, reminding him of that awful dream. His stomach lurched and his heart quickened with dread. He felt again as if Nik Koenig was haunting him, except that the man was still alive and well somewhere. Were these feelings some kind of warning to Erich that something ominous was going to occur, or was it emotional residue from the trauma that Nik had caused in the past? Either way, Erich didn't want Nik Koenig or anyone else interfering with these wonderful newfound feelings Kathe had brought to life in him. He took a deep breath, forced any negative thoughts out of his mind, and hurried down the hall. He found his sister in her sitting room, sketching.

"What are you up to?" Maggie asked, noting his light demeanor.

"Mags," he said, sitting across the little table from her, "when did you realize you were in love with Han?"

Maggie narrowed her eyes on him. "Erich?" she drawled. "Are you trying to tell me that you—"

"Just answer the question."

Maggie laughed softly. "I think in a way I grew up loving Han. I was just too stupid to recognize my feelings for what they were." Noting the grin that seemed permanently etched into Erich's countenance, Maggie turned to a fresh page in the huge sketch-book propped in her lap.

Erich leaned his forearm on the table and set his chin on it while he listened to Maggie talk on and on about the things she had gradually come to feel for Han through their adventures.

The door opened and Stefan peeked in. "Mother, have you seen . . . oh, there you are, Uncle Erich."

"Did you need something, Stef?" he asked as the child came to stand by his mother.

"No, I was just looking for you."

Erich and Maggie exchanged a knowing smile. It was increasingly evident that Stefan felt drawn to Erich, and there was a definite soft spot in Erich's heart for the child.

"It's Erich," Stefan announced, looking at the partially finished sketch.

"Oh, hush," Maggie scolded lightly. Then she motioned toward Erich. "Now that you know it's you, just put your chin back where it was and keep smiling." She chuckled and added, "The smiling doesn't seem to be a problem. What's going on?"

"I just had lunch with someone," he said as if it were nothing, but the sparkle in his eyes deepened. Combined with his questions, Maggie knew this someone must be special.

"So, tell me," Erich asked, "what made you think you were in love with Nik Koenig?" She saw him shudder slightly from the very mention of the name, but it seemed an important question to him and the happiness of his demeanor quickly returned. "Obviously it wasn't right."

Maggie grimaced. "Oh, don't remind me. I'd rather not talk about it."

"Seriously, Mags. What was the difference?"

"Well, at the time I certainly thought I loved Nik. But when I look back, I know that instead of listening to my instincts, I was ignoring them. He was charming and said all the right things—for obvious reasons. When I learned to really listen to my feelings and hear what they were telling me, I could see that I'd felt good about Han for years, and what I felt for Nik was almost . . . creepy." She shuddered herself.

While Maggie continued sketching, Stefan watched with deep concentration, and Erich briefly searched his feelings. He felt his smile broaden as his heart quickened. There was no degree of *anything* negative in what Kathe Lokberg had already spurred in him. He glanced at the clock. Seven seemed so far away.

"That's really good," Stefan said to his mother. "What are you going to do with it?"

Maggie smiled playfully at Erich. "Maybe I'll give it to the woman your Uncle Erich had lunch with."

Erich chuckled. "Before you do, we'd better be certain she wants to spend the rest of her life looking at my face."

"Who wouldn't when it looks like this?" Maggie turned it around to show him. "It needs a little work yet, but I've got the basic idea." Erich chuckled, and she added, "I'll call it *Erich in Love.*"

"Don't be absurd." Erich stood and ruffled Stefan's rust-colored hair before he moved to the door. "I only met her today."

"I'll get it framed for a betrothal gift," she said. He smirked and closed the door.

"What was that all about?" Stefan asked.

Maggie resumed her work on the drawing, adding details to the curls in Erich's hair. "I'm not certain, Stefan. But perhaps Erich's finally found a woman he could enjoy spending the rest of his life with."

"Do you think he'll get married and have children?"

"Eventually."

"Will they be my cousins?"

"Of course."

"Well, I hope he hurries."

"Why is that, son?"

"Because Gerhard and Hannah are boring."

Maggie chuckled. "Perhaps they think that *you're* boring. Just because you're different from each other, doesn't mean you can't get along."

"I know. They're just boring."

Maggie chuckled again and gave her son a quick embrace. "You're a very special boy, Stefan. One day you're going to do great things."

"Like my grandfathers?"

"Perhaps even greater," she said and he smiled.

Erich went to his room to freshen up and change. He found Theodor there, stretched out in a chair, reading a book.

"Good, you're here," Erich said. "I need to get cleaned up. And when we're finished, you'd best hurry to your father's home."

"Why is that?" Theodor asked dubiously.

"I met your sister earlier. I apologized for last night, and all. She invited me over this evening. Surely you don't want to miss it. You've been waiting for this for years."

Theodor prodded Erich with questions, but he refused to say

anything further. When Theodor left, Erich scowled at the time still left on the clock. It seemed like forever. Impulsively, he went to find his mother.

"Hello," he said, slipping into the library where she was perusing a number of books spread over a large table.

"Erich." She beamed and held out a hand toward him. Erich stepped toward her and took it, easing his arm around her with a firm embrace.

"How's your hand?" she asked gently.

"Better, thank you."

They kissed and she looked up into his face. A smile absorbed her countenance as she said, "What are you up to?"

"What do you mean by that?" He chuckled.

"You're positively glowing."

"What do you think I'm up to? Just guess."

Abbi narrowed her eyes, then her smile deepened. "Have you met someone?"

Erich laughed. "I would swear you can read minds, Your Grace. What makes you think I've met someone?"

"It was just a . . . hunch."

"Well, as usual, you're right. I had lunch with a lovely young woman, and I'm on my way to have supper with her."

"You like her," she said. It was not a question.

Erich laughed again. "I like her very much, yes." His expression sobered and he asked, "Mother, is it possible to believe, so quickly, that she could be the one for me?"

Abbi smiled serenely and urged him to sit beside her. With his good hand in hers, she looked into his eyes and said, "Do you remember the words to that song your father wrote for you?"

"Of course."

"What's the last line, Erich?"

He thought a moment. "A fire burns in my heart."

Abbi placed her hand over the center of his chest. "If you feel it, Erich, it's possible."

Erich couldn't explain the warm chill that rushed over his

shoulders as she continued. "Your father and I have been through some difficult things together, Erich, and we don't always agree, yet there is one thing we have no dispute over. What we felt for each other, right from the start, was more powerful than what it takes to rule a country. I believe all people are entitled to that kind of love, but many don't have the insight or determination to look past pride and fear to find it, or acknowledge it. You are a du Woernig. Your instincts are strong. Your heart is true. Listen to your feelings, Erich, and you will know. However, that doesn't necessarily mean it will be easy. It took me a long time to break through the walls your father had built around himself. I can assure you, however, that such a love is worth waiting for—and worth fighting for."

Erich smiled and embraced his mother again. "You are an incredible woman, Abbi du Woernig. I want a daughter just like you."

"I suppose that's possible." She laughed. "But in the meantime, you'd best get to that dinner appointment."

Erich glanced at the clock. His heart lurched at the realization he could be late if he didn't hurry. "Yes, I'd better. Thank you."

"Have a good time," she called as he hurried toward the door.

Long after he left, Abbi sat in quiet contemplation. She thought of Erich and could nearly feel all over again the childish excitement she'd felt when she'd first acknowledged her attraction to Cameron du Woernig. She laughed softly and returned to her books, grateful for the incredible son she'd been blessed with. She prayed that his future would hold the same joy for him as she'd found with his father.

Chapter Three

JUST KATHE

Erich knocked at the front door, wondering if he'd ever felt so nervous in his life. He recalled many such dinner invitations in the past when everyone had dressed like it was a royal occasion, and he'd been embarrassed to show up in an average dinner jacket. He'd endured many uncomfortable situations, but he'd never been so anxious—even knowing he was dressed appropriately.

Theodor answered the door himself, and Erich felt more at ease as they went together to the parlor.

"You remember my father, Karl," Theodor said as Karl rose to shake his hand.

"Yes, of course." Erich smiled. "It's good to see you again, Mr. Lokberg."

"And you, sir." Karl smiled in return.

"That must get confusing," Erich said as Theodor motioned him to the sofa, "with your son being named Karl also."

"We just call him Little Karl," Theodor said, passing a smile to his father.

"Nice place," Erich said, glancing around at the simple but tasteful decor.

"Yes, it is," Theodor replied. "I enjoyed growing up here, though I spend little time here now."

"How many years has it been since your wife passed away?" Erich inquired.

"About seven."

"And that is how old your son would be."

"That's right."

"You should bring him to the castle with you more often," Erich said. "Stefan really enjoys playing with Karl. Poor kid doesn't get much of a social life. For some reason he doesn't fit in easily with his siblings or the other children."

"You make up for that a great deal, I think," Theodor said thoughtfully.

"I enjoy having Stefan around," Erich said with warmth in his voice. "He and I seem to have much in common."

"Little Karl certainly likes him," Karl said. "He speaks of him quite favorably."

Theodor glanced at the clock and said, "If you will excuse me a moment, I'll see how dinner is coming."

Erich nodded and waved his hand to indicate he was completely at ease, and Theodor left the room.

"Would you like a drink, or something?" Karl asked.

"No, thank you, I'm fine," Erich said. He wondered for a moment how it might feel to be this man's son-in-law. The thought provoked a quiver somewhere inside. He had a difficult time believing that a woman could have such an effect on him so quickly. Was he letting his imagination run away with him? Wondering what Kathe was doing, his nerves increased. He began to wonder if he should be trying to make conversation, but Little Karl came in and rescued him.

"Hello there, Erich." The boy sidled up next to him on the sofa.

"You should show more respect to royalty," his grandfather scolded gently.

"He's fine," Erich insisted. "We're good friends, and . . ." His sentence drifted off when he looked up to see Kathe standing in the doorway. It only took one glance for him to know these feelings had nothing to do with his imagination.

"Miss Lokberg," he said, coming quickly to his feet. "It's been a long time."

She laughed softly as he took her hand and kissed it quickly. Their eyes met and he felt reluctant to let go.

"A long time, yes," she said lightly. "Uh . . . dinner is ready."

At the announcement, Little Karl bounded past them toward the dining room. Erich offered his arm, and Kathe smiled as she put her hand over it. He wondered what right Theodor Lokberg had to have such a stunning sister. Her simplicity was endearing and only enhanced her beauty. No jewels or elaborate gown to impress him. No curtsying before him. But she had a natural dignity and grace that reminded him of his mother.

As the meal commenced, Erich caught a subtle smirk from Theodor. While he tried not to betray what he was feeling, he sensed that Theodor knew: he was head over heels in love.

Dinner was positively the best he'd ever known. The food was great, the conversation better, and the butterflies he felt inside nearly outdid him. Now he knew why he'd waited so long to marry, and he blessed Theodor for his nagging.

Kathe tried not to look directly at the prince throughout the meal. The expression in his eyes overpowered her. She wondered why it had been so easy and comfortable to be with him earlier. But with her father and brother present, she felt certain she did everything wrong. In the hours prior to dinner, she'd tried to convince herself that what she felt was nonsense. But now as she discreetly observed him, chatting casually with the other men but looking often at her, she had to admit that what she felt was real—and it scared her. She couldn't deny that she was emotionally involved—almost against her will. But what made her believe that a man like Erich du Woernig would ever want to share his life with a woman so simple? It was preposterous and she knew it. Still, how could she not delight in the opportunity to be with him? However long this experience might last, she was determined to enjoy it.

When the meal was finished, Theodor stood and said, "Little Karl and I are going to clean the dishes. Erich, you must have Kathe show you the garden. She does it all herself. It's lovely on a summer evening."

"What an excellent idea." Erich rose and held out his arm for her.

Kathe would have been furious with Theodor had she not been feeling this way. As it was, she felt grateful for an opportunity to be alone with Erich.

Kathe placed her hand over his arm, delighted at what just touching him did to her. She led him down the hall to the side door and out into the summer air. The sky was just turning dusky, but there was enough light for her to show him the roses she was most proud of, and they walked together down the stone path while he held her hand possessively against his arm.

When there was no more to see, she sat on the little bench and he sat close beside her. As she became aware of him watching her intently, her heart beat quickly and she tried to avoid his gaze.

"So," she said in an effort to ease the tension, "how is ruling a duchy these days?"

Erich laughed.

"Did I say something wrong?" she asked quickly.

"Heavens no," he replied. "I fear you say everything just right."

"Why do you fear that, sir?" she asked.

"Erich," he said. "My name is Erich."

"Oh, but," she protested, "I'm certain it's—"

"Forgive me," he interrupted, "but I get tired of being called all of the things I'm called. It would be an honor to have you call me just Erich."

"That would be fine," she said soberly, meeting his eyes, "Just Erich."

Again he laughed. Her sense of humor tugged at his heart.

"May I call you Kathe?" he asked. "I don't want to call you Miss Lokberg, or even Katherine. It is Katherine, isn't it?" She nodded. "I'd like to call you just Kathe."

She laughed. "I'll call you Just Erich and you can call me Just Kathe."

He laughed with her, then took her hand into his, and the mood turned serious.

"Tell me you feel it," he said with the confidence of a prince, and Kathe's heart went mad.

"What?" she asked, trying to sound innocent.

"Tell me I'm not insane to believe I'm in love with a woman I just met earlier today."

Kathe met his eyes, searching for sincerity, and her whole being filled with an emotion so peaceful that waves of goose bumps enveloped her.

While Kathe's silence left Erich feeling vulnerable, he was surprised to see tears brim in her dark eyes. She turned away and blinked them back, but she said nothing. Instinctively needing to know where he stood, Erich touched her chin and turned her face toward his.

"Did I say something wrong?" he asked quietly. He hated feeling so exposed and uncertain.

Kathe shook her head and tried to think of something to say. But there were no words to describe what she was feeling, nor this combination of fear and delight. Her breath quickened when he moved a thumb gently over her cheek, then he briefly touched her hair. His face moved slowly toward hers and he closed his eyes.

"Oh, you mustn't kiss me," Kathe said abruptly, then she warmed with embarrassment at her outburst.

"Why not?" he asked in astonishment.

"Theodor is probably watching," she said breathlessly. "He'll never let me live it down."

Erich laughed and pushed his arm around her waist. "Nonsense. I'll fire him if he says a word." He kissed her soft and quick, and then he pulled back slightly to look into her eyes. "Better yet," he lifted his brows, "I'll give him a raise; keep it all in the family."

Kathe's eyes widened from his implication, but he kissed her again and she became lost in the consuming reality of his affection.

She could hardly convince herself this was real as his arms came around her, holding her close. As if she'd lost complete control of her senses, her arms moved by their own will around his shoulders, holding to him as if nothing else existed. He drew back, and she opened her eyes to find him watching her closely. The intensity in his expression was unnerving and she felt suddenly embarrassed.

"Oh, my," she said and shot to her feet, turning her back to him.

Erich scolded himself for being so bold with her so quickly. But it was difficult to hold back feelings that practically consumed him.

"Forgive me, Kathe." He stood behind her and spoke softly. "Sometimes I can tend to allow my position to make me a little overbearing. It's just that . . . what you make me feel is so . . . well, it's difficult to explain."

Although his words warmed Kathe, she doubted she was the first woman to have heard them. Afraid she was only setting herself up for an inevitable fall, she said firmly, "Please don't say things to patronize me, sir. I'm certain that most of the young ladies in Horstberg are quite in awe of you, and are willing to give anything you ask of them at the drop of a hat. But you cannot expect me to fall into line with the rest of them."

It took Erich a minute to absorb what he was being accused of. While his immediate response might have been to get angry or defensive, he reminded himself that she must have her reasons for feeling that way. His behavior with her had not been exactly proper when they'd only met just today.

"I can assure you, Miss Lokberg," he said kindly, "that the opinions or desires of most of the young ladies in Horstberg are of no consequence to me." She made no response, and he gingerly took her shoulders into his hands, whispering behind her ear, "You misunderstand me, Kathe."

"Then perhaps you should make your intentions clear, sir," she said, wishing she could control the eruption of butterflies inside her.

"Erich," he corrected. "My name is Erich."

"Forgive me . . . Erich. Perhaps you should make your intentions clear, *Erich*."

He chuckled tensely. "How does a man explain such things to a woman he's only just met without sounding like an utter fool? I only know that I've never felt this way before, and I want to spend the rest of eternity feeling this way."

Erich felt her shoulders rise and fall as her breath quickened. He sensed some kind of emotion, but her voice was steady when she said, "You're frightening me, Erich."

"What are you afraid of?" he asked, moving his hands down her arms and up again.

Kathe was amazed at his candor, but she fought to keep her wits and just answer the question. "I see no reason why we shouldn't be completely honest with each other. It's hard for me to believe that a man like you would be genuinely interested in a woman like me. There, I said it."

Erich turned her to face him. "What do you mean . . . a woman like you?"

Kathe was briefly silenced by the genuine alarm in his eyes. "Look at me, Erich," she said, though it wasn't so easy to speak firmly when she had to face him. "I'm a common woman."

"I know." He smiled. "That's what I like about you."

"I don't understand."

Erich touched her face with the back of his fingers. "I don't believe in mixing matters of the heart with social status and politics. It's like mixing oil and water. Eventually one always settles beneath the other. My mother has no royal blood, Kathe. My sister married a stablehand."

"She did?" Kathe was genuinely surprised.

He nodded. "Maggie's husband is a good man, and he's well suited to our family. What he was before he married her is irrelevant. They love each other."

Kathe took a step back as the reality of their conversation echoed through her mind. *Love. Marriage. Matters of the heart.* What was he saying? They stared at each other in agonizing silence while she attempted to understand what was happening. They were both startled when Little Karl came running out the door to announce, "Papa says to tell you they're having coffee in the parlor and you should come in."

"We'll be right there, Karl," Kathe said. "Thank you."

Erich smiled and offered his arm. "It would seem we've been unchaperoned long enough."

"Perhaps too long," she said wryly as they walked toward the door.

Kathe was grateful to be released from the conversation. It seemed the confusion of her feelings had only been getting her deeper into territory she wasn't ready to tread. Sitting in the parlor, she was glad her father kept Erich busy answering questions about politics and his family. Occasionally Erich caught her eye from across the room, and she couldn't deny the feelings he spurred in her. Could it be possible he'd been telling her the truth? She could hardly fathom the idea that Prince Erich of Horstberg might feel this same way toward *her*.

Kathe was lost in thought when she heard Theodor say, "Are you with us, sis?"

"I'm sorry. Were you talking to me?"

"I was just wondering if you're busy tomorrow," Erich said.

"Uh . . ." she stammered, wondering if she could tolerate this another day. How could she handle what being in his presence did to her, not to mention his probing questions and bold references? And yet the hours in his absence just today had seemed almost unbearable. "I . . . uh, well . . ." She was so confused she couldn't even talk.

"Oh, she's not busy," her father said, and Kathe glared subtly at him.

"Do you ride?" Erich asked.

"Yes, she does," Theodor answered for her.

"I can speak for myself, thank you." She scowled toward her brother. Then to Erich, "I ride adequately enough, you could say."

"Would you join me in the morning, then?" Erich asked.

"I don't know," Theodor teased, "she could get a bad reputation hanging around with the likes of you."

"No doubt." Erich smirked. "I'd love to have you join me," he added to Kathe. "Provided it's all right with your father, of course." He glanced toward Karl, then set his eyes on Kathe as he took a casual sip from his cup of coffee.

"It would do her good to get out," Karl said.

"Well then, I guess that settles it," Kathe muttered, coming to her feet abruptly. "Come along, Little Karl." She held out a hand toward him. "It's time we got you into bed."

"But I don't wanna—"

"It's already late," she insisted. "Don't argue with me."

Kathe returned to the parlor nearly an hour later to find the men still talking and laughing. She listened quietly as they countered ideas back and forth concerning some national dilemma. Again she was startled when Erich directed a question at her. "What do you think, Miss Lokberg?"

"I fear I'm not well informed on political matters, sir. You'll find me rather ignorant in that respect." She was hoping to convince him that she was not the kind of woman he should be interested in, despite her hope that he was not just idly toying with her.

Erich countered her theory with his easy reply. "Then you would have much in common with my sister."

Kathe managed a smile, and the conversation turned elsewhere. She was both relieved and disappointed when Erich finally left for the night, declaring he'd return in the morning to get her. He hadn't been gone long before she realized that the essence of himself that he'd left behind would make it very difficult for her to get any sleep.

Erich postponed going to bed by every means he could think of. When it couldn't be put off any further, he finally climbed reluctantly into bed, not feeling at all sleepy—exhausted, yes, but not sleepy. The day had been enormous in his eyes, and draining of his strength, but his mind spun in circles over the implications of his already complex feelings for Kathe. How could this be? Every element of logic told him he needed to be cautious and take his time. Still, an overpowering, unexplainable sensation rumbled inside of him with a sense of urgency and impatience. He had to ask himself if the feelings of urgency stemmed from this nagging sensation that Nik Koenig might erupt back into his life and put threats in place against him. Convinced that such feelings were only the residual effect of Nik's behavior years ago, he forced any thoughts of the fiend out of his head and was glad to think only of Kathe. If it was indeed possible to come to love a woman so quickly, and she was indeed the *right* woman for him, then time and caution seemed irrelevant. He'd been raised to use his head, examine logic and reason, and not overlook any important detail. Such tactics were mandatory in managing the affairs of an entire nation. He had also been raised—with equal emphasis—to trust his instincts and act on them, even when they sometimes contradicted all logic. Overall, he'd been taught that the right course was usually the place where his heart and his head could agree and feel at peace. Examining his heart, Erich knew exactly the course to take. Only certain aspects of logic and reason held him back. He wondered if this was one of those times he needed to abandon his tendency to overanalyze a situation and just follow his heart. Or if he was so wrapped up in the natural allure of Kathe Lokberg that he'd lost his mind.

Turning to prayer, he focused on trying to mentally communicate his dilemma to God. He'd also been taught that God would guide his life, and trusting in that guidance was most important of all. His parents had spoken of times in their lives when God's hand had been undeniably evident. Erich needed such undeniable evidence now, and he prayed that God might be merciful enough to show him the right path for his life at this time. Although he suspected that God would most likely let him know that he needed to be patient and give the matter some time—which would come across as no answer at all.

Erich finally slept and awoke with a sharp gasp and a pounding heart. Abruptly wrenched from a state of dreaming into full consciousness, he took a few minutes to slow his breathing and feel the beat of his heart return to normal. His mind frantically tried to recall the dream he'd been experiencing, until suddenly the image of it was so clear that he gasped again and a put a hand over the center of his chest while he attempted to take it in. His tendency to analyze and ponder kept him awake another hour or two before he drifted to sleep again, only to wake up abruptly following a repetition of the same dream. After it happened a third time, he rolled out of bed and dressed, knowing that dawn wasn't far off and that he couldn't possibly go back to sleep now.

Were these dreams the answer to his prayers? Were they the undeniable illumination of the path he should take? He only had to ask himself the question for his heart and head to both immediately agree. In fact, he both felt it and knew it with such certainty that the pounding of his heart returned as if to firmly add an exclamation point to the exactness of what he knew he needed to do. But he also felt the need to talk to someone about it, to share his dreams with a person he trusted. He'd learned long ago that he'd inherited some small degree of his mother's gift of dreams, but never had he dreamed anything with such force and emotion. Not even his eerie dreams of Nik Koenig had affected him so deeply. He'd heard his mother speak of her dreams and the feelings that accompanied them, feelings that made it clearly evident they were not just ordinary dreams but rather portentous in some way, and they needed to be acted upon. Erich now knew exactly what she meant.

Erich quickly considered the members of his family that he knew he could trust enough to share such private and sacred experiences. He was pleasantly reassured to know that he could talk to any one of them about this and feel understood. But in his heart he most wanted to discuss this with his father. He paced long castle hallways, knowing that his father was usually awake very early, yet he didn't want to go to his room *too* early and deny him of much-needed sleep. Erich knew it was common for his father to meet early with Georg and discuss pertinent matters before breakfast, after which the day would typically become very busy and chaotic. Even the servants worked fewer hours than the duke, since the servants worked in shifts, but the Duke of Horstberg was the only man who could make certain decisions, and he also needed to remain informed and aware of every facet of the politics and welfare of his country, and also of his family. And somehow he managed to do it. Erich felt intimidated at the thought of filling this man's shoes someday. So he didn't think about it. He just prayed that Cameron lived to be a very old man, and it would be many years before Erich taking over became necessary.

Finally, when Erich knew the duke would likely be awake, he knocked at his parents' bedroom door. Cameron pulled the door open quickly, already dressed.

"Well, good morning," Cameron said, clearly surprised to see Erich there so early. "Is everything all right?"

"Yes," Erich said. "It's good, actually. I just . . . wondered if we could talk."

"Of course," Cameron said immediately.

Abbi appeared at his side, tying a robe around her waist. "Oh, it is you." She hugged Erich tightly. "Good morning."

"Good morning, Mother." Erich kissed her cheek.

"We are going to take a little walk," Cameron said to Abbi, "and then I'll meet Georg in the office."

"Have a lovely time," Abbi said with a smile and kissed her husband before the two men left the room and walked together slowly down the stairs. They said nothing beyond comments on the weather until they had passed by the officers standing guard at the door of the duke's office.

When they were out of hearing range, they slowed their pace

and Cameron asked, "So, what's on your mind, son? I would guess you didn't sleep well."

"Off and on." Erich got right to the point. "I had a dream." Cameron turned to look at him while they kept walking. "The same dream three times, actually."

Cameron stopped walking, and Erich turned to face him. "Was this a good dream, or . . ." Cameron didn't seem to want to know if it was otherwise. And Erich had no desire to tell him of his haunting dream about Nik Koenig.

"Very good, I think," Erich said, keeping his focus only on Kathe. "But . . . overwhelming."

Cameron motioned toward a nearby doorway, and they entered one of the many parlors in the castle where they could have some privacy. Once they were both seated with the door closed, Cameron said, "Are you going to tell me about this dream, or—"

"If that's all right."

"Of course," Cameron insisted. "From what your mother tells me, they can be difficult to describe, but I am happy to listen and will do my best to understand."

"I knew you would," Erich said.

As if the connection had just occurred to Cameron, he asked, "Is this about the woman you went to see yesterday?"

"It is, actually." Erich gave his father a brief summary of what had happened the previous day, how he felt, and how he'd been praying prior to falling asleep.

"And then the dream," Cameron said with anticipation.

"Yes," Erich said, overcome with a fresh pounding of his heart. "It wasn't terribly complicated—just . . . powerful." He took a deep breath. "I saw the two of us together, and we were surrounded by brilliant light—almost blinding light. It was . . . perhaps . . . unearthly. It felt . . . like heaven. Literally . . . like heaven."

Erich was startled by hearing the sharp breath his father took. Their eyes met and Cameron echoed, "Literally?"

"Well . . . that was the feeling, but I see it to be metaphorical . . . of course."

"Of course," Cameron echoed again, but his brow was creased with a concern Erich didn't understand.

"Is something wrong?" Erich asked. "I just . . . wanted to tell someone about the dream. When I consider how it's made me feel, I don't have any doubt that she is the right woman for me, and I don't feel any need to move slowly just for the sake of propriety or any other reason. Actually, I feel more of an urgency to just . . . move ahead."

"Urgency?" Cameron echoed.

"Are you going to keep repeating what I say, or—"

"Forgive me," Cameron said. "I'm just . . . trying to understand. Your mother has always told me that the feelings that come with her dreams are perhaps more important than the actual dreams."

"Yes, I know."

"So . . . your interpretation of the dream would be . . ." Cameron motioned with his hand for Erich to summarize.

"She is the one, and there is no need for me to stew over it or waste time. I've been waiting for years to find someone to spend the rest of my life with. I'm moving forward. That's all."

Cameron took that in for a long moment before he smiled. "Well, then." He put a hand on Erich's shoulder. "That is wonderful news."

"It is, isn't it." Erich let out a breathless laugh. "Now, I just need to convince *her* that this is right."

"If it's right, it shouldn't take too much convincing."

"Oh, I don't know," Erich said lightly. "According to my mother, you required a great deal of convincing long after she knew it was right."

"True." Cameron laughed, his previous concern completely absent. "But I'm much more stubborn than the average person."

Erich drew in a deep breath. "Wish me luck, then."

"All the luck in the world," Cameron said, his voice expressing the love he felt for his son.

Erich stood up and Cameron did the same. "I suppose I will

see you later, then. Sorry I haven't been much good in an official capacity."

"Oh, you've earned some time off. And don't wait too long to tell me how it's coming along."

"Of course," Erich said.

They shared a quick embrace, and Erich hurried out of the room, but it only took him a few minutes to realize that it was still very early, and he couldn't show up at Kathe's door before breakfast. He returned to his own room, feeling suddenly exhausted from the lack of sleep, but he knew that attempting to rest now would be ridiculous. His mind naturally went to Kathe, wondering how she might be feeling about all of this. He couldn't simply assume that she would be agreeable just because *he* knew the direction that felt right to him. Although he had plenty of evidence that she felt something for him, he couldn't help being disturbed by her evident mistrust of his motives. When his thoughts only confused him, he got cleaned up and left a note for Theodor, telling him to see to the usual and take the rest of the day off.

It was still early when Erich knocked at Han and Maggie's bedroom door, but he knew his brother-in-law would be awake by now, and Han answered the door dressed for the day.

"Good morning," Han said and slipped out of the room.

"I hope I didn't disturb you," Erich said as they started down the hall.

"Oh, no. I need to meet my father in a while. Maggie sleeps late these days. Pregnancy, you know."

Erich nodded his understanding.

"What do you need?" Han asked, especially attentive, as if he sensed something unusual.

"I need some advice, I think. It's about . . . women."

"Ooh," Han teased. "Maggie mentioned that you were asking all kinds of questions. You've met someone?"

"Yes, I have, actually. It's about time, don't you think?"

"I'd say. So, what's the problem?" Han moved into a windowed alcove with a cushioned seat, and they both sat down.

Erich briefly debated over whether or not to tell Han about his dream, but he decided to use this conversation to test his theories with a more practical approach. "I can't deny that my feelings for her have blossomed very quickly . . . and it's difficult to know how to move forward exactly, but . . . I have to be honest with her, don't I?"

"That's a good theory, but such things can be sensitive. There was a long period of time when Maggie had no desire to hear my feelings."

"Yes, but Maggie's a shrew." Erich laughed.

"She's mellowed some," Han said wryly.

"Thanks to you."

"I'm already happily married, Erich. We were talking about you."

"Ah, yes, well . . . it seems that this woman is not necessarily trusting of my motives."

Han lifted an eyebrow. "What did she say?"

"She told me she couldn't believe that I would be interested in a woman like her."

"And what kind of woman is she?"

"She's just . . . a woman. Does my being a prince make that big of a difference?"

"Oh, you're hitting sensitive spots there," Han said, albeit lightly. "Those differences shouldn't matter, but unfortunately to many people they do. However, as long as the two of you are both the kind of people who can put the issue aside and marry for love, it should be irrelevant."

"All right. So, why would she not trust my motives? She implied that I was toying with her, and you know more than anyone that I have *never* toyed with women."

"She doesn't know that."

"She doesn't know otherwise."

"If she really likes you, she's probably *afraid* that you're toying with her."

Erich liked that theory—the liking him part, anyway. But it didn't solve his problem. "So, what do I do?"

"Well." Han thought a minute. "I'm certainly no expert."

"But you went through a great deal to win Maggie's trust."

"And yours, as I recall," Han said impishly.

"And mine," Erich admitted.

"Well, I'll tell you what my father told me. I had to find a way to make it clear exactly what my motives were. That's why I gave your father back the money and refused the job. It would have been impossible for Maggie to blame me of having ulterior motives."

Han looked at Erich closely and asked, "Is it serious, Erich?"

"Serious?" he echoed. "Good heavens, man, if she turns me away now, I'm doomed. I would rather rot in hell than live a day without her."

"Wow." Han chortled. "Well, in that case, I'd say you'd better make your intentions clear. If the woman wants commitment, give her commitment."

"What if I scare her off? We barely know each other."

"I'm certain you can find a way to make your intentions clear without making her feel trapped. If it's right, time is irrelevant. I waited a lot of years for Maggie to come around. She was worth waiting for."

Erich thought of the urgency he'd felt in his dreams that made waiting feel all wrong. But he recalled his mother's words just yesterday, and added more to himself, "Worth fighting for."

"That too," Han agreed.

Erich's mind drifted to Kathe, momentarily forgetting that he wasn't alone, and Han's voice startled him, "You've got it bad, boy."

"Yeah," Erich chuckled, "I guess I do."

"I know just how you feel."

"Yes, I suppose you do." He added severely, "Did you feel this way about Maggie when you were seventeen?"

"Well, feelings are impossible to compare, but I know I was obsessed with her. I was certain I would die without her, and time just didn't make it go away."

Erich sighed. "Maybe I would have been a lot more under-standing about the whole thing if I'd had any comprehension. If you felt like this, it's a wonder you didn't go insane."

"Maybe I did," Han chuckled. "Maggie seemed to think so at times."

"Well," Erich slapped Han's thigh, "I'm glad it all worked out."

"Me too. I swear I love her more every day."

"Even though she's a shrew."

"Ah," Han stood and stretched, "it takes a feisty woman to keep guys like you and me in line. Just think of our mothers."

"Good point." Erich laughed.

While Han was talking business with his father and Erich was waiting for breakfast to be served, Erich thought through the things Han had said as well as the advice he'd received from his parents. He also considered what he'd dreamed in the night and how it had made him feel. By the time he'd finished eating, he knew what to do, and the thought filled him with fresh excitement.

"Where are you off to?" Abbi asked when he rose from the breakfast table.

"I'm going riding with a certain young lady," he said.

Cameron comically pretended to choke on his food. "You're seeing her two days in a row?" he said once he'd pretended that he'd recovered.

"Yes," Erich said mischievously, "I am. I'm not certain when I'll be back, but I know you'll manage without me. I'll make it up to you, I promise."

"Get out of here." Cameron chuckled, and he exchanged a warm glance with his wife as Erich hurried from the room.

Kathe slept little following her evening with Erich du Woernig as her mind vacillated between fear and delight. She didn't know if it was possible to be in love with a man she'd just met, but when she put her fears aside and examined her feelings carefully, she couldn't question what her instincts were telling her. Recalling their conversation in the garden, she was embarrassed by her implication that his intentions were not honorable. On the other hand, a little embarrassment was worth having him know that she would not be trifled with. Still, she couldn't deny that a part of her just wanted to indulge in whatever delight this man might bring into her life. But she also had to admit to a deep fear that all of this was surely too good to last.

Confused and overwhelmed, she finally slept and awoke before dawn with the vivid memory of a strange dream circling in her mind. The implications of all she'd dreamed—combined with all that she felt—made her realize that Erich du Woernig showing up in her life was not just some kind of accident or coincidence. She felt as if she were on the brink of her own destiny, even if she could never find the words to explain how or why such feelings had come to life inside of her. It all felt irrational and ridiculous—and remarkably right. In spite of the strength of her convictions, she reminded herself that there was no reason to think that anything would transpire between them quickly. Or ever, for that matter. She needed to discipline her thoughts and feelings, although she was determined to enjoy her time with Erich and simply remain alert to her instincts.

At the breakfast table, she was surprised when her father pressed his hand over hers and looked into her eyes, saying with resolve, "He's a good man, Kathe. Don't go slamming a door in a man's face before he even knocks on it."

Kathe looked down, unnerved at how her father could read her so well. Were her concerns so obvious?

"I understand how difficult it was for you to lose your mother," he said. "And then to lose Leisl, as well. But you mustn't close off your heart because of it. I miss your mother dreadfully, Kathe, to this day. But she loved me, and I'd not trade a moment with her, even with the emptiness I feel now. It was worth it, and you and Theodor are living proof of how your mother and I felt about each other. Listen to your heart, girl. Maybe he's not the one for you. Maybe he is. And whether you marry a prince or a butcher is irrelevant to me. I just want you to be happy."

"Perhaps I would be more suited to a butcher," she said with a bite to her voice that she knew was an expression of her own nagging doubts.

"Don't underestimate yourself, Kathe. Perhaps His Highness sees in you what I've always seen."

"And what is that?" she asked, both curious and surprised.

"You have a natural dignity that many women simply don't possess. Like your mother before you, I believe you could conquer anything—especially for love."

"Even the next Duke of Horstberg?" Saying it out loud, the convictions she'd felt earlier seemed utterly ludicrous.

"You may have already done that," he said slyly. "With the way he was looking at you last night, I wonder if his heart isn't already lost."

Kathe glanced down timidly. The very thought turned her insides into mush.

"He reminded me much of Theodor when he first brought Leisl home to meet us."

Kathe's expression sobered. "But Theodor lost Leisl. And he swears he'll never marry again. What if I open my heart to a man, and he breaks it? Or even if he returns that love, what if something were to happen to him, or—"

"Kathe," Karl leaned a little closer, "there's no predicting the length of a man's life—or a woman's. And while we need to be prepared for the future, we can't live in fear of it. You must live while you can. Each day that two people spend together is a gift they give to each other. Follow your instincts. Savor the moment. If I had to go back and do it again, there is only one thing I would have changed."

"And what is that?" she asked. Already these feelings awakening inside gave her a bittersweet empathy for her father's loss of the woman he loved.

"I would have taken more advantage of the life around us. Instead of worrying so much about what was proper and what others might think, I would have taken every opportunity to experience something new and wondrous with her."

"But Father," she protested, "he's a prince."

"Yes," Karl smiled, "and a fine one at that. Matters of the heart are not always convenient, Kathe, but if you truly *listen* to your heart, there is no room for regret." He chuckled. "I'm not suggesting you go out and do something foolish, by any means. But you're a good girl. You know what's right. And when you commit yourself to one man, I'd bet that everything else will work itself out somehow."

Kathe thought about the things her father had said as she hurried to put the kitchen in order. She put on her best calico dress, wishing for the first time in her life that she had something finer to wear beyond her Sunday dress, which would likely be inappropriate for riding. Her father had often encouraged her to spend more money and time on herself, and she knew the funds were available. But she'd never seen much point in being so frivolous when all she did was go into town occasionally and work in the garden. But perhaps that was about to change.

With her hair braided down her back, Kathe hurried to answer the knock at the side door, knowing her father was already out in his workshop and Little Karl had gone down the street to play with a friend.

"Good morning," she said and pulled the door open. Just seeing Erich there left her a little breathless. All of her stewing and analyzing dissipated as her heart quickened at just the sight of him.

"Good morning," Erich repeated. "Did you miss me?" he added with a teasing smirk.

"Yes, actually," she said, and his grin broadened. "How's your hand?" she asked, nodding toward it.

"It's feeling much better, thank you, although I haven't actually looked at it today."

Kathe looked closer and recognized the bandage she'd put on it yesterday by the way she'd tied it. "Come in here and let me fix that for you," she scolded. "If you're not careful, it's going to get infected, and then you'd have to put it on your list with gunshot, coma, and . . . what was it?"

"Paralysis," he stated with a quick smile as he sat down in his appointed spot at the kitchen table.

"You still haven't told me about that." She unwrapped the bandage.

"It's all very tedious, I can assure you."

"Surely you're teasing me," she said with a little smile while she dabbed disinfectant onto his hand. She glanced up when he made no response. It wasn't so much the way he shook his head that unnerved her as the look in his eyes when he did. "You can't be serious," she insisted.

"As I said," his voice was toneless, "it's all very tedious, and not worth talking about."

"If you—" she began, but he interrupted her, holding up his good hand.

"I'll tell you about it some other time." He smiled. "Not today."

Kathe wanted to argue. The very idea of his having endured such serious ailments was unnerving, and she wondered why she would feel this much concern for someone she'd not yet known twenty-four hours. He smiled again and she didn't have to wonder. She was falling in love with him—plain and simple. *Falling?* She nearly laughed out loud at the thought. If she was completely honest with herself, she had to admit she'd fallen hard and fast the minute he'd sat down in that chair yesterday.

Within a few minutes she had his hand bandaged up neatly. They walked out to the stable together where he insisted on saddling her horse.

"She's a beautiful animal," Erich commented as he tightened the strap beneath the horse's belly. "My mother comes from horse-breeding people. We take great pride in our horses."

"So I see," she said, admiring his fire-colored stallion.

"Your mount, my lady." He held out a hand for her.

Kathe's hand tingled as it slipped into his. She was briefly uncertain as he bent his knee just underneath the stirrup, but he patted the knee with his free hand to indicate that she put her foot there. She hesitated a moment, then did it, and she felt nearly weightless as he hoisted her into the saddle with ease.

"Where did you learn to do that?" she asked as he put the reins into her hand.

"I grew up riding with my mother and sisters. They're all rather short." He smiled as he mounted, and she realized it was rare that he *didn't* smile.

"Lead the way," she said, and he trotted up the drive and onto the street, riding toward the foothills.

Erich observed Kathe discreetly as she brought her horse up to ride beside him. She'd claimed not to be an avid rider, but it was apparent she had a natural ability. She sat tall in the saddle, her back straight. Her full calico skirt was pulled up just high enough for her to straddle the horse, showing her lace-up boots. The dark braid hanging down her back nearly touched the saddle, and he wondered what her hair might look like if it were free. Being with her only strengthened his resolve, and in spite of the short time he'd known her, there was no question about his intentions. He knew he was doing the right thing. The problem would be convincing her that he hadn't lost his mind.

"A lovely view," he commented as they paused at the crest of a hill and looked back in the direction they'd come.

"Indeed," she said, then nodded toward the castle sitting against the mountain to the east. "You really live there."

"I really do."

"I've been there a few times, but not since Leisl died."

Kathe expected him to talk about the castle. The subject was wide open. Instead he said, "Her death must have been very difficult for you."

Kathe nodded and repeated his admonition from earlier. "Let's talk about that some other time."

Erich looked again across the landscape before them. They could almost see into town from here. "This is a beautiful valley," he said.

Kathe absorbed the depth beneath his words. She wondered how he might feel to know he would one day be solely responsible for a country. "The most beautiful," she added with sincerity. "I love Horstberg."

Erich smiled at her comment. It was the perfect opening for a subject he'd been wondering how to approach. "Enough to bear its name?"

Kathe glanced over at him sharply. His expression told her he wasn't joking, and her heart immediately raced.

"Allow me to reword the question," Erich said, decidedly nervous when she made no reply. Had he misunderstood what he'd seen of her feelings? Had he misinterpreted his dreams? Unable to back down now, he forged ahead with courage, his voice quivering slightly. "Will you bear *my* name?" Not even her eyes flickered. "Will you marry me?" he asked in exasperation.

Kathe felt suddenly so consumed with confusion and emotion, she couldn't face him another second. Not knowing how to react, she dismounted and walked away, but Erich did the same and followed.

"Are you telling me no?" he asked, trying to keep up with her.

"You can't expect me to answer such a question—*now.*"

"When?" he insisted. "If you want me to wait a week—a month—a year—fine. My feelings won't change." He wanted to add some explanation of the urgency inside that made him want to move forward, but he thought it best to stick with one issue at a time. He *knew* his feelings wouldn't change. He just didn't know how to convince her.

"How can you be so sure?" she asked, finally stopping to face him.

Foregoing the complicated version, he simply stated, "Instinct." He tightened his gaze on her and added, "I was raised on it. All my life my parents have told me how it feels to find real love. I've been waiting for it. I won't deny that I've found it."

"Love?" she countered breathlessly, unable to believe this was happening, and stunned to realize how deeply he was validating the conviction and urgency she'd been feeling about Erich that she had no way of articulating. Attempting to assert some practicality, she asked, "And what about my feelings? Do I have no say in this? You can't command me to marry you, Your Highness." She regretted that last sentence when she saw a glimpse of hurt in his eyes.

Erich withstood the bite of her words, not letting them deter him. He was not giving up that easily. He would not *ever* give up. Kathe turned to walk away, but he stopped her, taking her arm firmly. "Look at me, Kathe, and tell me that you don't love me." The widening of her eyes threw the words back at him, and he couldn't deny how crazy he sounded.

"You're taking a lot for granted," she said but turned her eyes downward, as if she was unable to do as he'd asked.

"Look at me!" he insisted. "If you don't feel it, all you have to do is say so and I'll leave you in peace." He felt as if he were lying. He knew he could never abandon what he felt, or the hope of a future with her. Still, his pride bolted forward as he added, "I'm not about to force my affections on any woman—*especially* you." Needing an answer to the question that was making his heart pound and his palms sweat, Erich lowered his voice to an imperative whisper. "Look at me, Kathe, and tell me you don't love me."

Kathe could hear herself breathing and knew that he could hear it too. She looked at him defiantly, wanting to tell him he was being arrogant and presumptuous. But to accuse him of that would be to deny her own relief that he'd been brave enough to give a voice to what she truly felt. Sincerity emanated from his eyes, and she felt herself soften with an undeniable truth that connected somewhere in the space between them. She glanced down again and breathed out the words on a whispered sigh, "I can't."

Erich took a breath of relief as his arms came around her. He closed his eyes a moment, just to absorb the reality, and pressed his lips to her brow.

"How can this be happening?" she asked softly, easing further into his embrace. "I don't understand."

"I don't understand it either, Kathe. But it's right and I know it." He drew back to look into her eyes. "I love you, Kathe Lokberg. It's as simple as that."

Kathe took a sharp breath and reminded her heart to start beating again. She wondered if she was dreaming. Erich du Woernig had just admitted he loved her. *Her.* Good heavens, he'd asked her to marry him! The reality was unnerving and she took a step back as if putting distance between them might help her see this more realistically.

"I'm not sure I can do it," she admitted.

"I'm not such a bad guy." He closed the distance between them and put an arm around her waist.

"It's not that," she said and impulsively touched those red curls. She'd wanted to since she'd first laid eyes on him. "Theodor has spoken nothing but praise of you. It's just that . . ." She hesitated and his eyes narrowed in question. "Erich," she said, "you will be the Duke of Horstberg. That's no life for a girl like me. Look at me. I'm . . ."

"Beautiful," he said when she faltered. "Let me tell you something, Kathe. I believe, because I've seen evidence of it, that good rulers are made of honest, hard-working men, and that's what I try to be. Good marriages come from love and mutual respect. Good marriages make good rulers better. I would require nothing of you as my wife beyond what you have already proven capable of handling. I want to marry you, Kathe, because I love you. This is what I've been searching for, but I wouldn't have asked if I didn't believe that I could make you happy. I'm not saying that life with me would be easy. My father professes almost daily that he would rather have been a blacksmith. But he's given my mother a good life, and they're happy. There are certain responsibilities attached to the du Woernig name, I admit. But I swear by all I hold sacred, with you by my side, I believe we could handle anything."

Kathe was speechless as she stared into his eyes. No matter which direction she forced her mind to go, she couldn't come up with one reason to tell him no that didn't sound shallow and impertinent. If he were a farmer, asking her to work side by side with him in the fields, she would do it. If he were a gypsy, asking her to leave her home and travel the earth with him, she would do it. She never would have believed in love at first sight, that feelings could be so undeniable, so consuming. But now, as she looked into his eyes, she could not deny that something beyond mortal comprehension had drawn them together. Instinctively, she believed that what he had said was true. For Erich du Woernig, she could do anything.

Erich began to feel vulnerable from her silence until his own adoration became overtly mirrored in her eyes. He impulsively went down on one knee and smiled shyly, saying again, "Will you marry me, Kathe?"

She laughed with tears in her eyes. "Yes," she murmured, "yes, I will. I will!"

Erich laughed as he stood and pulled her off the ground, turning around with her until they were both dizzy. He set her feet back on the ground, and they leaned against each other to regain their equilibrium.

"Oh, Kathe," he murmured and took her face into his hands, looking into her eyes as if he might find there the reasons she had changed his life so abruptly and unexpectedly. "I feel like I've waited my entire life for this moment . . . and I don't know what else to say. It's as if . . . I've always lived under the cover of clouds, and the sun has finally come out, but . . ." He laughed again. "I feel crazy, and yet . . ."

"More sane than ever?" she asked, bringing a hand to his face.

"Yes," he said firmly, realizing she meant the words to be applied to herself as well.

"This is not like me," she insisted.

"Nor is it like me," he countered.

"And yet here we are."

"Yes, here we are." His voice softened, and he leaned more toward her, slowly closing his eyes before he pressed his lips to hers. Nothing had ever felt so right and so perfect in his entire life.

Kathe lost her breath as she absorbed their kiss. She opened her eyes to see him gazing at her with the same wonder that she felt. Then he kissed her again, and she marveled at the intensity of his kiss, and more so at her own response. She heard herself moan gently and moved instinctively closer, threading a hand into his hair. He set her lips free only to press his over her face and into her hair.

"I'm not sure I can do it," she said again.

Erich looked at her and grinned. "I'm not asking you to marry me tomorrow. There will be time to prepare. I can assure you there is nothing to be concerned about."

He kissed her again, and what could she do but believe him?

"Come home with me," he whispered. "Right now. I can't wait to show you off."

"Erich," she took a step back, "not now. I'm not dressed to meet royalty."

He laughed. "Before this day is out, my sweet Katherine, you will realize the du Woernigs are just ordinary people."

He took her hand and ran back toward the horses, and she almost believed him. Erich du Woernig was so wonderfully normal that she couldn't question his ability to make her happy.

Kathe caught her breath as they rode up the hill to Castle Horstberg. "It's been so long," she said. "I'd forgotten." She smiled over at him. "I never would have dreamed . . ."

"That you would raise your children here?" he provided.

Kathe nodded subtly, trying not to appear too aghast.

"Well," he smiled with humble pride, "it is a quaint little place. Been in the family for years."

Kathe chuckled. "You are a funny man, Erich du Woernig."

"So I've been told," he said, and they rode beneath the huge arched gate. The horses' hooves echoed in the courtyard, and Erich helped her dismount when a servant came to take the animals to the stables.

"Are you sure I look all right?" Kathe asked as they came through the door.

"You look perfect," he said and stopped to kiss her briefly. "I love you. Don't worry. They will too."

Kathe became breathless as they stepped into the great hall where two huge staircases rose in different directions, with a balcony in between them. She'd never seen this part of the castle before, and she had an overwhelming desire to hover and move slowly, absorbing every detail as if it were a museum. But with her hand in Erich's, she was ushered quickly down a long hall.

"Do you ever get lost?" she asked, trying not to gape.

"Occasionally," he answered quite seriously, and she laughed.

Erich paused before a door where two officers in uniform stood. He greeted them comfortably, and Kathe could hear masculine voices laughing from within the room. He pushed the door open without knocking, and they entered holding hands. Three men came to their feet in unison, all of them as tall as Erich.

Erich savored the lengthy moment of astonished silence as Cameron, Han, and Georg all absorbed the evidence that Erich had brought a woman *here*. He'd never brought a woman to the castle, and he could well imagine what they all might be thinking. In spite of the conversations he'd had with his father and Han earlier, he doubted they had expected him to show up with this woman *today*. He wondered with sweet anticipation how his loved ones would respond to the news he had to share.

Kathe tried not to feel nervous as these men of imposing stature were all clearly taking in her appearance, and not at all discreetly. She squeezed Erich's hand tightly and felt him squeeze back, but her nerves were still on edge.

"This must be serious," one of the men finally said, and Kathe focused on the man who had spoken. She smiled to see a near replica of Erich, the main difference being hair color and age. He had to be Erich's father. She reminded herself that this was the Duke of Horstberg, and she discreetly pressed her arm around her middle to suppress a fluttering deep inside.

"Father," Erich said easily, "I would like you to meet Miss Kathe Lokberg."

"It's truly a pleasure, Miss Lokberg." The duke held out his hand and smiled warmly.

Kathe took it and nodded, and then she whispered to Erich, although they all heard, "Should I curtsy?"

Everyone but Kathe chuckled, and Erich said, "I don't think he'll care one way or the other." He then motioned toward a man near the duke's age and said, "This is Georg Heinrich, my father's highest advisor."

Georg nodded. "Miss Lokberg."

"And this," Erich said, slapping the third occupant of the room on the shoulder, who appeared to be closer to Erich's age but resembled Georg Heinrich a great deal. "This," he repeated, "is Han Heinrich, my highest advisor, and my brother-in-law. And they're all my best friends."

Han, too, greeted Kathe, and she saw him pass Erich a discreet smirk. Once introductions were complete, she glanced around the room and realized she didn't feel as uncomfortable as she might have expected. They all seemed normal enough, and very accepting of her. But when nothing more was said, Kathe's nerves began to rise again.

"We were just going to lunch," Cameron du Woernig finally said to break the silence. "You must join us, Miss Lokberg."

"Splendid idea," Erich piped in.

Kathe looked at him dubiously, but he offered an expression of reassurance, and they all went into the hallway. Erich put his arm around Kathe as they moved toward the dining room, and the others fell in step behind. She could almost imagine them speculating with hand signals, but she was too preoccupied with the thought of eating a meal at Castle Horstberg to worry about it. She was scared to death over what she had yet to face.

Kathe walked into the dining room and immediately saw two women and two children—a boy and a girl—just being seated. They *all* had red hair of varying shades. As they entered, she felt heads turning in her direction, eyes focusing on her. Kathe's nerves erupted all over again as Erich hurried her across the room toward them.

"Kathe, I would like you to meet my sister, MagdaLena Heinrich, but you should call her Maggie."

"Maggie," Kathe said, briefly stunned by his sister's beauty. She couldn't recall ever seeing such a conventionally beautiful woman in her life.

"And my mother." Erich took the duchess's hand and pressed a kiss to her cheek. The gesture warmed Kathe, and she became briefly distracted by it. She was almost startled when he added, "Abbi du Woernig, the Duchess of Horstberg." He smiled as he finished the introduction, "But then, you already knew that."

Kathe nodded, wondering again if she should curtsy. But Erich saved her by putting his arm around her shoulders and adding, "May I introduce Miss Kathe Lokberg."

"It's a pleasure, Miss Lokberg," Maggie said with a smile that reminded her of Erich.

"Oh, please, call me Kathe," she said.

Kathe was pleasantly surprised when the duchess took both her hands and quickly kissed her cheek. "It is so good to meet you, Kathe."

"And you," Kathe said. "I've heard so much about you."

"And I've not heard nearly enough about you." Abbi smiled toward Erich, an overt sense of wonder in her eyes. "I trust my son has been treating you well."

Kathe felt herself blush, but she managed to cover it quickly. "He's been a perfect gentleman."

"Imagine that," Han said with a smirk and kissed Maggie before he helped her with a chair. Kathe noticed then that Maggie was expecting a baby.

Erich introduced the children, Hannah age eight, and Stefan age seven, and he declared there was another child, Gerhard, who was currently down with a cold. He escorted Kathe to a chair and helped her with it before sitting beside her. She thought of him doing the same at *her* home, just yesterday. It was incredible to believe that life could change so quickly.

The duke kissed his wife before they were seated, and Kathe was beginning to understand what Erich meant about being raised with an instinctive desire to find love. It shone from his parents' eyes.

The talk was light and the meal delicious, once she got used to the servants. Erich met her eyes often, and if she felt nervous, he dispelled it with an obvious sparkle of love and excitement.

"So," the duke directed a comment to Kathe, "how long have you been acquainted with Erich?"

Kathe smiled timidly. "About twenty-four hours now."

Erich chuckled, and Cameron added more to Erich, "It's no wonder I've not gotten any work out of you." He smiled toward Kathe. "With such pleasant distraction, who'd want to be working?"

"I'd say he's earned a little time off," Han said. "I took off several months to be with Maggie."

"Ah, but that was hard work," the duke said, and everyone but Kathe chuckled.

"I'll tell you later," Erich whispered.

Kathe whispered in return, "Is he the stablehand that—"

"Are you talking about me?" Han asked lightly.

"Actually, we are." Erich said more to Kathe, "Yes, he used to be a stablehand, but he loves us anyway."

Han shook his head with a comical glare of disgust that made Kathe smile. "There are some things a person can never live down."

A minute later the duchess said, "So, your name is Lokberg. Who do I know that's a Lokberg?"

"You know Kathe," Erich said.

"Besides that."

"Theodor," Erich added. "Kathe is his sister."

Han erupted in laughter, and Erich glared at him.

"Forgive me," Han said, before laughing again until he pressed a hand over his mouth.

"Is something funny?" Maggie asked, seeming perturbed.

"Oh," Han chuckled, "it's just that . . . who'd have believed that Theodor Lokberg would have such a charming sister?"

"My thoughts exactly," Erich said.

"Tell us about yourself, my dear," the duchess said warmly with a sparkle in her eyes.

Kathe wanted to say everything just right, but the only answer she could think of was, "There is little to tell."

"Nonsense." Erich laughed, lifting his glass to her in a gesture of admiration. "She's witty. She's beautiful, as you can see. She's not afraid to put me in my place."

Kathe's eyes widened at this, but his father said, "Very good!"

"She has a beautiful garden," Erich continued. "She likes the roses especially; they are incredible roses. She's also a competent nurse." He held up his bandaged hand and smiled at her. "She's a marvelous cook. She can handle a horse rather well. She's going to be the next Duchess of Horstberg. She's a marvelous cook. Did I say that already? Oh yes, and she loves me."

An awed silence fell over the room as everyone—including Kathe—gaped at Erich in astonishment. He gave her one of his winsome smiles, and her heart quickened. She glanced around the table and saw emotion in every expression—even the children—but she couldn't be certain over the general reaction.

"Abbi," the duke finally said, "I'd swear I'm losing my hearing. Did he just say what I think he said?"

"What do you think he said, dear?" she asked, and a beaming smile broke across her countenance.

"I'd swear he said this woman loves him."

"I think that's what he said, Cameron."

"Is that true, young lady?" the duke asked Kathe. It was difficult to tell if he was teasing or not, and she wondered for a moment if he might be upset over all of this happening so quickly. She could almost imagine him telling Erich he was a fool to marry some common woman he'd only met yesterday.

Kathe felt Erich squeeze her hand beneath the table. With courage she lifted her chin and gave the only possible answer, "Yes, sir, I love him very much."

The Duke of Horstberg broke into a boyish grin that reminded her so much of Erich it made her heart flutter.

Following another brief silence while the reality seemed to sink in, Abbi du Woernig got out of her chair and rushed to embrace Kathe as if they'd known each other forever. Then she embraced Erich and said joyfully, "I knew it would happen. I knew it. She's beautiful, Erich."

The meal was briefly interrupted as Cameron stood also and walked around the table. He embraced Erich, then turned to Kathe and said, "Come here, young lady." She wondered how many women in Horstberg had been hugged by the duke as he put his arms around her with a warm chuckle. She turned around to be hugged by Maggie and then Han. And Georg. And then little Hannah. Stefan didn't seem interested in anything but his meal.

Everyone returned to their seats, and Erich was drilled with questions about their meeting and coming to this decision so quickly. She was surprised when he admitted that Theodor had been teasing him about marrying his sister for years.

"I told you that you should listen to your valet," Cameron said.

Erich looked momentarily astonished, and then he laughed, saying, "That is unbelievable." He turned to Kathe and explained briefly that Abbi's father had worked for a time as Cameron's valet and had told Cameron that he should marry Abbi. Kathe had to admit it was easier to feel that she fit in, knowing the royal family had many common connections.

After the meal, Erich gave her the "brief" version of a tour of the castle. It still took nearly three hours, and she was amazed by the size and grandeur. Late in the afternoon, they shared coffee in the drawing room with Maggie and his mother. Kathe couldn't help feeling in awe of these women, especially the duchess, who was quite literally considered a legend in her own time. She had to consciously remind herself not to stare at them. Both the duchess and her daughter were very beautiful women, but they had an essence about them that was difficult to define. Kathe felt especially affected by Erich's mother and longed to know her better. She tried to remain engaged in the conversation without letting on that this entire situation was completely beyond her ability to comprehend as being real. Then something eerily strange happened. At a moment when Kathe realized she was staring at the duchess and was about to turn away, she realized the duchess was staring back at her. Kathe couldn't force herself to look away.

At first she felt sure this woman was assessing all of the reasons that Kathe was not good enough for her son, and certainly not worthy of following in her footsteps as the Duchess of Horstberg. But Kathe looked deeper at Abbi du Woernig's expression and saw her own awe mirrored there. Kathe was almost moved to tears to feel a silent connection, an immediate bond, with this great woman. It seemed more that the duchess was attempting to figure out what it was about Kathe that had captured Erich's heart. And Kathe could never answer that question. She imagined herself decades into the future and doubted she would even then be able to understand what qualities she possessed that would make her fortunate enough to have won the heart of Erich du Woernig.

Kathe was wondering if they would stare at each other for the rest of the day when the duchess stood abruptly and said, "I think Kathe and I should take a little walk." She offered a smile that put Kathe at ease, and said to Maggie and Erich, "I'm certain the two of you can keep each other company and keep out of trouble for a few minutes."

"I suppose," Erich said, imitating a child who didn't want to be left with his baby sister.

Kathe felt the duchess's hand on her arm, and she was guided out of the room. As soon as they were in the huge empty hallway, with the door closed behind them, they moved at a slow pace, making it evident there was no destination in mind.

"My dear," Abbi du Woernig said, "we have all waited a very long time for this day."

Kathe almost feared that she might suggest she and Erich were moving too quickly, or that perhaps Erich needed to reconsider, especially when so much was at stake. But Abbi pressed her hand over Kathe's where it still rested on the duchess's arm. She looked directly into Kathe's eyes and smiled with perfect serenity. "It warms my heart more than I can say to see that he has finally found the right woman. His instincts are strong and true. I have no doubt that you must be a remarkable woman."

Kathe glanced down, not knowing what to say, and they continued to walk on very slowly.

"I hope that we can become good friends, my dear," Abbi went on. "With this betrothal you are as good as my own daughter now, and nothing could make me happier." Kathe looked up again, once more overcome with that feeling of awe and wonder. "Han was like a son to me from the cradle, so when he married Maggie, he already seemed like my own. Sonia's husband is a good man, but truthfully we barely know him, and they live so far away. I've looked forward to the day when Erich would find the love of his life, knowing that he would bring another daughter into our family." Abbi stopped walking and turned to face Kathe, putting her hands on Kathe's arms. "And here you are!" She smiled, and Kathe felt tears gather in her eyes. "May God bless you in this journey."

When it became evident that Abbi had nothing more to say, but they were still standing there, Kathe spoke with only a subtle tremor in her voice. "You're so kind. I never imagined . . . any of this . . . could happen to me. It's like . . . a dream."

Abbi laughed softly, and they walked on. "Dreams have a way of coming to pass," she said. "Enjoy every good moment of this one. There are many challenges in the life we lead, but it is also very rewarding. And remember that there was a time when I felt very much like you must be feeling. I certainly never would have imagined falling in love with a king, but being the mother of his children has brought me my greatest joy." She laughed again. "It's brought many adventures, as parenting does, but the best times of my life are when matters of state and politics fall to the background and I see that we are a family. Nothing means more than that. And now we are one step closer to being complete."

Kathe could only say, "Again . . . you are so kind."

"I am so glad to have you here," Abbi said, "but I don't think Erich will tolerate my dominating you for long. We should go back."

Walking the other direction down the hall, Kathe hurried to say, "You've raised a fine son, Your Grace. I haven't known him long, but I feel that I know him well. I never imagined that a man could be so . . . humble, and kind, and . . ." she laughed softly, ". . . and funny. He's very funny."

"Yes." Abbi chuckled. "He is, isn't he." She squeezed Kathe's hand. "And you must call me Abbi when we are not in public. Or call me Mother if you like; either is fine. But we prefer to save the formality for other times and places."

"Of course," Kathe said, and they reentered the room to find Maggie laughing over something Erich had just said, a scene that seemed to punctuate what Kathe had just said about him. Maggie smiled at Kathe as if they had always been friends, and Kathe felt that a true friendship with her was only beginning. As Kathe and Abbi were seated again and Erich took hold of Kathe's hand, she marveled at the reality. She had not only found a good man to share her life with, she had been given something she had lost a long time ago: a mother and a sister.

They all continued to visit, and Kathe found herself more relaxed and at ease. How quickly she had come to feel at home in a place and situation where she never could have imagined fitting in at all. Every trivial topic they discussed made her feel all the more drawn to Erich and his mother and sister. She loved to see the way Erich teased them, and she became increasingly comfortable as the women regaled her with funny stories from Erich's childhood. It was evident that he'd grown up much like any other boy, excepting certain requirements of royalty.

"So, where are you off to now?" Abbi asked when Erich rose and took Kathe's hand.

"The dungeon," he said, lifting his brows comically.

Abbi and Maggie both grimaced, but Erich rushed Kathe out of the room before anyone could comment. After traversing a small maze of hallways, they came to a significant-looking door. She watched as Erich looked carefully in both directions, as if to be assured that no one was in sight, before he lifted a vase off of a nearby table and reached beneath the doily on which the vase had been sitting to pull out a key. He carefully replaced the vase and made certain it all appeared as it had before, and she wondered over the precaution. From the same table he took up a lamp which he lit with a match that was also left there. With the lamp in one hand, he used the key to open the door, and he motioned Kathe to pass through. He followed and locked the door behind him with the same key. Kathe wondered again over the apparent security but chose not to bring it up now.

"It's not really a dungeon anymore," he told Kathe as she followed him down a winding stone staircase while he held the lamp high for her to see. She kept her hand on his arm to maintain her balance and wondered what on earth could be worth going down here for. At the bottom of the ancient staircase that seemed to go on forever, Erich opened a squeaky-hinged iron door with a great deal of aplomb, and she could see that inside was a laboratory. She watched with fascination as he proceeded to demonstrate the hobby he'd already told her much about at lunch the previous day.

"So, what's the greatest experiment you've ever done here?" she asked.

He smiled wryly and declared, "I make love potions."

Kathe touched his face and said, "I don't see any need for one."

Erich laughed and kissed her. Kathe relished the moment, enjoying his kiss that was quickly becoming so familiar, while she mentally tallied all that had happened since Erich had stepped into her boring and ordinary life. He looked into her eyes, and she could both see and feel the evidence that he was truly a prince, simply by the way he made her feel like a princess. But perhaps that was how all women felt when a good man made them feel so loved. Prince or beggar, it was love she could see when he looked at her. She had never imagined that she could be so happy.

Erich was thoroughly enjoying Kathe's company and not thinking of anything else when a sudden memory rushed unwanted into his mind. It had been years since he'd been in this room and the door had been slammed shut and locked. His surroundings had filled with smoke, and he'd awakened from a coma weeks later. It hadn't been the only time that his life had been threatened, but in that moment, the memory was so clear that he felt a sudden fear that he was putting Kathe's life in danger simply by having her in this room, even though the room had been kept safe for years. Recalling his dream of wandering empty castle halls and being shot by Nik Koenig, Erich wondered if he was putting Kathe in danger simply by bringing her into his life. The very idea made him sick to his stomach, and he had to force all such thoughts from his mind.

"Is something wrong?" Kathe asked, proving that she was sensitive to his mood even when he was trying very hard to conceal it.

"No." He forced a smile. "But let's go back upstairs. I can assure you there are many rooms in the castle much more appropriate for entertaining the future Duchess of Horstberg."

Erich led her carefully up the stairs where he relocked the door and returned the key to its hiding place. He was glad to take Kathe to a lovely parlor with sun streaming through the windows to illuminate a vase of fresh flowers on the table near one of the sofas. He watched Kathe inhale their sweet aroma and smile. In his heart he prayed that he could give her the life she deserved, and that loving her would not bring upon her anything but happiness and peace. But something deep inside lured him to believe that Kathe's life would be made much more difficult for knowing him and loving him. He reminded himself of his convictions in taking this step to move forward in making her a part of his life. It was right and he knew it. He needed to focus on that and try not to worry over things he could not control. But he wondered if she would be so pleased about becoming his wife if she knew even a portion of what he knew.

Chapter Four
MINGLING WITH ROYALTY

Kathe stayed to have supper at the castle, taking in the experience with the same amazement that had accompanied her throughout the day. With the men present, she had an opportunity to observe them more, and she loved their interaction with each other, with the women they loved, and as a family. One moment Kathe would feel so completely comfortable with these people that imagining her life among them was natural and easy, and the next moment she had to pinch herself discreetly to be certain she wasn't dreaming. She wasn't naive enough to believe that life could ever be like a fairy tale, and yet it seemed very much that way right then. She reminded herself that whatever good she shared with Erich would surely be balanced with many challenges. But for the moment she just tried to relax and take in all that was good. And there was plenty of that! She loved Erich. She loved his family—his parents especially. And it seemed they were more than pleased with Erich's choice of a future wife. For now, that gave her all of the contentment she needed.

After supper, every member of the family personally expressed their delight in meeting her and their hope to see her again very soon. As Erich escorted her down the lengthy main hall of the castle toward the door, he put his arm comfortably around her and asked, "Did you have a good day? You seemed to enjoy yourself."

"Oh, I did," she said with enthusiasm. "You family is wonderful!" She smiled and added, "You have your charms, as well." His answering smile sent butterflies into her stomach.

Erich rode home with her, declaring that he needed to take care of all this properly. Kathe felt a little nervous when she realized he meant speaking with her father about their marriage. He was right when he said that his own family couldn't all be aware of their plans when her own family was not—most especially her father. Kathe couldn't imagine her father having any objection, especially after the conversation they'd shared earlier, but she would be glad to have this over with.

When she and Erich were seated in the parlor with her father, Erich actually seemed nervous. But when he began to speak, she could see no evidence of anything beyond perfect confidence. She wondered if that came from his years of training to be a diplomatic leader. And yet his diplomacy was so genuine, there was certainly nothing false or patronizing in his behavior.

"Mr. Lokberg," Erich said firmly, "I would like to ask for your daughter's hand in marriage."

Kathe was a little taken aback by how Erich had come so quickly to the point, but she saw her father smile slightly. Karl said nothing for a full minute that felt much longer. Erich glanced more than once at Kathe while they waited patiently. She began to feel more nervous than Erich appeared to be, but he smiled at her and took her hand with silent reassurance, as if he knew that there was nothing to worry about.

"You know," Karl finally spoke, "there are some questions I've always figured I'd ask when this day came." He chuckled. "But I don't suppose there's any reason for me to ask what you do for a living."

Erich chuckled as well, relaxing. "No, sir, I would imagine that's pretty clear."

"And I don't need to ask about your family. They're rather well known."

"Yes, I believe they are," Erich replied.

"So, I only have one question." Karl's eyes tightened on Erich. "I know you won't have any trouble providing for Kathe's earthly needs, but will you do everything in your power to always see that my daughter is happy and cared for?"

"Yes, sir," Erich said with confidence. "As long as there is breath in me, I swear to you, she will never see a day without love and security."

"Well, then," Karl grinned, "you have my blessing, young man. But don't expect me to call you 'Your Highness' when I come to visit my grandchildren."

Erich snorted a laugh. "Heaven forbid."

"Do people really call you that?" Kathe asked.

"All the time, I fear," he answered. "Unfortunately it's considered proper and necessary, and I have to put up with it."

Kathe smiled at him, but she wondered what else they would *both* have to put up with that was proper and necessary.

They visited for a while with Karl, and then Kathe walked Erich out to the stable.

"What a day!" He chuckled.

"The happiest day of my life," she said.

"So far," he added and kissed her. And kissed her. And kissed her.

"Yes," she said breathlessly, "so far."

Kathe sat in the garden for a long while after he'd gone, just watching the stars and trying to comprehend the way that Erich du Woernig had changed her life. Nothing would ever be the same again. For a few minutes she carefully reexamined her feelings, her motives, and the enormous decisions she had made today. She had to ask herself if she was being impulsive or foolish, but as soon as the question appeared in her mind, the answers came firmly to confront it. She could never put into words how or why she knew this was the right path for her life, but she knew it with all her soul. And with that knowledge she could go forward and face whatever might lay ahead. With Erich du Woernig at her aside, anything felt possible, and everything felt right.

Erich resisted going to bed, not wanting the day to come to an end. He doused the lamps in his room and leaned his shoulder against the side of the window frame, looking out toward the valley below and thinking only of Kathe. He'd waited for so many years to feel this way, trying to keep believing that it was *possible* to feel this way. And now it had happened—and so quickly. A delighted little laugh escaped his lips, not to be heard by anyone but him. He felt deeply happy, and perhaps more importantly, he felt completely at peace. It was as if his years of adulthood prior to this day had been spent reaching toward these events, even preparing him somehow. And now that he and Kathe were together, with marriage on the horizon, his destiny—whatever it might entail—would fall into place. There was no reason to question his convictions over the matter. He already knew beyond any doubt that he was firmly on the right course for his life to be what it needed to be. And oh, how he loved Kathe! He loved her with all of his soul! With that thought firmly in his mind, and the accompanying feelings warming his heart, he forced away the fears that had confronted him earlier, banishing his frightful dreams and memories as if that might make them never have any viability in the future. Keeping his mind only on Kathe, he finally crawled into bed and drifted into a peaceful, dreamless slumber.

Erich woke early, feeling rested and eager to begin his day. He went for a brisk ride but didn't stay out too long, knowing there was another important conversation he needed to have. He wasn't disappointed to return to his room and find Theodor there, setting out Erich's shaving things.

"Good morning, Theodor," Erich said brightly.

"Been riding early?" Theodor asked.

"Yes, I had to get some fresh air before I go to that stodgy meeting."

While Erich shaved and Theodor laid out his clothes, Erich said, "Have you talked to your sister since dinner the other night?"

"No," Theodor said, becoming more alert.

"How about your father?"

"No," Theodor repeated. "I had the day off yesterday, remember? I spent it with friends. Why?"

"I was just wondering if you thought she liked me."

"It was difficult to tell."

Erich laughed, and Theodor gave him a sidelong glance. "Well," Erich said, "just so you don't have to wonder, she likes me. I was just curious to see if *you* thought she liked me."

Theodor leaned against the bureau and folded his arms. "You saw her yesterday, didn't you."

"All day," Erich said and laughed again. He was really enjoying this.

Theodor grinned with gratification and delight. "It would seem that you like her, too."

"Actually, I'm madly in love, or hadn't you noticed?"

"I suspected that you were impressed."

"Impressed? Oh, my good man"—he paused his shaving to look directly at Theodor—"there is no woman on earth like your sister."

"So, I was right, eh?" Theodor grinned smugly.

"As much as I hate to admit, it would seem I'm going to have to."

"Why is that?"

"Since we're setting a date this afternoon, I really should admit it, don't you think?"

"A date?" Theodor's voice almost squeaked.

Erich laughed again, and then he forced a sober expression and pointed a finger at him. "But don't think for one minute that you can quit your job just because you're my brother-in-law. I need you."

"You're serious," Theodor said a bit breathlessly after studying Erich's expression a long moment.

"Of course I'm serious. I asked your father for her hand last night."

"Well, I'll be damned."

"Oh, no." Erich smiled, but his voice remained very serious. "For this, Theodor, you will be richly blessed, I can assure you. I'm only wondering why you weren't more insistent about this two or three years ago."

"You didn't seem interested," Theodor said, and his tone sobered. "And to be quite honest, I don't think she was ready. She probably would have slammed the door in your face—literally. But that doesn't seem to be a problem now."

"No," Erich grinned and slapped Theodor playfully on the shoulder, "I don't see *any* problem now."

Erich walked into the meeting of the duke's advisory committee to a hearty round of congratulations. He looked at his father and Georg across the long table as everyone was seated. "You're a bunch of old gossips," Erich said.

The men all laughed, and Han leaned toward Erich, whispering slyly, "How does she kiss? Is it good?"

Erich chuckled and relished in the bubbling that erupted inside of him at the thought. "Oh, mercy yes!" he replied, and the meeting got underway. Erich tried to be attentive, but it was difficult to keep his eyes off the clock. He'd never found a meeting so tedious in his entire life.

In the middle of the afternoon, Kathe walked through the garden to her father's woodshop to take him a message that had just arrived. She stopped in the doorway when she saw Erich sitting on a stool with his booted feet on one of the workbenches, as if he'd been there for hours.

"You have a beautiful daughter," he said, smiling at Kathe, her father still unaware of her presence.

"Yes, I do. She looks much like her mother."

"Tell me, is she available?"

"I'm afraid not." Karl chuckled. "She's betrothed to some scoundrel."

Erich laughed and put his hands behind his head. "Tell me where to find the rogue and I'll challenge him to a duel."

"You are a funny man," Kathe said, and Karl looked up in surprise.

"So you keep telling me." Erich put his feet down and rose to greet her with a quick kiss. Kathe caught her breath to see that he was dressed differently. His boots and breeches were the same style, though much finer than what he'd worn yesterday. He wore a fitted striped waistcoat over a cream-colored shirt, and a satiny cravat was neatly tied around the shirt's high collar. The effect was almost heart-stopping. He was so handsome she could have spent the day just looking at him.

"Hello, my dear," Karl said to Kathe when she pulled herself away from Erich to kiss her father as well.

"Here's a message for you. It's about that custom order for Mrs. Dermer, I think."

"Thank you," Karl said and opened the folded paper to read it.

"How long have you been here?" she asked Erich as he put his arms around her and momentarily lifted her off the floor.

"Not long enough," he replied, "which is roughly around an hour or so. I've just been learning a few tricks of the trade." He nodded toward the workbench where Karl sat. "Your father's a genius."

"Yes, I know."

"So, what are you going to do now?" Karl asked, turning in his chair.

"I was thinking of starting some gossip, if Kathe is willing."

"Exactly how do we go about that?" she asked, not certain whether she liked the idea—whatever it may be.

"Well, you see, we go into town together. It's market day, you know, which is especially advantageous for gossip-mongers. We walk around, buy a few things—holding hands, of course. And before sundown, everyone in Horstberg will know that"—he raised his voice to mimic the probable gossip—"*Prince Erich is in love.* Although," he added more seriously, "I really just want to show you off; that's all."

Erich became concerned when her expression fell. "What's the matter?"

"I . . . I can't go into public . . . with *you.*"

Karl looked at her in astonishment. Erich asked lightly, "Are you embarrassed to be seen with me?"

"Don't be silly. Of course not. It's just that I . . ."

"You what?" her father asked when she faltered.

"I . . . I don't have anything suitable to wear to be seen in public with a prince."

"What you wear is absolutely irrelevant, Katherine, I can assure you," Erich insisted. "You look fine. Let's go."

"I've been cleaning house. I can't—"

"Kathe," her father interrupted gently, "your Sunday dress would do well, I think. There's no need to upset yourself."

"There, you see," Erich said. "Your Sunday dress would do well. Listen to your father."

Kathe sighed in exasperation and went into the house to change.

"Perhaps I'm being too overbearing," Erich said when she was gone.

"I think you're terribly good for her," Karl replied, concentrating on a tiny wood carving. "She became awfully reclusive when she lost her mother. It got a little better when Leisl moved in. She took Kathe under her wing, and they did things together. But when we lost Leisl . . ." Karl shook his head. "Well, Kathe just took over raising that baby. She's had a few gentleman callers now and then, but I think she scared them off; afraid of getting her heart broken again, I'd guess."

"Well," Erich chuckled, "I'm certainly *glad* she scared them off. I should have married her a long time ago."

Karl didn't move his eyes from his work, but Erich saw him smile. "You know, Erich," he said, and Erich liked the way he already felt like family to this man, "I'm certain you would buy her anything she needs or wants, and by all means, you should. I just want you to know that her lack of wardrobe is her own choosing. In truth, it's been an issue between us. I say she should take some money and buy herself something new now and then. She says it's silly to waste money on such frivolity."

Erich chuckled. He could well imagine her saying it just that way. Karl looked up at Erich. "Maybe *you* could get her to take some interest in being a lady. She's grown up with far too much masculine influence."

"There are certain social requirements that go along with me—or rather my position. But I don't want her to feel that she has to change herself for me. I just want her to feel comfortable. Perhaps I can turn her over to my mother and sister for such matters."

"Good idea," Karl said. After a minute he added, "I quite like you, young man."

"That's good, because you're going to be stuck with me for a long time."

Kathe hurried outside, surprised by her own nervousness. She paused partway between the house and the workshop to catch her breath before she slowly took the remaining steps and appeared in the doorway, wearing a dark blue dress with an intricate white lace collar. The usual braid was wound up and pinned at the back of her head.

"Very nice." Erich smiled with approval, and she felt a little less nervous. "You look beautiful, as always," he said, and she knew he meant it. "Can you ride a horse in that thing, or should we—"

"Plenty of room." She smiled patronizingly and lifted the sides of her skirt to indicate the full gathers.

"Let us go, then," Erich said, offering his arm in mock gallantry. "Good day . . . *Father*," he said to Karl.

"Have a good time." Karl waved and chuckled.

Kathe expected Erich to saddle her horse as he'd done the day before, but he motioned for her to mount his. "One horse is plenty for gossip," he said as he got into the saddle behind her.

Kathe unintentionally gasped at the reality of being so close to him. He brought one arm comfortably around her waist and took the reins with his other hand. She noticed then that there was no longer a bandage on his hand, but a quick glance showed her it seemed to be healing well.

"You all right?" he asked, guiding the horse up the drive.

"Oh, yes," she answered, wishing it hadn't sounded quite so dreamy.

He chuckled and tightened his arm around her. "Ooh, this is nice," he said. Kathe couldn't argue. Feeling him this close could make nearly anything tolerable, even being paraded before the people of Horstberg for the sake of gossip.

"This is ridiculous," she said for lack of anything better to say. "You can't seriously enjoy being gossiped about."

"Actually, I hate it. But I've learned to accept that it comes with being a du Woernig, and that makes it all right. And I must tell you, I'm not usually so concerned about such things. But for the last ten years I have not gone into public without feeling like some prize to be won. Women look at me as if I'm something they could win in a card game and hang on their wall. I have endured countless horrible social invitations from well-meaning people who believe their homely or garish daughters are destined to become royalty. And so, my dear Katherine, today I will settle it. Without saying a word, I will make it clear that *I* have found *my* prize, and the contest is over."

Kathe laughed and soaked in the dreamlike experience of his expressions of adoration toward her. Being paraded around town with him was seeming less ominous by the minute.

"You're a heartless man, Mr. du Woernig," she said. "Can you imagine how many women will be crying into their pillows tonight, knowing they've lost their chance?"

Erich chuckled and pressed a kiss to her neck. "Do you know what I love best about that?"

"What?"

"*You* don't even care whether I'm a prince or not. I'd go so far as to guess that you would probably prefer my being a blacksmith, or a farmer, or—"

"A chemist," she said.

"Yes, well . . . it would be much less complicated. But I am glad that you love me . . . in spite of my royal obligations."

"And you love me in spite of my common upbringing."

"Or perhaps because of it," he said.

The short distance from her house into town went slowly. Kathe realized they could have just as well walked, but she wondered if his prolonging the journey was for the sake of being close to her in the saddle. She certainly didn't mind.

Erich stopped the horse at the edge of the square and dismounted. Already Kathe could feel eyes turning toward them. He tied off the reins and put his hands at her waist to help her down, holding on to her longer than necessary when her feet touched the ground.

"You look beautiful," he said, offering his arm.

Kathe smiled and put her hand over it. He put his other hand over hers and they walked together into the square. It was a place she felt comfortable, but coming here had never been like this. She was amazed at the way people regarded them with deference. Everyone they encountered seemed to hold some degree of awe in his presence, and every greeting had a 'Your Highness' in it.

In the past she might have been surprised to see the way Erich du Woernig interacted with the commoners. But today it came as no surprise to see his warmth and congeniality as he exchanged small talk with the vendors, expressing sincere interest in their business.

"Wouldn't it be easier to just send out a proclamation or something . . . about your engagement, I mean?" she asked when no one was close by.

"Oh, we'll do that," he said, and her eyes widened. "But this is much more fun."

After nearly an hour, Erich bought some hot pasties and they sat on a park bench to eat them.

"How do you do it?" she asked. "You don't appear ruffled at all, while every person in sight is watching you."

"I grew up with it," he said. "My parents always handled it well. Although," he glanced around nonchalantly, "people seem a bit more interested today." He smiled at her and his eyes sparkled. "Today they're watching *you*. Don't worry," he added when she knew her expression betrayed her alarm, "I know exactly what they're thinking."

"Oh, really?"

He leaned closer and pursed his lips as if he were an old woman. "They're saying," he raised his voice comically, "'Isn't she the loveliest thing you've ever seen?" He changed his tone and turned his head slightly to give both sides of the imaginary conversation. "I wonder where she came from. She looks familiar. I'd swear I'd seen her before." Then the other side, "Oh, no. I'm certain he must have found her in some exotic place. She's probably one of those princesses from the Far East." Kathe smiled timidly, and he changed his voice again. "I'd always hoped he would marry my little Brunhilde; never mind that she doesn't know how to spell Horstberg, and she weighs more than him. They would still make an ideal couple."

Kathe laughed as she swallowed the last bite. Erich took her hand into his. "Your fingers are sticky, Miss Lokberg." She gasped when he put the tip of her finger into his mouth and licked it clean. Then another, and another.

"Erich," she protested softly, "people are watching."

"I know," he smiled and lifted his brows quickly. "Just think of the scandal we'll cause." In his gossip tone he added, "I never realized what a rogue he is. Do you think he's capable of ruling a duchy? Heaven help us all!"

Kathe laughed and was actually disappointed when he'd finished licking her fingers. "You are a funny man, Your Highness," she said.

"Nonsense," he quipped. "You would be amazed at the things people will say. I often read things about myself in the newspaper that I would have never known if I hadn't read them."

"Then I shall have to start reading the newspaper so I can discover what kind of man you aren't."

"Well," he said, "some of it's true—all the good stuff, of course."

"Of course," she laughed. He pressed her hand to his lips, and his eyes delved into hers. "What are you thinking?" she asked, marveling at how every moment with him was like an adventure.

"I was thinking about kissing you . . . long and hard."

Kathe smiled shyly and glanced away. "Not here, I hope."

"Perhaps another time," he said as they walked back into the square. "I think we've given them enough to talk about for one day."

They perused the wares for another hour or so. He tried hats on her and insisted on buying one that he declared would be perfect for working in the garden. He held silk scarves up to her face and settled on a deep red one that he swore enhanced the color of her eyes. Kathe tied the scarf around the crown of the hat and wore it throughout the remainder of their excursion.

When they finally left the square, Erich rode the opposite direction and up the hill to Castle Horstberg. They went first to find Erich's mother in her personal sitting room where the door had been left open. She appeared to be writing a letter at a small desk before they entered, and she looked up, a smile brightening her face.

"What a lovely surprise," Abbi said and came to her feet. She kissed her son on the cheek, then surprised Kathe by giving her a warm, tight embrace. Kathe felt a mother's love in the gesture and had to fight back the tingle of tears in her eyes.

Abbi insisted they sit down and tell her what they'd been up to. Erich told her all about Kathe's father giving his blessing for the marriage, and his loitering in Karl's workshop as if it had been a great adventure. He told his mother about their time in town and made her laugh more than once. Kathe interjected her own comments comfortably, loving the everydayness of such a conversation. She also loved the evidence that Erich and his mother shared such conversations as a regular habit. His tenderness toward his mother said a great deal about his character, especially when Kathe didn't feel at all as if what they shared would ever take anything away from her own relationship with Erich. Rather, she felt destined to share her own closeness with this great woman, and it added to her joy.

They all went together to the office where Erich knew no meetings or special business was going on at the moment. Abbi entered the room first, and Cameron rose to greet her with a kiss as if they were newlyweds. Han and Georg were also there, and it was evident they'd been busy at something that involved the papers spread over the huge desk, but all three men seemed glad to put the work aside, and they greeted Kathe with warm familiarity, as if she already belonged among them. They were all seated, and Erich gave them a condensed version of their trip into town, which made all of the men laugh boisterously.

Their conversation eased into the discussion of wedding plans, and they all looked over a very full calendar to set a date for the wedding. They settled on a Thursday less than two months away, and Kathe wondered how she would ever be ready.

"Will that be all right with your family, Kathe?" Abbi asked.

"Oh, my father said anything would be fine with him. And Theodor does whatever Erich tells him to do."

They also set a date for a social to celebrate the betrothal and make it official, and the duke declared that he was sending out the proclamation to have it posted all over the valley.

"I am officially unavailable," Erich said.

"And it's high time," Han declared.

Erich grinned toward Kathe, and she prayed the fairy tale spinning around her would never end. But then it became evident that living this particular fairy tale would require new clothes. She felt uneasy when it came up that Abbi and Maggie needed to take her shopping, and they needed to get right on it so that the dressmaker would have plenty of time to see that Kathe had the right wardrobe for all of the events coming up. She wanted to protest, but both Abbi and Erich assuaged her concerns as if they sensed her unease. She didn't admit that she had been stewing in the back of her mind about the forthcoming changes in her life—and the wardrobe that would be required. There was no question that her father would manage to buy her anything she needed; she had been more concerned about *what* to buy. But surely no one would know the answer to that better than Erich's mother and sister. She politely thanked Abbi and tried to focus more on her relief for their help rather than her discomfort over certain facets of what lay before her. And she told herself she needed to trust their judgment and not be difficult when everyone had been so perfectly kind and accepting.

The following morning, Abbi and Maggie came for Kathe, and she felt almost as nervous as she had when she'd first been told that Prince Erich was coming to dinner. When Kathe saw one of the ducal coaches in front of the house, she wished that Mrs. Burger next door was home to see it. But her widowed neighbor had left the country the previous week to stay with her sister for a couple of months. Kathe couldn't wait to see her again. She could well imagine the look on her neighbor's face when she realized who would be marrying Prince Erich.

For the hundredth time this week, Kathe had to remind herself she wasn't dreaming as she was seated in the luxurious coach with the Duchess of Horstberg and her daughter. They made her feel immediately comfortable in their presence—which wasn't a surprise—but Kathe felt the need to address her nerves over the purpose of their outing.

"It's really good of you to go with me," Kathe admitted as the coach went the short distance to town. "I must confess I'll be grateful for whatever advice you can give me."

"Maggie has a real gift for fashion," Abbi said. "But this is a *pleasure* for us, my dear. We've waited a long time for Erich to find the right girl."

Abbi's smile was so warm that Kathe nearly blushed. "I still can hardly believe it," she admitted. "It all seems too good to be true."

"That's the way real love feels when you finally find it, I believe," Abbi said.

They arrived quickly at a shop on Herger street where it was evident they'd been expected. Kathe quickly became overwhelmed with so many things to choose from; she felt nearly dizzy. But Abbi and Maggie managed to gracefully make suggestions without being overbearing, and still giving her the opportunity to voice her preferences. While Kathe had never considered the way color might affect a woman's appearance, Maggie was especially concerned about it. They experimented with different fabrics in the mirror, and Kathe began to see what she meant. The colors that brought out Maggie's beauty and enhanced the richness of her hair made Kathe look nearly sick. It was quickly established that greens and browns wouldn't work, but certain shades of blue were good. And pinks and reds did well. Yellow was atrocious on Maggie, but it gave Kathe a glow of radiance.

They took a break and walked to a nearby inn to have lunch. Kathe was intrigued by the contrasting feelings of being in their company. Just as when she'd been in public with Erich, she couldn't forget that she was in the presence of royalty by the way they were regarded and observed. And yet she felt as comfortable with them as if they were schoolmates, chatting and laughing. It was as if she'd known these women forever. Just like Erich, they were so wonderfully normal and gracious, she couldn't help but love them.

They returned to the dress shop and spent the afternoon putting together an order, making it clear to the dressmaker which items would be needed first. They finally left around four o'clock with Kathe's order consisting of two riding habits, one a deep blue pinstriped, and the other a burgundy red; several day dresses in a variety of fabrics, and two evening gowns. The first of these was to be picked up to celebrate the betrothal. There were also multiple pairs of shoes, gloves, a cloak, underclothing, and stockings. Kathe had only once suggested a concern about the cost for so many wonderful clothes, telling them that her father had gladly offered to buy her whatever she wanted, but Abbi had graciously assured her that she was considered a part of the family now, and such expenses were considered normal and customary. "If you weren't marrying into all of this ridiculous social life, you wouldn't have to worry about such things. The least we can do is pay for this stuff."

Kathe thanked them for a wonderful day, and when Abbi suggested there were many things they should discuss, Kathe promised to come to the castle in the morning. She didn't see Erich that evening since he was involved in a social event with visiting dignitaries, but it gave Kathe a chance to catch up on some things she needed to do and spend some time with her father. His obvious happiness on her behalf was warming, yet she felt concerned about neglecting the duties around the house that she had done for so long. He assured her they were managing fine, insisting that she enjoy every moment she could with her new family. He confessed that he'd been thinking for some time about hiring a live-in housekeeper, knowing that Kathe would be moving on eventually. At first Kathe wasn't certain if she liked the idea, but as they discussed it in length, she thought it would be good for her father, and realistically, she couldn't continue keeping house for her father and nephew.

Kathe talked with her father into the morning hours about her feelings for Erich, and the love and acceptance his family had shown her already. She marveled aloud on the wonder of it all, and his enthusiasm on her behalf made everything perfect.

A message arrived the following morning with the ducal seal, inviting Kathe and her family to a formal dinner the next evening at Castle Horstberg for the purpose of getting better acquainted. It was signed *Abbi du Woernig, Her Grace, the Duchess of Horstberg*.

Kathe wondered as she rode to the castle that morning if she had been neglecting to use their titles properly. It had come up briefly once before, but Kathe wanted some clarification on exactly what was proper so she wouldn't embarrass herself or anyone else. She was grateful to feel comfortable enough with Abbi to come right out and ask, and relieved when she was told not to be concerned. The duchess made it clear once again that she would prefer to be called Abbi—or even Mother—except when they were in public or involved in certain formal situations where using titles would be appropriate. She reviewed these things carefully with Kathe since many diplomats from other nations would be present at the upcoming social. Kathe felt a little unnerved to realize that Erich's betrothal was of great interest to many very important people, but Abbi's calm assurances soothed her.

They discussed many topics of etiquette that Abbi declared to be a lot of nonsense, but in order to avoid embarrassment, it just had to be done. Kathe felt some relief to hear the Duchess of Horstberg admit, with all sincerity, that she considered most of this kind of thing to be superficial and tedious.

"Then how do you do it?" Kathe asked. "How do you commit your whole life to something you don't enjoy?"

"Oh, I didn't say I don't enjoy it," Abbi replied. "I enjoy it because every little while, Cameron winks at me across the room, or he sneaks up behind me and whispers something in my ear to make me laugh. You see, Kathe, to us it's an occupation. We smile and do whatever it takes to keep Horstberg at peace and running smoothly, the same way your father goes out to his workshop every day and does his craft."

Kathe hadn't even realized that Abbi knew what her father did. She was freshly amazed by this woman's goodness and perception as she went on.

"And when I catch my husband's eye, it's as if we share a great secret. We both know why we do it, and we both know that real life goes on behind the social decorum; unlike some people, who believe the decorum *is* real life. There are many unhappy people in this business, and you'll be meeting them soon, my dear. It quickly becomes evident where their priorities are, and why they are so unhappy.

"And that is why," Abbi leaned closer and smiled, "it is such a good thing for Erich to marry someone like you, my dear."

"I don't understand."

"Do you have any idea, Kathe, what balance you will put into the ruling of this nation in years to come?"

Kathe's eyes widened. She wanted to suggest that the very idea of her contributing *anything* to a nation was preposterous. But the duchess went on.

"There have been countless women who would have been more than delighted to marry Erich because of the prestige, the wealth, the power, the social decorum. And what would he have had but an ornament? However, with a woman by his side who will marry him for love alone, and endure the requirements of such a life for the sake of love, he will stay grounded in what's real, and he will be happy. And I have seen for myself that happy men make better rulers."

"You're an incredible woman," Kathe said. "I only wish I had more of what it takes to be such a woman. For Erich's sake, I wish that I—"

"Kathe," Abbi interrupted, pressing a hand over hers, "let me share something with you. As a young woman, I rode horses.

That is all I did. I wore calico—the older the better, as far as I was concerned. And I refused to put my hair up."

"Surely you're joking," Kathe insisted.

Abbi laughed softly. "I assure you I am quite serious. And then, one day I met a man who changed my life."

"How *did* you meet him?" Kathe asked, imagining some magical encounter, not unlike hers with Erich.

"He found me nearly frozen to death in the snow," she stated. "But that wasn't actually the first time we'd met." Much to Kathe's relief, she went on to tell the story in detail of being snowed in for the winter with a man she didn't even know. She told how their love had grown, and how they had exchanged private vows with the intent of making their marriage official at the first possible opportunity.

"When I left the mountain in the spring," Abbi said, her tone growing more severe, "I feared that he might not even survive long enough to make our marriage public. I knew nothing about him. He had kept his identity from me for my safety. His brother was the duke at the time, and my involvement with Cameron could have been considered treason."

Kathe felt chilled as she saw a deep intensity come into Abbi du Woernig's eyes. She looked at Kathe as if she could see into her soul. "I gave everything to him, Kathe, but it was what my heart told me I had to do. As far as I knew, he was a common thief. I knew his life was in danger, and that was all I knew. At one point I had to accept the possibility that I might be left to raise our child without him."

Kathe unintentionally gasped and put a hand to her heart. The love she felt for Erich made her wonder how a woman could bear such a thing. And it made her wonder if *Erich's* life might ever be in danger, but she didn't know how to ask and she really didn't want to know.

"And I remember wondering," Abbi went on, "if I should have regretted the things I'd done to put myself in that situation. But I knew in my heart that what we shared was something most people only dream of. The circumstances with which we started our lives together were not normal or ideal by any means. Cameron needed the love I gave him to get him through; to give him the determination to reclaim his country from the hands that would have destroyed it. I had followed my heart, and I *could not* regret it. If he had never come for me, I would have raised his son with gratitude in my heart to have a part of him with me. I learned many things. I learned that right and wrong are not always black and white. And I learned that the moment I realized I loved Cameron more than life, I *gave* him my life. And I would have done whatever he asked of me, even if that had been raising his son to honor his memory."

Kathe was embarrassed by the tears that spilled down her face, until she glanced up to see that Abbi was crying, too. She watched Abbi dry her tears with a lace handkerchief, and then she smiled at Kathe.

"Obviously the story had a different ending," Kathe said.

"Yes," Abbi said wistfully, "in a matter of hours I went from wondering if the common criminal I loved was dead, to being crowned the Duchess of Horstberg. And I was *terrified* of the position. I felt certain I couldn't do what was expected of me. But with time I learned that God had not brought Cameron and me together by coincidence. If the love we shared was destiny, then I was certainly capable of becoming whatever being his wife required of me."

Kathe became lost once again in the fine details of Cameron du Woernig's reclamation of 1817. She especially loved the way Abbi told her that she knew Horstberg was in Cameron's blood, and he could not have been happy without having it a part of his life. Kathe knew that Erich shared those feelings with his father. As Abbi rambled on, Kathe couldn't deny the relief and comfort she'd found in these stories. If Abbi du Woernig had once been a common woman in calico, then Kathe could almost believe herself capable of being worthy of Erich du Woernig.

It was difficult to break away and go down to lunch, except

that Kathe knew she had a lifetime to spend with these people. They walked into the dining room a few minutes late. The men were laughing boisterously over something, and for a moment Kathe watched Erich while he was unaware. She admitted to Abbi in a whisper, "Just seeing him makes my heart go faster."

Abbi chuckled. "I know the feeling well. If not for Erich's red hair, I could almost believe he was Cameron all over again."

Erich and Cameron turned and smiled as if they'd sensed they were being talked about. As Erich helped Kathe with her chair, he whispered, "I've been going mad without you. After lunch I've got a mind to steal you away for a little serious necking."

Kathe met his eyes briefly, astonished by his boldness. It was difficult to tell whether or not he was teasing, but she couldn't deny the delighted tremor that erupted inside of her at the thought.

Through the meal, Abbi and Maggie talked on and on about the shopping they'd done the previous day and the plans they were making for the wedding and all that led up to it. But it was only when she met Erich's eyes that Kathe could feel that everything happening to her was real.

As soon as they were finished eating, Erich took Kathe's hand and whisked her away, declaring that his mother and sister had had more than their fair share of her, and it was his turn. He took her to one of the many parlors in the castle. It was impossible for her to keep track which it was. She stood in the middle of the room to absorb its lovely decor until he backed her toward the sofa.

"What are you doing?" she asked with a little laugh.

"Sit down, Miss Lokberg. I'm going to kiss you."

"Yes, Your Highness," she said and sat dutifully.

Erich laughed as he put one knee on the sofa beside her, and pressed his mouth over hers with immediate passion. "Oh, I've missed you," he said, pushing one arm around her waist. He kissed her again while he managed to sit beside her and maneuver her legs over his lap. The more he kissed her, the more preoccupied she became with the way it made her feel. She sensed his desires intensifying, and nearly expected him to become consumed with irreversible passion at any moment. But he seemed content to just hold her and kiss her, as if each time their lips met was a new experience to be explored and savored.

"I love you, Katherine," he whispered, his voice husky. He buried his face against her throat and eased her closer. "Do you have any idea the effect you have on me?"

Kathe pressed her hand into his hair. "Perhaps I do," she said and urged her mouth over his. She felt more than heard him moan, and a moment later she heard the door open.

Erich looked up but made no effort to let go of her, as if to say that he had every right to be holding her this way, and he had nothing to be ashamed of. His confidence inspired her, but she put her face to his shoulder, trying to force away the warmth of embarrassment. Whoever was entering the room, she didn't want to look at them.

Erich chuckled and said, "What are you doing, little man?"

"I was just wondering what *you're* doing," Stefan said. Kathe looked up. She could handle facing a child.

"As you can see," Erich said, tightening his embrace, "I am quite occupied."

"Are you going coursing today?" Stefan asked, and Erich smiled. He knew how much his young nephew enjoyed their little hunting expeditions, but it had always been more about spending time together than actually trying to bring home any game.

"Actually, I think I'll just kiss Kathe until suppertime—if it's all right with you."

Stefan sighed and shook his head with comical disgust, as if he were ten years older, then he left and closed the door behind him.

Erich laughed and pressed his face against Kathe's shoulder.

"If you keep this up until suppertime," she said, "you might find yourself compromised."

Erich looked into her eyes to see them sparkling. "Really?" he asked. "What exactly did you have in mind?"

Kathe laughed. "How would I know? I can assure you I am quite naive on such matters."

"How delightful." He smirked playfully in spite of the intrigue in his eyes.

"It would seem you'll have to teach me . . . about such matters."

Erich chuckled. "My dear Katherine, I've already taught you everything I know—and more, I believe."

Kathe tried to comprehend what he meant. "Surely you're joking. I find it difficult to believe that you've remained innocent into your thirties without dozens of women throwing themselves at your feet, offering all they have."

Erich ran a hand through his hair, and she thought he actually look embarrassed. "I can't deny that a few women have given me some interesting . . . propositions. But I never once took more than a kiss; I swear it. And there came a day when I stopped doing that."

Kathe leaned back but kept her legs over his lap. Watching his face, it became evident he wasn't joking. "You continually surprise me," she said.

"Why? Because you expected me to be some kind of philandering rogue?"

"Maybe."

"And you love me anyway?"

"Does love come under such conditions?"

"No, I suppose it doesn't," he admitted.

"However, trust is another matter. Rogue or not, from this day forward you are mine, and mine alone."

"Yes, Your Highness." He laughed.

"So, why did you stop kissing all those women who were throwing themselves at your feet?"

"I think it was when I realized that nearly every encounter I had with a woman was soon common knowledge. One girl actually told me she couldn't wait to tell her friends who she'd been kissing. It's embarrassing. I can just hear it." Erich picked up his gossip tone. "Oh, did I tell you he kissed me? He's not much for kissing, but he *is* a *prince,* so please tell everyone you meet that he kissed me. No, I don't like him at all, but he *is* a prince, and he *did* kiss me."

Kathe laughed until she realized he was watching her, an intensity in his eyes she'd never seen before.

"What?" she asked, resisting the urge to turn away. She could well imagine him being a very powerful man just by that look in his eyes.

"I was just wondering what it might be like to have you compromise me."

Kathe chuckled for fear of making a fool of herself otherwise. "I've not even known you a week, Erich du Woernig."

He pressed her hand to his lips but kept his eyes fixed on hers. "We are betrothed, Miss Lokberg."

"Then we have something to look forward to," she said, and he smiled.

Erich watched her eyes turn serious and he almost knew her thoughts were wandering to the same places his were. But he'd been raised to respect the bonds of matrimony related to intimacy. While a part of him wanted to explore these desires completely, there was something about the anticipation of such an experience that made waiting almost pleasurable in itself. Fearing he *would* compromise her if he wasn't careful, he steered his thoughts to the enormity of his feelings. He was amazed at how far he'd come in the years since he'd even considered marrying. For many reasons, he was glad to have waited until now, but there were ironies in his life that had been on his mind far too much. He debated whether or not to bring up the topic, but opted for the moment to just kiss her again.

Soon after lunch, Han entered the duke's office with his father, where they found Cameron searching frantically through his papers.

"Georg," Cameron said without even looking up. After all their years together, they could almost sense the other's presence. "Did you take one of the maps of the castle?"

"You mean the layout?" Georg asked.

"Yes."

"No."

"We had two copies of it, did we not?" Cameron asked, his voice growing more tense.

"We did." Georg remained calm, but Han sensed he was also concerned.

"Well, we don't anymore," Cameron said sharply, placing his hands on his hips in exasperation.

"There is only one possibility," Georg said. "We're too organized for it to be anything else."

"I know," Cameron said. "Blast!"

"I don't understand," Han said.

"It's most likely been stolen," Georg replied. "And it's been a long time since we've needed those layouts, so it could have been gone months for all we know."

"I always suspected that one of the servants was responsible for the little accidents we had back in forty-one," Cameron said. "We never did find out who it was, but I'd bet they're still working here, and most likely still associating with Nik Koenig."

"It's amazing," Georg remarked. "Even when we hardly see a sign of him, he seems to hang over us like some kind of plague."

"And I have a feeling we're in for a fresh epidemic," Cameron said. "I don't know why. I just do."

"Because a map was stolen?" Han asked.

"Exactly." Cameron's face was sober.

"Do you really think it has something to do with Koenig?" Georg asked.

"I don't know," Cameron said thoughtfully. "He's pretty much been minding his own business, but if I were to try and second-guess him—perhaps believing he thinks like his father—I would bet he's just waiting for us to get comfortable. Or perhaps for something unusual to happen that might have us distracted."

"Like what?" Han asked.

"Like a wedding," Georg put in, and only silence replied.

"This is ridiculous," Cameron chuckled tensely a minute later. "Absolutely nothing has happened. I'm getting all worked up over nothing."

"Except gut instinct," Georg said. "And when you and I get the same gut instinct, I tend to listen."

"Remember that, Han," Cameron said more lightly, as if in an effort to lessen the tension. "Good thought there."

"So, do you think there is still at least one servant here who is . . . well, you know?" Han asked.

"I wouldn't be surprised," Cameron replied. "But as I've said before, there is little to be done without any proof. And where do I begin to find the guilty servant out of the whole crew? Do you know how many people it takes to staff this place?"

"We just have to be careful," Georg said, "and do as we did before—trust no one."

"I always thought," Cameron said, "that amid the walls of this fortress, my family could find safety and refuge; we could be a defense against the problems we face. I still can hardly believe how we were undermined from the inside. I'm afraid I've just been reminded that I can't feel we are completely safe as long as Nik Koenig is alive."

Han looked to Cameron. "Don't you think Koenig took your threats seriously?" He recalled clearly the conversation in this very room between the duke and Nik Koenig. Cameron had made some bold threats in regard to his family remaining safe, but Nik had seemed to know that Cameron would not break his own laws, even for such reasons.

"To some degree," Cameron said. "Everything has been calm for quite some time, but perhaps we're getting too relaxed, too comfortable. Maybe that's what he was counting on. And when it comes right down to it—as much as I hate to admit—he was right to a certain extent; though I don't want him to believe that."

"What do you mean?" Han asked.

"I am governed by the law, and the law has restrictions. If I am to remain supported and respected by my people, I cannot disregard the law to satisfy my own motives." Cameron glanced at Georg. "It boils down to one thing."

"One du Woernig against another," Georg said.

Again, only silence followed the comment.

"Han," Cameron finally said, "will you find Erich and tell him I need to talk to him? It won't take long."

Han nodded and opened the door to leave, not liking the dread left hanging in the air.

"Oh, hello there," he said to Stefan, who was about to knock. "What are you up to?"

"I'm just bored," he reported, sauntering into the office. "I wanted to go coursing with Erich, but he said he's going to kiss Kathe all afternoon."

"Did he now?" Cameron asked with a little smirk.

"And where is Erich now?" Han asked.

"In the north parlor . . . kissing Kathe."

"I see."

Han and Cameron exchanged a quick glance before Cameron added, "I suppose I can wait a little while to talk to Erich. I doubt war is going to break out in the next hour."

"I sure hope not," Han said with light sarcasm.

Cameron asked one of the officers outside the door to go find Captain Dukerk, but to tell him it wasn't an emergency. With the order given, they all sat down, including Stefan, to focus on other matters at hand.

Ten minutes later, Captain Dukerk entered the room and took a seat when Cameron motioned to a chair. They exchanged some small talk as they usually did, most of which centered around the captain's report that Dulsie was doing very well. He and Nadine would be going to visit her in a few days, and it was always a joy to see how she was thriving in her new surroundings. Everyone present was glad to hear such a positive report since they had all shared a common concern for Dulsie for many years.

After a brief mention of the weather and some other odd tidbits of conversation, Cameron explained to the captain the dilemma over the missing layout to the castle, and they discussed the possible suspicions all over again. The captain said that even though they had no idea how long it had been since the layout had gone missing, he would still have the officers questioned who stood guard at the office door. He had records going back for months on who had done each shift. He would also have the servants questioned who had done the cleaning of the office. Records were always kept of that, as well.

"It might not give us the answers we want," the captain said, "but we have to at least try to find as much information as we can."

"I agree," Cameron said. "Thank you."

Han noticed how Stefan absently drew a picture of a horse during the discussion, but the boy was also listening attentively. With the child's ongoing desire to be in the office with the men, as opposed to playing with the other children, he had promised to never repeat what he heard in this room, and the men were all careful not to discuss anything too delicate when the child was present. But Han hoped now that Stefan wouldn't hear anything in this conversation that might make him feel alarmed. They had all grown so accustomed to him being there that Han wondered if perhaps sometimes they spoke too freely. He made a mental note to speak with Stefan later and make certain he was all right.

Captain Dukerk stood to leave but stopped and turned back before opening the door. "It occurs to me . . . I know we haven't had officers guarding the door that leads to Erich's laboratory for years. I assume the door is remaining locked, and only family members with the key can open it?"

"Erich assures me he keeps it locked," Cameron said, "but I will check with him and make certain."

"Just a precaution," the captain said and opened the door.

"I am completely in favor of precautions," Cameron agreed, but Han saw a faraway look in the duke's eyes that was haunting. Han's own memories of Nik Koenig's past crimes mingled with fears for the future, knowing the man's motives. If Han was feeling it, he could only imagine what Cameron and Georg were feeling. A glance between the two older men seemed to affirm what Han was thinking, but Cameron changed the subject, and they began discussing other issues. Stefan didn't seem to notice.

Erich looked at Kathe sitting close beside him and had to convince himself that it would be wise to engage in conversation. And they certainly had much they still didn't know about each other. He began by telling her about Dulsie and the lifelong friendship they'd shared. He felt comfortable telling Kathe all about Dulsie's situation and her struggles with it, knowing he could trust her completely, and she reassured him that she would never repeat anything he told her that was spoken in confidence. He was glad to be able to tell Kathe that through the regular letters he exchanged with Dulsie, he knew she was doing better than she ever had. She was blossoming with her new life, and she even had more than one suitable male admirer. He felt certain she would be able to find a good husband and a good life, and he was happy for her.

"I sent off a letter to her just this morning," Erich said, "telling her about our good news. I'm certain she'll be pleased, although you should know that I asked her to marry me and she turned me down."

Erich could see that Kathe initially thought he was joking, but when she noted his serious expression she said, "Well, I'm glad she didn't agree to it."

"As we all are," Erich said. "But still, you should know."

He went on to explain that when both he and Dulsie had been

getting older and nothing romantic was working out for either one of them, he'd believed that they could have a good marriage. He told Kathe that he'd meant it, even though he and Dulsie had both known they didn't share the kind of feelings that should ideally exist between a husband and wife.

"Still," he said, "sometimes we don't always get what's ideal, and I didn't know if I would ever find someone." He kissed Kathe's hand. "I'm glad that Dulsie had the wisdom to turn down my repeated proposals, and I'm glad that she's doing well. But I'm especially glad for me. In all selfishness, I feel like the happiest, most blessed man in the world."

"Is that selfish?" she asked, touching his face. "If it is, then we are both selfish. I too am happy and blessed. I don't think there's anything wrong with making each other so happy."

"No," he smiled and kissed her, "I don't suppose there's anything wrong with that."

Erich kissed her again, then had to remind himself of the boundaries that needed to be carefully kept between him and Kathe. He eased away and decided there were other things he needed to talk about with her, even if he didn't want to.

"There's something I want to ask you," he said, and Kathe felt intrigued.

"So, ask me."

"All right. Call it a hypothetical question. Let's just say, for instance, betrothed as we are, that something happened to me, and I became paralyzed."

He paused as if to let her absorb the idea, and she recalled his reference to once having been temporarily paralyzed. She still wasn't certain if he'd been teasing about that or not, but there was no questioning the severity in his eyes.

"I couldn't walk," he added, "nor could I father children."

Kathe's eyes widened. While his directness surprised her, she didn't feel uncomfortable. He reminded her of her father in that respect.

"All right, so you're paralyzed. What about it?"

"Would you still marry me? Would you want to spend your life with half a man?"

"You're serious."

"Yes, I'm serious," he insisted vehemently.

"Why are you asking me this?"

"Because it's important for me to know. But I need you to be honest with me."

"Would you expect me to be any other way?"

"No, I would expect you to be brutally honest with me, Kathe. That's one of many reasons I have for loving you."

"And what if I said *no*? Would you think less of me?"

"Kathe, I would not expect *any* woman to want to live her life with half a man—most especially you."

"Where do you get this idea of being *half* of who you are? Would your heart be paralyzed, your mind, your laughter?" She touched his face. "Your dimples?" He glanced away but didn't smile. "Erich." She touched his chin to make him look at her. "Is that what you think my love is based on? Whether or not you can walk and give me children?"

"There's more to it than that," he protested.

"Yes, I know what you mean. You don't have to say it. I am by no means experienced in such things, but I have observed a great deal in my life. I don't believe that intimacy is just a physical thing, any more than I believe that a happy marriage comes from two people walking down the aisle together. When I told you I would marry you, I gave you my life—for better or worse."

Kathe was surprised by the glisten of moisture that appeared in his eyes. She pushed a hand into his hair and asked, "And what if it were the other way around? What if I were bed-ridden the rest of my life, unable to give you children—you, who are supposed to have an heir?"

He pulled her into his arms almost fiercely. "For you, Katherine," he whispered, "I would give Horstberg away."

"But you couldn't." She drew back to look him in the eye. "It's in your blood. It's a part of you."

"Yes," he admitted, "but for you—"

Kathe placed her fingers over his lips to stop him. "Don't say it. I would never ask such a thing of you."

Again he hugged her tightly, pressing his lips into her hair. Kathe had to ask, "Why such a hypothetical question?" He pulled back and looked into her eyes. "What happened, Erich?" she added. "Does this have something to do with that temporary paralysis you mentioned before?"

Erich leaned back with a sigh. His eyes became distant. "It was several years ago. Maggie was expecting Hannah at the time, I believe. I walked into my laboratory, and I could smell something strange. I turned to leave and the door slammed in my face and locked, then—"

"What do you mean?" she demanded.

"I mean somebody slammed the door and locked it from the outside."

"But who would—"

"If we had known who, they would have gone before a firing squad." At her questioning gaze he clarified, "Because it was attempted murder."

Kathe was so stunned she couldn't speak. He looked away as he went on. "I remember banging on the door, and then getting dizzy; then everything went black. I woke up from the coma weeks later, in my own bed. I could feel nothing from the waist down. At the time, the doctor told me it could be temporary, or it could be permanent. I had good reason to believe that I would never walk again."

"And now," she said, "you must believe in miracles."

Erich turned to look at her, his eyes glowing. "Oh, yes," he said, touching her face, "I believe in miracles. I am alive. I am whole. And I have you."

"Erich," Kathe asked, hating the knot that formed deep inside at the thought, "why would someone try to kill you?"

"Because I am the heir to Horstberg and somebody else wanted it at the time."

Kathe leaned forward, her heart quickening. "You're *still* the heir to Horstberg," she stated as if he didn't know.

"Yes, I am."

"Did they ever find out who did it?"

"No," Erich said. He hated the way talking about this made him feel, almost as much as he hated the overt fear in Kathe's eyes. "Although we have a good idea who was behind it, we couldn't prove it. And we suspect this someone didn't actually do the dirty work."

"Does that frighten you—to know that this someone is still out there?"

"Yes," he admitted. "But I'm not going to stop living for fear of someone taking my life."

Kathe didn't like the reality of what he was telling her, nor the way it made her feel.

"But . . . I don't understand. Who would have done such a thing?"

Erich blew out a long breath. As long as it was open, he figured he'd better get it all out. "Probably the same person who had me shot."

Kathe pressed a hand over her mouth to keep from crying out. She had been blessed to have found love with a man more wonderful than she'd ever imagined. Now she was beginning to perceive that this man lived a precarious life.

"I was out riding," Erich said, knowing she wanted an explanation by the look in her eyes. "It was where I always ride. Obviously somebody had taken notice of my habits and hobbies. I was aware of some movement in the trees, but I saw nothing. I was shot. It hurt like the devil and I lost a lot of blood. But I survived it. There's nothing more to tell. I go riding in that very place all the time. There have been no incidents for several years. I'm certain it's in the past."

When Kathe just stared at him, shock and horror etched into her expression, Erich unbuttoned his shirt.

"What are you doing?" she asked.

He smiled slightly. At least he'd snapped her out of it. "Would you believe that I'm going to compromise you?"

"No."

"Well," he smirked, hoping to lighten the mood, "it was a nice thought."

He pushed the shirt over his shoulder to show her the scar.

"Good heavens," she gasped. The mark was not big, but it was deep and ugly. Erich took her fingers into his hand and pressed them there. "Does it still hurt?" she asked.

"It aches some when the weather is cold. Nothing serious."

He guided her hand over his shoulder to the back, and she gasped again as she felt a similar scar there. He turned slightly so she could see it. "The bullet went straight through, so I didn't get to keep it."

"Too bad," she said with sarcasm.

Erich pulled his shirt up over his shoulder and pressed her hand to the center of his chest. She caught her breath at the intimate implication in his eyes combined with the feel of his skin beneath her fingers.

"My heart is still beating, Kathe. And as long as it is, we will live life to its fullest—together. I will give everything I have to give—for you, and for Horstberg—as long as there is breath in me. I will not waste away the life I have in fear. And neither will you." He put his mouth over hers as if to seal the promise, and Kathe clung to him. He let go of her hand to pull her into his arms, but she kept it against his chest. She could feel the quickening of his heart, and forced any fear out of her mind. As his kiss deepened, she became distracted by the feel of his hand on her ankle.

"I'd wager that you have beautiful legs," he said.

"One of these days, I'll show you, and you can decide for yourself."

"I'll look forward to it." He kissed her again and eased her closer. "When that happens, I'll know you're trying to compromise me."

"You can count on it, Your Highness. But then, if I am your wife, you wouldn't be compromising me, now would you."

"What a pleasant thought," Erich said and kissed her again.

A knock at the door startled them both. In a split second they withdrew from each other and sat up straight.

"What?" Erich called, buttoning his shirt quickly.

Han peeked his head in the door and grinned mischievously. "Hi," he said. "What are you doing?"

"A little serious necking, if you must know," Erich said.

Kathe pressed a hand over her eyes to hide her embarrassment, and at the same time bit her lip to keep from laughing.

"I was hoping," Han said. "I've been wanting to catch you the way you caught me for . . . oh, about fourteen years now."

"So, I'm a late bloomer," he said. "What's your point?"

Han chuckled. "I just came to tell you that your father needs to see you. It should only take a few minutes."

"Tell him I'm necking," Erich said, and Kathe nudged him with her elbow.

"Actually, Stefan already did . . . more or less."

"Oh, that's great," Erich said with light sarcasm. "In a place this size, you'd think we could avoid being found."

"Perhaps we'll do better next time," Kathe suggested.

"There are a couple of great spots in the garden," Han said. Erich raised an eyebrow, and Kathe shook her head. They all laughed.

Kathe waited in the hall while Erich went into his father's office.

"What do you need?" Erich asked, closing the door behind him.

Georg answered him. "There's a layout of the castle missing. You wouldn't know anything about that, would you?"

"No," he stated, feeling an uneasy prickle from the way his father and Georg exchanged a concerned glance. All of his own fearful feelings that he'd been fighting to suppress rushed forward, and it took great discipline to keep his expression steady.

"We believe it's been stolen," Georg said. "And we have no idea how long it's been gone."

"Who would want a layout of the castle?" Erich asked. No one answered, and he sat down as he began to perceive the implication. "Someone who wants to move in. Someone like Nik Koenig."

"It's only a guess," Cameron said.

"But a logical one," Georg added.

"Georg," Cameron turned to him, "do those layouts have the concealed passageways and—"

"No," he interrupted.

Cameron sighed in relief. "Well, that's good. At least we have a few secrets."

"I thought this room was guarded twenty-four hours a day," Erich said.

"It is," Cameron answered.

"And when it's cleaned?" Georg asked.

"Well, if we know who cleans the office, that narrows it down, doesn't it?" Erich asked.

"Except that with the rotations in housekeeping," Cameron said, "there's still more than half a dozen maids who could be responsible." He repeated to Erich Captain Dukerk's plan to investigate these very issues, and added, "From now on I want two officers actually in the room while it's being cleaned as well, rather than just posted outside the door."

"But the layout is still missing," Erich said. "What do we do?"

Cameron said with severity, "We wait for the captain to complete his investigation, and we just stay alert. What else *can* we do?"

Erich felt chilled as this conversation mingled with the one he'd been having with Kathe prior to their interruption. But he knew Kathe was waiting for him in the hall, and he doubted there was anything else to be said now, anyway.

As Erich stood to leave, his father asked, "Also, are you still keeping the door that goes down to the dungeon locked? The captain asked about it."

"Yes, of course," Erich said and resisted shouting some kind of profanity over the implication. Instead he left the office and closed the door behind him, trying to leave his worries there. He found Kathe admiring a painting done by his mother. But then, the castle was full of those.

"Is something wrong?" she asked.

"No." Erich forced a smile. "Just business. Listen," he took her hand, "I need to go upstairs and get something, and then I'll take you home."

As soon as they arrived at Kathe's house, they sat down together on the garden bench. "I have something for you," Erich said. "It's not much to look at, but it has great sentimental value."

Kathe watched as Erich pulled a finely-etched gold bracelet from the pocket of his waistcoat. He slid it onto her arm, and she could see that it was old and a little tarnished but beautiful nevertheless.

"It's not so much for you to wear as it is a keepsake," he said. "But first I must tell you the story behind it."

"I'm listening," she said eagerly.

"My mother's mother was English. Her name was LeeAnna Eddington, and when Gerhard Albrecht asked her to marry him, he gave her this bracelet. When my mother was very young, LeeAnna was killed, and Gerhard left my mother in his father's care. Gerhard had a bit of a gambling problem. Well, he ended up working at the castle, and eventually became the duke's valet; the duke being my father, who was married to a woman named Gwendolyn at the time. Gerhard gave the bracelet to my father for safekeeping, not wanting to be tempted to gamble it away when he knew he had a weakness for such things.

"As I understand it," Erich went on, "one morning Gerhard was in the duke's bedroom when Gwendolyn came in. He knew the duke had been suspicious of her actions for quite some time, so he hid in the draperies to see what she was up to. My father's brother came into the room. They argued. He killed her."

"You mean *murder?*"

"Yes," Erich said. "Anyway, Gerhard saw everything and was prepared to testify, but things went awry. The rest is rather complicated, but my father was wrongly accused of the crime. He escaped from prison and spent a number of years hiding in a secluded mountain lodge. And while Gerhard could prove his innocence, he believed that my father was dead. And then my mother became lost on the mountain, and—"

"Oh, I know this part," she said eagerly. "Your mother told me how he found her in the snow and she stayed there until spring."

"That's right." Erich smiled. "When my father realized this was Gerhard's daughter, he gave her the bracelet, insisting that she never take it off. When she came down from the mountain, Gerhard saw the bracelet and knew that Cameron du Woernig was still alive. It took some careful maneuvering, but eventually Gerhard was able to testify on my father's behalf, and the duchy was reclaimed."

Kathe looked at the gold band around her arm in awe. "And you're giving it to *me?*"

"*You* my dear, are the next Duchess of Horstberg." He took her hand and leaned closer to her. "When I was sitting in that bed, believing I would never walk again, my mother gave this bracelet to me. She told me to give it to the woman I married. She gave me the hope that such a thing might still be possible. To me, it represents just that—hope. One day you can give it to one of our children, and who knows? Perhaps it will be the means once again of bringing a miracle to pass."

Kathe looked at the bracelet again, then pushed her arms around him tightly. "Thank you. It's beautiful. I will treasure it always."

Erich stayed to help pull weeds in the garden, and afterwards he helped her prepare a light supper which he shared with Kathe and her father. Little Karl was absent since his father had come to get him earlier to play with Stefan and spend the night at the castle.

Erich insisted on helping clean the dishes, although they played in the water so long that it was nearly bedtime before they were finished. Kathe walked him to the stable, and they reluctantly parted.

That night as Kathe tried to sleep, images of Erich's life-threatening incidents assaulted her relentlessly. She reminded herself that it was in the past and there was no reason for her to be concerned. But even in her dreams, she could see the bullet hitting him, and the laboratory door slamming closed, over and over.

Chapter Five
THE PREMONITION

Only a few days later, Erich was in the office with his father, Han, and Georg when Captain Dukerk came in to report the results of his investigation. As always, Erich was amazed at the captain's efficiency and dedication. He reported that officers guarding the door had been aware of maids going in and out of the room to clean it thoroughly once a week, always late in the evenings when no business was taking place. Their cleaning supplies were searched before going in and after coming out. All of the officers had wondered how something so conspicuous as several large sheets of paper rolled up could have been removed from the room.

"All of them were baffled except one," the captain said. "He said that he hadn't given it a second thought at the time, but he did remember one night when one of the carpets had been carried out by two maids in order to clean it. The carpet had been rolled up, so it wasn't searched. The duties are rotated among several maids, and the officer can't recall the specific date the carpet was removed." All the men sighed at the sensible explanation, and the captain continued. "This officer feels horrible, but I'm not holding him accountable. He did his job as he was ordered to. If it's anyone's fault that something was overlooked in his orders, it's mine."

"No one could have predicted this," Cameron said. "And what about the maids?"

"Not one of them will admit to anything," the captain said. "I confess that most of them were so nervous by the interviews that it's difficult to tell whether or not they're lying. I'm afraid I have nothing more than that to tell you."

They discussed how to proceed, with no choice but to accept that someone unsavory knew the layout of the castle—someone most likely associated with Nik Koenig. And there was nothing to be done about it. Captain Dukerk said that he was increasing shifts for his officers at certain places in the castle. They would also increase their efforts in undercover operations with the hope of discovering something helpful by mingling among certain types of people.

When there was nothing more to report, the captain nearly left, but Cameron suggested they all go to the pub instead. "I think we could use a drink," he said, promptly changing the subject of conversation as they headed out. Erich was glad not to be talking about the insidious hints of a threat hanging over them, but he had trouble not thinking about it.

The following day the duke had to attend a conference for border negotiations in Kohenswald. He asked Han to remain behind and go over some financial statements in regard to a certain economic concern. Han was relieved to not have to go. Not one of them ever enjoyed visiting that particular neighboring country, and Han felt like he'd been given an award by being asked to stay at home.

He was sitting alone in the office with the assigned paperwork when the duchess came in.

"Good morning, Mother." He smiled toward her as he stood.

"Good morning," she replied, leaning momentarily against the door.

"The others aren't back yet from Kohenswald. I'm afraid I'm the only one here."

"I know," she said. "That's why I came."

Han tried to ignore her severity and motioned toward a chair, saying lightly, "Then you're in luck. Please, sit down."

The duchess sat across the desk from him as he sat back down and crossed an ankle over his knee. "Is something wrong?"

She smiled, but her eyes remained intent. "I just wanted to talk to you." She folded her hands gracefully in her lap. "You seem to enjoy your work."

"I do, yes."

"Cameron tells me you're well suited for it. He's been pleased, so far as he tells me."

"Well, that's good."

"Yes," she said, and he felt certain she had a point she wanted to get to that had nothing to do with his job.

"You and Maggie are happy," she said. It wasn't a question.

"Well, I haven't come right out and asked her lately, but she certainly seems to be. I know *I'm* happy."

"I've told you this before, but I was so pleased when everything worked out for you and Maggie. I've loved you nearly like one of my own since the day you were born."

Han was momentarily too touched to speak. His thoughts strayed to his own mother and he had to admit, "You've made losing my mother almost bearable, you know. But long before that, I was always amazed at how kind you were to me. Even when Maggie hated me, you seemed to always say the right thing to let me know it didn't matter to you."

Abbi blinked repeatedly as if she were fighting emotion. "You're a good man, Han," she said. "And you have a beautiful family."

"Yes, I do." He watched her through a minute of silence while she was apparently lost in deep thought. "Is that what you came here to tell me?"

"In essence, yes," she said. "Although . . . there is something I wanted to share with you."

"Please . . . go on," he urged gently when she seemed hesitant.

"You're aware that I'm sometimes prone to strange . . . dreams."

Han unwillingly straightened his back and inhaled. This was not what he'd expected. "Yes" was all he said.

"And that they have in the past seemed . . . premonitory."

"Yes," he said again.

"Over the years, I have learned to recognize a certain . . . quality about these dreams. The memory of them does not fade with time, and there is a . . . feeling about them that I can't quite put into words."

Han was wondering why she would want to discuss this with him—alone—when she looked him in the eye and said, "I had a dream about you, Han."

Attempting to lighten the mood, he chuckled and said, "What awful thing am I going to do? Perhaps you should denounce me now and get it over with."

Abbi smiled. "Always a tease," she said, and then her expression became more severe than before. "I wanted to talk to you about it alone because . . . if it has significance, the implications are . . . disturbing."

There was no humor in Han's tone as he said, "Am I going to die?"

A chill raced down Han's back when she pressed a hand quickly over her mouth as if to hold back emotion. She shook her head adamantly while she gained her composure, and he began to feel frustrated when she didn't go on. Impatiently he asked, "Is someone else going to die?"

She set her eyes on him firmly. "It would seem that's the only possible explanation."

"Explanation of what?"

"In my dream, Han . . . you were wearing the crown."

Han held his breath. He felt momentarily frozen as he gazed into her eyes, attempting to comprehend the implication. His breath finally escaped with a noise of disbelief.

"That's not even funny," he said.

"I didn't say it was."

"It's absurd!" Han chuckled dubiously and pushed a hand through his hair. He leaned over the desk, saying intently, "I'm the stableboy, Your Grace."

Abbi's expression remained intent. "You're sitting behind the duke's desk, in the duke's chair."

"Only because he's not here!" Han retorted. A moment later, huge tears fell over Abbi du Woernig's solemn face. "Dear God, no," Han whispered as he began to perceive the reason for them. He stood abruptly as if the chair had suddenly burned him. Turning to face the window, he tried to think of a rational explanation that wouldn't discredit the respect she had for her dreams. "Maybe it's . . . symbolic," he said. "Perhaps I'll . . . I don't know . . . I'll do something to benefit the country, and that's all."

"I'm certain you will do many things to benefit the country, Han," she said quietly. "You already have. And I suppose it could be symbolic, but . . ."

"But?" he pressed, turning to look at her as she dabbed her eyes with a handkerchief.

"That thought occurred to me, but it just doesn't feel right. It feels . . . *literal*."

Han chuckled again and shook his head. "Forgive me, Mother, but how could it possibly be literal? I don't have a drop of du Woernig blood in me."

"Your sons do."

"So, there you have it." Han spread his hands for emphasis, then planted them on his hips. "My son will wear the crown. Erich will have seven daughters. It's symbolic."

"Hear me out, Han," she said gently.

He nodded and sat back down, wondering why he was letting this get to him.

"Cameron is not a young man."

"He's not that old either," Han retorted. "He's healthy and strong."

"Yes, he is. But no one can predict when a man's life will end, or—"

"And when he's gone, Erich will—"

"Han, listen to me. There is a point to this."

"I'm listening," he said, forcing himself to lean back and relax—or at least appear to be relaxed.

"Let's just say, for instance, that something happened to Erich, and he died without progeny. What would happen at Cameron's death?"

Han swallowed the knot in his throat. "Stefan would be the duke, but . . ."

"But Stefan is a child. Is that what you were going to say?"

Han nodded.

"And until he comes of age?"

Han said nothing. He didn't want to admit that this was making sense, and it scared him. "There would have to be a regent. You're his father, Han. And you know the business."

"Are you implying then, that something is going to happen to both Cameron and Erich before Stefan comes of age?"

Abbi sighed and resettled her hands on her lap. "It's only a dream, Han. Maybe it's just nonsense."

"And maybe it isn't. Why did you come here to talk to me about it if it's nonsense?" She didn't answer, and he added, "Do you believe it's nonsense?"

She hesitated before answering firmly, "No."

Silence hovered for several moments. "Was that all? Just me . . . wearing the crown?"

Abbi straightened in her seat. "No." She took a deep breath. "I could see the name *du Woernig* carved in a piece of granite, as if it were a gravestone. I was standing, looking down at it. You knelt on the granite and I placed the crown on your head. When you looked up at me, there were tears in your eyes. You stood and the granite crumbled into dust. The wind blew it away. I woke up cold."

Han wondered if the intense chill that rushed over him was

anything similar to what Abbi had described as a feeling she couldn't quite put into words.

Abbi sighed and said, "The du Woernig name has ruled Horstberg for many, many generations. But Erich is the last . . . unless he has a son."

"There's Nik Koenig," Han stated. "He's technically a du Woernig."

Abbi took a sharp breath. "Well," she said after a moment's thought, "if you're wearing the crown, we know *he* won't be wearing it."

"I'm not entitled to that crown—and I don't want it; not under *any* circumstances." He chuckled sardonically. "This is not what I bargained for when I married Maggie."

"Oh, but it is, Han. When you gave her your name, you took upon your shoulders the legacy bequeathed in her blood."

Han leaned forward. "I am nobody! I am the son of servants! People like me do *not wear crowns!* Do you understand what I'm saying?"

Abbi du Woernig shot out of her chair and set her palms flat on the desk. She leaned toward him and looked into his eyes as if she could see into his soul. "Now, you listen to me, young man," she spoke in a voice seething of power, yet so quiet he could barely hear her. "You have no less royal blood in you than I do. I committed my life, heart, and soul to Cameron du Woernig, having no idea he was the Duke of Horstberg. I am here because I *love* him—no more than you love Maggie. Do you think *I* got what I bargained for? It's not been an easy life, Han. The responsibilities are heavy at times. The heartaches have been many. But I have much to be thankful for. And for Cameron, I would give my life to Horstberg.

"Now," she continued less intensely, "I am certainly not going to take a dream and let it put me into a panic. I consider it a gift, and I must treat it as such. There is only one reason for this particular gift, as far as I can see. It is to prepare for something that may likely happen, even if it doesn't happen according to my perception. The way I see it, the du Woernig name will end with Erich. And that means *your* name, Han, will take its place. For generations to come, Horstberg will be governed by *Heinrichs*. Do you understand what I'm saying? Royal blood alone does not make a man a ruler. It takes knowledge, and integrity, and courage. You have those things, Han. You are a husband to the Princess MagdaLena du Woernig, and a father to Stefan Cameron Han du Woernig Heinrich. And you are the son of two of the finest people I have ever known. Don't let there be any question—your father has more knowledge, integrity, and courage than most men would ever dream of. *That* is who you are, Han Heinrich. And don't forget it for a moment."

Han sat in stunned silence. When she said nothing more, he cleared his throat tensely. "You must forgive me, Your Grace. I have much to learn."

Abbi straightened her back, then turned and quietly walked around the desk to look out the window toward the valley below. "We all have much to learn, Han. My intention was not to upset you—or myself. Maybe its meaning is something entirely different. Maybe it means nothing. I had a dream more than thirty years ago that still hasn't come to pass—though my memory of it has not faded. Perhaps this one will be equally slow."

"Either it will be before Stefan comes of age, or in the absence of Stefan and Gerhard."

"There is only one reason I've shared this with you, Han. You must be prepared. You must learn to treat yourself as one of us—completely—just as your father has. You must absorb the knowledge carefully. That is all I have to say. We will not speak of it again. And it will remain between you and me."

Han rose from his chair and stood beside her. "You won't tell Cameron . . . or Erich?"

"No. I believe that good men—and women of course—will leave this life when their time is done. We as mortals cannot change that. They must live as they always have—as if they could live forever. I won't take that away from them."

"You're a wise woman, Abbi du Woernig. I dare say that God would only give such gifts as visionary dreams to people like you."

She looked up at him with fresh tears brimming in her eyes. Han put his arm around her, and she pressed her face to his shoulder.

"You're a good man, Han," she said, wrapping her arms around him in a way that made him miss his mother—or perhaps feel closer to her. "Did you know," she looked up into his face, smiling slightly, "the day Maggie was born, I told your mother that I would like to see her grow up and marry you? We laughed over it and speculated about sharing our grandchildren, but at the time I don't think either of us really believed it would happen." She touched his face gently. "You are the best thing that ever happened to Maggie. I thank God for your persistence on her behalf."

"She was worth waiting for." He smiled and pressed a kiss to her brow.

Abbi's expression sobered as she said, "Stefan is a unique child, Han."

"Yes, he is. Sometimes I feel we have little in common." He chuckled. "I think he's smarter than I am already."

"You have much wisdom to guide him, though he seems quite drawn to both Cameron and Erich. He always has. Perhaps he knows instinctively that they are his mentors."

"Perhaps," Han said, unable to help the crack in his voice. The very thought struck something in him he didn't want to put into words.

They both turned toward the door at the sound of laughter coming from the other side. A moment later, Erich burst into the room with Cameron and Georg trailing behind him.

"Hello, Mother," Erich boomed, crossing the room to kiss her. Han observed the way she smiled as if nothing in the world was wrong, and then she laughed when Erich hugged her tight and briefly lifted her feet off the floor.

"Did everything go well?" she asked as Georg pressed a quick kiss to her cheek in greeting and sat in his usual chair.

"Quite well, actually," Cameron answered. He kissed her on the mouth and looked briefly into her eyes and smiled, as if they shared some secret. Abbi quickly touched his face before he sat down at the desk.

Han met Abbi's eyes. She discreetly put a finger to her lips, as if to seal their conversation forever.

"Did you miss us, Han, my boy?" Cameron asked, motioning Han toward his usual chair with an indication that they had business to attend to.

"Immensely," Han said in his usual light manner. Abbi slipped unnoticed from the room. As the duke's report of their brief visit to Kohenswald commenced, Han watched him closely, trying to comprehend life without him. Then he put his attention to Erich, who seemed completely absorbed in his father's every word, in spite of the way he toyed idly with a pen. The thought of losing them both was too incredible to believe. While the hole it would leave in his life was something he couldn't fathom, he tried to comprehend what the loss would do to Abbi. The thought was almost physically sickening.

"Are you all right, son?" Georg asked gently.

Han looked up at him, startled. "I'm sorry," he said. "I was just . . . distracted."

"Something on your mind?" Erich asked with genuine concern.

Han managed a smile. "Nothing worth repeating, I can assure you. Go on." He motioned toward Cameron, who looked equally concerned. Did they know him so well? Yes, he thought as Cameron continued. They were family. And by heaven and earth, he would do everything in his power to live worthy of all they worked so hard to uphold.

A short while later, Stefan slipped quietly into the room and sidled up next to Han's chair. Han put his arm around the boy and gave him a quick hug.

"Did you need something, son?" he asked quietly. "We're having a meeting."

"Oh, he's all right." Cameron grinned toward Stefan. "Rusty never causes any trouble."

"Come here, Stef," Georg said, sliding his chair back a little. Stefan hurried to occupy a familiar spot on Georg's lap.

"What were you talking about?" Stefan asked.

"Ah, it was getting boring anyway," Cameron said. "What have you been up to?"

"Just practicing the piano," he reported.

"Good boy." Cameron chuckled.

"I have a question, Cameron," Stefan asked.

Han smiled. With the time Stefan spent around the office, he couldn't just say "Grandpapa" without having both Cameron and Georg answer. He'd started putting their names along with it, until gradually the *Grandpapa* was dropped. Now Stefan spoke to his grandfathers as if they were business associates. Han recalled Abbi's dream. Perhaps they were.

Han missed Stefan's question, but he noticed the careful way Cameron answered it. He wondered how many sovereigns interrupted their meetings to humor a seven-year-old boy. They shared something special was evident.

Stefan kept his seat on Georg's lap as the meeting continued. He listened and quietly drew a picture that Georg was admiring over his shoulder while absently scribbling notes. Nearly an hour after Stefan had appeared, Han noticed him look up sharply toward Erich, who was grinning slyly at the boy. Han shook his head in amusement as Erich flipped a tiny rolled piece of paper at Stefan. A minute later, Stefan flipped one back. It hit Erich square in the chest, and Georg's present comment was interrupted by a histrionic wail.

"Oh," Erich groaned and fell off of his chair, holding his chest as if he were in agony. "He got me. The wretch got me." He performed a remarkable death scene while Stefan and Han tried not to laugh. Georg shook his head with a little chuckle. And Cameron laughed so hard he nearly cried.

The meeting fell apart after that, but Erich hadn't begun

playing until it was nearly time for supper anyway. When everyone was seated at the dining table and the usual conversation regarding the day's events had commenced, Han caught Abbi's eye. For a brief moment he could nearly feel the irony and emotion she had touched on earlier. She truly believed that she would lose her husband and son to untimely deaths, and there was nothing anyone could do about it. He discreetly put a finger to his lips, returning her promise of secrecy. Then they exchanged a smile. Whatever the future held, he knew they were in it together.

A week after Erich had asked Kathe to marry him, Theodor declared to Kathe that she had already practically moved into Castle Horstberg. She had quickly established a habit of spending more time there than she did at home, and they often saw each other in passing. Abbi and Maggie took her shopping again, and many of her new things were left in the room she'd been given that adjoined Erich's, with a sitting room between. As more days passed, she often used the room to rest or freshen up, and it was becoming easier every day to feel at home there.

When Kathe was with the women, Erich was either in his laboratory or seeing to his obligations. Erich and Han spent a great deal of time together, and little Stefan followed them almost continually. Kathe noted that Stefan seemed quite drawn to his Uncle Erich, and the two of them would often go coursing together without Stefan's father.

Kathe also became well acquainted with Lance and Nadine Dukerk. Erich stated when he first introduced them to her that they were Dulsie's parents, that Lance was also the Captain of the Guard, and that he had been a lifelong friend of both Cameron and Georg. Kathe was told they also had sons, but they were scattered with lives of their own, and she never met any of them. However, she quickly came to admire Lance and Nadine and to feel, as Erich did, that they were like family. It was typical that when Erich and the other men were busy with their work, Nadine would sometimes visit with Abbi and Maggie, which gave Kathe the opportunity to get to know her better. Kathe knew that Dulsie must surely be a remarkable young woman, simply because of the people who were her parents. She considered the secret that Erich had told her about Dulsie, and it made her feel nothing but compassion and admiration that these people were so good in spite of facing such challenges. And she was glad to hear continued reports that Dulsie was doing well in her new home. Kathe looked forward to meeting her and said as much to Nadine, who suggested that Dulsie would likely come to Horstberg for the wedding.

"Erich and Dulsie have been such good friends for most of their lives," Nadine said. "I can't imagine that Dulsie wouldn't be here to see him married." Dulsie's mother smiled warmly at Kathe and added, "We're all so happy that Erich has finally found such a wonderful woman."

"You're very kind," Kathe said and once again soaked in the pleasure she found in being surrounded by so many wonderful people. Erich had given her a family and many new friends, and she loved the time she spent with all of them.

Of course, Kathe most enjoyed the time when Erich was not working and they could spend time together. Cameron only required him to be present for the very important things, since he was understanding of what he lightly referred to as Erich finally finding a woman. The only difficult thing for Erich and Kathe was finding an opportunity to be alone together. It almost became a game to steal moments alone, but eventually they were always found.

Erich's kiss became familiar to Kathe, and she sensed a carefully guarded passion that made the prospect of marrying him all the more exciting. She marveled as Erich talked about the cathedral ceremony they would have, with a grand procession from the castle. And he often speculated over their honeymoon, starting in the Black Forest where Han had a cottage he would let them use.

Kathe became nearly as comfortable with the du Woernigs and the Heinrichs as Erich was. She'd been accepted so thoroughly that there was little choice. Even little Stefan, who of all Han and Maggie's children was the quietest, gradually took to Kathe. And he was thrilled with the prospect of being ring bearer at the ceremony, though he wouldn't admit it. He seemed more preoccupied with being able to spend time with Little Karl as much as possible.

Kathe's father had even come to feel at ease in the castle. He'd shared a number of meals with the du Woernigs, and he'd taken to bringing Karl and Stefan back and forth to play quite regularly.

As the social to celebrate their betrothal approached, Kathe began to feel nervous at being able to handle all that was expected of her. Talking it over with Abbi and Maggie helped, but she panicked when it became evident that there would be dancing. Maggie solved the problem when she and Erich took Kathe to the east winter parlor one afternoon. Erich moved back the furniture and Maggie sat at the piano to play. It didn't take long for Kathe to feel comfortable following Erich's lead, although she feared that doing it publicly would not be so easy.

On the day of the social, Kathe went to the castle early in order to get ready for the event. Just a while after lunch was finished, Erich took Kathe to the north summer parlor where he stood her in front of a beautiful mirror. Seeing their reflection together momentarily took her breath away.

"I have something for you," he said.

"Again?" she questioned.

He chuckled. "It's not nearly as precious as that bracelet, but I wanted you to have it nevertheless." He slipped a flat box out of his jacket pocket and held it in front of her. "Are you ready?" he asked.

"I don't know," she said. "You're making me nervous."

"No need for that." He opened the box, and Kathe drew in a sharp breath. She'd perhaps expected some piece of jewelry, but she had never even imagined that something so beautiful existed.

"It must be worth a *fortune,*" she gasped.

"A small one." He laughed. "Maggie told me you would be wearing red tonight, so I chose rubies to go with the diamonds. There are fifty-two stones all together; our ages combined." He paused. "The jeweler suggested that."

"Erich," she shook her head, "you can't give that to me."

"I just did."

"But it's so . . . expensive . . . and . . . when would I ever wear it?"

"Tonight," he said. "And about twice a month for the rest of your life. We could get another one for variety, if you like. Although there is a collection of family jewels that you are welcome to use."

Kathe looked at him dubiously, and he laughed. "Go ahead. Try it on." Kathe couldn't even bring herself to touch it. "Oh, for heaven's sake," he laughed and pulled the necklace out of the box. She realized then that there were also earrings to match. "Hold this," he insisted, and she took the box while he fastened the necklace around her throat. He turned her to face the mirror, and she gasped. She met Erich's eyes in the reflection, wishing she knew what to say.

"Here, give me your hand," he said and pressed her fingers over the jewels hanging below her throat. "See, they don't bite."

Kathe put her other hand over the top of his and moved it downward. She felt him catch his breath as she held it against her. "Do you feel my heart beating, Erich? It beats harder and faster because of you. And I ask myself, day after day, why you would choose me, of all the women in Horstberg."

"Because I loved you the minute I saw you, and I love you more every hour of every day. And because you love me—for who I am, not what I am."

Kathe turned to look at him, but he kept his hand firmly over her heart. "I don't know what to say. Thank you seems so trite."

Erich smiled. "If you can endure this dreadful social this evening for my sake, it will be more than thanks enough."

His eyes turned serious as he pressed her hand over his heart as well. "My heart beats for you, Katherine. Yours beats for me. Life can be no better than that."

He bent to kiss her, and she moved instinctively closer, as if nothing existed beyond the nucleus of their love.

The moment was shattered when the door flew open. "Oh, there you are," Maggie said, apparently oblivious to what she had interrupted. "We've got work to do, sister." She took Kathe's hand to pull her from the room. Erich couldn't help but chuckle as Maggie pointed a finger at him on her way out the door, saying sternly, "Now you just stay away. You can't see her until the social begins."

Erich gave a mocking bow, and the door closed, leaving him alone. He stood for a moment in the empty room and put a hand over his heart. Even in Kathe's absence, it still beat quickly. He thought of the words to the song that his mother had reminded him of. "A fire burns in my heart," he said aloud, and he could almost feel the warmth.

Maggie began by having her lady's maid, Klara, prepare a bath. While Kathe soaked in the steaming water, clouded with rose-scented bath salts, Maggie meticulously worked on Kathe's fingernails. She rounded the tips carefully with an emery board, then buffed them to perfection while they talked on and on, as if they'd known each other forever.

Kathe knew that her gown for this evening had been delivered to the castle, but Maggie hadn't let her see it until she was dressed in all new silk underclothing and silk stockings. It felt different from the soft cotton she was accustomed to, but she declared to Maggie with a smile, "I think I could get used to this."

Maggie claimed that Klara was gifted with styling hair, and while Maggie was getting herself ready, Klara twisted, curled, and pinned Kathe's hair until it was swept into a perfect, elegant twist.

"Oh, it's lovely," Kathe told her. "You *are* gifted. I can never do anything more than a braid and a few pins."

Maggie, too, raved about Klara's accomplishment, and then Kathe was presented with the new gown. Maggie and Klara gasped with approval as Kathe slipped into the red satin that almost appeared to be wrapped around her bodice and draped over the rest of her body, as if it had no stitching at all. Klara fastened the hooks beneath Kathe's arms while Maggie adjusted it off her shoulders. Kathe looked in the mirror and hardly recognized herself. She'd never seen so much of her throat and shoulders exposed, but she had to admit, "You do have good taste, Maggie."

"The color's perfect for you," Maggie replied. "And red does have other advantages, as you will see. Oh," she clasped her hands together triumphantly as she stood back to admire Kathe, "you look incredible. He won't be able to keep his eyes off you for a second. And all those poor souls who didn't win his heart will be crying in the corners."

"What poor souls?" Kathe asked.

"Oh, mercy. It seems that every ruler of every country we have any contact with has one daughter at least who would kill for Erich du Woernig of Horstberg. Not only do they want the man, they want the country and the title. Kohenswald especially would love to get their fingers in our pie. But it's not to be; at least not in this generation. Before Stefan grows up, I'll have to be sure and warn him."

"You've got some time left," Kathe chuckled.

Klara provided red-dyed slippers that felt almost as comfortable as the silk stockings. Then Maggie fastened the new necklace around her throat, and Kathe clipped on the earrings.

"How do you feel?" Maggie asked as they admired the final effect.

Kathe sighed and pressed a hand over her middle in an attempt to ease her nerves. "Like a queen," she said.

"As you should. You'll be very nearly that in a matter of time."

Kathe waited a few minutes while Klara put some finishing touches on Maggie's hair, and then they went together to wait just outside of Cameron and Abbi's room, where they were to meet Erich and Han before descending into the ballroom at the other end of the same hall. Kathe could hear the music of an orchestra in the distance. The reality heightened her nerves.

They had only been there a few minutes when Kathe heard the click of more than one pair of boots on the stairs, and Erich's voice saying, "Theodor practically abandoned me; said he had himself to get ready. Who invited him to this party, anyway?"

Erich and Han stopped at the top of the stairs, and for a long moment the world seemed to freeze. Kathe understood now why Maggie had said the red gown would be appropriate. She had forgotten that the ducal uniforms were red and black. But what Erich wore now was far more elegant than anything she'd ever seen on officers of the Guard. He looked so majestic, so regal—like some mythical god capable of conquering the world. But his eyes were sparkling and full of love as he overtly absorbed her appearance. She'd never felt so beautiful in all her life.

"I did," she finally said after his eyes had traveled slowly down the length of her and back up again.

"You did what?" he asked with a husky quality to his voice.

"I'm the one who invited Theodor."

"Oh, well." He smiled. "In that case, I'll excuse it."

Kathe looked him over again. "You seem to have done rather well without him."

"You seem to have done rather well yourself," he said.

"I had Maggie's help."

"I just picked out the gown," Maggie insisted.

"Let's get out of here, Maggie," Han said, taking his wife's arm. "They could probably stand there and look at each other for an hour."

Maggie winked at Kathe as she turned away on Han's arm and they walked toward the ballroom.

"Can I touch you?" Erich asked when they were alone.

"I was hoping you would," she said, holding out a hand toward him.

Erich took her hand reverently into his and brought it to his lips. Then Kathe caught her breath as he went down on one knee before her, pressing his forehead to her hand in a gesture of pure devotion. Before he came to his feet, Kathe realized his parents were standing nearby. There were tears in Abbi's eyes. Erich cleared his throat and glanced down, seeming briefly embarrassed.

"You look lovely, my dear," Abbi said, stepping forward to share a careful embrace.

"And you, Your Grace," Kathe replied, noting she also wore elaborate jewels with the deep green taffeta gown that brought out the green of her eyes.

Cameron pressed a kiss to Kathe's cheek, then touched it momentarily. "We are truly blessed to have you with us, my dear," he said.

"It is I who am blessed, Your Grace," she replied, kissing him in return. She took note of his uniform, much like Erich's but with more elaborate adornment. The duke and duchess walked past them, and Kathe was intrigued by the crown he wore and the red robe attached to the duke's shoulders that billowed out behind him. She could well imagine Erich wearing them one day.

"You are incredible," Erich said. "It seems to me that you were born to be the next Duchess of Horstberg."

"I'm not so sure about that. But for you, I believe I could do anything."

"Shall we?" he asked, offering his arm.

"Oh," Kathe pressed a hand over the sudden swarm of butterflies in her middle. "I'm nervous. What if I embarrass you, or—"

"That is impossible," he insisted. "If you handle everyone else the way you just handled my parents, there is nothing to be concerned about."

Kathe took a deep breath and put her hand over his arm. They walked together down the hall which curved and widened, opening onto a huge staircase that descended into the ballroom. Kathe held her breath when they hesitated at the top. She had seen this room before, but she never could have imagined a picture so grand as what lay before her now. In a glance, she absorbed the brightly lit room with the orchestra playing at one end. There were many people surrounding the perimeter of the room, drinking champagne, talking and laughing. And several couples were waltzing in the center, as smoothly as if they were floating on clouds. Kathe was amazed at the variety of elegant gowns and the jewels that caught the light, twinkling from every part of the room like stars. Some of the men were dressed in fine suits, but most were wearing elaborate uniforms in many different colors and styles representing the different countries Horstberg associated with for the sake of international relations.

When they stood at the top of the stairs for more than a minute, Kathe whispered discreetly, "What are we waiting for?"

"For the music to end," he said.

"Then what?"

"Just stay with me and look beautiful. That shouldn't be too difficult."

"When a woman is this nervous, *everything* is difficult." Erich chuckled, and she added, "Couldn't we just sneak off and find someplace to do a little serious necking?"

Erich smiled at her with blatant desire showing in his eyes. "With that gown you're wearing, it will take great self-discipline to not do a lot more than that."

Kathe was seized with an entirely different breed of butterflies as they shared a heart-stopping gaze. She nearly forgot where they were standing as her mind wandered into paths it had never gone before. And by the deepening intensity in his eyes, she felt certain his mind was in the same place. She was startled back to the moment when the waltz came to an end. Erich straightened his back and cleared his throat. She followed his example and willed her insides to stay calm.

From the direction of the orchestra, an elaborate fanfare sounded. Kathe felt all eyes in the room turn toward them, and there was a moment of hushed silence before Erich called in a voice of authority, "Ladies and gentlemen, may I present my fiancée, Miss Katherine Lokberg."

Erich turned to her and smiled. The crowd broke into cheers and applause, and the music resumed as they descended the staircase together. The duke and duchess met them at the bottom, and they exchanged embraces all over again. Her father approached as well, and Kathe laughed at the sparkle of joy in his eyes.

"You look like a princess, my dear," Karl said. "But then," he kissed her cheek, "to me you always did."

They fell into some semblance of a receiving line where she stood between Erich and his mother, and they introduced her to each guest individually. Kathe wondered how they remembered so many names and titles. Her head was nearly spinning, but Abbi seemed to sense this and occasionally whispered reassuring words in her ear. Erich kept his arm possessively around her while he told everyone how she'd been more than worth waiting for, and how there was not a more beautiful woman in all the world.

The duke kept her father next to him, handling introductions graciously. Kathe felt pride in her father for his efforts to fit in for her sake. She knew he would prefer not to be involved in such things, but he appeared to be enjoying himself. No one would ever guess he was a common craftsman, although Erich didn't hesitate to admit it whenever anyone asked about him. He spoke of her father with the same pride that he spoke of his own.

Kathe was grateful when they finally had that portion of the event behind them. The supper hour was announced, and they all went together into a dining room she'd not seen before. It was so long she could hardly see the other end. She noticed the children were present now, and Little Karl nearly beamed in his new suit as he was seated between his father and Stefan. Theodor winked at Kathe across the table and she felt warmed by all the love and support surrounding her.

Gradually Kathe began to relax as she realized this wasn't really so difficult. She felt confident that she could survive the evening without embarrassing herself. And it only took a glance at any one of Erich's family to feel completely secure and accepted.

When supper was finished, the adults returned to the ballroom, where Erich led her directly to the center of the floor.

"Why are we the only ones out here?" she asked, alarmed by the fact.

"Because this is *our* dance, my love. This party is in *our* honor, remember?"

"How could I forget?" She managed a smile and took a deep breath as he put one hand to her back, holding her tightly against him. She put one hand into his and placed the other against his shoulder, wondering if she could remember what he'd taught her.

"Just follow my lead," he whispered. As soon as the music began, it was easy to fall into step with him.

"That's what I've been doing all evening," she said.

"You don't need *me* in order to shine," he insisted. "You have more than enough light all by yourself, my love."

He watched her eyes as they danced, and she felt as if they were floating. "I think I could get used to living this way," she said. "As long as you're with me, I believe I could tolerate it."

"Good." He laughed. "It gets tedious after a while, but I must admit, I've never enjoyed one of these socials so much as I am right now. With you to look at, I could enjoy just about anything."

"Tell me I'm not dreaming," she said, feeling delightfully dizzy as he waltzed her around the full circumference of the room.

"You're not dreaming."

"Even if I were, it would be all right."

"Why is that?"

"What you have given me already could last me a lifetime."

"Heaven forbid," he muttered. "We have a lifetime yet to live together, my love. And live it, we will."

The music ended and Erich brought her to a graceful halt. They were applauded, but he seemed oblivious to his surroundings as he bent to kiss her.

"Break it up," Cameron said, taking Kathe's hand. He kissed it regally and added, "Now it's my turn."

"Your Grace." Kathe curtsied slightly. The music began and Kathe quickly learned that it was just as easy to dance with Erich's father. She noticed Erich dancing with his mother, and gradually the floor filled up with other couples. The duke spoke lightly to her, saying things to make her laugh, then he said quite seriously, "I trust my son is treating you well."

"He treats me like a queen, Your Grace."

"As he should," Cameron replied. "Let me put it this way. I'm told by many that Erich is very much like me. In a way, that pleases me. He's a good man and I'm proud of him. But there are things about myself that I'm not certain I would want my son to exemplify, yet I often see signs that he does."

"Such as?" she asked with mischief.

"Well," he chuckled, "I have a nasty temper, and Abbi tells me I can tend to be a little arrogant and overbearing. Georg says some of that is necessary to be a good ruler, and I'm certain he's right. He always is. But sometimes it's difficult to tell if those things are carrying over into my personal life."

The dance ended, but Cameron pressed her hand over his arm and moved deliberately off the dance floor to finish their conversation.

"You've not been beating your wife, or anything, have you?" she asked, then immediately wondered if he would consider it an inappropriate question under any circumstance.

Cameron laughed heartily and said, "No, my dear, I can assure you I try very hard to treat my wife well. But it's difficult to be everything such a woman deserves."

"She loves you very much."

"Did she tell you that?"

"Yes, but she didn't have to. It was evident to me the first time I saw the two of you look at each other."

Cameron smiled. "She is everything to me, Kathe. She's saved me . . . more than once. But there was a time when I didn't treat her well at all. She made me look at things about myself that I didn't want to see, and it was difficult to separate my anger toward my circumstances from my feelings for her. I've tried over the years to make up for that, but my work is often consuming, and I know it's difficult for her—even though she'll rarely admit it."

Cameron sat down at the edge of the room and urged her beside him, keeping her hand over his arm. "You be patient with him, Kathe, just as Abbi was with me. And while you need to allow him to fill his position, don't let him neglect you for the sake of it. Things have a way of balancing out when a man stops to listen to what a good woman has to say."

Kathe placed a kiss on his cheek. "Thank you."

"For what?"

"For raising him to be such a fine man, and for accepting me into your family. I never dreamed I could be so happy."

"The pleasure is ours, young lady, I can assure you."

"You're monopolizing her," Erich said, and they both looked up to see his expression of mock anger.

"I'm warning her," Cameron said in the same tone.

"What? Are you afraid I might be something of the scoundrel you once were?"

Cameron chuckled. "You're smarter than I thought you were." He pointed a finger at Erich and added, "You treat her well, young man, or you'll have to answer to me."

"Yes, Your Grace," Erich said, bowing ridiculously low.

"Get out of here," Cameron said. "I only wish I could live to say that to you."

"*That* is impossible," Erich said.

Kathe caught a look that passed between them: brief but unmistakably tinged with poignancy. She wondered how Erich must feel to know that everything he was raised to be could not take place until his father's death. And Cameron had to know that he would not be around to see his son achieve his life's purpose. But Erich had often said that he hoped his father lived a good, long time, and she appreciated the way they worked together as a team.

Kathe danced with several other gentlemen while Erich was kept busy elsewhere. She tried to enjoy it, but she wanted only to be close to Erich. Occasionally she caught his eye across the room, and he would wink or smile. She recalled what Abbi had said about that and just smiled back.

She was finally able to dance with Erich again, but when it ended, Han took her away from him. "It's my turn," he said. "Go talk to your sister. She's too pregnant to dance."

Erich joined Maggie at the edge of the room as Han swept Kathe across the floor. He looked back to see her laughing so hard at something Han had said that it was amazing she didn't trip. Grinning, Erich sat beside Maggie and took her hand.

"How are you feeling?" he asked Maggie as he sat beside her and took her hand.

"Fat!" she said scornfully, then she chuckled. "But it won't last forever."

"Yes, I know."

"You're happy," she said. It was not a question.

"Incredibly so," he replied, watching again as Kathe tried to laugh and dance at the same time. "He's telling her some of his bad jokes, you know."

Maggie laughed. "He'll probably scare her away."

"No chance of that," Erich insisted. "Did you—"

He was interrupted by a syrupy, "Why, hello there."

They looked up to see the Princesses Von Bindorf. Maggie scowled at them. Erich sighed. No one residing at Castle Horstberg liked these pretentious and arrogant women, or their father.

"Hello," Erich said, knowing he should stand, but he didn't.

"So you finally got snagged," Esmerelda said to him.

"How disappointing that must be for you," Maggie retorted. They both gave her a phony smile, and Anastasia added, "The valet's sister, I hear. It amazes me the way you people intermarry with your servants." She glanced obviously to where Kathe and Han were dancing. "Don't you fear that eventually the royal blood will get a little too . . . thin?"

"On the contrary," Erich said, barely maintaining a civil tone, "too much royal blood eventually turns to water. Interbreeding makes for good, strong stock."

The princesses both looked briefly appalled by his choice of analogies. Maggie bit her lip to keep from laughing. Erich just stared at them, silently daring them to push this any further.

"So, Maggie," Esmerelda said, "I see you're expecting again. Is this four now?"

"Yes," Maggie said.

"And tell me, do your children ever get confused about—"

"It amazes me," Erich interrupted, "how the context of your conversations hasn't changed in twenty years. Do you have nothing better to do? Perhaps you should spend some time examining *your* marriage requirements. Obviously your efforts to marry power and wealth have not brought about the desired results. Perhaps mingling a little with the stablehands would thicken up that blood of yours."

Maggie had to press a hand over her mouth to keep from erupting with laughter to see the shocked expressions of these girls she had hated since she was fifteen.

"I've never heard anything so rude and impertinent," Anastasia said.

"I have," Erich stated, glaring at her.

"If Horstberg survives the likes of you for another generation, it will be a miracle. I hope I live to see the day it falls. You don't even have the sense to be civil to a lady when you see one. How could you—"

"I can assure you," Erich said as he came to his feet with

Maggie's hand in his, "that when I *do* see a lady, I will be civil. Good evening."

Maggie could hear their gasps of astonishment as he whisked her to the other side of the room and got her a glass of champagne.

"It's a wonder we're not at war with those people," Erich snarled. "Those girls are every bit as bad as their father. I pray to God that Horstberg never sees the day when it has to come against them."

"Amen," Maggie said, then she giggled. "You were great. I wish you'd have been around me more when I was fourteen." He grinned in response.

Han and Kathe approached. "If you will excuse us," Erich said, taking Kathe's arm. "I think we're in need of some fresh air."

"Excellent idea," Kathe agreed, desperately wanting a break from all of this grandeur to which she was so unaccustomed.

A minute later they were walking through the castle gardens, admiring the stars. They said little, but Kathe felt content and secure with his arm around her.

"Cold?" he asked when she nuzzled closer to him. She shrugged her shoulders, not wanting to go back inside. "You should be," he said, "half naked as you are."

"Not exactly," she laughed.

Erich stopped and turned to face her. He glanced over her shoulder to be certain they were well out of view from the open doors to the ballroom. With purpose, he took her shoulders into his hands, then moved his fingers across her upper back. "I've been wanting to do that all evening," he admitted.

Kathe pushed a hand into his hair and lifted her mouth to his. "I've been wanting to do *that* all evening," she said.

"How scandalous you are, my lady," he smirked and kissed her again. She succumbed without protest as he eased her completely into his arms, nearly crushing her against him.

"Oh, Erich," she breathed as he slowly opened his eyes. "I wish that we had been married *today*."

"All in good time," he smiled and kissed her again.

Erich wondered how he had reached the age of thirty-one without ever experiencing such pleasure. Knowing they had much yet to share together, he blessed the day she had come into his life. He felt her soften in his embrace and he too wished they were already married. Still, the anticipation was sweet, he thought as he bent to kiss her throat.

"Oh, there you are," he heard Han say behind him. Erich straightened abruptly, and Kathe pressed her face to his shoulder with an exasperated sigh.

"If we weren't related," Erich turned and snarled, albeit lightly, "I'd have your hide. Can't a man kiss a woman in peace around here?"

Han chuckled. "Apparently not."

"Did you need something, or did you just come out here to annoy me?"

Han cleared his throat and spoke like some kind of royal messenger. "Your father wishes to make a formal toast before the guests begin dispersing for the evening."

"Tell him we'll be there in a few minutes," Erich insisted.

"Of course, Your Highness." Han bowed as he backed away, disappearing around the corner of the shrubbery.

Kathe looked up at Erich and they both laughed. "Tomorrow," he said, pointing a finger at her, "you and I are going where *no one* will interrupt us."

"Really?" Intrigue showed in her eyes.

"A picnic might be in order," he said, lifting one brow elaborately.

"Ooh, how nice. You come up with the place. I'll bring the food."

"Ooh, that *does* sound nice."

Erich noticed Kathe shiver involuntarily. "You *are* cold," he said and immediately began to unhook the jacket of his uniform.

"Oh, no, you don't have to do—"

"I'm too hot in this thing. It would seem we're in a position to help each other."

He removed the jacket, revealing a fitted white shirt with a unique collar, and black braces. She felt warmed by the gesture alone as he wrapped the fine coat around her shoulders and straightened it. "There." He smiled. "A ducal uniform has never looked better."

They walked slowly back toward the ballroom, where the orchestra's music emitted through the open doors. As they moved inside, Kathe felt eyes turning their way. But she concentrated on Erich at her side and managed to avoid a fresh onslaught of nerves.

Kathe wore his jacket the remainder of the evening and as he rode home with her in one of the ducal coaches. He kissed her at the front door of her home and only then did she give it back to him. Once the door closed, she hurried up the stairs to the landing, where she watched him discreetly from the window. He slipped the jacket on but left it unhooked as he climbed up on the box seat with the driver, and the coach rolled away.

"Did you have a good time?" her father asked from the bottom of the stairs.

"Oh, the most wonderful time," she replied as he came to stand beside her.

"Your mother would be so proud of you." He put his arms around her.

Kathe wondered if life could get any better, but the next day when Erich came to get her for their picnic, she began to believe it would just improve each day. He came through the back door and immediately pulled her into his arms, growling like some kind of beast. She laughed as he pressed her against the wall and kissed her as if they'd been separated for weeks.

"Mercy, woman," he said in a husky voice, "you've turned a prince into a beggar." Kathe laughed as he kissed her again.

"Good morning, Erich," Karl said lightly.

Erich took a step back, and Kathe actually saw him blush before he glanced down and chuckled. "Good morning," he replied.

"It's a good thing these royal betrothals don't last too long," Karl said before he walked outside. He added over his shoulder, "Have a good time, and be careful."

"We will," Kathe promised.

"I'm really going to get myself into trouble one of these days," Erich said.

"Just promise it will be me you'll get into trouble with."

"No question about that." He stepped back to absorb her appearance in a new burgundy-colored riding habit. "You look splendid, my love."

Kathe turned around at his insistence, and he made a noise of approval. She smiled as she put on her wide-brimmed hat with a burgundy silk scarf tied around it that hung down her back.

"I'm ready," she announced, and he took her hand.

Chapter Six
THREAT OF TREASON

Kathe and Erich rode together over the foothills, then through a covered bridge. "Stay right behind me," Erich ordered as he started into the forest.

Kathe felt a rush of unexplainable excitement as they passed over a fallen tree, then rode along a trail that barely existed between the closely rooted trees. She wondered over their destination, since Erich obviously was well-tuned to the course. She was beginning to think they'd never get there when suddenly the forest moved behind and a spacious meadow opened up before them. It was surrounded by trees, except for a long, high rock wall that ran along the uphill side.

Erich smiled at her as she halted beside him. He pointed to the shade at one side of the meadow created by the angle of the trees in the late-morning sun. "There," he said, and they rode that direction. He helped her dismount, tethered the horses, and then spread a blanket on the ground and motioned gallantly for her to be seated. They talked and laughed and ate until the sun was moving into afternoon, and Erich lay back on the blanket and closed his eyes. Feeling warm, Kathe removed her jacket and set it aside.

"Come here." He pulled off her hat and tossed it, urging her beside him. With her head on his shoulder, it was easy to relax, and the next thing she knew he was looking down at her, the sun at his back.

"We were sleeping together." He smirked proudly.

"So we were," she said through a yawn. "What are you doing?" she asked when he pulled out the ribbon at the bottom of her braid.

"I want to see your hair," he said, urging her to sit up.

Kathe said nothing as Erich unwound the braid and ran his hands through it to smooth it out. He'd always found something cozy in seeing his mother early in the morning or just before bed when her hair would be brushed out and hanging free—a contrast that wouldn't be apparent if women didn't wear their hair confined in public. But Kathe's hair was nothing like the women's he'd grown up with, which was much like his own. Beyond the subtle wave left by the braid, it hung straight and smooth like a dark waterfall, nearly touching the blanket where she sat. He moved to where he could see her face, and as trite as it sounded, he couldn't resist saying, "You are so beautiful, Miss Lokberg."

She smiled timidly. "I am counting the days until it will be Mrs. du Woernig."

"Me too," he said, bending forward to kiss her. With little effort he eased her back onto the blanket, and her hair spread out around her. He kissed her. And kissed her. He rummaged his hands through her hair, fascinated by how soft and thick it was. He buried his face in it, then rolled onto his back and brought her with him. Her hair fell around his head when she looked down at him. She relaxed her head against his shoulder, gently moving her fingers up and down his arms. While he toyed with her hair, she fell back to sleep. The sun moved down behind the trees while he relished just holding her close and gradually drifted off himself.

Kathe woke to realize it was early evening. She was beginning to feel hungry again and wondered if they should leave soon to get home before dark. She was digging quietly in the hamper for some bread and cheese when she heard Erich groan softly and realized he was dreaming. At first she found it amusing, but it quickly became evident that he was . . . what? Frightened? She was contemplating trying to wake him when he sat up so abruptly it startled her.

Erich came awake with a gasp, and his eyes focused on Kathe. She looked afraid, but just seeing her there prompted such relief that he sighed audibly and fell back onto the blanket.

"You were dreaming," she said gently.

"Yes," he admitted, pushing a hand through his hair.

"Tell me," she urged.

"It was nothing," he insisted almost sharply.

"I don't believe you."

Erich looked up at the concern in her eyes and took a deep breath. A part of him didn't want to admit it aloud, while something deeper nearly believed that sharing this burden would somehow ease it. She was the woman he loved, the woman he would spend his life with. There was no reason he shouldn't tell her, but still it came with difficulty. "I've . . . had the same dream . . . several times." *And others that are equally haunting,* he thought but decided to stick to the one he'd just had, the one that he'd dreamed over and over.

"What?" she asked, her concern deepening. She eased close to him and urged his head into her lap, gently pushing the curls back off his face. "Tell me, Erich," she whispered soothingly.

Erich pressed his hands around her back and nuzzled closer to her. "It's not very clear, really. I seem to be in . . . the dark. I feel afraid. And then, I hear glass breaking, and at the same time, it's as if a gun is fired, and the force of the shot throws me against a wall." He shifted his head in her lap so that he could see her face. "I mean . . . it's almost like I'm flying, then I hit the wall. And I wake up. That's it."

Kathe felt stunned. It wasn't so much what he'd said as the way it made her feel. "What do you think it means?" she asked.

Erich forced a chuckle. "It probably doesn't mean a blasted thing. It's a dream, Kathe; that's all."

Kathe looked into his eyes, wondering why there was a lack of sincerity there. From the moment she'd met him, she'd seen nothing in him but genuine honesty. Until now. She couldn't explain it, but her instincts told her he was holding something back.

"I don't believe you," she said. His expression fell so quickly there was no question that she'd hit on a sensitive point. "Erich?" she pressed when he said nothing. He looked at her as if he wanted to say something, but he turned his face into the folds of her skirt and sighed.

Kathe tried frantically to think how to bridge this sudden gap she was feeling between them. "Erich," she twisted her finger in his curls as she spoke, "everything came together so quickly for us, and neither of us have any question that it's right, but . . . sooner or later we've got to face the reality that we're committed for our lifetimes. And we can't buoy each other up through the struggles ahead if we don't start learning to talk about the things that really matter, and trust each other with those things. I want to be able to share my deepest feelings with you, Erich: my fears, my hopes. I want you to be able to do the same."

Erich looked up at her, and the sincerity had returned to his eyes. "You are an incredible woman, Kathe Lokberg."

She smiled timidly and touched his face, but he could see the concern still hovering in her eyes. He wondered how to tell her that she had just voiced his thoughts exactly, in a way he never could have put to words. He *wanted* to tell her his deepest feelings, his hopes, his fears. But he had to admit, "I'm almost afraid to say what I'm feeling aloud, Kathe. These feelings have been with me ever since I came out of that coma. I've often wondered if it was just a hangover from coming so close to death. But as the years have passed, it hasn't gone away. I fear that saying it aloud might make it more real."

"Or perhaps sharing it will ease the burden you've carried alone for so long."

"Perhaps."

"If you're not ready to talk about it, I understand. Please don't feel that you need to—"

"I think maybe I *should* talk about it. You see, I've never felt like I could tell anyone about this. My mother especially would have trouble with this, because—" He stopped abruptly and met Kathe's eyes to gauge her reaction. "Kathe," he sat up and looked at her closely, "my mother has . . . well, my father calls it the gift of dreams."

Her eyes narrowed, and he hoped she would not discredit the respect he had for his mother's gift.

"You see, on many occasions, she has had premonitory dreams. Sometimes they are literal. Sometimes they are symbolic. But in several instances, they have come to pass, so accurately that it's chilling."

"Like what?" she asked, more intrigued than skeptical.

"Well, she dreamt of meeting my father before it happened. And she dreamt of me before there was any indication that she and my father would ever marry. Things like that. But I also know she has dreams she won't talk about—things that frighten her."

It took Kathe a minute to put the pieces together and absorb what he was trying to say. "Are you implying then, that this recurring dream of yours is somehow . . . a presage?"

"I don't know what to think, Kathe," he said, but by the way he glanced down and pushed a hand through his hair, she felt certain he believed it—at least to some degree.

"What do your instincts tell you?" she asked.

"I don't know," he shook his head in frustration. "How do you know where unreasonable fear ends and instinct begins? I only know that I've come close to dying in the past, and I don't want to even consider the possibility that my life might be cut short . . . because of who I am, or any other reason."

Erich pulled Kathe urgently into his arms. "I want a lifetime with you, Kathe. I want to have a family, and to see our children grown."

Kathe didn't know what to say. How could she console him when the things he'd said left her feeling so uneasy? But perhaps her own fears were contributing to this anxiety. She had lost her mother to death, and then Leisl, who had all but taken her mother's place. Could she bear losing Erich? She couldn't even think about it. He had filled her life in a way that she'd never dreamed possible. How could she ever live without him?

"I love you, Erich," she whispered, and he held her tighter. She drew back and touched his face. "We have no way of knowing what the future holds, my love. But I won't waste away the life we share by fearing what tomorrow might bring. We will live while we can and make the most of each moment. That's all we can do."

Erich looked into her eyes, wanting to tell her how precious she was to him. Did she have any idea how she had assuaged his fears already? He only wished they had years behind them already, the way Han and Maggie did. But there was no good to be found in regret. He would do as she'd said and savor every moment with her.

"I love you, Kathe," was all he could think to say, but he believed she understood the true depth of his feelings.

"You know," he said, feeling more relaxed, "my mother tells me there are some dreams—one in particular, I believe—that she's had occasionally for over thirty years, and as of yet nothing's come of it. Maybe my dreams are just nonsense. But even if they aren't, there's no reason to believe that anything will happen in the near future."

"That's somewhat of a comfort," she said, but Erich could see that she still felt uneasy.

Erich touched her face with the back of his hand. "Whenever I got scared as a child, my father would sing me this little song. He tells me that he wrote it for me before I was born."

"Your father writes songs?"

"Only one or two that I know of. He plays the piano relatively well."

"And did he pass down his talent?" she asked with a smile.

"Not to me." He laughed. "He certainly tried to teach me to play, but it was hopeless. I can pick a guitar some, but it's pretty pathetic."

"You were telling me about this song. Were you going to sing it to me?"

"My voice is comparable to my ability with the piano, but if I teach it to *you*, then you can sing it to *me* when I get scared and my father isn't around."

"All right, teach me," she said, threading her fingers between his.

Erich cleared his throat and moved behind her, easing her back to his chest, encircling her with his legs. In a soft voice he sang the simple verses:

> *I know a place where snow falls white*
> *That's where I long to be,*
> *Where castle turrets strike moonlight*
> *And shine where I can see.*
> *I've known my love on mountains high*
> *Where meadows bloom in blue;*
> *I know my love is there for me,*
> *I know that love is true.*
>
> *There is a place where snow falls deep*
> *And warmth is near the hearth.*
> *Deep in my sweetheart's dreams I sleep*
> *There's comfort in this warmth.*
> *The world is cold and brash outside,*
> *I fear what it imparts,*
> *But I know my love is here with me*
> *A fire burns in my heart.*

Kathe turned to look at him as he finished, wondering how to explain the way his song had warmed her. She could almost literally feel the legacy of love passed down to him from his parents, as if he had just passed it on to her.

"That was beautiful," she said.

Erich impulsively pressed her hand over his heart. "My mother told me that when I found the love of my life, I would feel the fire in my heart. Do you feel the warmth, Kathe? It burns for you."

Kathe nodded and took his hand, pressing it over her heart. "I feel the warmth," she said and urged her mouth to his.

Reluctantly they packed up and went home, but Erich taught her the song as they rode through the forest.

After that day, going together to the mountain meadow became a common practice, as did their private gesture of pressing a hand over the other's heart. They would often ride up the mountain together whenever Erich could get away, or they would meet in the meadow where they talked and laughed and played like children. And at least once a day, they exchanged the evidence that their hearts were beating for each other.

Kathe was delighted when Maggie came to visit her one day, bringing a pencil drawing she'd done of Erich, which she'd had framed.

"Oh, I love it!" Kathe actually laughed to see the perfect likeness of him, his dimples showing, his eyes sparkling. "It's incredible how you've captured him so well."

Maggie told her the story of when she'd drawn it, and Kathe was moved to tears. They went upstairs together to decide on a place to hang it in Kathe's bedroom, and then Maggie stayed for lunch.

What little time Kathe spent at home, she enjoyed just looking at the drawing, loving the way it made her feel close to Erich, even in his absence.

On a particularly warm day, Erich and Kathe left the castle together on horseback, going to the nearby meadow where Erich had told her he rode often. She went ahead of him a little, humming the song Erich had taught her. Hearing a loud thud, she glanced over her shoulder and panicked immediately. Erich's horse had no rider. She halted and turned to see him lying on his back on the ground.

"No!" she muttered and galloped toward him, dismounting before the horse came to a complete halt. "Erich!" she cried, going to her knees beside him. She touched his face but got no response. "Oh, Erich, no." She shook him slightly, wondering what might have happened. Memories of his being shot catapulted into her mind. Had he been hit in the back where she couldn't see the blood? Had the sound been lost in her humming and the galloping of her horse?

"Erich!" she cried, her heart pounding into her throat. Never had she felt such fear! He showed no response. She thought of his dream. . . . *It's as if a gun is fired, and the force of the shot throws me . . . It's almost like I'm flying, then I hit the wall.* Or the ground, she thought. "Erich, please!" She pressed her face to his shoulder as a sob erupted from her throat. She wondered what to do. Should she ride back for help or . . .

Kathe's cry turned to a breathy scream when he rolled her onto her back and smothered her with a kiss.

Erich looked down at Kathe's stunned expression and laughed. But he stopped when it became evident she was anything but amused. Huge tears welled up in her eyes and a gaspy sob erupted from her throat.

"Damn you!" she hissed and drew back her hand, slapping him hard. She pushed him away and scrambled to her feet, running to catch the reins of her horse. Erich sat on the ground, stunned and rubbing the sting in his face until he realized she was riding away.

"Kathe!" he called. "Wait a minute. I'm sorry. I . . ."

She galloped past him, ignoring him completely. He whistled for his horse and cursed its slowness in answering his call as he saw Kathe disappear in the distance. He mounted and rode after her, wondering where she would go. He felt some relief as he galloped around a bend and saw her ascending the castle hill. While he tried to think of what would have made her so angry, he wished he'd thought his little practical joke through a little more carefully. He'd heard his father tell the story many times of his jumping off the roof of the lodge into the snow, pretending to be unconscious just to see how Abbi would react. The story always got a good laugh when it was repeated, and Erich just couldn't resist using the idea. But the joke had backfired, and he wasn't certain where to begin making amends—if she would even talk to him.

Kathe was tempted to ride home, but she was riding one of the du Woernig's horses and it didn't feel right to not take it to the castle. Her heart was still pounding with the vivid fear of losing Erich as she galloped into the courtyard and dismounted. A servant took the horse, and she hurried inside, hoping to find someplace to hide and be alone until she could calm down. If the fear weren't bad enough, she felt so angry with Erich that she would likely hit him again if she saw him before she could put these feelings into perspective. She couldn't believe she'd actually slapped him! She couldn't even imagine herself capable of such a thing. But she'd responded immediately to her deepest fears concerning the precariousness of Erich's life. And he'd had the nerve to put her in a position where it had become all too real. And for what?

Kathe stood for a moment in the main hall, wondering which direction to go. She knew the castle was full of alcoves and unused rooms, but she nearly feared getting lost. Impulsively she headed up the stairs toward her own room. She was familiar with that wing and felt certain she could find refuge there.

Halfway up the stairs, she nearly bumped into someone. The tears burning in her eyes made it impossible to tell who it was until she heard Abbi say, "Are you all right, dear?"

Kathe nodded, not daring to speak.

"You're trembling," she added, taking Kathe's hand. Abbi put an arm around her shoulders, and Kathe feared that Erich would come upon them before she could get away. She didn't want to see him right now.

Hearing the main door slam and echo in the distance, Kathe frantically moved away, barely managing a frenzied "Excuse me."

"Kathe!" Erich called from the bottom of the stairs, and she hurried on.

Erich was surprised to come upon his mother, standing on the stairs looking dazed. He paused a moment, feeling a need to explain, but he saw Kathe disappear from the landing and he hurried after her.

Kathe rushed into her room and locked the door, wishing she'd had time to find a more suitable place to hide. A moment later he pounded on the door. "Kathe. Talk to me, please."

She ignored him, pressing a hand over her mouth to keep from crying aloud as the fear and anger rushed out in torrents. When she heard nothing more, she hurried to lock the sitting room door, grateful that she had when he tried to open it a moment later.

"Come on, Kathe," he begged. "Just come out and talk to me. Don't make me beg through this door."

Kathe couldn't answer. She just sat on the floor and cried, trying to remain as quiet as possible.

Erich leaned his head on the door and groaned in self-punishment. For the life of him, he couldn't imagine why she would be so upset. His mother's hand on his shoulder startled him.

"Tell me to go away and mind my business," she said quietly, "and I will."

He stepped back and motioned toward the door. "Maybe *you* can get her to come out."

"What happened?" she asked, urging him away from the door where they wouldn't be overheard.

Erich sighed and pushed his hands into his pockets, feeling like a child again. "Do you remember that little joke Father always talks about . . . when he jumped off the lodge into the snow and pretended to be unconscious while—"

"Oh, you didn't!" she interrupted.

"I'm afraid I did. But I had no idea she would take it so hard. I didn't mean to upset her. I just . . ." He stopped when his mother moved to the bedroom door.

"Katherine," Abbi called gently, "you don't have to come out yet if you don't want to, but you should know that my son is an arrogant, insensitive idiot, and he ought to be slapped good and hard." Erich scowled at his mother, but she ignored him and went on. "I don't blame you a bit for being angry, and if I were you, I don't think I would talk to him for at least a week. It would serve him right. However, I doubt that any of us could tolerate living with him if you did that. He appears to be humble and wanting to grovel for your mercy and forgiveness. If you'll come out, I'll hold him by the ear so you can slap him, and then I'll . . ."

The door came slowly open. Erich held his breath as Kathe appeared, her eyes red and swollen. Her voice was raspy as she said, "I already slapped him; thank you anyway."

"Good for you," Abbi said.

"Whose side are you on?" Erich snarled.

"Someone's got to look out for the poor girl," Abbi insisted. "Nobody was there to look out for me when your father was behaving that way." She glanced at each of them. "Now, if you'll excuse me. Perhaps I should mind my business now and leave the two of you to—"

"Please stay," Erich said, watching Kathe's eyes closely. "Maybe you could help me tell her that I'm sorry. It was a stupid thing to do, but honestly, I didn't think it would upset her so badly. Tell her that I love her, and I will never do anything so cruel again as long as I live. I swear it."

"I think you managed that fine on your own," Abbi said.

"But she still looks angry with me." Erich glanced down sheepishly.

"Perhaps you should ask her why," Abbi suggested.

Erich cleared his throat tensely. "Why are you angry with me, Kathe?"

Kathe swallowed hard and attempted a steady voice. "I thought you were dead. I thought you'd been shot or something, and . . ." She faltered with emotion, but forced herself to get it out. "If you were anybody else, it might have been funny. But you are the heir to Horstberg, Erich du Woernig, and there is still someone out there who once wanted you dead."

Erich squeezed his eyes shut as it began to make sense.

"You've told me yourself about the threats against your life in the past. And with the dreams you've had, you can't possibly expect me to think something like that is funny." She faltered into tears again and leaned against the wall, trying not to make an utter fool of herself.

They were both startled when Abbi asked in a stern voice, "What dreams?"

Erich looked up to see his mother glaring at him, a distinct fear in her eyes.

"I'm certain it's nothing, Mother," he insisted.

Abbi glanced at Kathe, then back to him. "Apparently it is something."

Through the ensuing silence, Kathe's anger merged into compassion. She regretted letting that slip out, knowing Erich hadn't wanted his mother to know.

"What dreams, Erich?" Abbi repeated emphatically.

"There's no good in talking about it, Mother," Erich said gently. "You've said yourself that such things are sometimes better left unsaid."

Abbi looked into his eyes and absorbed his implication. She could hardly insist he tell her when he knew she kept many of her own dreams to herself. But she couldn't hold back the emotion as her own fears rushed forward to meet this new implication.

Erich felt chilled by the tears that rose into his mother's eyes. She might as well have come right out and said that she too had reason to believe something horrible would happen to him. While he was wondering what else to say, she turned and walked out of the room, leaving him alone with Kathe.

"I didn't mean to let that slip out," she said.

He shook his head. "It doesn't matter." Their eyes met, and fresh tears trickled down her face. "I'm so sorry," he said. "I wasn't thinking." He held out a hand toward her. "Will you forgive me?"

Kathe nodded and rushed into his arms, holding to him as if

she might never have the chance again. "Please don't let anything happen to come between us, Erich. Please."

"I intend to live a good, long time, I can assure you."

Kathe nodded stoutly, and nothing more was said about it. But something deep inside told her their time together would be brief.

"So tell me," Han said, putting his feet up on one of the empty chairs in the office, "why are we sitting here slaving away while Erich is off somewhere most likely necking . . . or something like unto it?"

"That's a good question," Cameron concluded.

"The same reason we were all here slaving away while you were off gallivanting about the world with Maggie," Georg said. "It's all for the sake of true love, I suppose."

"I suppose," Han said with dismay.

A minute later Cameron added, "We're not getting much done."

"I know what the problem is," Han suggested. "We've not been to the pub for three days. We're shirking our duties."

"Splendid idea," the duke said, slapping Han on the back. "What a good lad," he added to Georg. "You brought him up right."

At the pub Max greeted them in the usual manner, and everything seemed perfectly normal. But after the drinks were served and the only other people present had left, Max pulled a chair up to their table and sat down, straddling the back of it.

"Kind of quiet today," the duke said.

"You came late," he stated. "It's always quiet this time of day. And I'm glad you waited until now to come. I got something I need to tell you, and I don't want nobody else to hear."

The three of them became attentive as the innkeeper glanced around the empty room, then leaned forward and whispered, his voice barely audible, "One of the servin' girls," he began, "over-heard a conversation here—night before last. And . . ." he seemed hesitant to finish.

"Out with it, man," the duke insisted.

"There's treason underfoot, Your Grace. I hate to be the one to tell you, but you got to know."

The duke's face became intent and stern, waiting to hear the evidence of this.

"What she heard was," Max continued in an even softer whisper, "that someone is stirrin' things up against you, and whoever it might be is lookin' for men to back him up. She wasn't certain, but said she thought somethin' was said about a hundred men or better."

"Good heavens!" Cameron sucked in his breath and blew it out slowly, trying to recover from the shock.

"What were you saying a while back about gut instinct?" Han said to his father, who answered with a distressed expression.

"Do you know anything else?" Cameron asked.

"That's it," Max said. "But I'll keep my ears perked."

"Thank you." The duke put his hand over the innkeeper's where it rested on the table. "I will see you are rewarded for this."

"I don't want no reward, Your Grace," he said. "I just want to see you keep what's rightfully yours. Horstberg's never seen better years since you came back, and anyone who remembers the years when your brother was rulin' here would have to agree with me.

"Besides," he added as he stood, "you're my best customer. I don't want to lose that either."

Cameron managed a chuckle as the innkeeper left the table and a customer entered from outside, requesting rooms for the night.

Han waited for something to be said, but they all remained completely silent. A distinct dread fell over them as they finished their drinks and returned to the castle. The silence continued in the office until Erich came in late afternoon.

"What's the matter?" he asked. "You all look as though the world's about to end."

Cameron didn't answer, and Erich glanced toward Han in question.

Georg spoke up. "It appears a revolutionary force is building," he stated soberly.

"Here?" Erich squeaked. "In Horstberg?"

"That's right," Han said.

"The rumor is a hundred men or better," Georg added.

"Good heavens!" Erich exclaimed.

"That's what I said," Cameron interjected.

"Where on earth did you hear that?" Erich asked, hating the sudden smoldering in his stomach.

"The pub, of course," Han inserted. "Where else?"

"So what are we going to do about it?" Erich asked, and Cameron glanced up at him.

"If you've got any brilliant ideas, son, I'm listening."

Silence fell again. Cameron stared at his hands. Georg sat calmly, seeming deep in contemplation. Han could almost feel his father's mind working, while his own mind went unwillingly to Abbi du Woernig's dream. He felt a cold chill rush over his back but did his best to remain expressionless. Erich tapped a pencil nervously on the desktop, and Han drummed his fingers against his thigh, trying to push away his fears and think logically.

"We have to find out who's behind it," Han said, wanting to at least give a positive note—even if he didn't have a good idea. "Get rid of the instigator and you kill their motivation."

Cameron gazed at Han expectantly, and he fought for something else—*anything* else—to say. His mind ticked through what little they knew, and where the information had come from. Logic started to take over.

"Whoever it is must go to the pub," Han stated, and Cameron glanced dubiously at Georg as if to say this was going nowhere.

"That's right," Erich picked up on Han's idea. "Everybody who's anybody goes to the pub."

"If the barmaid heard what she did, surely she'll hear more. She's obviously loyal. Let's put her to work."

Cameron's eyes lightened a little. He glanced at Georg as if to say, *Why didn't you think of that?* Georg looked proudly toward his son.

"If we can find the instigator and pin anything at all on him," Han said, "we can nip this in the bud."

"I know who the instigator is," Cameron stated. "I can feel it in my blood."

"If Koenig is anything like his father," Georg interjected, "he won't leave enough of a clue to pin any of it to himself."

"But he can't be in it alone," Han added. "There's got to be someone tied to him."

"I think we're on the right track," Cameron said, and a glimmer of hope filtered over the room. "But we've got to be careful."

"Do we turn it over to the Guard?" Georg asked.

"No," Cameron stood up and turned to the window, "not yet. It's too sensitive." He turned to face Han and Erich. "I'm turning it over to the two of you. Find out who the link is between Nik Koenig and this revolutionary force. Get some evidence and have him arrested."

Han and Erich nearly smiled at each other. It almost sounded like the kind of games they used to play as children.

"Do you think you can handle it?" Cameron asked, sitting on the edge of his desk.

"Of course we can," Han said with confidence. "I'm going to start by having a talk with one of the greatest revolutionaries of our time. I'm certain he'll know how a man thinks when he's planning a revolution."

"Really?" Cameron looked surprised. "And who is that?"

Han turned toward his father and grinned. "Tell me, Mr. Heinrich, how does one go about overthrowing a duchy and doing away with the reigning duke?"

Cameron laughed.

"He makes me sound like some kind of criminal," Georg chuckled.

"There was a difference," Cameron added. "We never had anything but the best interest of the people in mind. I doubt that's where Nik Koenig's goals are centered."

"So, let's have it," Han said to his father. "We want to know all about it."

"Ah," Georg leaned back and crossed his ankles, "those were the good old days. We were in so much trouble. Eh, Cam?"

"Abbi thought I was some kind of thief," Cameron added.

"And she married you anyway?" Erich asked.

"Love conquers all." Cameron grinned.

"You know," Georg said, "I think that might be the key. It was making every effort to appear to be what we were not."

"Details;" Han said. "We want details."

Cameron and Georg both gave a wistful laugh and made themselves comfortable, reminiscing over the Reclamation of 1817, while Han and Erich listened to the story in a different frame of mind than ever before.

As Han became suddenly emerged in political affairs that he seemed hesitant to talk about, Maggie was extremely grateful for an extended visit from her sister. She had been keeping herself preoccupied with plans for Erich's wedding, but as her pregnancy progressed, she found it difficult to be involved and had to leave those details up to her mother and Kathe.

Having Sonia around was a delight, and they spent their days visiting and watching their children play. But Maggie lost all enjoyment when Sonia brought up an unexpected topic.

"You know, Mags," she began cautiously, "I've contemplated on whether or not to tell you this, but I feel you've got to know."

"What is it?" Maggie asked, hating her sudden uneasiness.

"I've heard the servants talking," she said, and Maggie didn't like this already. She knew this would be something she didn't want to hear. "You might as well have it straight out," Sonia hedged. "Whether it's true or not, it affects the way people see you."

"Get on with it," Maggie insisted.

"They say that Han is . . . well, that he's involved . . . with a barmaid."

"How ridiculous!" Maggie laughed tensely.

"I can't imagine that it would be true," Sonia said. "Still, you should be aware that . . ."

"Han would never do such a thing," Maggie insisted. "He loves me. I've no doubt of it."

"Then there's nothing to be concerned about," Sonia said easily. Maggie knew she was right, but she hated the nagging questions that remained at the back of her mind long after Sonia had returned to her home country of Schmautzberg. Maggie nearly brought it up with Han several times but decided against it. Memories came back of her mistrust of him when they'd been staying in Italy, and the struggles it had caused. She didn't want to repeat such a difficult episode. She had no reason to believe Han would be deceptive. But still, the uncertainty haunted her.

Why was Han gone so much in the evenings? Never in their married life had he spent so much time away from the castle. Erich was always with Kathe. Their fathers were often busy in the office as usual. But where was Han? He had told her it was a political matter that her father had put him in charge of, but he thought it was best she not know the details. She had trusted him. Why shouldn't she? He had never done anything to betray her trust—as far as she knew.

Thinking deeper on that time in Italy when the comtesse had attempted to entice Han into an involvement, Maggie felt a degree of comfort. Han had told Maggie then that he loved her and she was all he needed, and he had proven that over the years. Still, it needled her. Han seemed to love her as he always had, but when Maggie looked at herself in the mirror and saw only a woman well consumed with pregnancy, her panic deepened. Han was a handsome man—and he'd only become more so with time. Did he consider his wife still attractive after she had borne three children and was expecting another? Deciding she could bear her ignorance no longer, Maggie went to her mother for advice.

"How ridiculous!" Abbi said when Maggie repeated Sonia's gossip.

"That's exactly what I said," Maggie retorted.

"You know it can't be true. It wouldn't be the first time gossip had been started to cause us trouble. I don't believe it for a minute."

"But I . . ." Maggie couldn't bring herself to say that she still had doubts, but Abbi seemed to grasp the truth.

"If you must know," Abbi said gently, "then ask him. He's your husband."

Maggie stood and wrung her hands tensely. "I'm not certain I can. It sounds so accusing, so . . ."

"He has a right to know what's being said about him. You don't have to accuse him of anything. Just ask. There may be political things he can't discuss with you, but this is different. Two people who have shared so much can surely discuss such a thing."

"You're right," Maggie said with confidence. "I must ask him."

Maggie made up her mind to do it right after dinner, but much to her dismay, Han didn't come to dinner. Abbi's eyes across the table helped to reassure Maggie that everything would be all right. But as Maggie waited up far past midnight and still Han hadn't returned, doubts and fears began to blanket what little logic remained.

Feeling restless, Maggie checked on the children and found them all sleeping soundly. She became aware of some commotion outside and went to an upstairs hall where the window looked out to the courtyard. Something unusual was happening near the keep, but it was difficult to discern what. After a short while the commotion died down and all was quiet again.

Maggie went back to her bedroom, and in desperation she knelt to pray aloud. "Please help Han come home to me safely—wherever he is. Please allow there to be some explanation for all of this. Please help us to understand each other and bring it all into the open without—"

Maggie stopped her prayer when the door opened, and she came breathlessly to her feet.

"I'm sorry," Han muttered, "I didn't mean to interrupt."

"I was praying you would come home safely," she said.

"Efficient, isn't He." Han said quite seriously, glancing heavenward. Maggie said nothing and he added, "Is something wrong?"

Maggie shook her head.

"Well, I'm glad you're still up," he said, sitting down to pull off his boots. "There's something I need to tell you."

Maggie sat on the edge of the bed, her heart beating quickly.

"Now that it's over," he went on, "I don't have to keep it a secret anymore." He leaned back and smiled complacently. "We did it!" He laughed, but Maggie could only gaze at him dumbly.

Han could see her frustration and ignorance. He went to her side and took her hand. "Maggie, they just arrested the instigator of the revolutionary force that was conspiring against your father. He assigned me to the job and I did it! Well, actually he wanted Erich and me to do it together, but because of Erich's position, we thought it best for me to do the dirty work. I know I could have arranged for someone else to do it, but I wanted to do it myself. I didn't trust anybody else, or maybe I just wanted to see if I could pull it off."

Maggie smiled to see the pride and fulfillment in his eyes. Peace washed over her as something in his willingness to share this made it evident how much he loved her. Still, she made up her mind to talk to him about her concerns as soon as he finished telling her his news.

"Oh, Maggie!" He embraced her, then kissed her cheek, her brow, her lips. "I can't believe it. I was getting so tired of sitting around the pub pretending to have a good time, but it finally paid off. My connections to our contact must have appeared to be as we wanted it to. We found out who was behind it, and we got enough evidence to back us up." He laughed again. "All because men like to go to the pub and drink too much."

Maggie's eyes narrowed in question. Something in her yearned for this to be the explanation of the gossip she'd heard. Deciding she had to know and now was as good a time as any, Maggie took a deep breath and resigned herself to just ask and get it over with.

"I must apologize to you," he said softly before she had a chance to speak. "I'm afraid that in my attempts to defer suspicion that I was there for political reasons, I may have started some nasty rumors." A lump gathered in Maggie's throat. "I didn't do anything wrong, Maggie. I have nothing to be ashamed of, but I fear it may have appeared that way. I just want you to know . . . in case word gets back to you that . . ." He looked sheepishly toward the floor, and Maggie's heart swelled with love and pride. "Well," he went on, "you wouldn't believe it if someone told you I was . . . flirting with a barmaid, would you?"

Maggie was briefly stunned. When it finally sank in, she threw her arms around his neck as tears of joy and relief pressed into her eyes.

"What was that for?" he laughed.

"I love you," she whispered, touching his face, kissing his lips. "I love you so much."

"I love you too, Maggie, and if there's one thing I've learned from loitering around the pubs too much, I know more than ever that there is no better place than home with you and the children, and there is no woman so good and so beautiful as you are."

Maggie laughed and cried and held him tighter. Han felt a little baffled by her behavior, but he only pulled her close to him and kissed her warmly, so grateful to be home.

The duke made such a fuss over Han's accomplishments the following day that Maggie felt certain he was going to be given a medal for heroism or something. She nearly suggested it. If anyone deserved such an honor, it was Han. But to her, it was not for the same reasons. Politically, Han had done a great thing. By cunning and patience he had maneuvered an avid traitor out of the woodwork and dispelled a revolutionary force that surely could not function without their leader. But it was evident to Maggie that it had truly been a sacrifice for Han. Some men would have loved a good excuse to hang around the pubs and flirt with the barmaids, but Han had hated every minute of it. In Maggie's eyes, her husband's desire to be home with her made him a real hero.

Maggie was grateful to have it over. Not only did Han stay at home and seem more relaxed, but her father became less tense than she had seen him since word of treason had filtered to his ears.

Maggie saw evidence of this as she found Stefan seated at the piano with Cameron beside him. She waited silently in the doorway until Stefan finished his piece, then Cameron applauded and Maggie felt warmed by Stefan's timid smile.

"That was very good," she said and they both turned toward her in surprise.

"The boy is gifted," Cameron said, tousling Stefan's rust-colored hair with his hand.

"And he has a patient teacher," Maggie added.

"It's one of the pleasures in my life," Cameron smiled. "I can think of few things I'd rather do than be here with Stefan."

"Like what?" Stefan asked.

"I'll tell you when you get older." Cameron chuckled. "And how is Maggie today?" Cameron asked, taking his daughter's hand.

"As good as can be expected, I suppose," she replied.

"When's the baby coming, Mama?" Stefan asked.

"Not much longer," she answered. "Soon after your Uncle Erich gets married, I think."

"I hope it's a girl," Stefan said.

"Why is that?" Cameron asked.

"Hannah is a lot nicer to me than Gerhard is. I'd much rather have another sister."

Cameron chuckled. "I tend to agree. Sisters are nice."

"I'm afraid that's already been decided," Maggie said. "Whatever it is, we will love it just the same."

"Are we through now?" Stefan asked his grandfather.

"I believe so," Cameron answered. "You practice that piece twice a day until next week."

Stefan nodded.

"Run along," Maggie said. "I'm certain Grandpapa needs to get to work."

"Actually," Cameron said, "I promised Stefan I would show him something when we were finished. I have a trial to attend tomorrow," he added distastefully. "Today I'm spending some time with Rusty." Cameron tousled Stefan's hair again and Maggie smiled. He was the only one who called the child Rusty, but it seemed to fit the relationship they shared.

They walked together toward the door and Stefan turned to his mother. "We'd invite you to come along, Mama, but this is man to man."

Cameron grinned broadly and Maggie watched them move down the hall, hand in hand. It was one of those moments when the beauty of life struck her, and she couldn't help feeling grateful. There were no words to describe the joy Stefan had brought into her life—as he did to those around her. He was a unique child, small for his age, but intelligent, witty, and sensitive beyond his years. He could be intuitive and caring in a way that left Maggie in awe, and he had a look about him that could only be described as a man in miniature. At seven years old, he was masculine to the core. He wasn't exactly like any of the men he'd descended from, yet all of them found a unique fulfillment in sharing their life with Stefan.

"Stefan," Maggie called and he turned back without letting go of Cameron's hand. "You take good care of your grandfather."

"I will." He smiled with confidence, and they walked on and turned a corner so that Maggie could no longer see them, and she turned to go the other direction.

"Have you ever been to the highest turret?" Cameron asked Stefan.

"Is that where we're going?"

"Exactly. Do you think you can make it up all those steps?"

"If you can, I can," Stefan retorted.

"And why is that?"

"You're fifty-six years older than I am," Stefan stated.

"You're too smart for your own good." Cameron chuckled.

They went together to the central north turret, and Stefan followed his grandfather up the winding stairs. It seemed to go on and on, and they stopped a few times to catch their breath, but once they'd reached the top, the view was well worth it.

"Wow!" Stefan exclaimed, looking out the north window. "It's a hundred miles down."

"At least," Cameron said. "But come out here."

They stepped through a door, and a brisk wind greeted them. Stefan held Cameron's hand tightly as they circled around the balcony that surrounded the turret.

"Why is it so windy?" Stefan asked.

"It's always windy when you're up this high. Being at the top of the world has its drawbacks. Just like being the Duke of Horstberg is a much more turbulent life than, say, for instance, being a blacksmith."

"Don't you like being the duke?" he asked with genuine sincerity.

"It's not so much that as . . . well, it's just a lot of responsibility. And sometimes it's a precarious position to be in."

"What's precarious?"

"Chancy . . . risky." Cameron drew a deep breath and looked

around him. "But it does have its rewards." He pointed to the mountains before them. "As far as you can see is Horstberg. It's the same when you turn that way."

"What about over there?" Stefan asked.

"No," Cameron said. "Do you see that castle over there, just beyond the lake?"

"Yes."

"That's Castle Kohenswald. They're our neighbors. All of the land on the other side of the lake belongs to them."

Stefan turned back the other way. He liked looking at Horstberg better. After a long silence he said, "It's beautiful."

"Stefan," Cameron said soberly, "do you know what will happen if Erich doesn't have a son?"

"He'll be overrun by women," Stefan stated quite seriously, but Cameron couldn't keep from laughing at the incongruity of such a statement coming from a child's lips.

"I mean as far as the duchy is concerned," Cameron clarified. Stefan looked bewildered. "Do you know what will happen when I die?"

"Are you going to die?" Stefan asked in a panic.

"Not right away, I hope. But when I do, Erich will be the Duke of Horstberg, because he is my eldest—and only—son. But do you know what would happen if Erich died and he didn't have a son?"

"What?"

Cameron looked directly at him. "*You* would be the Duke of Horstberg, Stefan, because you are the eldest son of my eldest daughter. Everything you see would be yours." Stefan looked around him, then gazed at Cameron inquisitively. "I don't think it will ever happen," Cameron added with a smile. "Erich will probably have a whole slew of boys. But just in case, I wanted you to know."

"I'd rather be a musician—like you," Stefan stated, "or maybe an artist—like Grandmama."

"And so you will be," Cameron reassured him, "whether you are the Duke of Horstberg or not."

Stefan was silent a moment, then asked, "Can we go riding now?"

"I think that's a splendid idea," Cameron replied. He took one more look around himself and sighed before they went inside.

Stefan sat watching his grandmother paint, obviously fascinated by the way she was mixing colors to create a sunset that looked almost real to him.

The door opened behind him, and they both turned to see his grandfather enter.

Cameron offered the boy a smile, then focused his attention on his wife. Their eyes met, and Abbi could tell right away how much he needed her.

"Is the trial over?" Stefan asked.

"Yes, Rusty, it's over," he answered tonelessly.

"Run along now, Stefan," Abbi said. "Your grandfather and I need to talk."

Abbi watched Stefan leave with no hesitation, and Cameron leaned against the closed door, watching her intently. She rose from her stool and set the brush aside, wondering what had gone wrong.

"Tell me," she whispered.

"I hate it," he said brusquely, walking toward the window. "No matter how many times I sentence a man to death, it never gets easier."

"I assume he was found guilty."

"Quite."

"Treason?"

"He reeked of it."

"The jury was unanimous?"

"Yes. The evidence was staggering."

"And what about the judge?" she asked carefully.

He turned to lean on the sill and stuffed his hands in his

pockets. "My gut instinct told me he was guilty. I have to believe I did the right thing."

"Then there is nothing to concern yourself over."

Cameron turned away and pushed his hand through his hair.

"There's something else," she stated with certainty.

"He's going to be executed at sunrise. But what I really wanted to get out of him, I didn't."

"And what was that?"

"If only we could have connected his actions to Nik Koenig in any way, we could have the fiend arrested and be done with this."

"You told me he's been seen with him." Abbi sat back down.

"But that's it," Cameron said with distaste. "No matter what angle we took, he defended Koenig to the hilt. He swears that Koenig is nothing more than a friend, completely innocent of any political involvement. This man as much as admitted that he was leading an army with the intention of overthrowing the country. But for what purpose? What could possibly be his motive if someone like Koenig isn't behind him? There is no other person living who could make any claim to the throne—however questionable. Without Koenig's connection, it doesn't ring true. It doesn't make sense. Now this man is going to die, and we will be back where we started. Koenig will be able to gather his force back up with a butterfly net once this has subsided."

"I can see why it disturbs you," she said gently.

"Disturbs me?" Cameron chuckled humorlessly. "It scares the hell out of me."

"Maybe Nik Koenig truly isn't involved," she offered, trying to be objective.

"There's nothing but instinct to tell me that he is."

"And that's enough, I think," Abbi said. "Although there is some clear logic to your thinking, as well. You have proven many times that it takes instinct to be a good ruler." She smiled toward him. "And you are a good ruler."

Cameron's eyes turned wistful as he gazed at his wife. "Only because I have you," he said quietly. They were both silent a long moment. "Abbi," he added, "I would die without you. Every day I look at Georg and wonder how he even survives. If he loved Elsa half as much as I love you, then he has faced more than I could ever endure." He sighed. "I could not rule this country without you."

Abbi gave a soft laugh. "Well, I certainly couldn't rule it without you."

"I bet you could," Cameron said, knowing the true depth of Abbi's strengths.

Their laughter dissipated into a silence that hung heavily on what permeated the air between them. For thirty-two years Cameron had done nothing more than love her a little more each day. Her beauty still left him stunned, her unquestioning love for him was humbling.

"You need me," she said quietly, knowing by his eyes that the turmoil he felt within was presently unbearable.

"You always know," he whispered. Quietly he stepped toward her and pulled out the paintbrush that held part of her hair coiled at the back of her head. The thick red curls fell around her shoulders, and he set the brush aside. He took her hands into his and kissed them each in turn.

Without a word between them, Abbi led him by the hand to the bedroom they had shared for more than three decades. She locked the doors and closed the drapes, then stood before him as he sat to pull off his boots. The gray in Cameron's hair betrayed his years, as did the lines in his face. But the fascination in his eyes was as if he had never seen anything so beautiful before in his life.

Cameron rose to take her in his arms and kissed her as if there were no tomorrow. He thought briefly of Georg and the loneliness he surely felt each day, and he almost wished there was a way to share the rich blessings that Abbi bestowed upon his life. As he pulled her into his arms and urged her to the bed,

Cameron felt the weight of a country fall briefly away from his shoulders.

Abbi cherished her own renewal of strength from the way Cameron loved her, and inwardly she blessed the unseen power that had brought them together and made their lives so rich. She loved him so much.

Chapter Seven
A TRAITOR'S QUEST

Cameron nearly fell asleep with Abbi in his arms, and they were both startled when a knock came to the door.

"Who is it?" Cameron called, pulling on his breeches.

"It's Georg," came the reply, and Cameron glanced toward Abbi with concern. They both knew he wouldn't have come personally without good reason.

"I'm coming," Cameron said. He tossed Abbi's wrapper to her and put his arms into his shirt, making certain she was decent before he pulled open the door.

"What is it?" he insisted as Georg stepped into the room, not seeming surprised in the least to realize what had obviously transpired in the middle of the afternoon.

"We just had an attempted prison break," Georg stated.

"What?" Cameron shouted, pulling on his boots. "In broad daylight?"

Georg glanced wryly toward Abbi, who smiled timidly. "Some people aren't conformists," he said, and Abbi laughed softly.

Cameron glanced toward her in surprise, and then he caught the irony and chuckled himself.

"You said it was an attempt," Cameron said, buttoning his shirt. "I assume it failed."

"Quite."

"Our great traitor, I'm guessing."

"Very perceptive."

"Was anyone hurt?" Cameron insisted.

"Two of the four assailants were killed. One was wounded and arrested. The other got away." Georg paused. "One of our men was killed."

Cameron looked up sharply. "Who?"

"Yunger," Georg provided.

Cameron turned his face upward and squeezed his eyes shut. Abbi went to him and took his hand, knowing how it hurt him when such things happened.

"Isn't he the one who just got married?" Cameron asked dryly.

Georg only nodded. Abbi felt Cameron's grip tighten, and she returned it, trying to offer comfort.

"I will pay his wife a visit this afternoon," Abbi said quietly, "and see if there is anything she needs." Cameron nodded, appreciating the little things she did for others that meant so much.

"I think we'll have a little talk with our prisoner," Cameron said, moving toward the door.

"I suspected we might." Georg followed him, pausing to nod toward Abbi.

Cameron stopped at the door and turned back. "I love you, Abbi. Thank you for always being there when I need you."

"It was my pleasure," she replied gently, and Cameron knew he could face anything.

Georg explained in detail what had happened as they walked out to the courtyard and crossed it. Cameron had to agree that what they had been attempting couldn't possibly have succeeded. If they still believed Nik Koenig was behind this, it was almost as if he didn't want the prisoner to escape. He only wanted his cohort to see that they had tried.

"Rolf Grimm," Cameron demanded as he entered the keep.

"I think he's expecting you, Your Grace," the officer said, leading the way down the hall while he rummaged through his keys.

When the door of the cell was opened, Cameron stepped in and Georg followed. The officer remained in the doorway as a standard procedure. The prisoner didn't rise from his cot, and the officer shouted. "Get up, Grimm. His Grace is here to see you."

"How quaint," came a cynical reply as he swung his legs to the floor but remained sitting.

"I hear your friends paid a little visit."

"They tried."

"One of my men was killed in the process." Cameron lowered his voice. "How does that rest on your conscience?"

"I didn't kill him," he replied calmly.

"That doesn't hold you any less responsible. I'm certain the herd of sheep following you would do anything if you asked them to."

"They probably would," Grimm said proudly.

"They appear to be loyal," Cameron said, "but perhaps a little stupid."

"As many of your subjects must be," Grimm retorted.

"Keep it up and we'll summon the firing squad now."

"The sooner I get out of this wretched place, the better . . . *Your Grace.*"

"It wasn't meant to be an enjoyable place to stay."

"At least you've succeeded at something."

"The sooner you get to hell, the sooner the real punishment can begin. And that's all the less time I have to think about it. But before you go," Cameron said, making no effort to hold back his bitter tone, "I want to know who you're covering for. There's more to this than you're admitting and I know it." Mr. Grimm said nothing. "Who's holding the leash, Grimm?" Cameron demanded.

"What's in it for me?" he asked lightly. "What's it worth, Your Grace? My life perhaps?"

"That's questionable," Cameron replied, "but perhaps negotiable."

"Ah," Grimm chuckled, "don't bother. I'm not afraid to die for my country. It's a worthy cause."

"But you're not dying for it," Cameron stated distastefully.

"You're dying against it. I'm certain that will be noted on the other side."

"If there is another side," Grimm retorted.

"In your case, you'd be wise to pray there isn't. But in the meantime, you might reconsider telling me what I want to know. You won't lose anything by it. All you're doing now is sacrificing your life so some undeserving bastard can throw his power and greed around. If he fails or succeeds, you're still dead."

"Oh, he'll succeed," Grimm said with a sneer, and Cameron felt his fists clench. He knew they were talking about the same man. "And it is a pity I won't be around to see it, but then, neither will you."

"Your tongue is getting a little too sharp," the officer cautioned, but the prisoner just laughed.

"If I'm going to die, I might as well have my say." He turned to Cameron and looked directly into his eyes. "They may have failed at getting me out of here," he said, "but this is not the end. It is only the beginning. My death will be avenged, Your Grace, and before this is over, you will wish you had never seen my face."

Cameron didn't allow his expression to falter as he absorbed the depth of Rolf Grimm's threat. His voice lowered and his gaze hardened further as he spoke to the officer without taking his eyes from this traitorous fanatic. "I want him executed at sundown." Silently he turned toward the door, pausing only to say to Mr. Grimm, "And may your soul rot in hell."

Rolf Grimm was executed several hours before it had been originally scheduled, and for the first time ever, Cameron felt a degree of pleasure to witness a man being shot. If only he could be free of what Rolf Grimm had left behind. Instinctively Cameron knew it was not a bluff. The traitor's death would be avenged.

"What are you doing?" Erich's voice startled Kathe, and she nearly dropped the little shuttle in her hands.

"Ooh," she growled, "how did you get in here so quietly?"

"One step at a time." He smirked and walked into the parlor to kiss her. He sat beside her on the sofa and added, "Your father says I've been neglecting you."

"He's absolutely right," she insisted, albeit lightly.

"Business must be done," he stated, "but I can assure you that no one suffers when we are separated more than I."

Kathe scowled comically at him, then asked, "What kind of business?" She didn't like the prickly sensation at the back of her neck spurred by the brief hardness that passed through his eyes. Something was wrong and she knew it.

"Is it confidential?" she asked when he didn't answer.

Erich was tempted to lie. But the trial and execution of Rolf Grimm was public knowledge. It was the personal implication of the whole thing that disturbed him, and he simply didn't want to tell her. "It's not confidential," he stated. "But I don't want to talk about that right now." A moment later he added, "You didn't answer my question. What are you doing?"

"It's called tatting," she said, concentrating on the tiny shuttle in her hands as she maneuvered it to create the intricate lace.

Erich bent over to examine her work closer. "It looks difficult."

"I've been doing it since I was a child. A friend of my mother's taught me."

Erich made a noise to indicate he was impressed. "Talented as well as beautiful," he said, fingering the lace collar she had added to one of her new dresses. "I've noticed the lace you wear, but I had no idea you made it yourself."

"I'm just full of surprises." She smiled wryly.

Erich sighed and pushed his arm around her. "I've missed you."

"It's only been two days. And I was at the castle yesterday, having lunch with Maggie, but you were nowhere to be found."

"Yes, I heard about that. And it broke my heart. That's why I brought you a gift; although I confess it has selfish motives behind it."

Kathe set her work aside and gazed at him sideways. "Your gifts make me nervous. If it's dreadfully expensive or a priceless family heirloom, I don't think I can take the stress."

"It's neither." He laughed, coming to his feet with her hand in his. "I left it in the kitchen so that I could sneak up on you."

They walked down the hall until Kathe tugged on his hand to stop him. "Do you call that little chicken peck you gave me in the parlor a proper kiss for your betrothed?"

"Certainly not." He lifted his brows comically and pulled her close. She laughed when he lowered her back over his arm, kissing her long and hard.

"How was that?" he asked, still holding her back so far that her braid dangled on the floor.

"Very good," Karl said, and they straightened abruptly. Kathe put her hands over her eyes in embarrassment, shaking her head slowly.

Erich sighed with exaggerated frustration. "I seriously doubt that the average man has this much trouble kissing a woman in privacy."

"That's the idea, young man," Karl said, easing past them to go to the library. "When you're married to her, you'll have plenty of privacy." He glanced back over his shoulder with a smirk and added, "As if either of you were average."

"I think you'd better show me this gift," Kathe said, "before you get us both into trouble."

"Katherine, my dear, I was in trouble the minute I set eyes on you."

They entered the kitchen where a large box was sitting on the table. "Go on and open it," Erich insisted. "It won't bite you. I must confess, Maggie picked it out . . . although it was *my* idea."

"It must be something to wear," she said, lifting the lid and folding back the tissue.

"Very good," he drawled with exaggeration.

"Oh, it's beautiful!" Kathe exclaimed, lifting the red gabardine dress, adorned with black piping and black frog closures down the front of the bodice. She held it against her, noting the extremely full skirt.

"And, of course, you need a hat . . . or so Maggie tells me." He slid out a chair and lifted an elegant hat box up by its cord handle. Kathe set the dress aside and tentatively removed the lid, gasping with delight as she pulled out an adorable red hat, the style for riding, with a long black scarf hanging down the back.

"Try it on," he said, setting the box aside. Kathe put the hat on and turned for him, laughing at his obvious approval.

"Does this have a specific purpose?" she asked, wondering what great event she would have to endure now.

"It's for Reclamation Day, of course," he said.

Kathe's eyes widened in alarm. "And what exactly do I have to do?"

"Relax," Erich said, pushing his arm around her. "You will ride from the castle with the family, and then we just enjoy the festivities. Of course, we will participate in the folk dancing, but—"

"What folk dancing?" she interrupted.

"You know . . . they do it every year. It's the . . ." Erich stopped at the obvious ignorance in her eyes. "Surely you've been to the fair and—"

"Not since my mother died," she insisted, turning away from him.

Erich set his hands gently on her shoulders. "Losing her must have been very difficult for you," he said softly behind her ear.

"Yes, it was," she admitted.

"Do you think she would have wanted you to stop living in her absence?"

"No, but . . . everywhere I went reminded me of her."

"Come with me to the fair, Kathe, and we'll make new memories." She said nothing, and he added gently, "You will go with me, won't you? This holiday has special significance with my family, you know. You're a part of that family now. I want you with me."

"I'm not a du Woernig yet," she stated.

"As good as," he replied, turning her toward him. He touched her face and looked into her eyes. "Will you go with me, Kathe?"

She smiled at last. "Of course I will, but if I'm going to have to do this . . . folk dancing, you'd better start giving me lessons."

"Nothing would give me more pleasure." He smirked, then added, "Well . . . almost nothing."

Erich pushed back the table in the kitchen, and they spent the following hours practicing the simple dance. Erich had her laughing so hard a few times that she had to sit down and hold her aching side. When Kathe began to feel some confidence with the dance, an excitement budded in her at the thought of attending this celebration with him. While he was turning her around with his hand at her waist, she glanced over to see her father leaning in the doorframe, grinning broadly.

"Hello, Father," she said as Erich moved behind her and held her hands high.

"May I?" Karl asked Erich and deftly took his place, doing the simple steps fluidly. "It's been a long time," he said, turning with his arm around her waist, "but it would seem I've not forgotten it."

They finished together, and Erich applauded exuberantly. "Very nice," he insisted. "I take it you will be joining us at the fair . . . *Father*."

"Well," Karl shrugged, "I haven't been since my wife passed away, but—"

"Oh, not you, too!" Erich said. "I'd say it's about time the both of you got out and had some fun."

"I'd say you're probably right." Karl smiled and gave Kathe a hug. "Hey, little lady," he added, looking into her eyes, "I was wondering if you'd ever shown Erich the view out your window. I think he might find it interesting."

Kathe's eyes widened as she perceived his idea. She hadn't really thought about it, but she had to agree. With purpose, she held out her hand to Erich. "Come along."

Erich followed her down the hall to a staircase that curved gracefully upward. They entered the first door on the left, and he felt warmed immediately by the coziness of the room that seemed to speak of her personality.

"Ooh," he said, "this is nice. Maybe I should move in here with you."

"Not very convenient for your work."

"That could be advantageous at times."

"Well, I'm certain Father would let us escape here any time we need to."

"That's a nice thought." Erich turned to survey the room, surprised to see a large, framed drawing of himself.

"My sister has been here," he said with a comical scowl.

"Yes, she has," Kathe said, putting her arms around him from behind. "And on those days when that scoundrel I'm betrothed to abandons me for his work, I always have his handsome face to admire."

Erich made a dubious noise, then said, "So, show me this view before I throw you on that bed and kiss you passionately and have your father walk in on us."

Kathe led him to the window, which was situated into the corner of the room. He caught his breath at the perfect view of Castle Horstberg sitting majestically at the far side of the valley.

"I have often stood at this window," she said softly, "trying to imagine what it might be like to actually live in such a place. In a way, I think I believed that it was just a myth; that no one could really call such a magnificent structure *home*." Erich looked into her eyes and touched her face. "I never would have dreamed . . ."

"That it would be *your* home?"

"Precisely. It's nearly like a fairy tale."

"I only pray we will have a happily ever after," he said a little too seriously.

"As I've said before, I believe I could live a lifetime on what you have given me already."

"While I tend to agree, I would hope to be entitled to more than that."

He pressed his mouth over hers, pulling her completely into his arms. And miraculously, no one interrupted their kiss.

Reclamation Day dawned with fair skies. Kathe went early to Castle Horstberg to get ready and couldn't help feeling excited. She walked down the stairs with Abbi and Maggie to find the men waiting in the main hall, dressed in their uniforms. Erich's father wore the ducal robe and crown, and it wasn't difficult for Kathe to imagine Erich wearing them one day.

"You look superb, as I expected," Erich said warmly, offering his arm.

Kathe smiled in return and the family moved out into the courtyard. As soon as the duke appeared, the Captain of the Guard called the troops to attention. Maggie was escorted to one of the ducal coaches, along with Hannah and Gerhard, both of whom preferred not to ride horses in the procession. The rest of the family mounted the waiting animals, and the livery servants moved back. As Cameron lifted his gloved hand, the captain responded with a command. A drum cadence began and started them on their slow trek toward the village.

Kathe felt nervous at first by the grandeur of the entire thing. But as she observed the casual manner in which Erich rode closely beside her, she gradually relaxed and enjoyed the experience. She noted Cameron riding just ahead of them, conversing easily with his wife on one side and Georg on the other. Han and Erich were joking with each other as easily as if they were sitting in the parlor. Erich often turned to her with a wink or a smile, and she had to admit she was glad to be at his side.

Nearing the center of town, their attention turned more to the crowds lining the sides of the street.

"Just smile and wave," Erich said discreetly. She noticed how naturally Abbi was doing just that, and occasionally blowing a kiss. It was easy to follow her lead, and after a few minutes she actually felt comfortable. She was twice given flowers by children, and managed to hold them in her hand with the reins.

When they finally arrived in the market square, they were seated where they could observe the entertainment. The day flew by with enjoyment and laughter, and Kathe realized she was truly beginning to feel like a part of the family. In the weeks since she had met Erich, she had to admit she had adjusted rather well to something she had once believed she could never do.

The only dark spot in the day came when she heard Erich say with disdain, "What is *he* doing here?"

"He lives here," Han answered scornfully, "just like the rest of us."

Kathe turned in the direction of their focus and saw a young, dark-haired man approaching with a middle-aged woman on his arm. They were obviously coming to converse with the duke, and Kathe sensed Erich becoming tense. She was surprised when this man said exuberantly to Cameron, "Uncle! How are you?"

The duke shifted in his seat and asked, "Is there something you need?"

"Actually, no. I only wished to introduce you to my mother."

"How charming," Cameron said in a voice that indicated it wasn't.

Cameron stole a quick, discreet glance toward Abbi, grateful to feel the calming effect her presence always had on him.

"Your Grace," the woman said with a glint in her eye that he found disturbing.

"Miss Koenig," Cameron nodded civilly, wondering if the woman had any idea what kind of a man her son really was. But then, if she had been involved with Nikolaus du Woernig, he wondered what kind of woman *she* was.

"It's Mrs. du Woernig," she said with a snippy voice and an arrogant tilt of her chin.

"You must forgive me for being ignorant of my brother's escapades . . . dead that he is."

"And were he not," she glanced obtrusively toward Abbi, "the circumstances here would be very different."

"Were he not," Cameron stated, and Klarice Koenig looked back at him with eyes that seethed with hatred, "Horstberg would have long ago fallen into the hands of its enemies. My brother was a suave, charming man, able to make a woman believe just about anything. But the fact is, he was a greedy tyrant with no comprehension of ruling this country."

"You don't know what you're talking about . . . *Your Grace.*" The title dripped of sarcasm, and Cameron got a glimpse of why Nik Koenig behaved the way he did.

"I see now where your son gets his manners," Cameron remarked.

"My son will fulfill his father's legacy and avenge his death, as surely as I'm standing here."

Kathe tightened her hand in Erich's. She was only able to put little pieces together, but it was evident the situation here was not good.

"Are you threatening me, madame?" Cameron asked coolly.

"Come along, Mother," Nik said, and for a moment Cameron almost thought he looked embarrassed by her behavior. "This is getting nowhere."

"Listen to your son, madame," Cameron said. "It will get you nowhere." He nodded toward Nik and added, "And you listen to me, young man. Believe me when I tell you that your father was not a nice man." He glanced toward Klarice. "It seems that your parents were well suited for each other. Still, if he had minded his business, you could have grown up with a very wealthy— albeit obnoxious—father. His death was a result of the choices he made. Bear that in mind while you are choosing what you do with what he left to you."

"Save your sweet little speeches for the people who follow

you blindly like sheep," Klarice hissed. "I'm not fool enough to believe that you are what you say you are."

"Come along, Mother," Nik insisted and urged her firmly away. Once they were alone, he added, "Saying such things to him will not help your cause any."

"Perhaps not," she snapped, "but it certainly made me *feel* better."

"You're a bitter woman, Mother. At times I could almost fear what you will drive me to."

"If it weren't for me, you'd *never* achieve your quest. If you want to be the Duke of Horstberg, then shut up and listen to what I tell you."

"*My* quest?" He laughed cynically. "I'm beginning to wonder whose quest this really is."

Klarice ignored him as she stopped and turned back briefly to where the royal family was seated. "I hope they enjoy the remainder of the celebration. It will be their last day of public glory, I can assure you."

"Dare I ask who that was?" Kathe asked after a long minute of silence among the family.

"That, my dear," Cameron volunteered, "is the thorn in my side."

When he said nothing more, Kathe turned to Erich, hoping for an explanation. "I'll tell you later," he said, but by his tone she wondered if he would.

A few minutes later the folk dancing began, and Kathe became caught up in the mood of celebration. She danced one set with Erich, then her father, then Theodor. She danced with Han, then with the duke. On the last set, Erich insisted she dance with him again since it was tradition to spend the remainder of the evening with your dance partner.

The day ended with a magnificent display of fireworks while Erich held her close from behind, and she leaned her head back against his shoulder, holding her hat in her hand.

"Did you have a good time?" he asked as he opened the side door of her home to escort her in.

"The most wonderful time," she said.

Erich kissed her warmly, but when she drew back, there was question in her eyes.

"What?" he asked.

"It's later," she stated. He looked baffled and she clarified, "You said you would tell me later . . . about the thorn in your father's side."

Erich's expression faltered immediately. "Must we talk about that now?"

"Do you have an appointment or—"

"No, of course not."

"Well then, now seems a good time." He said nothing, and she added, "I get the impression you're keeping something from me."

Erich sighed and folded his arms, looking at the floor. "Give me one good reason why I should burden you with the tedious details of political matters."

"Because I am almost your wife," she stated. "Is that a good enough reason?" He didn't answer and she went on. "Do you consider it a political matter . . . this obvious friction between your father and the man I am assuming is your cousin? It would appear to be more a family matter."

"In this business, family and politics are very closely related."

"You keep telling me that I'm as good as a member of your family. Is there anyone else in the family who doesn't know what's going on?"

"No," Erich had to admit. But again he was silent.

Kathe sighed in exasperation but reminded herself to be patient. "It's apparent you don't want to talk to me about this. Is there a reason?" He looked at her intently and she clarified, "Don't you trust me, or—"

"Of course I trust you."

Kathe recalled Abbi saying that Cameron had once kept her in ignorance for her safety. While it seemed unlikely, she asked anyway, "Will my ignorance benefit me in any way?"

"It might keep you from worrying."

Kathe took a deep breath. "So, you don't want me to know because you don't want me to worry."

"That's right," he stated firmly.

"Then there is reason for concern." It wasn't a question.

Thoughts tumbled quickly through Erich's mind as he met the worry in her eyes. While a part of him wished he could keep it from her forever—as if withholding the whole truth from her might prevent the circumstances from affecting their relationship—he knew in his heart that this was likely to get worse before it got better. And she was right. She was entitled to know what was going on. He thought of his mother's involvement in political matters. She remained abreast of everything. It was evident his father spent a great deal of time talking to his wife about his business.

"Maybe we should sit down," he said quietly.

Kathe motioned toward the parlor, and they walked down the hall in silence. She sat at one end of the sofa and he sat at the other, crossing his ankle over his knee and pushing a hand through his hair. Kathe tossed her hat onto a chair and turned to face him directly.

"We're sitting," she said when the silence grew too long. She tried to tell herself that this was probably not as serious as she was assuming. But could she deny this instinctive uneasiness? Frustrated by her ignorance, she was relieved when he finally began.

"Several years ago," he said, tapping his fingers on his thigh, "Maggie came home one day to announce that she was in love with a man she'd met. His name was Nikolaus Koenig."

This was not the beginning Kathe had expected, but she relaxed when it became evident he was willing to talk.

"I was there when Mr. Koenig walked into my father's office for the first time. He was supposed to be there to request permission to court Maggie. Instead he announced that he was the son of my father's deceased brother, Nikolaus. He made it clear that his intentions were to get what his father 'should have had.' My father had no knowledge that Nikolaus had married before his death, but Koenig had documents to prove it."

"And these were the people speaking with your father this evening."

"That's right. Apparently they *are* du Woernigs, and somehow Nik is convinced that he should have a great deal more than the allowance my father is giving him." Again Erich pushed a hand through his hair, and she knew he didn't want to go on. "I'm not going to bore you with the details, Kathe. The bottom line is this: We have no proof, but we have every reason to believe that Nik Koenig's main objective in life is to become the Duke of Horstberg."

"But how can he possibly do such a thing?" She nearly laughed at the absurdity, but the seriousness in Erich's eyes silenced her.

Erich cleared his throat tensely, knowing he had to get to the point. "It was very soon after Mr. Koenig's appearance in our lives that I was shot, Kathe."

Kathe's heart started to pound as it began to make sense. "Then he's the one . . . He's that person you told me wanted you dead."

"We have no proof," he stated. "But the coincidences are too incredible to discredit. There were several accidents—and some near misses—that were obviously intended for myself and Maggie."

"But why Maggie? What would—"

"At that particular time, she was pregnant. If she had lost the baby, or if she had not survived, it would have eliminated a possible heir." He looked at her and stated a hard fact, "If I die without progeny, Maggie's eldest son would be the duke."

"Stefan," she stated.

"Yes, Stefan. Although, all of this happened before he was born. The problems stopped when my father confronted Koenig with some pretty harsh threats. But recently . . ."

Erich glanced at Kathe, then shot abruptly to his feet. "Why can't I just be a normal man?" he erupted. "Why can't I have the opportunity to begin a normal life with the woman I love instead of facing this damned revolution? I shouldn't have to be telling you this, Kathe. We should be—"

"What did you say?" she asked breathlessly, standing to face him. He looked briefly stunned. "Did you say *revolution?*"

Erich squeezed his eyes shut and pushed his hands behind his back. "Yes, I said *revolution.*"

Kathe took a deep breath and reminded herself to stay calm. "What exactly does that mean, Erich?"

Erich walked slowly across the room and began trifling with the knickknacks on the mantle. "In my youth, I was subjected to endless hours of lessons in world history. I hated it, but I managed to take it seriously. I believed my parents when they told me that the things I learned from the past could affect the future of my country. They told me that I might be called upon to make impromptu decisions that could affect many lives, and my knowledge of the mistakes and successes of others would make it possible for me to make those decisions correctly. How clearly I remember studying *revolution.*" In a toneless voice he repeated a definition that had obviously been deeply ingrained. "The overthrow or renunciation of one government or ruler, and the substitution of another by the governed." He chuckled without humor. "My father and Georg were actually revolutionaries. That's what we were celebrating today. I mean, the fair has been observed for centuries, but my father made some adjustments to the celebration when it became the vehicle to help bring him back to power. In 1817, my father and Georg maneuvered the country out of his brother's hands, and my father took back the throne. But you see, his motives were for the benefit of the people. He was taking back what rightly belonged to him. I seriously doubt that Nik Koenig's motives are so pure."

Erich's expression became more solemn than Kathe had ever seen. With distant eyes he went on. "I will never forget the day my history tutor cited many examples in history of revolution. I don't remember many of the names, or the dates, but I remember the stories. Those stories haunted me. I actually had trouble sleeping for days afterward as the faces of the people I love somehow meshed into those stories of royal families being executed . . . beheaded . . . violated . . . imprisoned." Kathe felt almost physically ill as he continued. "Women and children tortured and murdered because some revolutionary fanatics decided to take every precaution that the bloodline would end."

Erich blew out a long breath. "And now? Now . . . some revolutionary fanatic has deemed himself worthy to be the next ruler of Horstberg. It's really a rather insignificant country, you know. It's nothing but a dot on a world map. But ruling it represents wealth and power nevertheless. And while I, like my family, would often prefer a simple life, my father would rather die than see this country fall into the hands of a tyrant. He loves the people he rules. He works hard for their happiness. And most of them know that. But there are some who are weak-minded enough to believe that every problem in their life would be solved if anybody else were at the helm."

Erich turned to look at her, again putting his hands behind his back. Wearing his uniform, with that hard severity in his expression, she could well imagine the power he was capable of.

"At this point in time, my dear, there is rumor of a revolutionary force of a hundred men or better building right here in Horstberg."

Kathe unintentionally gasped, but it didn't seem to deter him now that he'd gotten the momentum to lay out all the facts.

"Han managed to uncover the leader of this movement, and enough evidence to have him executed. But he went before a firing squad without giving us any evidence of who was above him, holding his leash, so to speak." His eyes hardened on Kathe as he stated, "Georg tells me this man looked my father in the eye and made it clear that he truly believed someone would succeed at overthrowing this country, and that my father would not live to see it."

Something died a little inside of Erich as he absorbed the horror in Kathe's expression. But he'd expected it.

"I didn't want to tell you, Kathe . . . even though I knew that your finding out was inevitable. But nothing will ever be the same between you and me. The day I asked you to marry me," the crack in his voice nearly broke her heart, "we had our whole lives ahead of us, and nothing between us to keep us apart. But now . . . our relationship will always have a bitter edge. I have a prayer in my heart *constantly* that we will be able to overcome this triumphantly, and see this revolutionary force disbanded, once and for all. But if I am completely honest, I have to admit that it would take a miracle."

Erich watched the tears spilling down the face of the woman he loved, and he had an urge to just sit down and bawl like a baby. It wasn't fair, and it wasn't right. But he couldn't change it. He was only a man. And this was real life. He couldn't expect fairy tales, as much as he would like to, for Kathe's sake, if nothing else.

While he was wondering what he might say to console her, a subtle smile crept into her countenance. She drew back her shoulders as if she could take on Nik Koenig's army single-handedly. With a firm voice she said, "As I understand it, you are a man who believes in miracles."

Erich shook his head in disbelief. "You are an incredible woman, Kathe Lokberg. Any woman in her right mind would escort me to the door and express her relief at not having exchanged vows prior to discovering the horrible things attached to my life. But you . . . I lay despair and futility into your lap, and you pass me back hope and a smile."

Kathe rose and moved into his arms, holding him as if she might never have the chance again. "I love you, Erich du Woernig." She looked up at him. He kissed her, allowing the turmoil within him to seep into it. Her response said more than words ever could of her love and commitment as well as her acceptance of him in spite of the struggles he was bringing into her life.

"I love you, too, Kathe," he whispered against her face. With her in his arms, he could almost believe that everything would be all right. She had the ability to make him believe in miracles.

Chapter Eight
ELIMINATING PROGENY

"Are you feeling any better today, Father?" Maggie asked, and Cameron's head shot up from his breakfast. "You've seemed a little down since that execution," she clarified in response to his blank expression.

"I'm fine." He smiled, but Maggie knew that everyone felt the tension.

"Han and I are going into town this afternoon," Maggie went on. "Would anyone like to come along?"

"What will you be doing?" Abbi asked.

"We're taking Hannah and Gerhard to be fitted for their clothes for the wedding."

Erich's face lit up, as it always did when the forthcoming event was mentioned.

"I already did that," Stefan said distastefully.

"Do you want to come along anyway?" Han asked him.

"Stefan's coming with me," Erich announced.

"We're going riding this morning," Stefan added proudly. "And this afternoon I've got to practice the piano."

Abbi said to Erich, "Isn't Kathe coming this morning?"

"Yes, but I told her she would have to occupy herself until Stefan and I return from riding." Erich smiled warmly at Stefan, and the boy was obviously pleased.

"Do you want to go into town, Mother?" Han asked Abbi.

"Thank you, dear," she replied, "but I think I'll paint this afternoon, and then I'll be here if I'm needed."

"Come along, Stefan." Erich rose to his feet.

Stefan picked up his riding crop and donned his hat, pausing barely to kiss his mother before he skipped away.

"Hey!" Han called to him. "What about your old papa?"

Stefan grinned and ran back to hug his father and they were off.

"He is such a joy," Abbi said. Han and Maggie could only agree.

"Are you going to be the Duke of Horstberg?" Stefan asked Erich as they headed out.

"I sure am," he replied.

"Are you glad?"

"Ah, I don't mind."

"But do you want to be the duke?"

"Let's just say I'm well prepared to be the duke. I'm certain I'll have a good life." He attempted to squelch thoughts of the present threats against Horstberg continuing throughout his life.

"You'd rather be a chemist," Stefan stated.

"Perhaps," Erich said, "but I can do that as well—just for the fun of it."

"I can't decide if I want to be an artist or a musician," Stefan said thoughtfully.

"I think you should be both."

"Do you think I can?"

"Of course." Erich laughed. "You can be anything you set your mind to being."

"Do you love Kathe?" Stefan asked.

"Very much," Erich replied, surprised at the question.

"I hope the baby is a boy," Stefan added methodically.

"I thought you wanted your mother to have a girl."

"Not that baby!"

"What other baby is there?" Erich asked.

"The one Kathe is going to have when you get married."

"Oh," Erich chuckled, "that baby. Why do you hope it's a boy?"

"So I don't have to be the Duke of Horstberg," Stefan said.

Erich looked toward him in surprise. "Don't you want to be?"

"Cameron says that it's precarious."

"That's a pretty big word."

"Isn't he right?"

"I suppose precarious could describe it at times. But it's not so bad."

"I'm not worried. I know Kathe will have a boy."

"Well, I certainly hope so." Erich chuckled again, and his thoughts turned to Kathe. He reminded himself to believe in those miracles.

"I'll race you," Stefan said when they reached the meadow. Before Erich could reply, Stefan heeled his stallion into a gallop.

When the first shot was fired, Erich's heart went mad. Stefan stopped and turned, looking bewildered while Erich raced toward him. With the second shot, Stefan fell, and Erich was over him like a protective lion. He felt a bullet braise his back as he leapt from the horse, wondering if either of them would ever live to be the Duke of Horstberg.

Shots continued from the trees. Erich could see nothing from where he lay, instinctively pretending he was dead, hoping and praying that this would end before he was.

Stefan lay completely motionless in his arms. "Please no," he whispered, but he didn't dare move even enough to see if Stefan was alive.

The shots finally ceased, and Erich heard a distant rustling in the trees. Then silence—a deathly silence that forced Erich to finally move and look around. Pulling back, relief washed over him to see Stefan, eyes wide with fear but very much alive.

"Are you all right?" Erich asked.

"My leg hurts, Uncle Erich," he said, obviously trying to sound brave. "It hurts bad." Tears welled up in Stefan's eyes, and Erich felt like crying himself. Before Erich moved away to check the problem, he realized his breeches were wet and glanced down to see blood gushing from Stefan's thigh. Erich attempted to subdue his rising panic. The last thing he needed was for Stefan to go into shock. Erich quickly removed his waistcoat, tore it, and bound it around Stefan's thigh. He then glanced around and realized the horses were gone. Panicked, he gave a shrill whistle. Nothing happened, but when he whistled again, his well-trained stallion came trotting out of the trees toward them.

Erich sighed with relief. They were alive, and they had transportation. He figured if the other horse didn't return to the castle, he would send someone to look for it.

"All right now," he said to Stefan, trying to sound positive, "we're going to get you home and then everything will be all right."

He came carefully to his feet, but Stefan apparently noticed him grimace. "You're hurt too, Uncle Erich."

"I'll be fine," he said. "I'm more worried about you."

Erich was grateful that Stefan was small for his age as he carefully pulled him into his arms and set him on the horse. The child gritted his teeth and moaned with each movement, but once Erich was in the saddle behind him, Stefan relaxed and held onto him tightly.

A sick dread rose in the pit of Erich's stomach as they rode toward Castle Horstberg. He could almost literally feel the strength draining out of Stefan. The makeshift bandage was already saturated with deepening red, and blood seeped into Erich's clothes and dripped over the saddle.

Stefan was too little to even have that much blood, Erich thought, but he tried to remain cheerful to keep from frightening him.

"We're almost there," Erich said, managing a smile.

"Is this was Cameron meant," Stefan asked weakly, "when he said it was precarious?"

Erich bit his lip and swallowed hard. "Yes, Stefan, I think this is what he meant." He paused and attempted a positive note. "But we'll be all right. I've been shot before, you know."

"You have?"

"In the shoulder. Long before you were born. And another time they tried to shoot me and missed."

Stefan said nothing, and Erich realized the child was barely conscious.

"Help me!" Erich ordered to anyone who was there as he rode into the courtyard. A servant hurried out to take the horse, and three officers of the Guard appeared.

"Good heavens, sir! What happened?" one of them asked as he helped steady Erich's dismount with Stefan in his arms.

"Someone's using royal heirs for target practice again," Erich snarled. "Get a doctor!" he ordered, and one of them hurried away.

"Find his parents," Erich ordered, "or my parents—anybody!" Another officer ran into the castle entrance.

Erich glanced down at Stefan, steadily weakening in his arms. "I'd like to know what kind of perverse mind would want to shoot a child," he muttered to the officer at his side.

"If I knew, I'd strangle them personally," he answered angrily, holding the door for Erich.

"Han!" Erich shouted, knowing it was ridiculous to think he could hear it. He sank involuntarily to his knees, suddenly feeling weak. "Where are they, dammit?" he muttered, then he shouted at the officer, "Find him!"

"We're home, Stefan," Erich said gently when they were alone, and the child's eyes came languidly open. "Everything's going to be all right." Stefan made no response, and Erich pulled him close, unable to hold back the emotion any longer. "Oh, please don't leave us, Stefan. We need you. We all need you so much."

Stefan attempted a smile, but his eyes closed again. A sob erupted from Erich's throat as he frantically searched for any evidence of life. He kept his fingers pressed tightly against the faint pulse in Stefan's neck while tears fell over his face.

"Hang on, Stefan," he cried. "Please, hang on!"

Erich looked up at the sound of footsteps and saw Han running down the hall with Cameron and Georg at his heels.

Han's pounding heart dropped to the pit of his stomach as the reason he'd been summoned came into view. For a moment he was stunned, unable to move, unable to think. All he could see was the blood. He'd never seen so much blood in his life! Erich looked up at him, tears streaming down his face, and Han could already hear the words in his mind. *He's dead.*

Erich looked back to Stefan. "You're father's here," he said gently, and Han sank to his knees with relief when Stefan's eyes came open.

"It all happened so fast," Erich cried as Han took his son. "I hurried back as soon as they stopped shooting at us, but . . ." His explanation faded into emotion as Han looked into his eyes. With all they had shared in their lifetime, a moment had never been so poignant.

"Dear God, help us," Cameron muttered as he appeared at Han's side, startling him.

"What happened?" Georg demanded.

"He was shot," Erich managed. "I sent someone for the doctor."

"Get him upstairs," Georg ordered, helping Han to his feet. He'd barely started down the hall when the women came running from the other direction. Erich bit his lip to keep from crying out when Maggie went hysterical. She screamed and cried until Cameron took her by the shoulders and shook her gently. "Look at me, girl," he insisted. "Now, take a deep breath and calm down. Your ranting isn't going to help him."

Maggie took hold of her father and pressed her face to his chest, sobbing uncontrollably.

Abbi glanced at Erich, as if to assure herself he was all right. He stood and nodded, and she left Maggie in Cameron's care to hurry after Han and Georg. Only then did Erich realize Kathe was there. She'd obviously been with Abbi and Maggie when they'd gotten the news. The shock and horror in her expression provoked a whole new bout of emotion. He moaned as he held out a hand toward her.

Kathe willed her heart to stop pounding as she rushed into Erich's arms, oblivious to the blood on his hands and clothes. He took her fingers into a trembling hand, holding them so tightly it hurt. Meeting her eyes, he pressed her hand to the center of his chest, saying in a shaky voice, "It's still beating, Kathe."

She buried her face in his shoulder and sobbed nearly as hard as Maggie had. A minute later the doctor arrived, and Cameron took Maggie upstairs to wait. Erich eased Kathe closer, inwardly thanking God that he was still alive, and praying that Stefan would survive. He was startled at the pain he felt when she put a hand on his back, and he winced.

"What's wrong?" she demanded, pulling away. He said nothing as she looked at her hand and gasped to see fresh blood there. "Good heavens," she muttered, turning his back to her view. "You're hurt as well."

"It's nothing," he insisted. "I forgot all about it until you touched it."

"It's bleeding too much to be nothing." She scowled at him. "You need to have the doctor look at this."

"He's very busy at the moment," Erich snarled.

"Then let *me* look at it." She took his hand and headed up the stairs. Though her heart was still beating hard from the reality of coming so close to losing him, she was determined to keep this as light as possible. She knew his concern was with Stefan at the moment, and he didn't need her emotion adding to the burden.

"Your dress is ruined," he said as they entered his room, leaving the door open.

Kathe glanced down at the blood smeared over the yellow fabric. "It will come out if I soak it long enough. But this," she motioned toward his shirt, "could be hopeless." As she unbuttoned it for him, she added, "Is this what Theodor does?"

"I can usually manage taking off my own clothes."

"All the same," she managed a smile, "I think I should very much like his job." Their eyes met as she untucked the shirt from his breeches and pushed it over his shoulders. But there was nothing romantic in the gaze they shared, only poignancy and fear.

"I assume a bullet did this," she said, pulling his shirt off from behind.

"Unless it was one hell of a bumble bee."

Kathe forced back her emotion and managed a little laugh as she tossed the shirt on the floor. "Why don't you sit down and—"

"Because I'm covered with blood," he interrupted.

Kathe glanced at his breeches. "I think I'll wait in the hall while you change. I wouldn't want you to embarrass me."

Kathe caught a hint of a smile as she closed the door. She'd only been outside the room a minute when Theodor came bounding up the hall.

"I just heard what happened," he said. "Are you all right?"

Kathe shook her head vehemently and forced a smile. "But if I start crying again, I'll never be able to stop, so don't make me talk about it."

"Is Erich—"

"He's getting changed. He could probably use some water to clean up and . . ."

Theodor nodded and went into the room, leaving her alone. Kathe went to her room and changed, leaving the stained dress soaking in cold water. Then for another ten minutes she paced the hall outside Erich's door, fighting not to think about the reality. The bullet that had braised Erich's back could have pierced his heart had the aim varied a few inches. She jumped when the door came open and Theodor appeared with Erich's soiled clothes.

"I'll get you something to put on that wound," he said and hurried down the hall.

Kathe entered Erich's room to find him staring out the window, wearing clean breeches and nothing else. The damage from the bullet looked bloody but wasn't bleeding anymore. She put a hand on his arm and he started.

"You're still shaking," she said.

Erich held up his hands and looked at them. "Yes, I am." He looked into her eyes. "If he doesn't make it, I'll—"

"Shhh." Kathe put her fingers over his lips. "He's alive. You're alive. And for the moment, that's all that matters."

Erich pulled her into his arms and held her tightly. She was briefly distracted by the feel of him without a shirt, but she forced her mind to the reason she was here.

"Now, let me look at this," she said, turning him around. "Ooh," she grimaced, "it's not deep, but it's nasty looking."

Theodor came back with some medical supplies and helped Kathe treat and bandage the wound. She was wrapping long strips of gauze around his torso to hold the bandage in place when Abbi appeared in the doorway.

"Good heavens," she said. "I didn't know you were hurt, too."

"It's nothing, Mother," Erich insisted. "Is Stefan—"

"The doctor's with him. It's difficult to know at this point how bad it is." She walked toward him. "I take it you were hit, as well."

"It just braised him," Kathe reported. "It's not deep."

"Thank God for that," Abbi said, taking Erich's face into her hands. "Are you all right?" she asked intently. He knew what she meant. Erich shook his head and she pulled him close.

"Has Maggie calmed down yet?" Erich asked.

"Your father is with her."

"Han and Maggie must hate me," he added.

"It's not your fault," Abbi insisted.

"Then why do I feel this way? I should have never taken him there. If I hadn't—"

"There's no good in that." Abbi took his chin into her hand and looked into his eyes. "Stefan will be fine, but even if he isn't, you must know it was not your fault and you did all that you could. If the duke blamed himself every time one of his people was hurt or killed in defense of his country, he would be too lost in guilt to be able to rule."

Erich nodded willfully and embraced his mother.

"Put on a shirt," Abbi told him, "and we'll go see how Stefan is doing."

Erich donned a shirt and boots, and Kathe held his hand tightly as they followed his mother to the hall outside Stefan's room. Maggie was crying on Han's shoulder, her hand holding tightly to her father's. Georg was sitting at Cameron's side, looking almost as glum as he had when he'd lost his wife. The men looked up when they approached. Maggie was oblivious.

"I tried to get him out of the way," Erich said, mostly to Han, "but it was too late."

"He surely wouldn't even be alive if you hadn't been there," Han replied.

"I knew something would happen," Cameron muttered as Abbi guided Erich to a chair across the hall. "But I didn't think it would be like this."

Kathe sat close to Erich and felt his grip tighten around her hand. Following minutes of grueling silence, Cameron demanded to hear what had happened, and Erich told all that he knew.

Kathe saw the duke's eyes harden, and Georg bore an expression of intensity that was almost frightening. Beneath their concern for Stefan's life was a deep-seated bitterness.

"What's the point?" Georg asked. "Are they trying to scare us, or do they really believe they can eliminate all the heirs to Horstberg? It's preposterous!"

Cameron nodded in agreement but nothing more was said. The time dragged on while they all wondered what could be taking so long. The entire family came to their feet in unison when the door finally opened and the doctor appeared.

"The bullet's out," he reported. "I'm afraid it was deep, but as far as I can see at this point, he's going to be fine."

Maggie nearly collapsed into fresh tears as embraces of relief were shared among the family.

"I've given him something to help the pain that will probably put him to sleep soon. But I think he would like to see his family first."

The doctor motioned them into the room, and Maggie rushed to Stefan's side, pressing her face carefully to his. Han knelt beside the bed and brushed the child's hair back off his brow. Erich fought back his own emotion as he observed them. Stefan was so pale he almost looked dead, but he opened his eyes and smiled, first at his parents—then his eyes focused on his grandparents, hovering behind them.

"Grandmama," he said so softly they could barely hear him. "Am I going to die?"

"No!" Cameron insisted. "You're not going to die, Stefan."

"Everything's going to be fine," Georg added.

"Is Erich—" Stefan began weakly.

"I'm right here," Erich said, easing a little closer. "I'm fine."

Stefan smiled again and closed his eyes. Maggie gripped Han's hand tightly as she kissed Stefan's cheek. "You sleep now, my little man," she said. "You'll be all better in no time."

Kathe could see the love and concern in Erich's expression as he watched his young nephew. Silence hung uncomfortably until Erich hurried out of the room, Kathe's hand firmly in his.

"Where are we going?" she asked as he hurried down the stairs, nearly dragging her along.

"I've got to get out of here," he replied, and Kathe knew they were going to the mountain meadow.

He went first to the office and scribbled a quick note for this father, leaving it on the desk.

"Do you think we should?" she asked while he was saddling his stallion. "I mean. . . what if—"

"We'll be careful," he interrupted tersely.

Erich helped Kathe mount before getting into the saddle behind her and taking the reins. He said nothing as they galloped through the trees, but Kathe could feel his anguish. The reality of death hovered so close she could almost taste it. More than once, tears burned into her eyes, but she discreetly wiped them away and tried to swallow her emotion, not wanting to upset him further.

In the meadow, Erich dismounted and pulled Kathe into his arms with desperation.

"Talk to me, Erich," she whispered. "It's just you and me, now. You can tell me how it *really* feels."

"How can I when . . ." Erich stopped and squeezed his eyes shut. Emotion tainted his voice as he finished. "In spite of everything that's been happening, I suppose I . . . wanted to believe . . . it wouldn't happen . . . again."

Kathe sat down in the high grass and drew her knees to her chest, urging Erich to sit next to her. He eased close beside her, his longs legs nearly encircling her. She played idly with the leather of his bootleg while he seemed lost in deep thought.

"Tell me what you're thinking," she urged.

"I wish I could explain it."

"Try," she encouraged.

Erich took a deep breath. "When that first shot rang out, it was like all the memories assaulted me instantly. The coma. The shootings. The paralysis. All of it. But as difficult as it was before, I thought of you and wondered how I could ever bear leaving you when our life together has just begun."

As Erich voiced Kathe's deepest fear, the strain of holding back her emotion suddenly became too great, and tears fell unrestrained down her face.

"I was terrified," he admitted with distant eyes. "But in a split second, all of my fear shifted to Stefan." Erich felt momentarily embarrassed when he started to cry, until he looked at Kathe and knew he wasn't crying alone. "He doesn't deserve it," Erich said sadly. "He's just a child. Even with everything I have to lose,

I would have given my life in a minute for him. I felt so helpless. Just so . . . *blasted helpless.*"

"You did all you could."

"That's just the point." He looked skyward and noticed clouds darkening overhead, but he didn't care. "What can a man do when there's a price on his head? How is a man supposed to feel, knowing that his birthright is so . . ." Erich thought of Stefan's words and his voice trembled, "so precarious?" A moment later he added, "I'm sorry. I don't mean to burden you with—"

"Your burdens are my burdens," she replied.

"It's just a little . . . unnerving at the very least, to come so close to crossing the line between life and death—and seeing someone I love come even closer."

"You love Stefan very much."

"I do," he admitted serenely.

"He is a wonderful boy."

"I have to wonder what kind of life he will have if he's being shot at when he's only seven. What kind of life will any of us have if Horstberg is . . ." He couldn't bring himself to say it.

Kathe forced herself to have courage. She could cry later. "You mustn't worry so, my love," she said, almost managing a smile. "Be grateful that you and Stefan are both alive. And make the most of the life you have." She pressed his hand to her heart and looked into his eyes. "We're alive. We're together." She covered his mouth with hers, unable to hold back the desperation she was feeling, wondering if they would ever make it to their wedding day, alive and together. He ran a hand over her hair, holding her in a grip that left her powerless. She gasped as his lips touched her throat.

Kathe felt only too eager for passion to engulf her and make her forget the fear. She became so consumed by the sensations he aroused in her that she was hardly aware of the way he eased her back into the high grass, kissing her like he never had before. Thunder sounded in the distance and startled them both. Erich looked down at her for a long moment, and then he eased away from her and sighed. Kathe felt the ache of sudden separation and grasped his hand as if it might keep him from moving too far.

"Forgive me, Kathe," he said. "I shouldn't let myself get so carried away."

"It's all right, Erich." She leaned up on one arm to look down at him. "Or didn't you notice that you weren't the only one getting carried away?"

Erich smiled, but not nearly enough to show his dimples. His sadness tugged at her, and she laid her head against his shoulder, wishing she could assuage it somehow.

Thunder sounded again, closer this time. "I think it's going to rain," Erich said.

"I hadn't noticed," she replied. Their eyes met, and something lurched inside of her at the realization that he had nearly died today.

"I love storms," she said, looking up at the darkening sky to distract herself from thoughts that were making her insides churn. Sporadic drops of rain began to fall and she added, "But perhaps we should get back."

Erich eased her closer. "I don't want to go back. I feel safe here."

"Have you got any options?"

"If I did, would you love me more?"

"How could I possibly love you more?" She looked into his eyes again, fighting the urge to cry—again.

"I don't know." He smiled at last. "But we'll try it anyway."

Erich stood and helped Kathe to her feet as he whistled for the horse and it trotted toward him. They both mounted, and Erich galloped toward the high rock wall that rose against the uphill side of the meadow.

"Where are we going?" she asked as the rain worsened.

"I'm giving you an option," he replied with mischief in his voice. He dismounted and glanced around before he carefully pulled back the thicket to reveal a crevice in the rock.

Kathe said nothing as he helped her dismount. He slapped the horse, and it disappeared into the crevice. A fluttery excitement enveloped her as Erich led her carefully through, pausing only to cover the opening from behind. They came to a plateau, mounted the stallion again, and rode a short distance. Kathe was surprised to see the lodge appear, and she wondered what she'd expected. They rode into a little stable across from it and dismounted. Erich removed the horse's saddle and secured it in a stall. Kathe watched him in silence, feeling somehow as if these moments would become precious in her memory . . . as if the blessing of observing Erich du Woernig doing a simple task would be brief.

The rain was coming down hard as they ran together toward the lodge. He smiled at her before he opened the door and they stepped inside. She was grateful to see that at least he was more relaxed now. Glancing around the common room in which she stood, Kathe immediately loved it.

"Little family secret," Erich said. "It comes in handy at times. I was saving it for our wedding night." His smile grew wider. "But necessities do arise."

"This is where your parents were snowed in together."

"That's right."

"Your mother told me the whole story."

Erich pulled his boots off, muddy as they were, then bent to unlace Kathe's shoes and set them aside.

"How gallant you are, my love," she said, and he smiled up at her. Again her emotions responded, and it took great willpower to hold back the pressure forming in her eyes.

"You are soaking wet, Miss Lokberg." He took her hand and started up the stairs. "Let's see if we can find something for you to wear while your clothes dry."

Kathe caught her breath as they entered the bedroom at the top of the stairs. The minimal furnishings were simple and well chosen. Her eye was drawn first to a cozy window seat, and then to the brass bed. Despite the room's practicality, it was comfortable and had a warm atmosphere. Erich knelt by a trunk near the bed and opened it.

"There's a number of odd things in here," he said. "I'll let you find something that will work. Let me hurry and build a fire, then I'll give you some privacy and you can change."

He went downstairs to find some kindling and matches and returned to see Kathe unwinding her wet hair. While he split kindling with a knife, he couldn't help glancing at her every few seconds. The passion he'd barely managed to hold back in the meadow rushed forward to taunt him as she moved her hands methodically through her hair to smooth it. He knew he should force any such thoughts away, but at the moment, being distracted by Kathe was the only thing that kept him from thinking about the precariousness of his own life. And Stefan's.

Erich knelt by the fireplace and forced himself to concentrate long enough to get the fire burning. "I think there's a hairbrush around here somewhere," he said.

"I found it, thank you."

He glanced up to see her pulling it through her hair. *She was so beautiful.* But something pierced him through as he wondered if their time together would be over in a heartbeat. Clearing his throat in an attempt to clear his head, Erich turned his attention back to the fire.

"Who else knows about this place?" Kathe asked, fighting to maintain some normal conversation, hoping it would appease the rumbling emotions inside her.

"Only my parents . . . and Georg."

"Not even your sisters?"

"My father brought me here when I came of age. He told me its purpose was for the duke to find refuge and solace. And since this lodge kept him alive for several years, he respects its secrecy and asked me to do the same. Of course the family knows there is a lodge, but they don't know how to find it."

"How . . . intriguing," she said, feeling almost chilled by the significance of this place.

Erich concentrated on the kindling as it began to burn. He carefully placed some larger pieces of wood on the grate and waited for them to take hold of the flames, his thoughts wandering back to the incident with Stefan. He closed his eyes and heard the bullets whizzing past. He felt Stefan's weakness. And the blood. How could he ever forget all the blood? Then his mind darted to images he'd seen in dreams, as if the messages of the night were meant to somehow prepare him to face the end of his life. The anguish seemed more than he could bear. If he was going to die, why couldn't he just go without warning like most men? Why did he have to be tormented with premonitions and feelings of dread that wouldn't relent?

Kathe watched Erich closely as he stoked the fire, wondering where his thoughts might be. When he closed his eyes and anguish filled his countenance, she didn't have to wonder. Seeing the evidence of his own internal torment, the emotions she'd been fighting to hold back rushed forward. The horror she'd wrestled with since the moment she'd seen Erich covered in blood suddenly overpowered her, tremoring from the deepest part of her into every nerve. Her chest tightened. Her breathing sharpened. She began to shake and wondered how she could avoid drawing attention to herself, which she knew would only upset him further. She was contemplating the distance to the door when Erich looked up at her.

"Kathe. What is it?" he said, moving abruptly toward her.

The concern in his eyes shattered what little self-composure she had left. She gasped as he took hold of her shoulders and looked into her eyes. Her breathing became so sharp that it strangled her voice.

"Kathe," he demanded with that regal air of his, "whatever is wrong?"

"Someone . . . someone . . ." Just trying to put the words together in her mind intensified her emotion. Everything blurred as her eyes misted over.

"Out with it!" He shook her gently.

"Someone . . . is trying to . . . kill you."

Erich forced back his own fears and attempted to soothe her. "They didn't succeed, Kathe. It's all right."

"It's . . . not all right," she cried, and he could feel her whole body shaking. "Look at me, and . . . tell me . . . that you believe in your heart . . . he will not succeed. Tell me . . . that he . . . won't . . . prevent you from . . . seeing another year." She practically shouted, "Tell me!" Her voice softened. "Tell me and I'll believe you. I'll believe anything if it will keep you alive."

Erich looked into her eyes while logic battled with hope. The battle was brief, and hope took its last breath. He wanted with all his heart and soul to tell her what she wanted to hear. But even searching his deepest feelings, he could find nothing to make him believe he would see another year. At the moment, another week seemed a miracle.

"Tell me!" she screamed, startling him from his thoughts. He bowed his head, unable to look at her. Hot tears burned into his eyes, and he squeezed them shut, feeling the moisture sear a trail down his cheeks. He felt Kathe's trembling hands take hold of his face and lift it to her view. But he couldn't open his eyes. He knew his eyes would tell her the truth.

Kathe absorbed his expression and the tears on his face. Her heart dropped with a hard thud to the pit of her stomach. The sharpness of her breathing settled into an eerie breathlessness as if a harsh wind were blowing in her face.

"Look at me," she whispered, but his eyes remained closed. "Look at me!" she ordered in a tone of voice she'd learned from him, a man with natural authority. For a split second she imagined herself a duchess, standing by his side to rule a country. But the image passed quickly. In her heart she knew it would never be. This was all just a fairy tale, a brief escapade of romance and adventure. And there would be no happily ever after.

Erich forced his eyes open. He blinked to release a fresh swell of tears spurred by the anguish in Kathe's expression. He didn't have to tell her what he was feeling. She already knew.

With urgency, he took her hand from his face and pressed it to his chest, wanting her to feel the evidence of his heart beating.

Kathe heard a sob break the air before she realized it had come from her. Reading the truth in Erich's eyes, she felt the world crashing down around her. She collapsed under its weight, but Erich caught her in his arms, breaking her fall. She wondered what she might do when he wasn't there to catch her. She took hold of him and sobbed again.

"We have now, Kathe," he murmured, touching his face to hers, mingling their tears together. "We have now."

Through the mist that blurred her vision, Kathe searched frantically for his kiss. His lips met hers with an urgency that soothed her emotions by the way it matched them. Love for love. Anguish for anguish. He shared her life, her heart, her soul. As long as his heart was beating, hers would beat with the same rhythm. She felt her feet come off the floor, and then the bed beneath her. The room spun like a tornado, with Erich at the center in the calm eye of the storm. Anguish turned to ecstasy, fear to elation. Through this tiny slice of forever, he was hers, she was his, and the world couldn't come between them. She knew it wasn't right. She knew there were risks. But something bigger and deeper took hold of her senses, making her believe there might never be another opportunity to be with him this way. She needed him now, before anyone had another chance to steal his life and the power it represented.

Kathe looked into Erich's eyes, in awe of the reality. This man who loved her was a prince. He had the ability to hold a country in the palm of his hands. His very being spoke of majesty. His power showed in his eyes. Yet his touch was gentle, and his commitment to her complete. He loved her. She knew it even when he didn't say it. At such moments, she could feel his power dissipate behind a soft, genuine love that shone in his eyes, uninhibited and full of life.

For Erich, the experience was so perfectly ethereal that he believed heaven was a place where he could be with Kathe forever. The love they shared was so intense, so complete, he found it possible to believe that it could transcend the limitations of this worldly existence, where death had the power to come between them. Even the precariousness of his life took on a different perspective, knowing the full measure of her love. He'd never imagined any earthly experience could be so stirring.

"I love you, Kathe," Erich cried, so grateful to have lived until now, if only to partake of this moment. He loved her as if there were no tomorrow, then held her as if eternity lay before them.

Long after it was over, neither of them spoke, as if words would only bring them too close to reality. The only sound that broke the stillness was the beating of rain on the roof, and an occasional crackling from the fire. Erich lay staring at the ceiling, Kathe's head against his shoulder. His mind sorted through the evidence of all that threatened himself and his loved ones. Then he forced his thoughts to the present. Here, with Kathe in his arms, they were safe, and the reality of his fears seemed distant. He began to wish they could stay here forever, and then his mind wandered into a desire to just take her and leave Horstberg. He had the money. They could run away together and be safe from the threats against his life. But at what price? Could he ever turn his back on everything he'd been raised to be? The more he thought about it, the more he realized it wasn't an easy question to answer. At one time he would have unwaveringly said that *nothing* would make him turn his back on his country. But that was before Kathe. His love for her had changed his perspective, and the dilemma pounding in his head almost provoked physical pain.

As his thoughts became more disturbing, he was relieved to hear Kathe's soft voice break the silence. While she idly moved her fingers over his chest, she sang perfectly the little song he had taught her.

I know a place where snow falls white
That's where I long to be,

Where castle turrets strike moonlight
And shine where I can see.
I've known my love on mountains high
Where meadows bloom in blue;
I know my love is there for me,
I know that love is true.

There is a place where snow falls deep
And warmth is near the hearth.
Deep in my sweetheart's dreams I sleep
There's comfort in this warmth.
The world is cold and brash outside,
I fear what it imparts,
But I know my love is here with me
A fire burns in my heart.

Erich felt tears leak into his hair as she finished. "That's incredible," he whispered. "My father wrote that song before I was born, and yet it's as if he wrote it for us . . . now."

"Perhaps your father felt very much the same way at the time."

A new perspective settled into him as he contemplated the idea. At this moment, it wasn't difficult to imagine Cameron du Woernig living in this lodge, banished from the world, wanted for a crime he didn't commit, while his brother ruled Horstberg very badly. What kind of turmoil had he endured, alone here for three years? And then Abbi had come into his life. Erich had heard the story countless times of the way Abbi had changed him, given him the courage and conviction he needed to face his responsibilities. Cameron du Woernig *could* have taken Abbi and run away where no one would ever find them. But he had stayed. He had fought for what he believed in. He had honored the blood in his veins. And Erich would do no less. Not in spite of Kathe, but because of her. He would fight with everything inside him to keep Horstberg safe and free, with whatever life was left in him.

Nothing would ever be right if he willingly turned his back on his country. He could never be at peace.

With purpose, he eased Kathe closer. He was still afraid of what awaited him in the valley below, but he was no longer confused. Without even realizing it, she had reminded him of who and what he was. He turned slightly to look into her eyes, and a moment later she pressed his hand over her heart. "Can you feel it, Erich?" she asked. "Can you feel the fire in my heart?"

"I feel it," he murmured.

"Whatever happens," she said, touching his face as if to memorize his features completely, "it will burn forever."

Erich sighed and pulled her close, wondering how he could feel so much joy when the prospect of the future seemed to hold nothing but despair. As if to answer his silent plea, Kathe spoke close to his ear in a hushed voice. "No matter what we might feel or believe, Erich, we must do everything we can to stay safe and be together. Perhaps we might be given a miracle yet."

Erich looked into her eyes again, marveling over the hope she gave him. If nothing else, the intimacy they'd shared made him determined to fight for a life with her, and for her—if such a thing was possible.

"Erich," she said, lifting up on one elbow, "is this not where your life began?"

He touched her face. "Yes, I believe it is."

"Well, if Cameron du Woernig overcame his obstacles in order to have a life with Abbi, surely you can do the same."

Erich pulled her closer. "I'm not so sure I have the courage and determination my father had. Sometimes I wonder if my life has been too easy in some respects. I'm only grateful that I have my father at my side. I believe he and Georg are capable of working miracles. And Han's not terribly stupid either."

"Then we have nothing to worry about. Our lives are in capable hands."

"So they are," he agreed. He rummaged his fingers through her hair and pressed his lips to her brow.

"Erich," she said again, "what if there are . . . results . . . from this?"

"My dear Katherine, we will be married before there is time enough to know."

Kathe hugged him tightly. "That's a nice thought."

They drifted to sleep while the rain persisted on and off outside. Kathe's next awareness was of Erich jolting awake with a gasp.

"Are you all right?" she asked through the darkness.

At the sound of Kathe's voice, Erich relaxed and took a deep breath. "I was . . . dreaming," he finally answered.

"The same dream?" she asked, trying not to sound upset.

"Actually, no." He sat up and swung his legs over the side of the bed, pressing his head into his hands. "This was different."

Kathe sat behind him, wrapping her arms around his chest, laying her head against his back, taking care to avoid touching him where he was wounded. "Tell me," she urged gently.

Erich took another deep breath, attempting to calm his quickened heart. "I could see you . . . but you seemed . . . distant. I touched you, but you didn't respond. You seemed terribly upset, and I tried to comfort you, but it didn't do any good. It's like I was there—but I wasn't. And that's it. It was more the way it made me feel. It was as if I'd lost you—but not really. Temporarily perhaps."

"As long as it's temporary," she said lightly, hoping to ease his anxiety.

Erich turned and pulled her into his arms. "I don't want to lose you, Kathe," he whispered. "I would die without you."

"No," she said, *"I* would die without *you.* I firmly believe that if I lost you, I would die of a broken heart."

She laughed softly, but Erich didn't see any humor in it. And looking into her eyes, he knew she was only trying to appease his own fears. With urgency, he kissed her. The trauma of the day seeped into it. But she answered it with comfort, and he could do nothing but kiss her again.

Kathe immersed herself in his love once more, forcing herself to ignore the possibility that they might never have this opportunity again.

It was nearly midnight when Erich got Kathe home. He returned to the castle expecting everyone to be asleep, but he'd barely come in when his parents erupted from the main drawing room.

"Where in heaven's name have you been?" Cameron shouted while Abbi put her arms around Erich as if she'd feared never seeing him again.

"I had to get away," he stated, not the least bit apologetically. "I left a note for you so you wouldn't—"

"I know what the note said. But for the love of heaven, Erich, you nearly got killed this morning," Cameron shouted louder. "And you go off gallivanting through the forest? Your mother has been sick with worry. I think you owe her an apology."

Erich nodded firmly.

"See to it," Cameron added and walked away.

Erich was silent until his father had gone. "He has a lot on his shoulders right now," he said to his mother.

"Yes," she agreed, still holding him tightly.

"Forgive me, Mother." He returned her embrace firmly. "My intention was not to worry you."

"I know. It's all right. Actually, I think your father was more worried than I was. I knew you needed to be with Kathe." She drew back to look at him. "You were with Kathe?"

Erich nodded, hoping she didn't sense the change in him. As if she'd read his mind, she added, "You seem more . . . at ease. It would seem your time with her was well spent."

Erich nodded again. "She has a way of helping me put things in perspective."

"I dare say she was terribly upset."

"Yes, but . . . even though she's terrified, she smiles and gives me hope."

"She has a great deal of courage, I believe," Abbi said.

"Not unlike you," he added warmly.

"If she's like me," Abbi chuckled softly, "she's crying into her pillow right now."

"You may be right."

"I'm glad you found her when you did, Erich."

"So am I. I only hope we'll have a future together. I pray this doesn't get worse before it gets better."

"And what does Kathe have to say about that?"

Erich looked directly at his mother. "She reminds me that I'm a man who believes in miracles."

"And do you?" Abbi smiled.

"Yes," he admitted, "I would have to say there are many miracles in our lives, but . . ."

He glanced away, feeling the same old doubts rush in to squelch his hope.

"But?" Abbi pressed.

Erich looked into his mother's eyes, wondering if he should tell her his deepest fears. He settled for simply saying, "Perhaps some miracles just aren't meant to be."

Erich recognized the emotion in her eyes. He'd seen it there before. It was as if she felt the same foreboding that he did. But she was equally reluctant to admit it.

"How is Stefan?" he asked, knowing there was nothing more to be said otherwise.

"Mostly sleeping, which is just as well for the time being."

Erich nodded. "I'll see him in the morning. I'd better get some sleep."

"You've had a long day," Abbi said and squeezed his hand.

Walking slowly toward his room, Erich contemplated the circumstances all over again. But his thoughts quickly strayed to Kathe. He felt an inner ecstasy to recall the intimacy they'd shared. And that alone strengthened his resolve. He would do everything in his power to make it through this and remain alive!

Maggie lay close to her son in the darkness, playing idly with his thick, rusty hair while he slept. The night dragged incessantly and she couldn't even force herself to not worry. And the child moving within her made it nearly impossible to relax. Somewhere in the middle of the night, Han came in quietly and sat beside her.

"I woke up and you were still gone."

"I didn't want to leave him alone," she whispered.

Han bent to kiss her brow. "How are you feeling?"

"About the same."

He pressed his hand over her rounded belly and smiled. "You get more beautiful all the time."

"I don't know how I could possibly be comely in this condition."

"Oh, but you are," he whispered. "You go through so much to bear my children. And it makes you all the more beautiful."

Maggie's eyes filled with tears, and she turned them toward Stefan. "I would die to lose him, Han," she muttered.

"We won't lose him," Han assured her. His eyes too rested on his son, and his expression filled with love and pride. "He will grow up tall and strong and make us very proud."

"He's such a good boy," Maggie added, touching his peaked face. She turned to Han. "He is so much like you."

Han chuckled. "I didn't think he was at all like me."

"To others it might not be obvious." She smiled. "But I can see you in him. Every now and then it comes through. How could I help but love him?"

Han squeezed Maggie's hand and eased onto the bed beside her. With a lamp burning, they both drifted to sleep and awoke when Stefan began to stir. Expectantly, they watched him come awake in the lamplight. A quick glance at the clock told them it was just past four in the morning.

"Mama," Stefan whispered, and Maggie took his hand.

"I'm here, my darling."

"How are you feeling?" Han asked.

"Papa. My leg hurts."

"I don't doubt that," Han replied.

"How do you feel other than that?" Maggie asked.

Stefan stretched and yawned, then proclaimed, "I'm hungry."

Han and Maggie laughed and embraced, knowing he would be fine.

"I'll go see if I can find you something to eat." Han came to his feet and stretched with a noisy yawn. Before he reached the door, they heard an explosive noise—not loud, but distinct.

"Erich," Maggie gasped as Han shot out the door.

Erich found it impossible to sleep as his mind became absorbed in the hours he'd spent with Kathe. He missed her dreadfully already, but he indulged in the memories of all they'd shared, longing for them to be married. Against his will, his thoughts wandered into his fears. He tried to convince himself that things were not as bad as they appeared, but he knew in his heart they were worse. He only had to think of Stefan's present condition to fully grasp how bad it could get.

When his thoughts began to get the better of him, he got out of bed, deciding to read, if only for a distraction. He moved through the dark to the table by the window, where he knew there was a lamp. The glass chimney felt dirty—almost greasy—as he removed it, and he wondered if the maids were getting lazy. As he struck the match and set it to the wick, he inhaled a vague, strange odor. Working with chemicals had made him especially tuned to smells, and it only took a split second to know that something wasn't right. Instinctively, he bounded across the room and dove to the floor on the opposite side of the bed, at the same time inwardly scolding himself for being so paranoid. A moment later, the lamp exploded, spraying shattered glass and oil.

With his arms over his head, Erich briefly contemplated the sound of glass breaking in a recurring dream, and the following explosion. Had that dream just saved his life? A chill rushed over his back.

"Thank you, God," he muttered, realizing he wasn't harmed. He looked tentatively over the bed to assess the damages, and his already-racing heart jumped into his throat. The table where the lamp had been sitting had crumbled, and everything within several feet of it was disheveled or broken. The drapes and some of the debris were on fire, but the shattered glass prevented him from getting too close without first putting something on his feet. As he crossed the room, attempting to beat the fire out, he tried to imagine where all that broken glass would have gone if he'd been standing over the lamp when it had blown up.

He was startled but relieved when Han threw open the door. "What happened?" he demanded. "Are you all right?"

"I'm fine!" Erich shouted. "Don't get too close. There's glass on the floor. Get some water!"

By the time Maggie appeared in the doorway, they had the fire out.

"What in heaven's name . . ." she gasped.

Erich slumped onto the bed and pressed his head into his hands. "The lamp blew up," he said.

"Blew up?" she shrieked.

"It's a miracle you're in one piece," Han said, looking around himself at the damage.

Erich sighed and willed his heart to slow down. "I've been hearing that quite a bit lately."

"I'm going to get Father, and—"

"No," Erich interrupted his sister firmly. "Let them sleep. Their room is too far away for them to have heard the blast.

Everything's all right." He glanced around the room. "I wonder what other little surprises are waiting for me in here."

"Maybe you should sleep elsewhere for the time being," Han suggested.

"I think maybe you're right," Erich said, but the fear hovering inside him didn't go away when he closed the door to his room and left it behind. He attempted to sleep in one of the guest rooms but knew it was futile. As soon as he knew his parents would be awake, he got dressed and went to their room, knocking lightly at the door.

"Good morning," his mother said, pulling it open as she tied a wrapper around her waist. Seeing his expression, her brow furrowed.

"What's wrong?" Cameron came behind her, buttoning his shirt.

"There's something I need to show you," he stated.

They walked together to the wing where Erich slept, saying little between them. Methodically, he opened the door to his room and motioned them inside. Abbi gasped and put a hand over her mouth. Cameron erupted with a breathy, "What the . . .?"

"The lamp blew up," he explained. "I thought I could smell something unusual just as I lit the wick. I don't know if it was instinct . . . or paranoia . . . or what . . . but I moved away fast and the thing just . . . blew."

"It's a miracle you're alive," Cameron said.

Erich sighed and stuffed his hands into his pockets. "Yes, but . . . how many miracles is one man entitled to?" He met his mother's eyes and felt chilled by the blatant fear he saw there. It seemed so out of character for her that he wondered again if she knew something he didn't; something she'd dreamt perhaps. He wanted to ask, but a deeper part of him just didn't want to know.

Chapter Nine

RETREAT

rich went to Stefan's room before breakfast. He felt so relieved to see him awake and hungry that he laughed out loud.

"So," he said to his nephew, sitting on the edge of the bed, "what's the first thing we should do when you get on your feet again?"

"I want to shoot the crossbow," Stefan said.

"We haven't done that for a long time."

"I suppose you'll still have to cock it for me."

"Probably." Erich chuckled. "I can barely cock it myself. But one day you'll be able to do it."

"I'm glad I'm not going to die," Stefan added after a brief silence.

"So am I," Erich said earnestly. "So am I."

After breakfast, Erich went to a meeting of the advisory committee, where it was impossible to ignore his uneasiness. The major topic of discussion was the possibility of revolution, and the threats against himself and Stefan. When the meeting finally adjourned, Erich went down to his laboratory to pass some time while Kathe caught up some things at home. Descending the stairs, he reminded himself that he had much to be grateful for, not the least of which was Stefan being alive. But Erich was only in the laboratory a minute when the dread struck again in the pit of his stomach. He had no doubt that someone had been there, tampering with the chemicals. But how could that be? He kept the door from the hallway always locked. Could someone truly have found his hiding place for the key? The very idea made him feel ill when he considered how he'd nearly died down here before. Since that time, no one beyond him ever came here, except Han on rare occasions. And Erich knew he wouldn't have left things this way. Despite how disorderly the room appeared, Erich knew it like the back of his hand. And something was wrong.

Memories flooded back of going unconscious in this room amid billows of smoke. He could almost taste the reality of waking up with weeks of his life gone, and then wondering if he'd ever walk again. A physical tightness developed in his chest when he added to that his encounter with the lamp just this morning. Without a second thought, Erich turned and left the room, closing the door tightly. He stopped to catch his breath before he began his ascent and realized this was affecting him worse than he wanted to admit.

Erich stayed close to the center wall as he went carefully up the steps. In his mind he could only see Kathe. She had taken his life from good to better, and he wanted a future with her. She increased his instinctive desire to survive, and he needed her.

Erich didn't put the key back in its usual hiding place but kept it with him as he went straight to his father's office, relieved to find him there with Georg. Cameron removed his glasses and looked at Erich sternly. "What's the matter?" he asked.

Erich glanced down, almost wishing his father didn't know him so well. He didn't want to tell him, but knew he had to. It was an unspoken rule between them that all such things had to be voiced.

"I was just in the laboratory," Erich stated.

Cameron's eyes hardened a little, seeming to expect what was coming. "And?" the duke insisted when Erich didn't continue.

"Someone's been down there. The chemicals that just arrived weren't touched; that box hasn't even been opened. But some other things were and I . . . well I . . . I should probably just go clear it all out and start over . . . and . . .”

“I thought you always kept the door locked,” Cameron said, sounding angry. But Erich couldn't blame him. He knew this was fear talking, even if it sounded like anger.

“I do keep it locked, but . . .” Erich hesitated, realizing now that his decision might not have been very well thought out, and his father might now be angry with *him*.

“But?” Cameron urged.

“The key is bulky, and sometimes I would forget to bring it, so I . . . hid it . . . near the door, and . . .”

“Dammit!” Cameron stood and turned his back, leaning his hands on the sill of the huge window.

Georg displayed his usual ability to remain calm under nearly any circumstance. He asked Erich where exactly he'd hidden the key and suggested what Erich had figured out in the last few minutes—that the maids would be required to dust that little table regularly, and someone had likely found it there.

“I'm so sorry,” Erich said. “I just . . . didn't think.”

Cameron sighed but still didn't turn around. “It's just an over-sight, Erich.” He sounded more calm. “People make oversights all the time. Heaven knows I've made many of them. Why didn't I think to have officers *in* this room while the maids were cleaning? After all these years why can't I figure out which people working for me are committing treason? Did I just get too comfortable with time passing? Questioning my own oversights makes my head nearly burst. I fear Nik Koenig will undo us in the end simply because some stupid, silly thing didn't occur to me. But such oversights shouldn't put the lives of the people we love in danger.”

“No, they shouldn't,” Georg said with compassion.

Cameron turned around and sat back down, his aura weary and deeply concerned.

Erich took a seat himself, feeling a little unsteady. To fill the silence, he said, “I have the key with me now, and I'm not going down there until I can clean it all out. But I can't do it right now. I hardly slept at all last night. If they don't kill me, they'll drive me insane."

"I don't want you to do it now," Cameron insisted. "And when you *do* clean out the room, there will be officers on watch and nearby. Just . . . don't go down there at all for now."

"My thoughts exactly," Erich said. He took a deep breath and rose to leave.

"Where are you going?" Cameron asked.

"I need to see Kathe."

"You're not stepping outside this castle," Cameron retorted.

"Oh, yes," Erich snapped with sarcasm, "this castle is such a *safe* place." He met his father's eyes, and the trauma of the past two days was evident. "I need her," he said more softly.

A glance passed between Cameron and Georg. "We'll send someone to get her," Cameron said gently. "I'd prefer you stay here."

"I'll go," Georg volunteered. "I could use some fresh air, anyway."

"Thank you, Georg," Erich said.

"No problem." Georg smiled as he passed by him and left the office.

"Are you all right?" Cameron asked as Erich sat down again.

Erich chuckled tensely and pushed his hair behind his ear. "This whole thing has got me a little shaky, I must admit."

"It's got all of us a little shaky," Cameron added. "When Kathe gets here, I need to talk with the both of you."

"About what?"

"We'll talk when she gets here," he said. "In the meantime," Cameron stood from behind the desk, "why don't we go see how Stefan is doing. Poor little tyke. It's a miracle he's alive." He slapped Erich on the shoulder. "And you too, for that matter."

"Well," Erich managed a smile, "I believe in miracles . . . I think."

"Then there's hope, eh?"

They walked together down the hall, and Erich was glad to feel the tension between them ease and to hear his father sounding in a better mood. But he knew they were both just exerting a great deal of self-discipline to keep their true fear from showing.

Kathe answered a knock at the door and was surprised to see Georg Heinrich. Although Erich's family had paid visits to her home, she had never seen Georg here.

"Georg." She smiled pleasantly while she couldn't help wondering if something was wrong. "Come in."

"Thank you." He stepped inside.

"What can I do for you?" she asked, motioning him toward the parlor.

"I can't stay," he said, sitting on the edge of a chair. Kathe sensed something severe in his countenance, and her nerves increased as she sat across from him.

"What's happened?" she insisted. "Is Erich—"

"Erich's fine," he assured her, and she drew a calming breath. "But it's evident someone has been tampering with the things in his laboratory, and . . . there was another incident early this morning."

Kathe's eyes narrowed. "What kind of incident?"

"A lamp in Erich's room exploded when he lit it. He was—"

Kathe shot to her feet and pressed a hand over her heart. "Are you sure he's all right?"

"Of course. I just saw him, but . . . His Grace didn't want him to go out under the circumstances. He asked that I come and get you."

"I'll be ready in five minutes." She rushed up the stairs, trying to fight back the tears that had plagued her most of the night.

Erich walked out to meet Kathe when she rode into the courtyard with Georg. He helped her dismount and held her tightly while a servant took her horse.

"Are you all right?" she asked.

"I am now." He smiled and kissed her quickly.

"I believe your father wants to see the both of you," Georg said as he dismounted and walked past them.

"Yes," Erich replied, "we'll be right in."

"What about?" Kathe asked, noting the way Erich's brow furrowed.

"I don't know. He wouldn't tell me." They walked inside together and slowly down the hall. "But he gets very upset when people try to kill his children."

"I can't say that I blame him."

Erich and Kathe passed the officers flanking the door and entered the ducal office to find Georg sitting in his usual chair, wearing deep concern. Cameron was gazing out the window, his back turned to them as they were seated before the huge desk.

Without preamble, the duke said, "I feel it's necessary to postpone the wedding."

"What?" Erich protested. Kathe squeezed his hand tightly. "We can't do that. We—"

"Georg and I have discussed this in great length." Cameron turned and looked hard at his son. "Under the circumstances, it just has to be."

"But why?" Erich leaned forward. "I don't understand why we can't—"

"I'll tell you why," Cameron shouted, and Kathe winced. She'd heard her father shout occasionally, but it was evident that Cameron du Woernig was a very powerful man. "I've got a missing layout for this castle, a crew of servants I can't trust, and my home is booby-trapped. Captain Dukerk has had the servants questioned again this morning, and they've all been threatened severely. No one will admit to anything that even gives us a lead to follow. There is a revolutionary force present in the valley, and the heirs to my duchy are being threatened with their lives. That's why!"

No one responded, and Cameron sat down. In a calmer voice

he went on to explain, "I cannot take my family through town in a grand procession and leave us all exposed like sitting ducks. It's as simple as that."

Erich exchanged a panicked glance with Kathe. "All right," he said firmly, "I can't argue with that. Let us get married privately . . . here at the castle. We don't need the procession." Another quick glance told him that Kathe approved of the idea. But a harsh uneasiness crept down his back as he observed the concern that passed between his father and Georg.

"Erich," Cameron leaned his forearms on the desk and looked at him closely. His eyes shifted briefly to Kathe and it was evident that her presence made him hesitant. He turned back to Erich, cleared his throat, and said firmly, "It's difficult for me to admit this aloud, son, but Georg and I have talked this through and . . . when we consider every possible repercussion of what is taking place, the bottom line is clear." He glanced briefly again to Kathe, and Erich thought he looked as if he were going to cry. "Kathe will be safer if she is not your wife."

It took a moment for the implication to set in. "Dear God, no," Erich cried and leaned back, suddenly weak. Kathe came abruptly to her feet and turned away, wrapping both arms around her middle as she felt a literal sickness smoldering inside her.

"Are you saying," Erich's voice raised angrily, "that you honestly believe it will come to that?"

"I don't know *what* it will come to!" Cameron shouted. "But all we can do now is prepare for the worst and hope for the best. It's ridiculous. It's unfair. And by heaven and earth, I *hate* it! But at the moment there's not a blasted thing I can do about it beyond protecting my family and my country to the best of my ability. At this point, you should consider Kathe the *lucky* one. She doesn't have this damnable curse of *being* a du Woernig."

Kathe pressed a hand over her mouth, attempting to hold back her emotion. But a harsh whimper erupted into the silence nevertheless.

Erich rose from his seat and put his arms around her, aching to take away her anguish. She buried her face against his shoulder, barely able to keep from sobbing.

Cameron leaned his elbows on the desk and put his head into his hands, sighing loudly. Georg said calmly, "We must keep you safe at all costs, Erich. Not only because we all care for you very much but also because you represent the hope of this country in the next generation. Only you have the right and the knowledge to rule Horstberg the way it should be done. There are a lot of people out there who need you to be there for them. We've discussed many times the poverty and horrendous working conditions that resulted in the brief time that Nikolaus ruled. We must do everything we can to preserve the rights of the people—and you are the key."

Erich absorbed Georg's words but then retorted tersely, "I suppose that means I can't just run away and elope."

"I wouldn't blame you if you did," Cameron said, his voice softer now. Something close to despair seethed in his eyes.

"But if I am any kind of a man," Erich said, "with any kind of integrity, I will not turn my back on Horstberg without a fair fight." He said it as if he resented it.

"I did that once," Cameron said. "It's not worth it, trust me. But if it comes to the worst, that may be an option. Better that than . . ." He stopped with a quick glance toward Kathe.

"What Georg said is right," Cameron finally said. "We must ensure your safety. That's why I'm sending you away."

"What?" Erich protested again, and Kathe turned to look at the duke, wiping at her tears.

"With what I've got to worry about," Cameron stated, "I don't need to sit here and wonder when you're going to run into another accident. If you are tucked safely away, I can concentrate on more pressing matters."

"Where?" Erich insisted. He didn't like this at all.

"You know where."

"Then I'm taking Kathe with me," he insisted, holding her tighter.

"We need her here," Georg interjected in his usual, calm, compassionate manner. "Under the circumstances, we feel it's best to make everything appear normal. If whoever is behind this believes you are gone, then they'll start looking for you, and they may move with more drastic measures. We will continue to behave as if you are still here, and we want Kathe to visit regularly as she has been."

"I apologize," Cameron said more to Kathe, "but I'm afraid the two of you will have to be separated for a time." Then to Erich, "Be ready to leave at midnight and tell no one. And in the meantime," he added, putting his glasses on as if to conclude the meeting, "please be careful."

Erich stood for a minute, wishing he could come up with any possible alternative. When he couldn't, he quietly left the office, his arm securely around Kathe's shoulders.

Once Erich and Kathe had left, Georg said to Cameron, "Do you really believe they want to kill every possible heir, or are they just trying to keep us off balance enough to make us vulnerable?"

"Well, if that's the case, it's working, isn't it," Cameron growled. "As I see it, it's irrelevant at this point whether they succeed at doing away with my heirs or not. If they *do* manage to take over the country, they'll just line up the survivors and kill us all anyway."

"God forbid," Georg muttered.

"Amen," Cameron added, and they said nothing more.

"I'm afraid," Kathe said when they had moved away from the officers standing guard at the door. "I don't want to be away from you, Erich. I—"

Erich put his fingers over her lips as they walked slowly down the hall. "I'm afraid, too, Kathe," he admitted. "But my father is the Duke of Horstberg. I learned a long time ago that whether I agree with him or not, when it comes to matters of political security, I have to concede to his authority. And as much as I hate to admit it, he's right. He knows what he's doing. We have to trust him."

Kathe nodded her understanding and forced back her fear, attempting to be positive. She would not waste away their time together now by blubbering with emotion. She could cry all she wanted after he was gone.

She was surprised when he took her to the chapel, but she had to admit that she felt a little better after they had sat together there in contemplative silence for over an hour.

"Kathe." His voice, though soft, startled her as it broke the air. "Do you believe there is life after this one? Do you think it's possible that our spirits live on somehow?"

Kathe lifted a hand to his face, then pushed it into his hair, toying idly with the curls. "When I lost my mother, I remember initially being overwrought with despair. I was only a child. She had been the center of my life. I remember my father telling me that he believed she lived on, and we would be together again one day. But something in me couldn't believe it . . . as if not being able to see or taste the evidence made it impossible to accept. And then . . . late one night, I was sitting in the chair in my room, just staring out the window. I couldn't sleep. I remember feeling this darkness around me . . . as if the loneliness would swallow me. And then . . ." Her eyes grew distant and she laughed softly. "It's funny. The memory is so clear—as if it happened only yesterday. I remember wishing with all my heart that there was a God, and that life went on, because if I had to believe that my mother was gone from me forever, there was no point in living. And then, it was as if in an instant the darkness was gone. I felt this indescribable peace, and . . ." She looked into Erich's eyes. "I've never told anyone this before."

"Why not?" he asked, mesmerized by the ethereal aura about her.

"Maybe because it sounds so . . . unbelievable."

"Why? Because you couldn't see it or taste it?"

"Yes, I suppose that's why."

"And yet you say the memory is so clear. Would something you imagined stay with you that way?"

Kathe smiled. She liked the theory. "Anyway," she went on, her eyes becoming distant again, "at the same moment this peace washed over me. I felt my mother's arms come around me. I don't know how I knew it was her, but I *knew*. The sensation of her touch was *real*. And while I was sitting there, marveling that this was happening, I remember expecting it to end. And while I don't think I had any real sensation of time passing, I know that it lasted long enough for me to *know* it wasn't my imagination."

Kathe turned to look at Erich, surprised by the moisture glistening in his eyes. "Yes," she added, "I believe there is life beyond this one. I believe that my father's being without my mother is only temporary—just as Theodor being without Leisl is."

Erich pulled her close to him, holding her tightly. "Then whatever happens," he said, feeling an undeniable peace, "we will be together . . . eventually."

Kathe drew back to look into his eyes. She nodded firmly, afraid to speak for fear of erupting with fresh emotion. Closing her eyes, she pressed her forehead to his, as if doing so could make him read her thoughts and feel her love for him.

They finally drew away from their reverie when Erich noticed it was time to eat and his family would be worried if he was late.

Throughout the meal, nothing appeared out of the ordinary, but the tension was evident. After spending some time with Stefan, Kathe and Erich walked together through the gardens, saying little. It seemed there was nothing to be said that wouldn't add to the anguish.

"Where are your thoughts?" Kathe asked, if only to break the silence. She could well imagine being without him tomorrow, wishing she had said a hundred things today.

"I keep thinking of being with you yesterday in the lodge," he admitted, and his lips twitched upward. "I never dreamed it could be so incredible."

Kathe stopped between two long rows of shrubbery and looked into his eyes, silently agreeing, willing herself not to blush as their thoughts mingled intimately.

"While I'm gone," he said, "just think about how good it will be when we're married."

Kathe nodded and tried to smile, but she couldn't hold back her emotion any longer. She pressed her face to his shoulder, attempting to hide the tears.

Erich pulled her close, muttering close to her ear. "I've never felt so helpless."

"I'm sorry," she murmured, "I don't mean to burden you with—"

"Your emotions are not a burden to me, Katherine." He lifted her chin and looked into her eyes. "I love you. Whatever happens, you must remember it."

Kathe nodded firmly, relieved when he took hold of her and kissed her in a way that spoke of the intimacy they had shared. A familiar desperation seeped into it, and she wondered what it might be like to experience passion without the fear of losing the one you loved. As his kiss deepened, he urged her closer as if he could make her a part of himself and take her with him.

Erich felt the emotion in Kathe's kiss that she was hesitant to show. While desire to have her again consumed him, the poignancy of what lay between them was suddenly overpowering. His own emotions erupted from deep in his chest and an anguished moan slipped into his kiss. The emotion stifled his passion, leaving him suddenly weak.

Kathe exhaled sharply when Erich dropped to his knees, pressing his hands to her lower back, and his face into the folds of her skirt. While his emotion was evident, she felt a surge of compassion. As difficult as it was for her to imagine losing him, she could not comprehend how it might be for him to realize his life was in danger. Gently, she pushed one hand into his hair and the other over his shoulder, urging him closer. He looked up at her like a child seeking comfort, and she touched his face, wishing there was something she could say to give it. A moment later he came to his feet, taking her hand.

"Come along," he said. "Let's go inside."

They passed a maid in the hall and went into the library. Without a word, Erich gently pushed her back onto a large sofa, obviously made to accommodate long reading sessions with comfort.

"I love you, Kathe," he murmured, stretching out beside her. In one agile movement, he eased her close to him, fusing her mouth to his, holding her as if the world might end at any moment. A calming warmth fell over them as his kiss became languid and savoring, then he gradually drifted to sleep, his face pressed to her heart. She wondered if he'd gotten any sleep at all last night as his body seemed to slump into complete exhaustion. Kathe reveled in holding him close until her own lack of sleep escorted her into slumber, holding him tightly against her.

Abbi shot her head up from the letter she was writing to Sonia. The sudden urge to check on Erich was not strong by any means, but it was something she couldn't ignore. While she hurried down the hall, wondering where to find him, she recalled feeling this way several times a day when her children were young. It was rare when these maternal urges led her to prevent some potential danger or led to the discovery that the children were doing something they shouldn't be. Usually she would see that everything was in order, and she would return with peace of mind to whatever she might have been doing. She recalled the countless times she had risen from a comfortable bed to peek in on her children, just to be assured that they were sleeping soundly. She would touch their soft hair and press an undetected kiss to their little faces, then return to her bed with the assurance that all was well.

Abbi's children were fully grown. Her daughters had children of their own, and Erich had long ago passed the age of needing his mother to check up on him. But recent events had put her on edge, just as they had the rest of the family. Though, for her, the maternal instinct had resurfaced harshly. She couldn't deny the vaguest urge to see that he was safe, hoping perhaps that she could somehow prevent whatever horrible thing might happen to end his life prematurely. She put the matter into God's hands, knowing that she was not capable of changing a man's mortal destiny. But on the chance that God might prompt *her* to do something to make a difference, she could not deny her feelings.

Abbi cursed having to live in this huge castle as she searched for half an hour, wondering where he could be or if they had inadvertently crossed paths. She began to feel panicked, fearing that something truly *was* wrong, and at the same time scolding herself for her paranoia.

She opened the door to the library, expecting it to be as unoccupied as every other room she'd peeked into. Then she sucked in her breath to see a booted leg draped over the back of one of the sofas. Quietly she closed the door and crept closer. A smile absorbed her to see Erich and Kathe tangled together, sleeping soundly. Relief rushed out with a long sigh, and she indulged in just watching them. Their love for each other was evident in the way they clung together, even in sleep. Knowing the feelings she shared with Cameron, it wasn't difficult to imagine what they were struggling with right now. Her heart could break on their behalf if she thought too deeply of the conflicts they were enduring. But for the moment there was nothing but peace surrounding them, and she prayed in her heart that they would be able to sustain each other enough to get through whatever lay ahead.

Abbi moved close enough to touch her son, unable to resist the urge to push her fingers through his curls like she'd done when he was a child. He was oblivious to her touch as she bent and pressed a gentle kiss to his brow. She watched him for a long moment, then felt suddenly like a guilty child when Kathe opened her eyes and looked up, as if she'd sensed someone there.

Abbi brought a finger to her lips, indicating that she stay as she was and not wake Erich. She slipped quietly out of the room, leaning for a couple minutes against the outside of the library door, grateful for a moment of complete tranquility in the midst of all this madness.

Kathe stayed until late, feeling as if each minute ticking away was bringing her closer to doom. While Georg waited to escort her home, she and Erich found it difficult to say good-bye. Once at home and alone in her own room, Kathe finally let her emotion spill without restraint. She was grateful that her father left her to herself. There was nothing he could say or do. In her heart, she honestly wondered if she would ever see Erich again.

Erich stood in the courtyard for several minutes after Kathe had ridden away with Georg. It was almost tempting to wish that he'd never met her. If he had never known the fulfillment and joy she'd given him, he wouldn't be feeling the intensity of this heartache. But how could he possibly regret what she had brought into his life? The thought of his life ending without ever experiencing such things was devastating. Attempting to balance it all out in his head, he could only feel poignancy and confusion.

Long after they normally would have gone to bed, Erich, his parents, and Georg were sitting in the office, quietly discussing the details of their plan. Georg had already talked privately with Theodor, instructing him to go about his day normally, making it appear as if Erich were still there. When there was nothing more to talk about, Cameron went with Erich to pack his things. He insisted on not letting Erich go anywhere in the castle alone that he might be a part of his regular routine. The debris had been cleaned out of his room, but the damage was still evident.

It was almost midnight when they quietly went to Stefan's room and found him sleeping. Erich held the child's hand a few minutes, wondering if he had any idea of the bond they shared. Cameron then led the way to Han and Maggie's room and knocked quietly at the door.

"What?" Han pulled the door open abruptly. "Is Stefan—"

"He's fine," Cameron insisted. "We were just there. We need to talk to you."

Han motioned him inside where Maggie was tying on a wrapper. "What's going on?" she demanded.

"Erich came to say good-bye," Cameron stated after he'd closed the door. At their astonished expressions, he added, "Until something can be done about this, we're not going to risk his being here any longer."

"Where are you going?" Maggie asked Erich, with no effort to disguise her concern.

Erich glanced at his father, not certain what to say.

"That's irrelevant," Cameron said. "I can assure you he will be safe . . . for the time being. While he is gone, we will manage to make it appear to the servants that he is still here, and they just won't happen to see him. Theodor is doing the majority of making his room look used, and his meals eaten, but we will need to do our part. Is that understood?"

"But won't they see him leave?" Maggie asked.

"No," was all Cameron said. "Now go back to bed," he nodded toward Han and Maggie. "And keep a close eye on the children."

Han nodded firmly as Cameron peered carefully into the hall. They each embraced Erich before he and Cameron slipped quietly out of the room.

Cameron felt a degree of relief to know that Erich was safely tucked away, and making it appear that he was still around kept the family occupied. Stefan made remarkable progress in his recovery, but Han and Maggie kept a close eye on him, as well as the other children. The children were not left without a member of the family close by, and precautions were taken with everything that Stefan ate or drank.

Kathe continued to visit the castle regularly, grateful for Maggie's companionship in these days without Erich. She appreciated Maggie's attitude that it was only temporary, and eventually this would be over and they would be reunited. Though they had not been told where Erich was, Cameron reported daily that he was doing fine.

"Where do you suppose he is?" Maggie asked Kathe one evening while they were having coffee after dinner.

Kathe had wondered if Erich might be at the lodge where he had taken her during the storm. But he'd said it was a secret, and she didn't dare say anything about it, even among the family. She focused her attention mostly on the tatting that kept her busy in quiet moments, and she was relieved when Han answered for her.

"I have no idea. And I'm equally baffled by how your father got him out of the castle without being seen. He manages to keep in touch with him daily, without leaving the castle himself."

"Why don't you ask him?" Maggie inquired.

"If he wanted me to know, he'd have told me by now. I'm certain we'll find out sooner or later."

"Of course, Father is preoccupied with other things," Maggie said to Han. "And *your* father has hardly shown himself lately."

"I believe the duke has him busy. It seems that Rolf Grimm's death did little more than slow down this revolution business. We have word that something big is in the making."

"Do you really think it could happen?" Maggie asked, instinctively pressing a protective hand over the baby growing within her. "I mean that a . . . a revolution could overthrow Father and . . ." She trailed off, not wanting to voice what it meant to them as a family.

"Right now," Han said, "it doesn't look good."

Maggie met his eyes solemnly, and they both turned to Kathe, who appeared to be lost in despair as she set the tiny shuttle aside and wrung her hands together tensely.

"You're not doing so well these days," Han said, snapping Kathe out of a daze.

She managed a smile. "Oh, I'm all right . . . considering."

Maggie reached over and took Kathe's hand. "I'm certain everything will be fine."

"I pray," she answered quietly, and then her tone lightened. "At least Stefan is doing much better."

"So good," Han chuckled, "he can hardly tolerate being in bed all the time. I've told him every story I know a dozen times."

"Karl keeps asking about him," Kathe said. "Perhaps he could come with me tomorrow and keep Stefan entertained."

"That's a splendid idea," Maggie replied. "Franz's son Russy has been spending a lot of time with him." Kathe knew that Franz was one of the servants who had worked closely with the family for most of his life, and Russy was one of the children who went to school with Maggie's children. "And Stefan certainly likes Russy, but he's such a quiet child. I think that Karl and Stefan are more suited to each other."

"I dare say there's a good balance in his life between the two," Han added.

"There is something Karl keeps asking me that I should talk to you about," Kathe said. "He wants to give Stefan a gift, but it's a bit unusual. I should ask your permission first."

"Let's hear it," Han said with enthusiasm.

"Well, Little Karl has a friend down the street with a litter of puppies and . . ." She stopped when Han grinned. "Does that mean it's all right?"

"I think it's a splendid idea," Han said.

"Just as long as you clean up after it," Maggie added to her husband.

The following day, Kathe brought her nephew to see Stefan, and Karl paraded into the young prince's bedroom with a big box that he placed before him like a royal treasure.

"A gift?" Stefan said with wide eyes. "For me?"

"Of course it's for you," Karl replied. "So open it, Your Royal Highness." He used the title facetiously.

"Be polite," Kathe admonished, but Han glanced at Maggie and smiled.

Stefan pulled the lid from the box and his eyes went wider. He laughed as he put his hands inside and pulled out the wiggling puppy.

"I love him!" Stefan exclaimed, and he both laughed and grimaced as the puppy licked his face. "Can I keep him in my room?" he asked. "Can I, Papa?"

"We already talked to Ruthild, and she said it would be fine. Ruthild's family always had dogs, and she tells me she knows very well how to care for them."

"Oh, thank you, Karl," Stefan said, and Karl beamed.

"His name is Lucky," Karl declared, and the adults left Karl and Stefan in the care of Lucky.

Kathe sat busily tatting in the parlor of her home. Theodor peered in, startling her, "I'm taking Karl to the castle. Do you want to ride along?"

"No, thank you," she said, concentrating more intently on her work. "I'm not going today."

Theodor sat down beside her. "Are you all right?"

Kathe glanced at him sharply. She wanted to snap at him and tell him to mind his business. But his concern was so genuine she could only shake her head quickly, hardly daring to speak.

"This is difficult for you," he said.

"Difficult?" She tossed her work aside and pressed a hand over her eyes. "I can't go up there and smile and pretend that everything's all right, while I wonder if I'm ever going to see him again. I can't do it!"

"I believe you've made this easier for Her Grace, if nothing else."

Kathe sighed. "And she has been there for me, I know. But I just can't go today. I can't."

"I understand." Theodor stood to leave the room, pausing to ask, "Is there anything I can do?"

Kathe thought about it. "Actually . . . if you will tell Abbi . . . Her Grace . . . that I'll see her soon. Just tell her I'm a little under the weather. She'll understand."

Theodor nodded and left the house, taking Little Karl with him. Kathe attempted to continue her tatting, but her thoughts became more and more absorbed with fear, and longing, and heartache. She finally put her work away, needing a distraction. She took to scrubbing the kitchen floor, even though the new housekeeper her father had hired strongly protested. When that was finished, she figured she'd better stay out of the woman's way or they'd be at odds. So she spent the afternoon in the garden, but even that had lost its fulfillment as she ached to be with Erich. She paused more than once to gaze toward the mountains, wondering if he was there, as lonely and afraid as she.

Late in the evening, Kathe wandered to her father's workshop where he was busily engaged in finishing some custom orders.

"How is it going?" she asked, fidgeting idly with an assortment of carved boxes he'd made.

"Not as quickly as I would like it to," he replied. "It always seems to go this way. Either I don't have enough work, or I have too much." When Kathe said nothing more, he asked, "And how are you, my dear?"

"I . . . miss him," she admitted. "It's as simple as that."

"And you're afraid," he stated.

"Yes."

Karl put down his work and turned to look at her. "And tell me, Kathe, if you were to go back and start over, knowing what you know now, would you have done it any differently?"

Kathe looked her father in the eye, saying without any hesitancy, "No. Even if I never saw him again, I wouldn't trade what we've shared . . . not for anything." She hurried to wipe away her tears.

"I'm glad to hear you say that, Kathe. You've followed your heart, and it's taken courage, I know. But that man's put life back into you, girl. Don't you ever forget the way he made you feel, and what you were willing to do to have a life with him."

"And what if my life with him is over?"

"Katherine," he leaned forward and pressed his hands together, "it's not over until you stop loving him; until you stop living for him. Do you think my life with your mother is over?" He smiled slightly. "Oh, no. I live for her. I live the way she would want me to live. But Erich is still very much alive, Kathe. It's not over."

Kathe lay awake far into the night, contemplating everything her father had said, trying to put all the pieces together and make sense of it. She could not predict or control the future. She had no regrets concerning the past. But what of now? Now . . . Erich was alone, probably in that lodge this very minute, and . . .

Kathe gasped aloud as the idea erupted into her head. At first it seemed preposterous, but as she milled it around a little, the risks seemed irrelevant in balance to the present circumstances.

It only took a few minutes for Kathe to throw a change of clothes and a few personal things into a bag. She pulled on a practical skirt and blouse and threw a lightweight gray cloak around her shoulders. Going quietly downstairs, she slipped into the library to leave her father a note.

I've gone to follow my heart. I hope to be away a few days. Please don't worry. All my love, Kathe.

Excitement pumped through her veins as she saddled her horse and went as quietly as possible up the long drive. A partial moon gave her enough light to see where she was going without being so bright as to make her conspicuous. She wondered as she started across the foothills if someone might have connected her to Erich and be watching her. She discreetly doubled back after going through the covered bridge and waited for several minutes in the shadows to be certain she wasn't being followed. She did the same thing after entering the forest, and once more upon reaching the high meadow. She felt confident that her leaving had gone undetected as she searched for the opening in the rock wall. She found it more quickly than she'd expected to, and laughed aloud as she pulled the thicket back and guided the horse through. She turned back to cover the entrance, then moved carefully up through the crevice. Recalling Abbi's story of Cameron finding her in the snow, she realized now that this was where Abbi had nearly frozen to death.

Kathe's heart was beating almost painfully when the lodge appeared in the moonlight, and she halted the horse abruptly just to look at it. What would she do now if he wasn't here? She felt briefly afraid, but then she recalled that only Georg and Erich's parents knew of this place. And the last she knew, they were all at the castle. Drawing courage, she took her horse into the little stable and managed to find a lamp and light it. She laughed with relief to find a stallion there. Although it wasn't Erich's; she figured they had wanted his absence to go undetected, so his own horse would have remained at the castle.

Kathe removed the saddle and secured her horse in a stall with food and water, and then she doused the lamp, closed up the stable, and moved stealthily to the lodge. The door was locked as she had expected. Knowing she only had one option, she took a deep breath and pounded hard with her fist, hoping she wouldn't regret this. She waited a minute then pounded again. She heard vague signs of movement on the other side of the door, but it didn't open. Trying to read what he might be thinking, she wondered if he might be afraid to open it, uncertain of who it was.

"Erich," she called. "Please tell me you're in there. It's me, Kathe." She knocked again. "Please, Erich. If you—"

The door opened so abruptly it startled her. For a moment she felt uncertain, unable to see anything but a shadow. Then she heard him laugh.

"What in heaven's name are you doing here?" Erich pulled her inside and slammed the door. He laughed again as he latched

270   Elizabeth D. Michaels

the door and pressed her against it, kissing her wildly, touching her face, her hair. She wrapped her arms around him and laughed from the pure joy of being with him.

"I had to see you," she murmured. "I couldn't bear it another day. I was careful to make certain I wasn't followed."

He kissed her again. "You are an answer to my prayers, my darling Katherine. I thought I would die without you." He lifted her into his arms and carried her up the stairs, his familiarity of the lodge guiding him through the darkness.

Kathe laughed as he tossed her onto the bed, and immediately he was beside her. For the moment nothing mattered beyond his kiss, his touch, his presence. She had believed that their time together previously could not be bettered, but the intensity of their emotions only enhanced the experience. And then she drifted into a perfectly contented sleep, wrapped in Erich's love, wishing that time could stand still.

Erich woke to bright daylight, alone in the bed. He sat up abruptly, his heart pounding with panic. Had she left? Had he dreamed it? Then he saw her shoes on the floor and collapsed back onto the bed with a sigh. While he was relishing in the reality that she was here with him, he heard noises in the kitchen below. He hurried to get dressed and went quietly down the stairs, peeking around the corner to see her stirring something at the stove.

Kathe screamed and then laughed when Erich took hold of her from behind. "Must you sneak up on me like that?" she growled in mock anger, and she laughed again.

Erich pulled her back against his chest and nuzzled his face into her hair. "I feared it had only been a dream," he whispered.

"If you dreamt it," she said, "it was a premonition." She turned in his arms, and he kissed her warmly.

"I fear that breakfast will burn," she said when he finally set her lips free.

"Surely you didn't come all the way up here to cook for me," he smiled.

"No," she laughed, turning back to the stove, "but we have to eat. And if what I found in that pan this morning is any indication of *your* cooking abilities, you could starve without me."

"I won't argue with that."

They sat at a little table to eat a simple breakfast, mostly in silence, until Erich asked, "How long can you stay?" When she didn't answer right away, he added, "Not nearly long enough."

"Well," she said, trying to be positive, "I know your parents want me to keep appearing at the castle for the time being. So far it's been working, I suppose. No one seems to have noticed that you're gone. But honestly, I just couldn't spend another hour there without you . . . not without some rejuvenation," she finished with a smile.

"So, how long can you stay?" he asked again.

"I don't think the world is going to end if I'm not in Horstberg for a few days."

Erich closed his eyes momentarily in relief. "And what of your father?" he asked.

"Are you trying to talk me out of staying?" she asked.

"Heavens no!" he exclaimed. "But I have enough people trying to kill me without getting on your father's bad side."

Kathe attempted to take it as he'd meant it—lightly. She forced a smile. "I left him a note. I told him I'd gone to follow my heart. Believe it or not, I think he'll understand."

"Yes, I believe he will." He took her hand across the table and pressed it to his lips. "I wish it would snow, good and hard."

She laughed. "It's not even autumn yet."

"I know, but if we could arrange getting snowed in here together, there wouldn't be anything anyone could do about it until May."

"It's a nice thought," she said. "But for now, I will be content with what we have."

Erich smiled, albeit sadly. "I love you, Kathe. I'm so glad you came."

She laughed. "I'm glad you're glad. I didn't want to make things worse."

"Not for me, you haven't."

They finished breakfast and cleaned the dishes together. Erich purposely splashed water on Kathe repeatedly, and she retaliated until they were both soaked.

"My dear woman," he said when the last dish was finally wiped dry and put away, "you mustn't wander around all wet like that."

"And why not?" she asked, tossing the dirty water out the window.

"Because it's driving me mad," he growled and pulled her into his arms. She laughed as he kissed her, and they spent the remainder of the day just being together as if nothing else existed. Together they prepared a meal in the evening and shared it. When the kitchen was cleaned, they walked together out to the stable to see that the horses were cared for. He showed her the pigeons kept there and explained how they were used for communication as he tied a message onto one of them and it flew away.

"What did the message say?" she asked.

"It's just to let them know I'm fine. I'm supposed to indicate that I'm alive every so many hours."

"And what do they tell you?" she asked.

"That nothing has changed," he stated. "But I don't want to talk about that."

They sat together near the lodge and watched the stars come out.

"It's a beautiful night," she said.

Erich pulled her closer and arched his head to look skyward. "Yes," he admitted, "it's a perfect night. Although," he laughed, "I think I would prefer snow."

"Where do you suppose Kathe is?" Cameron asked at the breakfast table when there were no servants in the room.

"She probably couldn't bear being here without Erich,"

Maggie commented. "I can't say that I blame her. This place has begun to feel like a monastery."

"I hope she's not ill," Abbi said. "Perhaps I should go and see her."

"That would be fine," Cameron said. "But go in a carriage and take Georg with you." Abbi agreed to the precautions, but when she and Georg arrived at the Lokberg residence, Kathe wasn't there.

"I'm sorry you missed her," Karl said with no apology as he showed them into the parlor.

"May I ask where she is?" Abbi asked.

"You certainly may," Karl replied, "but I'm afraid I can't tell you."

Abbi and Georg exchanged a concerned glance.

"Excuse me," Karl said, leaving the room. He returned only a moment later and handed Abbi a piece of paper.

Abbi read aloud for Georg's benefit, "'I've gone to follow my heart. I hope to be gone a few days. Please don't worry. All my love, Kathe.'"

Abbi looked over at Karl as he said, "I assume she is with Erich . . . wherever that may be."

"When did she leave?" Abbi asked.

"The night before last."

Again Abbi exchanged a glance with Georg.

"Well," Georg said, "as long as she wasn't followed, I don't see any harm in her being there a few days. And I'm certain she would have been careful."

"When was the last time you heard from him?" Abbi asked.

"Just before we left," Georg reported. "Everything was fine."

"I don't suppose it's any of my business where they are," Karl said. "I just want to know that she's all right."

"If she's with Erich," Georg said, "she's all right."

They stayed to talk with Karl for nearly an hour, and Abbi was relieved to know that Kathe's father was supportive of the circumstances when he could have easily been angry to have his daughter involved in such a precarious situation.

Cameron wasn't happy to learn that Kathe had likely gone to the lodge, but Abbi reminded him of how all of this must feel to Erich, and he finally relented that it was good for them to be together.

Abbi kept a prayer in her heart for them, wishing only that this nightmare could be over and her son could be married and find some happiness beyond this. They needed a miracle.

Han sat just outside the door, watching the children play in the castle gardens. He was briefly drawn into nostalgia as he watched them climb a tree that he had often climbed with Erich as a child. Occasionally Maggie and Sonia had joined them. The tree had grown bigger, but the children's laughter felt familiar, and the memories kept him from thinking too hard about this smoldering fear that his sons' lives were in danger. While Maggie stayed upstairs with Stefan, he had relinquished his work to his father and the duke so that he could keep an eye on the other children. Little Karl was currently in the tree with Gerhard and Hannah. Theodor's son had been spending a great deal of time with Stefan, but Maggie had suggested that he should get out for some fresh air with the other children, while Stefan got some rest. As they laughed and scurried through the leafy branches, Han had to admit it was a good idea. And then he heard the limb crack, only an instant before he saw a child fall. It happened so fast that he didn't know whether it was Karl or Gerhard until he'd run across the lawn to where Hannah and Gerhard were scrambling down from the tree.

"Are you hurt?" Han asked Little Karl, but the child was fighting so hard to catch his breath, he could neither speak nor cry.

Hannah and Gerhard both started to cry as Han carefully scooped Karl into his arms, praying inwardly that he was all right. Within minutes Theodor was with his son, and Karl had regained his breath enough to make it clear that he was hurting badly.

"I am so sorry," Han said while they waited for the doctor.

"What are *you* apologizing for?" Theodor retorted, rocking Karl back and forth.

Han pushed a hand abruptly through his hair. "Every time something happens, I tell myself it has to be the last. This place is like a battleground. It's no place for children to be playing."

"He'll be fine, I'm sure," Theodor said, smiling through his concern. But a few minutes later Georg came to report that it was evident the branch had been purposely weakened.

"Blast!" Han snarled. "We're lucky it didn't kill him."

The doctor repeated the same when he saw how far the child had fallen. It was determined that Little Karl had a broken arm and a few cracked ribs, which pained him terribly. While the arm was being set, Han waited in the hall with Theodor.

"I feel awful about this," Han said. "If I had—"

"Listen," Theodor interrupted, "you people have treated me nearly like family since my wife died. I don't want to see my son hurting more than any other father, but I'm grateful he's all right, and I'm not going to begrudge or regret the opportunity he's had to be with your children."

"But with everything that's been happening, I shouldn't have—"

"Han," Theodor put a hand on his arm, "we're in this together. I'm sure my sister would agree."

Han nodded, knowing there was nothing to undo what had been done. Still, he couldn't help wishing he'd kept the children closer, safer. But what could he do? Lock them in a closet? It was all so ridiculous.

The children were upset over the incident long after Theodor had taken Little Karl home. Han just cuddled with them on Stefan's bed and told them a long story while Maggie gazed out the window, her brow furrowed with concern. He wanted to tell her everything would be all right, but he wasn't so sure.

"Snow *would* be nice," Kathe said, laying her head against Erich's shoulder, warm water lapping against her throat. Erich had one leg hanging out of the bathtub, his arms wrapped tightly around her.

"A lot of it," Erich added.

"Do you ever think about what it might have been like for your parents when they were snowed in here?"

"I've thought about it a great deal lately," he admitted. "I can't imagine how my father survived here for three years before my mother showed up. I was already close to insane when you showed up."

"So was I," she said. "I don't want to leave, Erich."

"Then don't," he insisted. "I can't think of one good reason why you shouldn't stay. We can send a message and have them let your father know you're all right. I suspect he's already figured out that I've compromised you."

They reluctantly got out of the tub when the water began to cool, and then Kathe packed a picnic and they went to the upper meadow to spend the afternoon, lounging in a mass of wild-flowers while the horse grazed nearby. When they returned to the stable, there was a message waiting. Kathe saw Erich go tense as he read it.

"What?" she demanded.

Erich glanced at her, concern showing in his eyes, and he cleared his throat to read aloud, "Coming for Kathe at midnight. Don't—"

"How did they know I was here?"

"Do you think it would be so difficult to figure out?"

Kathe sighed. "Go on," she insisted.

"Don't let her come down alone." They exchanged a sharp glance, and he continued, "She is needed. Karl has been hurt."

"What?" she gasped. "Which one? My father or—"

"It doesn't say. That's it." He handed it to Kathe, and she read it again as if she could somehow make sense of it. She looked into Erich's eyes, so torn that she nearly felt physical pain. When tears crept into her eyes, she hurried toward the lodge, not wanting him to see them. She sat on the edge of the bed and let the tears fall, wondering what had happened at home, wondering if she would ever see Erich again beyond this day. She became so lost in thought, she was surprised to look up and see Erich standing there. He lifted one hand to wipe away her tears. She bowed her head forward when the tears wouldn't cease.

Seeing the evidence that Kathe shared his anguish, Erich found it impossible to hold back his own emotion. The full spectrum of his circumstances swept together and hit him square in the chest. Succumbing to weakness, he went to his knees and pressed his face into the folds of her skirt, crying like a child. He cried without restraint until the emotion merged into a numb helplessness, and he sat on the floor with his head in her lap while she idly trailed her fingers through his hair and over his face. With every fiber of his being, he wanted to tell her that they would get beyond this, that they would have a life together. But in his heart he didn't believe it. If they had *anything* beyond these moments together, he would be grateful. But if he combined logic with his feelings, he had to admit that he doubted he would ever see her again.

"Kathe," he said without looking at her, "if I don't make it through this, you must—"

"You have to make it through this," she insisted. But he looked up at her with such intense sadness in his eyes, she had to turn away.

"Kathe, listen to me." He took both her hands into his. "I'm not claiming to be able to predict the future, but I know what my heart is telling me. And I can't sit here and pretend that I have anything more to give you than what I already have."

"I'm not giving up that easy," she cried.

"I'm not giving up, Kathe. I just have to tell you that whatever happens, you must never—ever—forget what we shared."

Kathe looked into his eyes, trying to absorb the full depth of what he was trying to tell her. The emotion bubbled out of her like a volcanic eruption. "How could I possibly?" she murmured and fell apart.

"You must go on, Kathe. Promise me."

"My life is yours, Erich," she cried. "I'll do whatever you tell me to do."

"Then you must live, Kathe—with or without me. Find happiness and purpose. You must promise me."

Kathe shook her head, crying uncontrollably, not willing to admit this might be their final hours together. Erich took her by the shoulders and shook her gently, nearly shouting in her face, "Promise me, dammit! The only thing that makes this bearable is knowing that you will find peace without me if that's what it comes to. Do you hear what I'm telling you?"

"I can't live without you!" she muttered. "I can't!"

"You might have to!" he said through clenched teeth. "Now, promise me!"

Kathe compelled herself to nod, whimpering forcefully, "I promise."

She collapsed into his arms, and they held each other and cried. He made love to her with a desperation that far surpassed anything he'd ever experienced in his life. Then he held her close to him, surrounded by an almost deathly silence as the time ticked away, like the calm before the storm.

Chapter Ten

THE CHOICE

By midnight, Kathe had her bag packed, and she'd insisted on straightening up the lodge and leaving everything in order. They cleaned the dishes together after a late supper, and then they sat at the table, with a lamp burning low, sharing coffee from the same cup.

"I'm certain they're doing everything they can," Kathe said, if only to break the torturous silence. Erich nodded and took a long sip, and the quiet set in again.

"Who do you suppose is coming for me?" she asked, tapping her fingers against Erich's arm.

Erich put his hand over hers to stop her fidgeting. "Most likely Georg. Beyond my parents, I believe he's the only one who knows the way. He regularly delivered supplies here to my father during those years of exile. He's also very cautious and thorough . . . and he's always willing."

Kathe glanced at the clock. "Is he punctual?"

"He'll be here soon," Erich stated, as if his coming meant nothing.

"Then I suppose we don't have time to—"

"No," he said tersely, and then his voice softened. "Or maybe we could make him wait."

Seeing a hint of his dimples, Kathe smiled. She pressed a hand to his face, then leaned over the table to kiss him. He urged her onto his lap, kissing her over and over, until the knock at the door startled them. Erich briefly held her against him, saying softly, "Yes, he's punctual."

Kathe forced herself away. Erich rose and opened the door.

"Hello, Erich," Georg said, stepping inside. "Kathe," he nodded toward her, and she attempted a smile. Georg quickly embraced Erich and added, "That was from your mother."

"Did she give it to you personally?" Erich asked lightly.

"Actually, yes," Georg smiled before his expression became severe. "How are you?"

Erich shrugged his shoulders, hardly daring admit to the truth verbally for fear of causing a scene. "I'm more concerned about Karl. What happened? Was it Little Karl or—"

Georg glanced at Kathe. "Little Karl fell out of a tree in the castle gardens."

"Is he—" Kathe began.

"He's going to be fine," Georg assured her, and she relaxed somewhat. "He's got a broken arm and some cracked ribs. Under the circumstances, we've got Theodor awfully busy at the castle, and your father is—"

"Yes, I know," Kathe interrupted Georg's obvious attempt to apologize for taking her away. "His work has been very consuming lately. Besides," she forced a smile toward Erich, "what do they know about taking care of a hurt child?"

"Could you help me outside a few minutes?" Georg said to Erich, and they left Kathe alone to straighten what was already straight, and attempt to compose her threatening emotions.

"What else is going on?" Erich asked Georg as they approached the stable.

"Karl's fall was not an accident," he stated. "The tree limb had been weakened."

"Heaven help us! What next?" Erich muttered.

"Beyond that it's been pretty quiet, but we have a couple of spies that have been able to infiltrate this force that's brewing. Unfortunately, they can't get anywhere near the top, so we still have nothing that will help much. We only know that more men are joining every day."

"Why can't I just challenge Koenig to a duel and get it over with?" Erich snarled. "I think I'd prefer it to all this hiding and sneaking around."

"If only it could be so easy. But then, that puts everything at a fifty-fifty chance. I don't like those odds."

"And what are the odds as it stands?" Erich asked, wondering if he wanted to know.

"That all depends," Georg said in a tone that indicated he would say nothing more.

"Good heavens!" Erich exclaimed when he saw the three pack horses waiting to be unloaded. "How long am I staying?"

"It's hard to say." Georg began unloading the food and supplies, and Erich hurried to help him. "But this is just a precaution. We have to be—"

"Thorough. Yes, I know. Just promise me one thing, Georg. If you're going to leave me up here to get snowed in, send Kathe back."

Georg chuckled. "If it comes to that, we'll see what we can do."

It was a simple statement, but it gave Erich some hope. It only took a few minutes to unload the supplies and get Kathe's horse saddled. Erich rode with them to the ridge and helped Kathe dismount. He held her tightly while Georg urged the horses through the crevice, then turned to take Kathe's hand. She took a few steps forward, then turned and ran back.

"One more minute, please," she cried, and Erich held her so tightly it hurt.

Kathe finally forced herself away, and Georg helped her into the crevice, turning back to say to Erich, "I'll keep you informed. You take care of yourself."

"You take care of my lady," Erich said.

"The very best care," Georg added, "I can assure you."

Long after they were gone, Erich stood alone in the darkness, a thousand thoughts tumbling through his mind. The loneliness struck so suddenly, so intensely, he fell to his knees and wrapped his arms around his middle, groaning aloud. He lost track of the time as he knelt there on the ground, wondering what the future might hold. He finally returned to the lodge, reminding himself to be grateful that she had come, that they had been able to spend these days together. If only that could be enough.

Han declared that Lucky had been well named since the puppy made Stefan's recovery come along even faster. Gradually a healthy color returned to the boy's face, but since he had to remain in bed due to doctor's orders, Lucky occupied Stefan's time and kept him company.

A week after Lucky's arrival, Maggie brought her son a glass of milk by request. As always, it came straight from the kitchen by her own hand to be certain that it was safe. She noted that Stefan drank half of it and left the rest on the bedside table before falling asleep.

Early the following morning, Maggie and Han were just coming awake when they heard their son scream.

"Mama!" Stefan yelled, and Maggie hurried into the room with Han close behind. "Mama!" he cried as she approached his bed.

"What is it? What's wrong?"

"Mama!" He pointed toward the puppy, lying motionless on the floor. "Lucky won't wake up."

Han knelt beside the puppy, and it took little to surmise that he was dead. He sighed and swallowed hard. It took great courage to look his son in the face and say, "I'm sorry, Stefan, but he's gone."

Stefan turned to his mother's shoulder and cried while Han carefully picked up the puppy and took it away.

"It's all right, darling," she muttered, stroking his head, "we'll get you another puppy."

"But I love Lucky," he sobbed.

Maggie held Stefan until Han returned. He stood by the bed, wondering what could have possibly happened. Glancing down, he saw the cup on the floor and something inside him wrenched.

"Stefan," he said carefully, "when did your cup fall on the floor?"

"In the night my milk spilled," he replied, then sniffled. "Lucky licked it up."

Maggie tried to choke back the cry that came from deep within as Han met her eyes with terror in them. Stefan looked to his mother in surprise as a pathetic whimper escaped her lips.

"I thought you brought him his milk," Han said.

"I did," she said breathlessly.

"I only drank part of it," Stefan said, "and set the rest on the table. In the night I reached for it, but it spilled and I went back to sleep."

"I guess Lucky wasn't so lucky after all," Han said, and Maggie gave him a scolding glare. He glanced toward his son and added, "But Stefan was."

Maggie put her hand over her mouth in an effort to suppress the emotion aching in her throat. When she realized her efforts were futile, she rushed from the room so she wouldn't upset Stefan any further.

"What's wrong with Mama?" Stefan asked.

"She's just upset that Lucky died," Han reassured him. "I'm going to go talk to Mama. I'll come back in a while and tell you a story. Now, don't eat or drink anything unless one of the family brings it to you."

"I won't," Stefan said, and Han left the room.

Cameron and Georg both came to their feet when Maggie flew into the office wearing a nightgown and wrapper, her hair down.

"I can't take it anymore," she cried. "Must we go on day after day, wondering if we will all survive until the next?"

"What happened?" Cameron insisted.

"Do you think if they . . . if they . . ." Her emotion flooded forward. "If they do away with Stefan, will Gerhard be next? If my baby is a boy will they kill it too?" She hit her fists on the desk and cried out, "How much do we have to sacrifice for this country?"

Cameron was too stunned to demand what had brought this on. He could only put his arms around his daughter and let her cry, hating the reality of her questions. Georg met his eyes across the room, and an unspoken empathy passed between them.

Han burst into the room, then stopped. Maggie remained oblivious to his presence as she cried like a child on her father's shoulder.

"Perhaps you could tell us what brought this on," Georg said quietly.

Han bowed his head and swallowed hard. "Stefan left half a cup of milk on the bedside table. It spilled in the night and the puppy licked it up. The puppy is dead."

Panic leapt into Georg's eyes as he looked at Cameron again with dread. Maggie eased away, and Han put his arm around her while Cameron stood silently with his arms folded.

"What did you tell Nik Koenig once about hunting him down and hanging him?" Han asked bitterly.

Cameron swallowed hard, and Georg answered for him. "I fear that any aggressive move now would only put this force of his out for vengeance, and we'd be worse off in the long run. We have proof of nothing."

"Too bad the Italians didn't execute him while they had the chance," Han added.

"What happened?" Abbi rushed into the room, having heard the ruckus.

Han repeated the story, and Abbi sat down carefully as she absorbed what this meant.

"You know what we have to do, Georg," Cameron said.

"Yes, I know. When?"

"Tonight."

Cameron sat behind his desk and looked around at the expectant faces of those he loved, all waiting to hear what he and Georg had already discussed as a possible option. He reached his hand out to take Abbi's before he spoke.

"Maggie," he said softly. "We're going to get you and the children out of here. It is not worth the risk any longer. If you are safe, we can concentrate on handling the rest straight on. Do you understand?"

"Yes," she said, and her eyes moved to Han.

"He's got to stay with me," Cameron answered her silent question. "But it's only temporary. Hopefully, we will get this under control very soon.

"Han," he added, turning toward him.

"Yes?"

"I want you to help Maggie and the children pack some things . . . practical things." Han nodded.

"Cameron," Abbi said with concern, "you're not going to . . ."

"I most certainly am."

"But she . . . she could have the baby soon."

"It won't be for a while yet."

"She's been known to come early before. Cameron, she's—"

"They've got to get out of here! We're being undermined from the inside and . . ." He stopped himself and softened his tone. "I'm sending you, as well. You can take care of her."

Abbi's eyes widened, but she made no protest.

"I know you already know this," Georg said, "but remember, no one else—no one—must know. It is essential if this is to succeed."

Han and Maggie nodded their understanding.

"Han, you keep an eye on Stefan." Cameron rose and moved toward the door. "I'll come and get you when it's time to go. Come along, Abbi, we have things to see to."

Abbi followed Cameron out, while Han and Maggie returned to Stefan's room.

"Han," she said in the hallway, "I'm so afraid. I don't want to leave you."

"It won't be for long," he said as reassuringly as he could manage. "I don't want you to go. But our fathers know what they're doing. We must trust them."

"I know," she whispered.

"After all," he added lightly, "they did arrange our marriage."

Maggie smiled, and they moved into Stefan's room to find him looking depressed and upset.

"Stefan," Han said in a jovial tone, "your Grandpapas thought you might enjoy going on an adventure." The child's eyes widened. "Would you like that?"

"Can I get out of bed?"

"Yes, but you'll have to be careful. I know you can't walk, but do you think you can ride?"

"Of course I can. When do we get to go?" he asked.

"Not until Grandpapa tells us it's time to go, but we'll pack some things for you so you're ready. You mustn't tell anyone however, or you'll ruin the fun."

Stefan nodded firmly, and Maggie squeezed Han's hand. Han moved close and held her, trying to offer comfort, but he was dying inside to think of being without her and the children. And amidst it all, he wondered what Horstberg might suffer through all of this. If that weren't bad enough, that wretched dream of Abbi's just had to pop into his mind at moments like this. He didn't know what it meant—if anything—but he didn't like it.

At half past two in the morning, the servants had all retired and Castle Horstberg was mostly dark. The duke went to Stefan's room to find Han and Maggie waiting with the children.

"Come along," he whispered, "quietly."

Han picked up the bags while Maggie held Gerhard and Hannah's hands, and Cameron lifted Stefan up to carry him. They went to the room where the duke and duchess slept. Abbi was there waiting.

"Say your good-byes," Cameron said softly to Han. "I'll need you to come with me—right now."

Han turned to Maggie, who was already crying, and hugged her desperately.

"I love you," Maggie whispered. "Be careful. Don't get hurt. I need you."

"I'll be fine," he smiled, but she saw mist in his eyes. "You take care of that baby . . . and you too."

"I will."

"I love you, Maggie."

They held each other again, and Cameron cleared his throat.

Han knelt down to embrace Hannah. "Be careful, Papa," she said.

Han nodded. "You help your mother now, princess. And remember how much Papa loves you." He turned to Gerhard. "Do you think you can be good to your brother?" Gerhard begrudgingly nodded, and Han chuckled. "I love you, son. You're five years old now, and I'm trusting you to take good care of Mama and Stefan . . . and Hannah, too."

Gerhard hugged his father tightly, then turned to Cameron. "Can we go on our adventure now, Grandpapa?"

"In a few minutes," Cameron replied.

Han took Stefan in his arms. "I love you, son. I'm counting on you to be very brave and watch out for the family while I can't be with you."

Stefan nodded stoutly.

Han turned to the duchess and hugged her as well. He turned again to Maggie, kissed her desperately, despite the spectators, then left quickly with the duke. He followed him for what seemed like forever, until they came to the south turret and began winding up stairs that went on and on. Entering the room at the top, Han was surprised to see a cote of pigeons, writing material, and very little of anything else.

He watched silently as the duke wrote a short message stating: *Coming with five. Be prepared to receive them. Leaving now.*

He folded the paper very small, then tied it to the leg of a pigeon, which flew from his hands out a high window into the night.

"You wait here, Han. Erich's waiting for that message. You should get a reply before long. If the reply says: *Waiting,* shine that lantern in the window and cover it twice for the signal." Han nodded. "If the reply says: *Don't come,* shine the lantern but do nothing with it."

"I understand."

"If everything is all right, we'll be leaving with your signal; then you've got to wait—and it will be quite some time, so make yourself comfortable—until you get another message that says they've arrived safely. When you get it, send another back that acknowledges you've received his message. Can you handle it?"

"Yes, sir," Han stated with confidence.

"Good," Cameron said. "I'm off then. After you send the final message, meet me in my office. We've some things to discuss. If I'm not there, wait. We'll get some sleep tomorrow."

Han nodded, and Cameron turned to leave. "Father," Han said, "tell her once more that I love her."

"I will," Cameron smiled, then left Han alone with the pigeons.

Cameron went back to his rooms where the women and children were waiting. Abbi seemed calm and at ease, and the children were excited, apparently not at all tired after being awakened at two in the morning. But Maggie seemed distraught.

"Han said to tell you he loves you," Cameron said right off, and Maggie showed a degree of relief. "Come on, let's go."

Maggie glanced once more at the painting she had been admiring while they'd waited. It was an abstract piece—her mother's first, and her father had often called it, *Our Horstberg.* It was a fair depiction of the valley, with the castle and the river and many other details, yet she wondered where her mother would have ever seen it from that perspective.

Maggie didn't notice what her father was doing until she heard the children gasp, and she turned to see that a tapestry had been pulled aside, and part of the stone wall had opened like a door. Cameron stood aside gallantly and smiled toward Abbi. "You first, my dear. Surely you remember the way."

"I'd rather not think about the last time I went through here," she replied. Holding a lantern, Abbi went through the door, and Gerhard followed with Maggie close behind, quite in awe of the narrow passageway they were walking in. Cameron sent Hannah ahead of him then came last with Stefan in his arms.

"How are you, Rusty?" he asked.

"This is fun," Stefan replied.

Cameron chuckled. "Are you all right, Maggie?" he called ahead.

"It's a bit stuffy," she replied, "but I'm fine."

The passageway seemed to go on and on. At last they stopped, and Abbi called back. "How do I get this open?"

"Push on the stone that sticks out a little at the bottom . . . to the left."

Maggie heard her mother groan, soon followed by stone sliding against stone, and fresh air struck them. They came into the darkness at the bottom of the hill that supported the castle, and when the opening they'd just come through was closed, it was impossible to see it from the way it blended into the hillside.

Georg was waiting with horses and the lantern was quickly extinguished. "Have you seen the signal yet?" Cameron asked as they helped everyone mount.

"Not yet."

They waited for a few minutes while Georg occasionally strained his neck to look up. "That's it," he said, "let's go."

They rode slowly and quietly as Georg had instructed, with him at the head of the party and Cameron riding behind.

Maggie noted they were soon in thick forest on a trail which seemed unused and barely wide enough for a horse to pass through. Her curiosity was driving her mad, but Georg had told them to be still, and she dared not speak. She didn't know where she'd been expecting them to go, but this was not it. Thinking it through, she wondered if their destination was the mountain lodge where her parents had met. Rather than taking too much time to speculate over it, Maggie's thoughts went to Han. Already she missed him dreadfully. She grew weary and a deep ache seeped into her back. She was wondering if they would ever arrive at their destination when a huge meadow opened up and the trees moved behind them.

Georg broke into a gallop with instructions for them to follow more slowly. Maggie could barely see him dismount below what looked like a long ridge. When they rode closer to him, he was pulling thick foliage away to reveal a crevice in the rock.

Cameron helped them dismount, and then he took Abbi's hand and smiled. "You first, my love. This is where it all started."

"Really, Cameron. You say that every time we come here."

"Well, it's the truth. Isn't it, Georg?"

"It's the truth," Georg said, taking Stefan out of the saddle. "But I'll never forgive you for having such a good time while I thought she was dead."

"This must be the famous spot," Maggie said to her father, "where you saved Mother's life."

"Your mother can tell you about it all over again," Cameron said as he disappeared into the narrow crevice, holding Abbi's arm firmly. "You'll have lots of time for things like that."

They were gone for several minutes before Cameron reappeared and took Hannah, then Gerhard. While Maggie remained with Georg, she said, "When you get back, tell Han that I love him."

"I will." Georg kissed Maggie on the cheek.

Cameron returned again and took Maggie's arm. "Be careful," he said, "you're the most fragile one."

She held on to him tightly, realizing they were climbing through a narrow rock crevice that went steeply upward.Georg followed close behind carrying Stefan, and at the top, he turned Stefan over to Cameron and went back down.

"Bring the horses through," Cameron shouted, and Maggie heard Georg ushering them somewhere behind her.Cameron helped everyone mount again, then called to Georg, "Wait right there. I won't be long."

Cameron took the reins of Abbi's horse and led it while walking through sparse forest that was now oak and beech trees rather than the thick pines they had been in earlier. Maggie and the children followed close behind.

They rode only a few minutes before the smell of chimney smoke hit Maggie's senses. Suddenly the trees moved behind, and sitting in the moonlight, against a steep rise of the mountain, was a lodge, larger than the cottage where she and Han had stayed in the Black Forest. They all dismounted, and Abbi moved naturally toward the door before stopping.

"What are you waiting for?" Cameron asked.

"You always carry me over the threshold when we come here. That's what I'm waiting for."

Cameron laughed and picked up his wife, and then he kicked open the door and carried her in. Erich was there to greet them, full of hugs and smiles.

"I'm sure glad to see you," he said. "This place is torture, being alone."

"I don't feel a bit sorry for you," Cameron said with a smirk, and he went back out to get Stefan.

"Hey!" Erich laughed when Cameron brought Stefan through the door and set him on the sofa. "You look great."

"We've been on an adventure," Stefan said.

"Did you get all of the extra bedding and food that Georg brought up?" Cameron asked Erich.

"I've got it."

"You have everything you need, then?"

"We'll manage," Erich said.

"You let me know if you need anything and we'll find a way to get it here."

"I could really use Kathe," he said a little too seriously. "But I think it's going to be a bit crowded."

Cameron put a hand on his shoulder and said quietly, "We're doing everything we can."

"I know." Erich forced a smile. "We'll keep in touch."

Cameron patted him on the back, then gave Maggie and each of the children a hug. "I'm going to miss you, Abilee," he said, using his wife's full name as he took her into his arms.

"I've never been here without you." Tears showed in her eyes.

"It won't be too long . . . I hope."

"I've heard you say that before." She smiled sadly, and he chuckled with very little humor.

"I love you," he whispered and kissed her.

Cameron gave a few more instructions to Erich, then left in the night to return with Georg.

"Well," Abbi said, "let's get settled in here so we can all get some much-needed sleep. Maggie, you must have the bed. It's upstairs. Come along."

"There's only one bed?" she asked.

"That's right."

"But where are the rest of you going to sleep?"

"I will use one sofa, and Stefan the other. They're quite large and comfortable. Erich's made bedrolls for Gerhard and Hannah near the sofas, and Erich—"

"Gets the floor," he called after them.

Abbi turned and smiled. "Your father wouldn't feel a bit sorry for you," she said.

"I suspected he wouldn't." He smirked.

"Now run along and get that message sent to Han," Abbi said.

"Tell him I love him," Maggie cried impulsively.

Erich gave a comical nod of disgust and left the lodge, calling over his shoulder, "I don't feel a bit sorry for you."

Han realized the duke hadn't been kidding when he'd said it would take a long time to get the reply. It was only his anxiety over the situation that kept him awake, and he was more than a little relieved to see the pigeon finally appear. Quickly he removed the message which read: *Five received. All is well. M loves you.*

Han sighed, feeling incredibly lonely as he scribed a quick reply: *Message received. H loves M.*

Abbi awoke soon after dawn by habit. She could see from the sofa where she was lying that the children were sleeping soundly, but Erich wasn't there. She sat up and turned to see him standing near the window.

"Are you all right?" she whispered, startling him.

"I didn't mean to wake you," he replied softly.

"You didn't wake me." She moved to his side and put her arms around him. "Are you all right?" she repeated.

Erich smiled at his mother. "It's nice to have you here."

"I missed you, too. But that's not what I asked."

Erich turned back to gaze out the window.

"You're missing Kathe," she said, and he nodded. "She was here."

"Yes, she was here."

"I thought the lodge looked in terribly good order . . . considering."

Erich chuckled. "She has a way of smoothing over my rough edges."

"She has been a blessing in your life." Abbi touched his face. "For that matter, she has added something to *all* of our lives. She is a marvelous addition to our family."

Erich couldn't help the cynical tone as he retorted, "Yes, but it's not *safe* for her to be a du Woernig, so . . ."

"I know this is difficult for you."

"This is hell for me, quite frankly. Part of me just wants to steal her away in the night and never look back." He sighed. "But I could never do it."

"Never?" she questioned. "What if Horstberg were lost to you, and there was no going back?"

He thought about it. "I could only answer that if I knew it were true. At this moment, I feel as if a piece of my heart has been torn out. I imagine Nik Koenig controlling the welfare of all those people and my stomach just turns to knots."

"Then you can understand the anguish your father experienced through the years he was banished."

"Yes, I believe I can . . . at least to a degree. But I'm not sure I have the same strength and courage. I feel more like a lost little boy."

"I believe he felt much the same way, Erich. It's a difficult position to be in." Abbi saw something uncertain come into his eyes, and she asked, "What else is troubling you?"

As always, Erich was amazed by her perception. "There are moments, in spite of the way it tears at me, when I just *want* to turn my back on all of it." He inhaled deeply. "Am I less of a man because a part of me wishes I didn't have to be responsible for a country? I long for a life free of complications." He chuckled humorlessly. "At this point, I just long for a life." His tone became severe. "I wonder sometimes if I really have what it takes to be the ruler of a country. In spite of my training, I fear I will never be able to fill my father's position . . . even if the opportunity came."

"Erich," she said gently, "fears and doubts are human. They make us look at ourselves and take inventory. You cannot possibly understand a lifetime all at once, and you mustn't be hard on yourself for feeling confused and discouraged under the duress of such circumstances."

Erich didn't look convinced. She continued gently, "If you trust in your feelings, and follow your instincts, I believe that you will find peace . . . even if things don't work out the way you might want, or expect them to."

Erich looked into his mother's eyes and hugged her tightly. "Where do you come up with such wisdom?"

Abbi chuckled humbly. "I just struggle through my life like everybody else. I only know that my instincts have never let me down if I truly listen to what they're telling me."

"And what do your instincts tell you about what we are facing now?"

Erich saw something briefly pass through her eyes that sent a chill down his back. It was quickly replaced by perfect confidence as she stated, "I'm certainly no prophet, but I believe that Horstberg will be at peace . . . eventually. What may happen in the meantime, we have no way of knowing."

"And what about me, Mother? What do your instincts tell you about me?"

Erich wondered if he imagined the emotion that passed quickly over her expression before she glanced down. "You must follow your own feelings, Erich. What do *you* believe?"

"I don't know." He sighed. "Is it instinct or my own fears and doubts that tell me I will never wear that crown?"

Abbi only tightened her hold on him, leaving his question unanswered.

Life in the mountain lodge quickly fell into a routine. And Maggie hated it—mostly because she missed Han. She was grateful for the training Han had given her in the Black Forest, which made it easier to adjust to being without servants. She did her best to keep busy and help her mother with the meals and upkeep, but her pregnancy was getting more uncomfortable by the day, and she found it difficult to do little but lie down, which was becoming terribly tedious.

Erich did well in keeping the children entertained, and he had them outdoors much of the time during the days. In the evenings, they found diversion sitting by the fire while Abbi told them about her experiences in this lodge. Maggie and Erich had heard it all before, but being here made it more fascinating, and the children were enthralled and full of questions.

"Did Grandpapa really save your life when you got lost in the blizzard?" Gerhard asked.

"He certainly did."

"Why was he hiding here?" Stefan asked.

"Because his brother had framed him for a crime, and he couldn't stay in Horstberg."

"I hope you don't ever do that to me," Stefan said to Gerhard.

"Of course he wouldn't," Maggie insisted.

"Was Grandpapa handsome back then?" Hannah asked.

"He still is." Abbi laughed softly.

"Did he kiss you?" Hannah added.

"He certainly did."

"He'd have been a fool not to," Erich piped in.

"Why did you have to stay here all winter?" Gerhard asked.

"When the pass through the crevice is full of snow, you can't go through it."

"What if it snows before we can go home?" Hannah sounded fearful.

"I think we will be able to go home before then," Abbi assured her. "And I think it's time you children went to sleep."

They reluctantly got into their makeshift beds, but there was a chorus of complaints until Erich said to his mother, "Do what you used to do when I didn't want to go to sleep."

Abbi smiled at him, then said to the children, "If you all hurry into bed, I'll sing you a song that your grandfather wrote for Uncle Erich before he was born."

The tactic worked, and Erich grinned as he turned to help Maggie up the stairs.

"How are you feeling?" he asked as she sat slowly on the edge of the bed.

"Awful. As if it weren't bad enough to be in this condition, I have to be without Han. This is his baby, you know. He should be hearing me complain and rubbing my feet. He should be every bit as miserable as I am."

She said it lightly, but Erich didn't miss the reality in her eyes. If she missed Han half as much as he missed Kathe, he could well imagine her misery.

"Would you unlace my shoes?" she asked. "I simply can't reach them, and my feet are killing me."

"It would be a pleasure, Your Highness." He chuckled and knelt on the floor to remove her shoes. He rubbed her feet while she rambled about how swollen they got being pregnant in the summer, as opposed to being pregnant in the winter.

"Oh, you're almost as good at that as Han is. I'll have to tell Kathe to insist on a foot rub when we get back."

"Why don't you do that," he said, liking the idea of being with her at all. "Tell me what the two of you did together after I left."

"What was there to do?" she asked. "I'm too fat to do much of anything. The castle was like one big booby trap. We hardly dared move. Of course, she made a lot of lace. She can sure release nervous energy with that little shuttle, I'm telling you."

Erich continued to rub his sister's feet while his mind conjured up a clear image of Kathe.

"She really is a wonderful girl, Erich. I wonder what we ever did without her. It's a pity you didn't find her years ago."

"Amen," he murmured, wondering how long this dreadful waiting would go on.

"I want the servants watched," the duke said firmly to his

highest-ranking officers, gathered around looking glum. "If one of them leaves the castle, I want them followed."

"We will have to put the men on double shifts," Captain Dukerk stated.

"Do whatever you have to," the duke insisted. "If anyone from this castle goes anywhere near Nik Koenig, I want to know about it immediately."

"Yes, Your Grace," the captain replied.

"That's all for now," the duke added, and his men filed out.

"Do you really believe that will solve the problem?" Georg asked.

"No," Cameron nearly shouted, "I don't! But I don't know what else to do!" Georg said nothing and Cameron bowed his head, drawing a deep breath. "I'm sorry, Georg."

"There is no need to apologize. I know how you feel."

"Yes, I suppose you do." Cameron sighed. "And you should also know that you've always been the brains behind this operation. If you don't know what to do, then I certainly don't know what to do."

Georg sighed as well. "Maybe we should have had the servants followed a long time ago."

"Maybe we should have," Cameron said. "But stewing over what we should have done isn't going to do us any good now."

"It's inevitable, isn't it." Han piped in, playing idly with the drapery cord that hung near his chair.

"What is?"

"War. We're going to have to fight."

"I pray we come up with an alternative before that happens," Cameron said grimly.

"Now that's a good idea," Han said, coming to his feet.

"Where are you going?" Georg asked.

"To pray," he said. "Where else could I possibly go?"

Georg stood up and followed him.

"Where are *you* going?" Cameron asked.

"I'm going with him."

Cameron came to his feet and followed them to the castle chapel, where they all sat in contemplative silence for the better part of the afternoon.

Cameron lay in the middle of the huge bed, staring blankly into the darkness above him. The nights he'd spent alone here in the past thirty-two years were few, and he hated it. No matter how he tried, he just couldn't sleep.

The banging on his door came as a welcome reprieve.

"Who is it?" he called, pulling on his breeches.

"It's Captain Dukerk," came the reply.

"What?" Cameron demanded, opening the door as he slid into a shirt.

"We've come upon something that might interest you."

"Wait for me in the office. I'll be right down."

"Yes, sir," he said, already on his way down the hall.

Cameron entered his office and stopped abruptly to see the little maid sitting in a chair, nearly trembling, while two officers stood at attention on either side of her. It was easy to tell what had happened. A quick nod from the captain confirmed it.

"Heidi, isn't it?" the duke asked, placing his hands behind his back.

"Yes, Your Grace," she said quietly.

"Dare I ask what you're doing out and about at three in the morning?"

She silently turned her eyes to the captain, and he gave her a hard glare. "The duke asked you a question, miss," he said sternly.

"I swear to you, Your Grace," she blurted, "I don't have anything to do with this. I swear it."

"Simply answer His Grace's question," the captain added after Cameron sighed impatiently.

Heidi turned fearful eyes toward the duke. "I went out to

meet a friend. While I was there, these brutes," she eyed the officers at her sides, "barged in and arrested me."

"Who was . . . this friend?" Cameron asked.

Again Heidi turned to the captain, as if to ask if she really
had to answer that. "Speak up, miss," he insisted.

"Nik Koenig," she said with her head bent forward.

"I see," Cameron said, pretending to be surprised. "And to
what does Mr. Koenig owe the pleasure of your nocturnal visit?"

Heidi drew back her shoulders. "I love him, Your Grace. And
if you want my opinion, I think your assumptions that he is—"

"If His Grace wanted your opinion," Captain Dukerk said
brashly, "he would ask for it."

"That's right," the duke agreed, and he bent forward and
looked the maid right in the eye. She turned away, and he said,
"Look at me!" She did, and he lowered his voice. "I want to know
if you have any knowledge whatsoever concerning the accidents
that have taken place in this castle. And bear in mind, miss, that
you are as good as under oath. If I find out you have lied to me
in any way, you will pay sorely."

The duke waited quietly without taking his eyes from hers.
Finally she answered, "I already told you. I have nothing to do
with this."

"Let me rephrase my question," Cameron said. "You are
being accused of treason. If you are guilty, we will find out
whether you tell us or not. There are two things that can happen
to people found guilty of treason. The first, and most popular, is
a firing squad. The second is the exchange of one's life in return
for valuable information."

Cameron watched her eyes closely, and instinct told him
she was lying. The fear in her expression went far too deep for
genuine innocence. But mingled with the fear in her eyes was a
subtle defiance, an undeniable arrogance that reminded him of
her boyfriend.

"Do you wish to change your statement?" Cameron asked.

Heidi hesitated. "No, sir, I don't."

Cameron leaned back and drew a heavy sigh, wondering what Nik Koenig did to make his acquaintances so blasted loyal. Or was she more afraid of Mr. Koenig than she was of him?

"If you will excuse us for a moment," Cameron said.

Cameron nodded toward Captain Dukerk, who followed him out of the room.

"What do you think, Lance?" he asked quietly when they were alone in the hallway.

"If it's true that she loves him, she's got to know something."

"Yet I can't just assume she's lying. If I put her in the keep, what good will it do me? I suspect he doesn't love *her* nearly as much as she thinks he does. He would probably just leave her to rot." They remained thoughtfully silent a moment until Cameron said speculatively, "If I were to pretend that I believe her and we let her go, perhaps we could find out more eventually. If she went to see him once, surely she will again."

"I can have my best team keep an eye on her. They do well at going unnoticed."

"Sounds good to me," Cameron said. "Let's do it."

Cameron went back into the office, and Heidi trembled visibly as he set his eyes upon her.

"I'm going to assume you're telling me the truth," the duke said, and she held her breath. "If I discover otherwise, I'm certain I'll be seeing you again."

"Do I still keep my job, Your Grace?"

"If you've been honest with me, there's no reason why you shouldn't." Cameron folded his arms. "You may leave."

"May I see to my previous appointment," she asked, coming to her feet, "or will I be arrested again?"

Cameron only motioned casually toward the door, and Heidi was apparently oblivious to the challenge in his expression.

"Heidi," Cameron stopped her, "take some advice. Find your-self a nice guy. Nik Koenig is nothing but trouble."

Her eyes betrayed that she didn't dare say what she wanted to, and then she scurried down the hall.

Cameron glanced toward Captain Dukerk once they were alone. "I know you're well aware of what we're up against," Cameron said.

"Yes, sir."

Cameron sighed. "It's been more than thirty years since you and I have had to face something so ominous."

"It has been a good thirty years," the captain said.

"Yes, it has. I just want you to know, whatever happens, I am deeply indebted to you. You've been a true friend, Lance."

"And you have been the same to me, Cameron."

Cameron smiled. The two of them shared a deep and special bond for a number of reasons, and he very much appreciated the way they always used given names when they were alone or with family. Still, that couldn't begin to express the gratitude and devotion he felt toward this man who had never let him down in all the years they'd shared—both professionally and personally.

"Whatever you decide to do," the captain said, "I'm behind you all the way."

"Yes, I know. And that means more to me now than it has since the night you . . ."

Cameron hesitated, and Lance added, "Killed your brother. Yes, I know."

"And saved Abbi," Cameron added. "And the country, for that matter." He sighed as the memories hovered too close to the present situation. Changing the subject, he said, "So, how is your family, Captain? I know your youngest was ill."

"He's doing fine now, thank you."

"Glad to hear it," Cameron said. "And what have you heard from Dulsie?"

Lance's face brightened. "She doing very well; better than I'd hoped, I'm glad to say. She's being courted by a fine young man. I've met him and I must say I was impressed. She's told him everything about her past and he is completely accepting of her. I've never seen her so happy."

"I'm very glad to hear it," Cameron said. "At our age, I dare say little means more than knowing our children are happy and well."

"I would agree," Lance said with a solemnity that brought to mind the present situation and how it was affecting their families. "I should tell you something I never thought I'd say, but . . . I'm grateful at the moment that my children have moved out of the country."

"I agree."

"I wish the same was possible for your family," Lance said.

"It might come to that," Cameron countered, and both men sighed at the same time, as if their thoughts were in perfect unison.

Cameron forced a lighter tone. "And how is your sweet wife? With all that's been going on, I haven't seen her for a while."

"More beautiful every day."

"Ah," Cameron smiled, "it seems to happen that way, doesn't it."

"It certainly does. I take it Her Grace went with the others."

"Yes," Cameron said.

"Then I pray this will all be over very soon."

"Amen," Cameron muttered and went back to bed.

"Excuse me, sir." Klara breathlessly stopped Han in the hall.

"What is it?" he asked, noting her distraught expression.

"One of the other maids was just hurt in the garden. I heard her cry out and went to see and . . . and . . . I think she's hurt bad, sir. One of the archways in the garden wall collapsed and . . ."

"Take me to her," Han insisted, following Klara down the hall. He wasn't surprised when she led him to an area in the garden where the children usually played. He felt relatively certain this accident had been intended for one of them. Han surveyed the situation quickly then told Klara, "You stay with her. I'll send for the doctor and get someone to move her inside."

When everything was under control and the injuries were reported as minor, Han checked out the scene of the accident again before going to the duke's office.

"What's wrong?" Cameron asked as soon as he saw his face. Captain Dukerk was also there, and his expression was grave as he waited for one more dire report.

"One of the maids was hurt in the garden. It doesn't appear to be anything serious—some bruises, but . . ."

"But what?" Cameron insisted, seeming more upset than usual.

"I believe it was intentional."

"Yes?"

"I think it was intended for one of the children."

Cameron sighed and pushed his hand through his hair. "Well, let's thank heaven they aren't here."

"There is something else," Han said, and Cameron drew his eyes up intently.

"You know the little maid that you believe is responsible?"

"Heidi?"

"She's the one who got hurt."

Cameron's eyes narrowed as the incongruity struck him. He sat down hard and ran his finger over his cheek thoughtfully.

"I want all of the servants evacuated."

Han said nothing, almost thinking it was a joke. When he began to see that it wasn't, he questioned, "You're serious?"

"I am quite serious. The captain and I have already been discussing the possibility."

"Where will we send them?" Han asked.

"Give them all an advance of some pay. Most of them have relatives or friends in Horstberg; in fact, many of them don't actually live at the castle. Send the ones who don't have a place to go to the inns and pubs. We'll take care of the expenses in advance. Coordinate with Lieutenant Joerger on the details."

"Also," the captain said more to Cameron, "I wanted to tell you that Nadine has gone to visit Dulsie, and she will stay there for the time being. I didn't want her here . . . with all that's happening."

"Of course," Cameron said and sighed. "You bring up an important point. We also need everyone who lives in the castle apartments evacuated."

Han knew well enough that the apartments were used by families of high-ranking officers and servants. He'd grown up in one of them. But he knew they were talking about a great deal of people. "Again," Cameron added, "if they have nowhere to go, we will make arrangements. If I have to pay for it personally I will—anything to keep them as safe as possible."

"I can help with the arrangements," Captain Dukerk said and came to his feet. "We should see to it right away."

Han knew the reasons but still found himself asking, "Why must we take such drastic measures?"

"I won't have anyone else getting hurt," Cameron said. "That's why."

Han knew there was something more. He had to ask, "And?"

Cameron faced him directly. "The captain just informed me that one of the men sent out to keep an eye on Mr. Koenig's girlfriend came in this morning with a bullet in his gut."

Han swallowed hard, and Cameron went to the window. Bringing his hands behind his back, he continued, "Nothing was discovered concerning the maid, but he did manage to tell us what he did find out before he . . . died."

"Dare I ask?" Han said quietly. With all they had been through, he couldn't recall Cameron's voice ever sounding quite so despaired.

"Rumor has it that there is a force equal to, if not greater than, the Guard. And they have plans to invade the castle sometime in the coming week."

Han said nothing. That number of men was far more than they had initially believed were involved. What could he possibly say to the Duke of Horstberg when Horstberg was on the brink of possibly being destroyed?

"Have the servants and all of the apartments evacuated," Cameron repeated. Han left with the captain to see to it.

Cameron sat quietly in his office until Georg came to join him. Then they both sat quietly.

Distant noises drew Cameron to the window, and he watched as the castle gate groaned to a close.

Cameron commented. "I don't ever recall seeing it shut since the night we reclaimed the castle, and that was only for a short while. In all my years, there has been no need."

"That should say something of the success you have had as a ruler," Georg attempted to offer a positive note.

"And now?" Cameron turned toward him.

"Now we will pray that your success will continue."

"Georg?"

"Yes, Cam?"

"If a captain is to go down with his ship, where does that leave us?"

"With a terrible choice," Georg replied, and Cameron said nothing more.

Theodor entered the parlor of his father's home where Little Karl was sitting on the sofa, drawing pictures in a sketch-book that Stefan had given him.

"Papa! You're here early."

"Hello, Karl." Theodor smiled. "And how are you feeling?"

"My arm hardly hurts anymore, but my ribs still hurt, so Kathe says I need to sit as still as possible. But she said I can sit in the garden with her tomorrow and help a little bit."

"That's great." Theodor hugged the child carefully and looked up to see Kathe in the doorway.

"What's wrong?" she asked, noting his expression.

"You keep working on that picture," Theodor said to Karl. "I'm going to help Kathe for a few minutes."

He walked toward the kitchen, and Kathe followed. "What's wrong?" she repeated, wringing her hands nervously. "What's happened?"

Theodor sat down at the table and motioned for Kathe to do the same. She moved methodically to a chair, her heart pounding as he met her eyes gravely. "Is Erich—" she began to ask, but he interrupted.

"I assume Erich is still fine . . . wherever he is."

"And the family? Are they—"

"I haven't seen the women or children for days."

Kathe's eyes widened.

"The duke and Han and Georg have been taking meals in the office. I think the rest of them are gone. I assume they went wherever Erich is."

"Most likely," she muttered more to herself, trying to imagine the entire family existing in the lodge.

"And," Theodor continued, "the duke just had all of the servants dismissed temporarily."

"Dismissed?" she gasped. "Whatever for?"

"I don't know." Theodor shook his head. "But whatever's going on, it must be serious. Perhaps the rumors are true."

"What rumors?" she asked warily. While it was evident she probably knew more than he did, she was curious as to what he *did* know.

"From what I hear, the threat of revolution is imminent." Theodor took her hand across the table, startling her from deep thought. "You're frightened," he stated.

"Yes, I'm frightened. What if . . ." She couldn't bring herself to say it.

Theodor squeezed her hand, attempting to offer comfort, but Kathe stood abruptly to find something to occupy herself with; otherwise, she would fall apart. Her longing for Erich was only emboldened by the questions that haunted her unceasingly. If the country did fall to the hands of revolutionaries, what would happen to her future? Where would that leave Erich and his family? Would she ever see them again? It was all so unsettling that she could feel nothing beyond despair.

Abbi awoke with a fearful gasp, and then she sighed when she realized where she was. A quick glance told her that all of the children were well and sleeping soundly.

"What is it, Mother?" Erich's voice came from the darkness.

"I'm sorry," she whispered. "Did I wake you?"

"No," he answered. "Is something wrong?"

"Just a bad dream," she replied.

Erich's heart quickened at the thought. "Why don't you tell me about it?" he urged, wondering if he wanted to know.

Abbi hesitated, then said quietly, "It was the same as before. You remember. The castle lost its soul. I was walking the halls as if they went on forever, but no one was there." Erich heard her emotion through the darkness and squeezed his eyes shut, wanting to block out the fear and dread he was feeling, not to mention the memory of his own dreams.

"Was that all?" he asked, trying to keep his voice light.

"Someone was in pain," she whispered. "I don't know who, but someone I love was in a great deal of pain."

Silence prevailed for several minutes before Erich asked, "Will you be all right?"

"Yes, of course," she replied. "Try and get some sleep."

Erich said nothing more, but Abbi knew that he was as restless as she and that their heads were spinning with similar thoughts. The unspoken fears were sinking in a little deeper each day. Messages were received from the castle regularly, but they were short and cryptic, and rarely did anything personal come through. Still, it was evident that things were getting worse. They had been informed that Nik Koenig had a substantial revolutionary force, and by word of an espionage courier, who had given the message with his last breath, they were planning to invade the castle and take over, with confidence that they would succeed.

Though it was rarely voiced, Abbi grew increasingly fearful of what might happen. The waiting and wondering seemed endless and tormenting.

When word came that a servant had been injured by one of the traps, as Cameron called them, Abbi became terribly upset. Word came only hours later that Cameron had dismissed all of the servants temporarily to avoid bringing further harm to anyone; the apartments had been evacuated, and the castle had been sealed off. Only officers of the Guard were carefully allowed in and out as their shifts changed.

The dream was coming to pass, Abbi thought over and over as she stared into the darkness above her. The castle was losing its soul. But when would they discover the source of the pain?

Han walked stealthily down a long hallway, hating the deadly quiet of the castle that had set in since the place had been closed up. He found Cameron sitting quietly in his office, staring blankly at a layout of the castle with despair in his eyes.

"Any messages from the mountain?" the duke asked.

"No. I assume everything's fine."

Cameron made no response, so Han asked, "What do we do now . . . Father?" He and Maggie had been married for years, but he still said it as if it were somehow comical.

"I wish I knew." He gave a chuckle with no sign of humor. "I wish I could think of an alternative—*any* alternative—to handle what is facing us. I have tried to think of any other feasible possibility, and I'm thwarted. I suppose we have no choice. Damn!" he hit his fist against the desk.

"Does this mean we fight?"

"Unless you can think of something better."

"I could try," Han managed a smile, "but . . ."

"Well, we might as well just face it. We can't wish it away. We're just going to have to give it all we've got."

"Maybe we have them outnumbered," Han said, hoping to offer reassurance.

"But that doesn't mean they won't win. And in the process, it's all just a lot of senseless killing. It's a waste. My men don't deserve to lose their lives because of that bastard! Their families don't deserve it. But the end is nearing, I'm afraid. And I'm only grateful the women and children are safe." He sighed. "Well, at least the women and children in *our family* are safe. I feel sick with worry over every other family in Horstberg. I've wondered if we should have officially posted something to notify the citizens and have them on the alert, to give them some kind of warning. But my gut tells me that any such information would only give more leverage to the revolutionaries." He sighed again. "I don't know. I really don't know. And that's what I hate most of all. I rule this country. I should know what to do."

"I'm afraid I don't know, either," Han said, praying with all his soul that he would never find himself in Cameron's position.

Cameron stood to leave the room.

"Where are you going?" Han asked, hating this helpless feeling.

"I'm going to find your father and the captain," he said. "If we're going to fight, we've got to make it good. You wait here. We'll be back to discuss this, and then I'm having all of the Guard called in."

Han nodded, and Cameron left the room. Sitting on the edge of the desk with a heavy sigh, Han glanced down at the layout of Castle Horstberg spread out there, praying he could think of something that might give them an option. When a long scrutiny didn't bring any brilliant ideas, Han leaned back and studied the office carefully, not certain if he was hoping the walls would give him an answer or if he was just absorbing the memories.

Chapter Eleven

THE INVASION

Cameron found Georg in the turret with the pigeons, staring blankly at a paper in his hand.

"What is it?" Cameron asked, concern creasing his brow.

Georg silently handed it to him, and he read: *We are praying for your safety. We love you all.*

"Why does it make me feel as though I'll never see them again?" Cameron asked.

"I don't know," Georg said, "but I was just thinking the same."

"Come along, Georg," he said, trying to push the fears away, "we're not going to give up without a fight. We've got work to do."

They walked quickly to the duke's office and entered to find Han smiling.

"Got any ideas?" Cameron asked hopefully.

"We could hide." Han managed a chuckle.

"Now that," Georg said dramatically, "is a good idea."

"Very noble!" Cameron added.

"How noble is it to leave our families to—"

"Don't say it, Georg. Those choices are too hard to face."

They were all silent a long moment until Han admitted he had a bit of a battle plan, and Georg and Cameron listened attentively.

After hours in the office, Cameron sent Han to find the captain and see that all of the officers of the Guard were called in, and the castle was made ready for battle.

Abbi gave Erich the brief message that she had felt urged to write, hoping to give the other men some comfort, and then she went upstairs to see if Maggie needed anything.

"How are you feeling?" she asked.

"Not very well," Maggie confessed. "I keep getting this pain that . . . Oh, Mother. I think this is it. Oh," she grimaced, "there it goes again. It's getting worse."

"Erich!" Abbi went to the landing and shouted down to the common room below.

"What?" he appeared immediately.

"Send another message: 'It's time!'"

"Oh my!" Erich ran out the door and to the stable. He knew what the two simple words meant. That was the cue they had decided on to let those in the castle know when Maggie was going to have the baby, and they needed the doctor. It was almost dark when Erich let the pigeon go, and after double the expected time it took to usually get acknowledgment, he went back into the lodge.

"Did they get it?" Abbi asked, pausing on her way up the stairs when he came in.

"I've heard nothing," he said soberly, and Abbi took in a sharp breath.

"Is Mama going to have the baby now?" Gerhard asked.

"It looks that way," Erich answered. The children's faces became mutually distraught as they heard Maggie cry out.

"Erich," Abbi said, "do you think you can—"

"Get the children dinner and put them to bed?"

Abbi nodded warmly, appreciating his perception.

"I'll do my best," he said easily. Noting again their distressed expressions, he added, "It appears a few distraction tactics wouldn't hurt either."

Abbi left the children in Erich's care and went upstairs to be with Maggie.

Erich didn't have any trouble finding something to feed the children. He'd learned how to cook relatively well with a few lessons from his mother. The hard part was answering all the questions while attempting to sound like everything was all right.

"Is Mama going to have the baby right here in the lodge?" Hannah asked.

"It looks that way," Erich answered.

"Is it going to be a boy or a girl?" Gerhard added.

"We'll have to see."

"Will Mama be all right?" Stefan asked.

"Of course she will."

"Why didn't the doctor come?" Stefan persisted. "Mama said when it was time that Doctor Furhelm was going to come here and help with the baby."

"Perhaps he's busy."

Erich was relieved when he finally had dinner fixed and they were all so hungry that they stopped talking and started eating. He played a guessing game with them while they got into their nightclothes, then taught them a folk song that they sang a few times together before he knelt with them to say their bedtime prayers. Once they were lying down, he extinguished the lamps.

"I'm going outside for a few minutes," Erich said. "You go to sleep now. It's late. And remember, even if you hear your mother crying, that doesn't mean anything is wrong."

"Because it hurts to have a baby," Hannah stated what he'd told them a few times already.

"That's right," he said, and they all settled down.

Erich felt certain a reply would be waiting by now, but he soon discovered it wasn't. Thinking that perhaps something had happened to the pigeon, he sent a duplicate message, then waited an adequate length of time. Still nothing came, so he went back in to check on the children. Gerhard was snoring like an old man, and Hannah was sleeping soundly. But Stefan still lay awake.

"I know something's wrong," the child said, and Erich felt cornered. How could he tell Stefan that his mother was in labor without any physician to help her if she needed it, and the where-abouts of his father and grandfathers were unknown?

"Why won't you tell me what's wrong?" Stefan asked.

"You're too smart for your own good," Erich replied, but the air still hung heavy with Stefan's question. "If I knew what was wrong," Erich said gently, sitting beside him and taking his hand, "I would tell you. We haven't got a reply to our message. That's it. We don't know what's wrong."

Stefan remained silent, and Erich took that as an acceptance of the circumstances.

"I wish Papa was here," Stefan said.

"So do I."

"Papa always tells me stories when I'm scared."

"Are you scared?" Erich asked.

"Are you scared?" Stefan countered.

"Yes," Erich admitted, "I am."

"Do you want me to tell you a story?" Stefan asked.

Erich had to chuckle. "I wish you would."

"I can't tell them as good as Papa. But here goes." Stefan cleared his throat elaborately, just as Han would, and it made Erich miss him all the more. "Once upon a time," Stefan began, and Erich held the child closer, "there was a beautiful princess who lived in a castle, but she fell in love with an evil man and wanted to run away and marry him. The king didn't know what to do, so he hired the stableboy to kidnap the princess."

Erich grinned, realizing he'd heard this story before. "Did your father teach you this story?"

"Of course," Stefan said proudly. "Now let me finish. The stableboy kidnapped the princess and took her to the Black Forest, and they fell in love and lived happily ever after."

"Is that all?" Erich asked, realizing that for some reason he felt better.

"Of course that's all. They always end with happily ever after."

"Of course," Erich whispered, wishing inwardly that real life could be the same.

Stefan drifted to sleep, and Erich eased carefully away from him. He went upstairs and knocked quietly on the bedroom door, and Abbi came into the hall to talk with him.

"They're all asleep . . . finally." He paused. "Still no message."

"Get back out there," she said. "They check the turret regularly. It's got to come soon."

Erich nodded. "Is Maggie going to be all right?"

"So far everything seems fine, but . . . Just get back out there."

Erich turned to do as his mother told him while she went back in the bedroom.

Maggie's labor intensified, and she grew nervous when the doctor didn't come. But Abbi kept assuring her it couldn't be too much longer. She was certain they had just been in such a panic to get a doctor that they hadn't thought to reply.

Hours into the night, Abbi took Maggie's hand gently into hers. Knowing she needed to have courage and give Maggie nothing but positive reassurance, she spoke carefully and clearly, stopping occasionally to allow Maggie to endure her labor.

"Maggie, my darling," she said. "The baby is getting closer and . . . we have had no reply from the castle. There must be some kind of problem there, Maggie, but . . . I have helped deliver babies before. I'll make certain that everything is fine."

"I want Han," Maggie said. She felt reassured enough about the delivery of the baby. Her thoughts were more in turmoil over the whereabouts of her husband.

Abbi tried to smile. "I'm sure everything's fine. You must think about the baby right now. It's going to take a lot of hard work to get it here."

Maggie only groaned with pain. Abbi took it that she understood the circumstances, and she heeded her own advice and went to work, concentrating on this baby.

When the worst of the labor hit, Maggie cried out Han's

name repeatedly and begged her mother to find him. Abbi tried to remain calm, but something inside felt more afraid than she ever had in her life as she wondered what might be happening that could make a message go unanswered for so many hours.

Castle Horstberg stood majestically in the predawn light of an August day. Nik Koenig rode with his well-instructed band of revolutionaries up the winding road that led to the principal gate, and with the ancient method of battering ram, broke down the gate.

The center courtyard was unexpectedly peaceful, but Nik felt anticipation . . . like the calm before the storm. Their first destination was the armory, and with weapons held ready, they broke down the entrance and were surprised to find it empty. Though it was a bit disappointing, it didn't take Nik too much off guard. He felt confident that he knew what Cameron du Woernig was thinking. He already knew the servants had been dismissed and all civilians had been evacuated. With everything quiet so far, he knew the royal family and the Guard were most likely waiting inside the main area of the castle, waiting to defend their home. Obviously they had taken everything from the armory there as well.

Confident that the battle would be easily won, Nik and his men approached the principal entrance to the residence and had partially broken through when the Captain of the Guard appeared.

"What do you think you're doing?" he shouted.

Nik laughed as his men easily brought Captain Dukerk into bonds, despite his protests.

"We have a hostage," Nik grinned, and the captain glared at him. "And you keep your mouth shut, Captain!" he threatened.

The elaborate door broke loose, and with deft efficiency, the men moved inside and spread out in all directions, having studied the plans of the castle carefully.

Nik kept the captain close by as he made his way to the duke's office, waiting for signs of the great battle at any moment. He found the office empty, and with one of his men holding a threatening gun toward the captain, they waited at this pre-appointed rendezvous for his officers to come and report that the family had been taken into custody, and the Guard had been outdone. He became impatient by an apparent stillness and felt relieved when a report was finally made.

"Sir," a burly man entered the office.

"What is it?"

"The castle is empty, sir."

"Empty?"

"Yes, sir."

"They're hiding," he said with a touch of self-satisfied humor. "Find them! You know this place. Find them!"

"Where are they, Captain?" he asked pointedly when the man had left.

"Who?"

"The family."

"I don't know. They were here last night."

"And where are the Guard? You can't hide that many men."

"Most of them left," he said sheepishly.

"Left?"

"They didn't like the duke's orders, so they left. If you'd been watching the castle carefully, you surely would have noticed that many men leaving."

Nik ignored the comment and asked, "What exactly were the duke's orders?" Nik was becoming more amused by the moment.

"He didn't want any bloodshed. He said there were other things more important to him than this blasted duchy, and you could have it."

Nik felt briefly stunned, but triumph quickly took over. "Why are you still here?"

"I've worked hard to keep this job," the captain insisted. "I'm not about to let it go just because the duke made the choice to take the cowardly way out."

"Why didn't you say that before?" Nik laughed.

"You told me to shut up." Captain Dukerk actually smiled.

Nik laughed boisterously. He would never have dreamed it could be so easy, but the triumph was glorious, nevertheless.

"There is no one in the castle, sir." The same man appeared and gave his report. "All we found was a brood of pigeons, sir."

"Pigeons?"

"Yes, sir. This same message was on two of them."

Nik took the small paper and read aloud. "It's time!" Then he laughed again as he bent over the desk and scribbled something, then handed it back. "Send that on one of those pigeons. That's a good place to start spreading the word. Oh, and . . ." The man stopped and turned. "Post the proclamations as we discussed, and then send for Heidi and my mother. We should celebrate."

The man smiled and left the room.

"You know, Your Grace," Captain Dukerk said, and Nik grinned, "you could use a good captain . . . with experience. If you'll untie me, we could perhaps arrange it."

"And what guarantee do I have that you will remain loyal?"

"A raise in salary wouldn't hurt."

Nik laughed again, then untied the captain, and he sent the man who had been holding him at gunpoint away. "Repair the gate and seal off the castle," he ordered, "then tell the men to have a drink . . . on the duke. But don't let them hurt anything. This is my home now."

"Yes, sir," the man smirked and left to carry out his pleasant orders.

Erich wandered back and forth between the lodge and the stable throughout the duration of the night. He hated the stable because of the incessant waiting for the pigeon he'd given up on. And he hated the lodge because of the obvious anguish going on upstairs. He was terribly glad the children were sound sleepers and oblivious to Maggie's labor.

He was almost relieved to come through the doorway and hear his mother's voice, "Erich, are you there?"

"Yes."

"I need you," she said, and he hurried up the stairs. His momentary relief at being needed soon dissipated as he entered the bedroom and the reality struck him.

"I can't do this," he tried to whisper to his mother so Maggie wouldn't hear.

"You've got to," she insisted, and he said nothing more. "Now sit there against the headboard and let Maggie lean back against your chest." He attempted to do as he was told, but she stopped him. "Wait until the . . ." Abbi paused and seemed to hold her breath while Maggie clenched her teeth and groaned.

Erich went tense as he observed Maggie's pain, but then it seemed to subside and he quickly did as his mother had told him. He barely had Maggie positioned against him when the pain struck her again and she gripped onto his thighs, inflicting only a degree of the pain he knew she must be experiencing.

"Now put your arms beneath hers and . . ." Abbi opted to show him rather than explain it, placing his hands over Maggie's belly. Erich met his mother's eyes, wanting to tell her he was afraid, but there was every bit as much fear in her expression as he felt inside.

Abbi turned her attention to the other end of the bed, where Erich was grateful that everything was concealed by the sheet spread over Maggie's knees. Erich recalled Han telling him that this was an unforgettable experience. He was trying to remember what else Han had said when he felt Maggie go tense from the pain and Abbi ordered, "Push down with your hands." He hesitated, afraid of not doing it right. "Push!" Abbi demanded. "She's tired! You've got to help her!"

Erich did as he was told, trying to recall if he'd ever seen his mother so upset. After a few contractions, Erich began to get the feel of what they were doing, and with confidence he pressed down hard.

"It's almost here," Abbi cried, pushing hair from her brow with the back of her hand. "Come on now, give it all you've got—both of you."

Maggie cried out in what seemed unbearable anguish, and Erich felt the mound beneath his hands move out from under him. Instinctively he wrapped his arms around his sister and held her as she fought to catch her breath and the air hung with expectancy. He saw his mother take a deep breath and could tell she was very busy, and then a high-pitched cry pierced the room and Erich felt warm chills overwhelm him.

"It's a girl," Abbi whispered and began to cry, holding the infant up for them to see. Maggie laughed and cried as she took the baby into her trembling hands, and Erich looked on in awe.

"Isn't she beautiful, Erich?" Maggie said.

"She is," Erich answered, barely audible. Suddenly he missed Kathe more than ever, and the reality of the other aspects of their lives struck freshly.

"She has red hair," Maggie said.

"What a surprise," Erich chuckled dryly, easing away from Maggie. "Is there anyone in this family besides Father who doesn't?"

"Thank you, Erich," Abbi said gently, and he embraced her.

"I'll go check the stable," Erich said, and Abbi nodded.

It was barely dawn when Erich walked for what seemed the hundredth time toward the stable and he saw the pigeon flying in. He ran and almost caught it mid-air as it flew through the window. He hadn't known what to expect, but what he read left him stunned. Unwillingly, he sank to his knees in the straw, tears burning in his eyes. After several moments of staring numbly at the words written there, he forced himself to stand and move toward the lodge, knowing he had to tell his mother.

Abbi barely had the worst of the mess cleaned up and the

baby wrapped in a blanket when she heard Erich call for her. Quickly she left the baby in Maggie's arms and ran out the bedroom door. She stopped halfway down the stairs when she saw Erich standing solemnly near the door with a paper hanging limply in his hand and tears streaming over his face.

"What?" she asked, her voice trembling.

Silently, he held it out for her. She stepped down hesitantly and took it. Mist filled her eyes and she had to blink several times to take in the whole of what it said.

Whoever you are, for obvious reasons your message was not received. Castle Horstberg has been overtaken and is now under the reign of Nikolaus Koenig du Woernig.

Abbi felt Erich's arms come around her, and she weakly fell against him, sobbing helplessly. "They wouldn't have given up without a fight," she cried.

"I know," Erich whispered.

"No," she sobbed. "It can't be. Oh, please . . . no!"

Erich only held her tighter, trying to comprehend that they were fugitives now. Questions tumbled through his mind. Hopeless, unanswered questions that drove the agony deeper. How was he going to care for all of them? Could they survive up here without any support from below? Where was Kathe? Would he ever see her again? Where was his father . . . his dearest friends? He closed his eyes and could almost see their bodies being desecrated in some kind of triumphant ritual.

"I must see to Maggie," Abbi said, pulling back and wiping at her tears. "We must get control of ourselves before the children wake up."

"You look out for Maggie," Erich said, grateful for the distraction. "I'll handle the children."

Abbi nodded gratefully and tried to compose herself, but the tears came again, and they could do nothing for the moment but cry in each other's arms.

Maggie attempted to ignore the prominent soreness as she admired her new daughter. She wished that her mother would come back. She wanted to know what Erich had called her for. She wanted Han to see his daughter. Her mind was in a turmoil. The baby was so beautiful. She was so relieved to have it over. But the fear and worry were intolerable.

When Abbi came into the room with Erich close behind, Maggie knew something was terribly wrong. Between the two of them, they told her what had happened, and Maggie felt a painful lump wrench into her throat as she cried out Han's name over and over.

Abbi tried to soothe her while she bathed the baby and cleaned up the room, crying silent tears as she did. Erich left the lodge and stood numbly outside the door.

Maggie finally calmed down and lay exhausted yet unable to sleep as a blanketed ache overcame her. She stared numbly toward the window with her hand against her baby, who slept close beside her.

When the room was tidy and Maggie slept at last, Abbi walked to the stairs, sat down, and wept, grateful that the children were still sleeping. The door below came open abruptly, and Abbi looked up, startled. As the mist cleared from her eyes, she realized Erich was smiling.

"Oh, Mother," he cried, "you won't believe it. I thought we'd been found. I thought we were all dead, but—"

"Don't upset your mother," Georg said, coming through the door and patting him on the back.

Abbi wept harder and swept down the stairs into Georg's arms, and he laughed and turned her around.

"Georg! You're alive. Oh, Georg. I don't believe it!" Abbi laughed and cried and held him close. "Where is Cameron?" she asked fearfully.

Georg parted his lips to answer as the door came open again and Erich ushered his father into the lodge. Abbi went into his arms and the tears only increased. "Oh, Cameron," she cried,

"I thought I would never see you again. I would die without you."
He laughed and kissed her madly, then a familiar voice boomed
from outside just before Han appeared in the doorway.

There was an ominous outpouring of laughter, kisses, and
embraces until Han said, "Where is Maggie?"

"She's upstairs," Abbi said quickly, deciding to let him find
out the good news for himself.

Han took the stairs three at a time. His heart beat madly as
he pushed open the bedroom door. He almost felt weak when he
saw her, lying with her back turned.

Maggie had come awake, hearing indiscernible noises downstairs. But with a combination of physical soreness and emotional
numbness, she had ignored the distraction and lay with her eyes
closed, crying silent tears.

Hearing her name whispered, she felt certain she was
dreaming until it was repeated. "Maggie," Han said more loudly.

Ignoring the pain, Maggie turned and did her best to sit up,
trying to convince herself he was real.

"Han!" she cried out, and he flew to the bedside, pulling her
into his arms and kissing her.

"Oh Han! We got this message . . . We thought you were dead.
Oh, Han . . . I love you!"

"And I love you." He chuckled. "Actually, I am dead. This is
my ghost you're kissing."

"Oh," she laughed, "you can't fool me. I know a man when
I hold one."

He chuckled again and pulled her closer, and she groaned
from the pain.

"What's the matter?" he asked.

She remembered. "Oh, Han . . . look!" She turned slightly
to look at the baby. His eyes followed, then widened as a smile
spread over his face.

"It's a girl, Han. She's beautiful."

Han laughed as he pulled the baby into his arms, sitting carefully on the bed next to Maggie while they both admired her.

A knock came at the door. Maggie called out, and her parents, Georg, and Erich came into the room, all gathering around the bed, full of admiration for the new baby and grateful that they were all alive and together.

"Cameron," Abbi said at last, "you must tell us what happened. Why did you—"

"Before you even ask, there is something I must tell you . . . all of you." Cameron glanced solemnly around the room.

"Last night while I was sitting in my office, I was reminded of a night in my life . . . the night you and I were married, my dear," he briefly focused on Abbi, "when I was faced with the worst decision of my life. I will never forget the turmoil I felt while I stood there so helpless, while Nikolaus held you there with a knife at your throat, and he made the choices clear. It was either you or the duchy. I remember feeling like a traitor for that brief moment before Captain Dukerk killed him. I was ready. I had made the choice. I was going to keep you.

"I selfishly decided then that I had already sacrificed too much of my life for Horstberg, and I would not give you up. Fortunately, things turned out well, and I was able to keep both. Now I have given another thirty-two years of my life for Horstberg, and I decided last night that if a decision had to be made, I would choose to be with my family and see them cared for.

"I don't know what will happen for certain, but whatever does, we are together. I love you all," he added, and for the first time in her life, Maggie saw her father cry. She couldn't believe it. The Duke of Horstberg had sacrificed his country to the hands of a wretched man to save himself and his family. But she was proud of him. Traitor or not, she loved her father. And she was more grateful and happy for the love and unity present in this room than she ever would have been to hear that Horstberg had been saved.

"But what will we do?" Erich asked, and Cameron looked down abruptly.

"We talked about it and came to the decision to take a number of the family jewels and a fair amount of money with us. We've buried it in the forest and . . ." He paused deliberately and looked around to survey the expectant expressions of his family. "We'll give it some time and most likely have to find a way out of the country and make a fresh start elsewhere. As farmers if we have to, I suppose."

Cameron bowed his head in shame, but Abbi took his hand, and he looked into her eyes.

"I love you, Cameron du Woernig," she said with strength. "I love *you,* no matter what!"

Cameron smiled warmly, and the family huddled together with a prayer of gratitude that they were together.

"Grandpapa!" Stefan called from the doorway, and both Cameron and Georg turned to see him hobbling toward them with a crutch Erich had made. Stefan laughed and hugged both his grandfathers at the same time.

"I knew you would come," Stefan declared. "I just knew it. Papa!" he cried when he saw Han. "You're here too!"

Han laughed and picked Stefan up, then moved toward the bed.

"See there," Han said, "you have another sister."

"Oh, good!" Stefan exclaimed. "I wanted another sister."

Han laughed and hugged him tightly while the family all gathered closer to get a better look at the new baby.

"How did you get her delivered?" Han asked, just now realizing their message hadn't been received.

Maggie turned her eyes to Abbi. "Mother did it," she said proudly. Cameron's expression filled with pride as he embraced his wife again.

"Erich helped too," Maggie said, and they all glanced around to realize Erich was no longer there. Cameron slipped away to go find him.

"What are you naming this one?" Han asked Maggie.

"That's easy. She will be named for her grandmothers. Elsa Abilee Heinrich."

Abbi noticed a distant sadness seep into Georg's eyes, and she reached out to take his hand. "You're missing her," she whispered.

"Always," he replied.

"She would be proud," Abbi added, looking toward the baby.

"Yes." Georg smiled. "She would."

"You don't look very happy," Cameron said, startling Erich, who was leaning against a stall in the stable.

"I'm very grateful you're alive," Erich said, "don't get me wrong."

"I'm grateful I'm alive too. But it's not easy to face what we've lost."

"I could be content being a farmer," Erich said, and Cameron felt proud of him, "though I must confess it leaves a hole inside me." Noting his father's expression, he added, "I guess I don't have to tell you that."

Cameron shook his head, and Erich felt an urge to cry on his father's behalf. He couldn't comprehend what he must be feeling. His choice had obviously been a difficult one. In a way, he was relieved. The future was uncertain, but at least the waiting was over. There was only one problem. Looking directly at his father, he asked, "What about Kathe?"

Cameron bent his head forward and took a deep breath. "Right now, there's nothing we can do."

Erich looked toward him sharply. "And I'm just supposed to sit here and wonder if I'll ever see her again?"

Cameron said nothing.

"What am I supposed to do?" Erich shouted. Still, he didn't get a response, and impulsively he came up with his own answer. "I've got to go get her."

"You can't," Cameron stated, trying to remain calm.

"I have to," Erich protested.

"You're a fugitive, Erich. You can't show yourself down there."

"Better that than to be without her."

"Don't do something stupid and get us all killed," Cameron said grimly, and Erich's eyes narrowed. "Didn't you study your history, boy? It's happened before and it could happen again. When fanatics take over a country, the first thing they do is destroy the bloodline that could threaten their keeping what they've just gained. If we are found, we will be slaughtered. All of us. If you stop to think about it, you'll know it's true."

"You don't have to remind me. I've thought of little else for weeks." Erich turned abruptly and slammed his fist against the stall.

Cameron watched with empathy, wishing he could tell him that he knew how he felt. Still, the reality couldn't be denied. In a softer voice, he said, "I don't know what we're going to do yet, son. I can't guarantee you'll ever see her again."

"And what if it was Mother?" Erich shouted. Cameron tilted his head in question. "If the woman you loved was down there, what would you do?" Cameron couldn't answer. That fine line of making unbearable choices was creeping up again. "Tell me!" Erich demanded. "If Kathe and I were married, would she be here with us now? We should have been married by now, Father."

"As I said before, she is safer without your name right now."

"Is she really? Because she's not technically a du Woernig yet, does that make her any less a part of the family? Do you think her association with me went unnoticed? Can we really leave the country without her?"

The desperation pushed through, and Erich blurted out the question that had been haunting him since he'd seen that message written by Nik Koenig's hand. "What if she's carrying my child?" Cameron's eyes widened, and Erich lowered his voice, not caring what he'd just admitted to. "What do you think they will do to her if she's carrying my child? Legitimate or not, it's *my* child. And you're talking about *fanatics* who would do anything to be sure our bloodline is annihilated!"

Cameron retorted with a controlled shout, "How could you have been so stupid? With what we have been up against, what made you think you could do something like that and not put her at risk?"

"I had no reason to believe I would ever see her again," Erich said in an attempt to justify himself. "I had no reason to believe I'd live long enough to have any life with her at all."

"And that is exactly the point," Cameron insisted. "If you *had* been killed, what would she have done if there is a child involved?"

Erich sighed and hung his head. "It was foolish and irresponsible, I know," he admitted. "But we have been dealing with incredibly difficult circumstances here. What's done is done. I made a mistake and I admit it. But we cannot leave her at their mercy. We can't!"

Cameron sighed in obvious frustration. "Give me another twenty-four hours, son," he said. "By then we'll make a decision on what we're going to do, and we'll find a way to get her, even if we have to kidnap her in the middle of the night."

Erich nearly slumped with relief. If he had his father's support, he knew he could do anything. "Thank you," he said. "You can't know what this means to me."

"Oh, yes, I can," Cameron said. "There was a day when I was a fugitive, your mother was pregnant with you, and I had nothing. If my brother had known at that point whose baby she was carrying, I shudder to think what he would have done. It was my greatest fear. Far beyond my concern for anything else, I feared for your mother's safety. In spite of being my wife, she was completely ignorant of the situation, and if we had failed in taking over the country, her ignorance could have saved her from accusations of treason." Cameron paused and gave the purpose for his little story. "That's why I didn't let Kathe know what was going on. If she's questioned before we can get her, she'll have nothing to tell them."

"You're a genius," Erich said.

Cameron chuckled. "It was Georg's idea. Georg has the brains."

Erich chuckled as well, but Cameron turned serious again as he said, "Erich, I have to apologize to you."

"Whatever for?"

"I have just thrown away everything that I ever promised to give you."

"No," Erich said, reaching out to grip his father's hand, "you have given me everything a son could ever want from his father, and that has nothing to do with Horstberg."

They shared a firm embrace, and Erich could almost believe that everything was going to be all right.

Kathe dusted in the library while her father was bent over the big table, going over some plans for a custom project he was working on. She heard the side door open and close loudly and Theodor's distinctive stride bounding up the hall. Even before he appeared, she knew something was wrong. Time seemed to freeze for a long moment when he appeared in the doorway, and she and her father both met his distressed expression.

"What?" Karl demanded.

Theodor handed him a piece of paper, glancing hesitantly toward Kathe. "These were posted all over town," he reported.

Kathe put a hand over her pounding heart as she watched her father read it, and then he handed it to her without meeting her eyes. With courage, she read: *Let it be known that Horstberg is now officially under the reign of Nikolaus Koenig du Woernig.* Kathe didn't bother to read on as her knees weakened and she sank unsteadily into a chair, the proclamation falling to the floor. The revolution was over. They had lost everything. Karl put his arms around her, and she collapsed against him.

"This is unbelievable," she heard Theodor mutter. "It's a nightmare."

"Do you think they're still alive?" Kathe asked, her voice trembling.

"That depends on how well hidden they are," Theodor said. "But the duke and his advisors were still there when—" He stopped at the sharp glance from his father.

"Kathe," Karl said in a hushed whisper, as if he feared the walls might overhear, "are they well hidden? Do you know where they are?"

"It would be practically impossible to find them if you didn't know exactly where to look."

"Then you *do* know," her father stated.

Kathe nodded. Her father and Theodor exchanged a sharp glance. "What?" she demanded, missing what seemed obvious to them.

"Katherine," her father said in a way that reminded her of when he'd told her that her mother was dead, "they could use you . . . to find them."

Kathe's breath quickened. The fear became tangible, even painful. All at once she recalled Erich talking about royal families being executed, and the duke saying that she would be safer if she weren't a du Woernig. But the whole country knew she was betrothed to Erich. Would they use her against him? Would they force her to betray him?

"Kathe," her father startled her from her thoughts, "I wonder if you would be safer with Erich, but I wonder if they might already be watching you. If Erich and his family are safe, we can't risk having you lead them to wherever they're hiding, but . . ."

"But?" Theodor questioned when he didn't finish.

"I don't know," Karl said. "I'm thinking."

"What will I do?" Kathe muttered. "I'll never see him again."

"Knowing Erich," Theodor took his sister's hand, "he'll be every bit as desperate to see you as you are to see him." He added more to his father, "I say if she stays in and we keep a close eye on her, we just need to be patient. We'll keep the guns loaded and the house locked. If there is any possible way for Erich to contact her, he will." She felt a light of hope, and Theodor smiled. "And it might not hurt to have a bag packed, just in case. He'll probably be in a hurry."

Kathe silently absorbed what he was saying, and she smiled. "Will you forgive me," she said intently to her father, "if I have to leave here and never come back?"

"Forgive you?" Karl laughed. "Why should I forgive you for leaving me with the satisfaction of knowing that you are the happiest woman alive wherever you may be?"

Kathe laughed and wrapped her arms around her father's neck, then she hugged Theodor and went upstairs to pack a bag.

Nik Koenig sat in his new office with his feet on the desk, admiring his surroundings. The door opened and he grinned.

"Good day, Your Grace," Heidi said, curtsying deeply before giggling and coming to sit on his lap. Nik laughed and kissed her.

"Now that you're the duke," she said, "I might be willing to forgive you for what you did to me."

"And what is that?" He smirked.

"I've still got the bruises!" she scolded.

"Ah yes, so sorry." He lifted his chin carelessly. "I did get a little upset when you told me they'd found out about us. But you must admit it did give your feigned accident some credibility. It kept you out of prison." He smiled and touched her chin. "All of that's in the past now," he added.

"You can't know how relieved I am," Heidi said. "You'd better be good to me after all of the mischief your mother put me up to all these years."

"Good to you?" he laughed. "I'll make you the Duchess of Horstberg, my dear. Just give me some time. We'll live like a king and queen."

Heidi laughed, and Nik kissed her until a throat clearing interrupted them.

"Mother," Nik said, pushing Heidi aside and coming to his feet. "Do you like your new home?"

"Indeed," Klarice Koenig smiled, glancing around. "Your father would be proud of you, Nik. You've done well."

Nik smiled proudly, and Captain Dukerk came into the room.

"Why don't you two run along and have a look around," Nik said, "while the captain and I get settled in."

Klarice and Heidi slipped into the hall, and the captain nodded politely toward them.

While the captain took Nik on an extended tour of his new home, Nik found it amusing to see that the men were all helping themselves to the vast supply of the duke's liquor. If it ran out in one room, there was usually a tray in another that had a few bottles there for the taking.

"Have a drink, Captain," Nik offered congenially as they looked freely through some of the ducal records that were kept in the principal library.

"Later," the captain replied. "I never drink while I'm on duty."

"Good policy," Nik said, and the captain smiled. Nik liked the natural rapport between them.

After his extended tour, the captain left him on his own. Nik was further amused to see that everyone had all but passed out from their drinking. He considered having a drink himself, but he felt quite drunk from his success and opted to thrive on the real feelings for the time being. He found his mother sleeping soundly in one of the bedrooms and Heidi in another. Making himself comfortable next to her, he sighed complacently, feeling good about the day's events . . . and quite exhausted. Overwhelmed with triumph, he fell asleep.

Abbi noticed that her husband seemed extremely tense. She wondered if he was regretting the decision he'd made already, and she felt compassion for him, knowing how difficult it must be. He spent a great deal of time outside, but Abbi left him alone, knowing it was probably just as well. The lodge was more than crowded with everyone here, and the new baby, however joyous, hadn't allowed anyone much sleep.

Abbi had just finished preparing the children something to eat when Cameron came inside and met her eyes intently.

"You need to talk," she said quietly, and he nodded.

Abbi turned to Georg to ask if he could watch out for the children. Before she could speak, he motioned toward the door with his hand. "Run along. I can handle this."

"Are you sure?" Abbi asked.

"No problem." He smiled, and Abbi followed Cameron outside.

"Where are you going?" Erich asked, passing them on their way to the stable.

"Your mother and I are going riding." Cameron kept moving.

Abbi watched silently as Cameron saddled only one horse, then helped her mount and climbed into the saddle behind her. With ease, he stirred the stallion out of the stable, and they galloped toward the upper meadow.

"Just like old times," Abbi said as Cameron halted and helped her down.

"Not quite," he retorted with an edge to his voice.

She waited for him to say something, knowing he needed to talk. When he didn't right off, she knew he wasn't ready, and she opted for small talk instead.

"Same wildflowers every year," she said, glancing around. "Same handsome man." She smiled up at him, attempting to lighten his mood.

"Not quite," he repeated, the edge deepening.

"Of course, we don't have Blaze," she said.

"I dare say every horse we own has a little of Blaze in it. Best stud we ever had." Cameron remarked, and Abbi was glad to see that her distraction was working. "Even the cavalry horses are mostly . . ." He stopped, and Abbi saw a shadow pass over his face as he bent his head.

"What is it, darling?" she whispered.

Abbi sensed the tension and nearly expected him to start shouting as he usually did to release his emotions. But he only looked up at her with deep sadness in his eyes, saying softly, "We don't have a cavalry anymore." He squeezed his eyes shut and turned his face skyward. "We don't have a blasted thing."

"That's not true." Abbi reached up to touch his face. Searching deeply for the right thing to say, Abbi sat down in the tall grass and urged him to sit beside her.

"I remember," she said softly, "the day I realized I was in love with you." His eyes widened, surprised by the topic. "As you put it back then, you were a man with nothing—not even a name. But even then, Cameron, we had each other."

Abbi took his hand into hers, knowing that her words could in no way compensate for his loss, but at least she could help him see the good.

"Look how blessed we are, Cameron. We are all alive. We are together. We have a beautiful posterity." She paused, and emotion seeped into her voice. "I thought you were dead, Cameron. There is no way to describe how it felt to think of facing my life without you." Cameron looked into her eyes and pulled her tears away with his fingers.

"If I had to make the choice," she said, "I would take you over Horstberg. Traitor or not, I won't hesitate to say it."

"And you love me still," he asked, "even though I am a traitor?"

"I loved you when I thought you were a thief. Why shouldn't I love you now?" She touched his face and fresh tears came. "I love you more than life, Cameron du Woernig."

"You are priceless, Abbi girl," he muttered, pulling her into his arms. "I love you so."

He held her a long moment before pulling back. "What will we do, Abbi? Do we leave the country or . . ."

"Can I tell you what I have been thinking?" she interrupted.

"Please."

"Until things have settled, aren't we far safer here than anywhere else?"

"But fall is coming. Once it snows . . ." He stopped when he saw her smile.

"Precisely," she said. "They can't get to us if we're snowed in. Granted, it could be a long, hard winter with all of us living in such close quarters, but if we're well prepared for winter, we can survive and . . ."

"And *then* leave?" he asked, only slightly cynical.

"Perhaps," she said quietly, "but I was more thinking on the order of . . ." Abbi paused and watched his face carefully. "Cameron, could you ever be at peace, knowing that your country was . . . Well, let me put it this way: if you and Georg reclaimed the country from Nikolaus, think what you could do with Han and Erich, as well. We'll find a way to get Kathe up here safely. We can stay hidden until the new government gets comfortable. We can make contacts with the right people. You know we'd have tremendous support. Perhaps we could somehow leave the impression we've left the country and given up completely."

Cameron's eyes widened, and a smile absorbed him. "You are too good to be true," he said. "After all we've been through, you would still sacrifice so much, put so much on the line, to try and get it back?"

"I would."

"Why?"

"Because I know from experience that Horstberg is in your blood. It is what you need to be truly happy. I want you to be happy. We will find a way."

Cameron silently absorbed her words, and Abbi saw

moisture well up in his eyes. "Yes," he said, "we will find a way." He laughed and embraced her as if they were newly in love all over again.

"I love you, Abbi." He kissed her, and Abbi laughed and held him close. "Now this," he added, "is like old times."

Chapter Twelve

RECLAMATION

Nik Koenig awoke to find Heidi still sleeping soundly. He got dressed and left the room, glad he'd not awakened her, and he went to talk to his mother, knowing she had big plans for this day. She too was sleeping, so he moved downstairs, admiring his surroundings as he went. While there had been many times when his mother's ambition had concerned him, the glory of his triumph was sweet. His pleasure increased more each moment he spent within these great walls.

An indiscernible chill ran down his spine when he looked in room after room and found all of his men still lost in drunken sleep. He brushed it off, knowing they'd had quite a celebration— and it was well deserved. They had worked hard over the past months, waiting for this day. He actually felt proud of himself to realize that, in reality, he'd outsmarted the duke rather than overpowered him.

Nik found his way to the kitchen and helped himself to something to eat, thinking he'd have to call the servants in and get things back to normal. With his stomach full, he wandered aimlessly, admiring his new home and what it represented. He began planning the changes he would make and decided they must get to work just as soon as everyone recovered from their hangovers.

At the realization of hours passing and the castle still remaining silent, a dread crept into him as he went into the library.

"You're all alone." Captain Dukerk startled Nik from behind.

"You shouldn't sneak up on me like that," Nik chuckled.

"Things are a bit quiet," the captain added easily.

"Yes," Nik said, "everyone got drunk; still sleeping it off, I suppose."

"They're not sleeping."

Nik smiled. He felt certain this was a joke.

"They're all dead," the captain added soberly.

"That's ridiculous!" Nik insisted. He pushed his way past Captain Dukerk and almost ran down the hall, determined to prove him wrong.

The captain followed Nik solemnly from room to room, watching him as he futilely tried to wake his men, his lover, his mother. Even the men who had been left to guard the doors and the main gate would not respond. Each attempt increased his exasperation, and the glory of triumph dissipated into a sick trepidation.

"This is your doing!" Nik pointed an accusing finger at Captain Dukerk, who remained intently calm.

"I had nothing to do with this. I simply reported that they were dead. One never knows what will happen when someone drinks something they're not . . . accustomed to."

At the realization he'd been outdone, Nik's first thought was to take what he could and get out of there. Heart pounding, he ran back to the duke's office, knowing that's where the safe was. Surely it held more money than ten men could spend in a lifetime.

The captain followed him into the office, and Nik demanded, "Where's the safe?"

"I believe it's behind that painting of your grandfather," he answered coolly. "The key to it is in the desk."

Nik found the key and smiled to see it there. He was about to offer the captain some kind of bribery, but the captain spoke first, "It's perhaps too bad you didn't decide to have a drink last night yourself."

Nik turned and looked at the captain, who seemed complacent. He wondered why it had taken him until now to remember who this man was. Lance Dukerk had been his father's closest friend for many years—and also the man who had killed him.

"Too bad," Nik taunted. "Too bad for you and your wretched duke. But I seriously doubt you'd have the guts to finish me off the way you did my father."

"Oh, there's no need for that. He murdered my sister. So far I've got no personal score to settle with you."

"Well, as soon as I get this safe open," Nik said, removing the painting and grinning to see that he'd found it, "I'll be gone before you know it."

"I can't let you do that," he replied easily.

"But you're unarmed, Captain." Nik put the key in and turned it. "How very foolish."

"I don't need to be armed," he said just as Nik reached up to take hold of the handle on the safe. "I'm counting on what the duke told me to count on." Nik glanced briefly at him, then pulled the lever just as the captain added, "Human nature."

Captain Dukerk felt certain that Nik Koenig figured out what he meant. There was a brief look of fearful enlightenment just before he disappeared through the trap door in the floor.

Cameron and Abbi returned to the stable full of laughter, but Cameron sobered when he saw a pigeon there, bearing a message.

Abbi held her breath as he opened it, knowing it could only be bad news. She was surprised to see him smile. A smile so broad and complacent that she felt completely baffled.

"What?" she demanded.

"It looks like it's for you." Abbi's eyes narrowed in question as she reached out to take it, her hand trembling. "From an old admirer," he added.

Abbi looked down and read: *My dearest Abbi, Everything is perfect! All my love, Lance.*

Abbi gave a baffled chuckle. "I don't understand."

"You remember Lance," Cameron said, positively smirking.

"Yes, dear," she said dubiously.

"You nearly married the man, if you'll recall."

"Yes, dear," she grimaced slightly.

"Of course you know he's the Captain of the Guard."

"Yes, dear."

"And he sent that message."

"Yes, of course. But . . ."

"From the castle."

Abbi gave him a sidelong glance, infuriated from his tormenting her.

"You see, my dear," Cameron said, pausing to let out a boisterous, triumphant laugh, "that is the message we decided on so that I would know for certain it came from him."

Abbi began to grasp the implication, but there were so many questions tumbling through her mind that she didn't know which to ask first.

"Come along," he said, taking her hand, "let's go inside."

Han sat with Maggie on the bed, admiring their new daughter.

"You'd think I'd get used to it after three," Han said. "But number four is every bit as wonderful as the others."

Maggie smiled. "I dare say Elsa won't take any love from the others. She'll just create more love for us to give her."

Han kissed Maggie warmly and then turned his attention back to little Elsa.

"Han!" Cameron's voice boomed from below.

"I'm up here!" he called.

Cameron bounded into the room with Abbi close behind and a piece of paper in his hand. Han stood to meet him.

"Han," he laughed, "you scoundrel. You did it!"

Han laughed, too. The duke embraced him, then slapped him on the shoulder.

"What did he do?" Maggie asked, baffled.

Cameron ignored her and went to the landing. "Everybody come up here," he called. "It's time for a family conference."

Han and Cameron both kept laughing as everyone came into the room. Georg was the only other one who seemed to know what was going on, and all eyes turned expectantly to Cameron. "We did it!" he almost shouted. "Or rather . . . *Han* did it."

"He did *what?*" Abbi asked in exasperation.

"Horstberg is saved, my love," Cameron said, pulling her up off the floor.

Everyone was obviously pleased with the news, but still they remained baffled.

"You see," Cameron said, "Han came up with the idea to give them exactly what they didn't expect, and then wait for them to do what they obviously would."

"I don't understand," Erich said.

"Well, I don't know the details yet, but according to the communication we decided on, I have to assume from Captain Dukerk's message that everyone is dead."

"Everyone?" Abbi asked skeptically.

"Everyone who was into something they weren't supposed to be." Han grinned. "It only took some of the odd things from Erich's laboratory to—"

"You didn't use the—" Erich interrupted.

"Don't worry," Han chuckled. "We knew you'd said things had been tampered with. I just used the stuff from your last shipment. The box was still unopened, and I mixed it upstairs."

"Mixed what?" Stefan asked. Unlike Gerhard and Hannah, he was listening to this attentively.

"The poison, of course," Han said. "We put poison in all the liquor. What do men do when they want to celebrate? They drink."

"I can't believe it," Abbi said breathlessly.

"You're a genius, Han." Erich slapped him on the back.

"I wonder if they used my trap door," Han said to Georg.

"Whether they did or not," Georg said, "it was a good idea."

"Let us in on it," Maggie insisted.

"I found a crack in the floor of the office," Han said, "and I realized there was this ancient trap door in front of the safe. We made a minor repair and set it. If anyone did try to get to the money, they are no longer."

"So you see," Georg said, "we just left and let Castle Horstberg take care of itself."

"We won this battle," Cameron said, "and not one of my men shed a drop of blood for the cause. In fact," he laughed, "they had the day off."

Cameron then turned soberly toward Han and finished, "Thank you, my boy. You well deserve the position you hold. Horstberg will be in good hands with you and Erich working as a team to lead it."

Han smiled humbly.

"Why didn't you let us in on your little plan?" Abbi asked.

Cameron turned grimly to his wife. "If it hadn't worked," he said, "we didn't want all of you to be disappointed. Better that we expected the worst in this case."

"If any of them would have had the insight not to eat or drink anything available," Georg added, "we would be here with nothing."

"Stuck here for the rest of our lives," Erich interjected.

"This is a nice place," Cameron protested.

"Nice for the two of us," Abbi said, "but it is a bit crowded."

"I should get a reply back to the captain," Cameron said, but he paused to glance around the room, and Abbi's words from the meadow came back to him. "We are so blessed," he said quietly, "with or without Horstberg."

"All the more blessed with it," Abbi provided. "It would seem that God is with us in this."

"Amen." Cameron smiled down at her, and then he gathered his family around him, and they knelt in humble prayer, expressing gratitude to the unseen power that had miraculously saved Horstberg and preserved their lives.

"Kathe!" Theodor called, coming through the door. "Kathe! Where are you?"

"I'm here," she said, coming into the kitchen. "What is it?"

"Come in here," he said excitedly. "Sit down. Sit down. Listen to this."

Kathe did as she was told, wondering what on earth he had to be so happy about. Theodor cleared his throat elaborately and began to read the paper in his hand. "'Let it be known that the revolutionary force of Nikolaus Koenig has been defeated and the family du Woernig will be returning to fulfill their rightful obligations.'"

"Oh!" Kathe gasped, and her hand went to her heart. "Oh, Theodor!" she cried with sheer joy, jumping up to throw her arms around him. He twirled with her and laughed. Feeling dizzy and suddenly weak, she slumped into a chair. The relief was so immense she couldn't hold back her tears. With her brother's arm around her, she cried out all of the fear and loneliness she'd hardly dared feel. It was over! Erich was safe! She'd never been so happy in all her life.

When she had quieted, Theodor said, "Listen. There's more."

"Where did you get this?" she asked.

"The Guard were posting them about town. Not those scruffy revolutionaries who brought out the last proclamation. These were the Duke's Guard, fully uniformed," he said proudly. "Men I know."

"Go on," she urged, "read me the rest."

"Yes, of course." He scanned the page to find his place. Theodor cleared his throat again and read: "'I am happy to report that there were no casualties suffered by the Guard or royal family, but those involved in the treasonous efforts of Nikolaus Koenig were all killed.'"

"How do you suppose they did that?" Kathe asked.

"I'm sure we'll hear all about it eventually," Theodor assured her.

"Read on."

"'If there is anyone who can assist us in claiming and identifying those deceased, please report to Castle Horstberg immediately. Bodies not claimed will be given proper service and burial by the Guard. All servants of Castle Horstberg are requested to report to duty as soon as possible.' That's it," Theodor finished. "It's signed by Captain Dukerk."

"Oh, it's so wonderful!" Kathe exclaimed, and she nearly ran from the room.

"Where are you going?" Theodor asked. "I thought we should celebrate or something."

"Oh, we will," she said, "but first I've got to unpack my bag." She smiled. "I'm staying in Horstberg forever."

"Are you sure you can ride?" Han asked, helping Maggie down the stairs.

"Of course I can," she insisted. "I feel fine. After four babies, I'm an expert at this. I'll take it easy once we're home."

When Han and Maggie entered the common room, Cameron said, "Now that you're all here, there are some things you should know." Everyone listened attentively. "We need to get back for obvious reasons, but things might still be a little unsettled. There were well over a hundred bodies found in the castle, and I'm certain it's no small job to get that taken care of.

"The captain informs me that most of the servants are back, and things have been cleaned up and repaired fairly well, but we still may be in for some surprises. Who knows what they did?

"Georg has suggested, and I believe he's right, that it is wise and appropriate that we arrive in town when we can be seen so that the people will know everything is as it should be. It will be a long ride, but we'll stop and stretch on the other side of the forest. Any questions?"

"Is today market day, Grandpapa?" Hannah asked.

"Yes, it is," he replied. "That's why we chose today to go down."

"Can we stop and buy a cinnamon bun?" Gerhard asked.

"We'll have to see," Maggie told him.

"Are you sure you're up to it?" Georg asked Maggie.

"Oh, yes. "I'm fine, really. Han's going to carry Elsa through the forest and I'll take her from there. We'll be fine."

"When are we leaving?" Stefan asked.

"As soon as we get things cleaned up," Abbi told him. "So let's get busy. And we'll try to make ourselves look as presentable as possible."

"Come on, everybody," Erich said impatiently. "Let's go."

"Uncle Erich is in a hurry," Stefan said to Hannah.

"I know," she replied, "he just wants to see Kathe."

"You're too smart for your own good," Erich said, and he hurried them along to do their tasks.

"You know," Abbi said to Cameron as they moved into the kitchen, "we'll be getting back in time for the Day of Horst."

"Really? How appropriate." He smiled. "We could use a celebration."

"Yes, we didn't properly celebrate our wedding anniversary. Can you believe it? We've been married . . ." she paused to think.

"Thirty-two years," Georg provided on his way out the door.

"And I suppose we'll be having another wedding within a week or so," Cameron added.

"Did I hear that correctly?" Erich called from the other room.

Cameron peered around the corner. "As soon as you get that dungeon of yours cleaned out, I think we'd best get you married. Otherwise we may have a scandal on our hands."

Erich only grinned with a trace of guilt and went back to work.

"We must let Sonia know as soon as we get back so that she can be here in plenty of time."

"We will," Cameron said, and with no warning, he pulled Abbi into his arms and gave her a hungry kiss.

She laughed. "What was that for?"

"I can't wait to get home," he whispered, "to that ridiculously huge bedroom of ours that we don't have to share with anybody."

While Cameron and Georg were busy loading the pack horses, Abbi sought out Han in the stable.

"Hello, Mother," he said. She smiled and put her arms around him with a forceful hug. "What was that for?" he chuckled.

"Today, Han," she said with tears brimming in her eyes, "you wore the crown."

Han's expression sobered. "Do you think that's all it meant? Do you think it's over?"

"No one can ever tell what struggles might lie ahead, Han. But we have triumphed this time, and we must make the most of the life ahead of us—whatever it may bring." She hugged him again. "I just wanted you to know that I'm proud of you, Han."

Abbi turned and walked away. Han took a deep breath and tried to comprehend the reality of all that had happened. A minute later, Erich came into the stable. Without a word spoken, they exchanged a firm embrace and shook forearms. What they shared was no small thing, and Han was grateful for whatever the future might hold for them—all of them.

The market square in the center of Horstberg was full of bustling people, just as it was every Wednesday when citizens came to buy and sell their wares. There was an extra excitement in the air as people chattered and speculated over the miraculous happenings of the past week, and it was a general consensus that the people were grateful Nikolaus Koenig had failed.

A murmur of excitement rushed through the crowds as someone spotted the little procession approaching town. Cheers and applause greeted the royal family as they rode through the cobbled streets and into the square. Cameron du Woernig led the procession with all the dignity he was known for, with the duchess close by one side and Georg Heinrich on the other. His children and grandchildren followed, and it was quickly evident from the baby Princess Maggie carried that there was a new addition to the family.

Erich scanned the crowds desperately with his eyes, searching for that familiar face he had missed so much. Not far into the square, he heard his name rise above the din and turned abruptly.

"Erich!" Kathe called, fighting her way through the crowd. "Erich! I'm here." Tears pressed into her eyes when he saw her, and she couldn't get to him fast enough.

Erich slid abruptly down from his horse and moved through the crowd toward her. He'd never wanted anything as bad as he wanted to hold her right now.

"Kathe!" he cried as she came into his arms, and the crowd around them cheered and laughed with delight.

"Oh, Erich," she whispered, touching his hair, his face. "You're safe. I missed you so badly."

"You're so beautiful," he replied. "It's so good to be home."

Cameron glanced back to see the reunion and figured this was as good a time as any to stop. He held up his hand, and the horses halted in unison. The crowd quieted down as people realized the duke had something to say. It became unusually quiet in the market square, and Cameron was struck with an embarrassing reality.

Abbi glanced toward him in question when he started to chuckle, and he leaned toward Georg and whispered, "You forgot to write me a speech, Georg."

Georg only grinned and shrugged his shoulders while the silence continued.

"Well," Cameron said loudly, "we're back!" The crowd roared with approval before quieting again. Cameron laughed and added, "Are you glad to see us?"

Abbi gave a pleasant smile of embarrassment, but the crowd didn't seem to mind the informality. They cheered as if he'd given the speech of a lifetime.

"We're certainly glad to be here," Cameron said when they quieted again. Feeling an onslaught of emotion, the Duke of Horstberg bowed his head slightly, and then he squared his shoulders and lifted his chin. "God bless us all."

The cheers resumed. Cameron stirred his horse forward, and the rest followed. Erich helped Kathe mount and got into the saddle behind her. As a family united, they rode toward Castle Horstberg.

Epilogue

Castle Horstberg was found in near perfect condition with few signs of the ordeal remaining. The surprise came when Captain Dukerk reported that Nikolaus Koenig was not dead. His encounter with the spiked pit had left him paralyzed from the waist down. But much to Nik's dismay, the doctor claimed he was likely to live for years, though he would have to face a trial for his treasonous actions and the outcome remained to be seen.

In the meantime, the du Woernigs were his only remaining relatives. After much thought and talking it over with his family, Cameron gave Nik exactly what he'd wanted all along—his father's room. With a strict nurse, a homely maid, and a stack of good books, the duke told him to mind his manners or he'd have watered-down soup for the rest of his life—though the duke believed he would likely be executed for treason, and they would all be out of their misery.

Soon after the family's return, Theodor brought Karl to the castle, and they presented Prince Stefan with two puppies from the same litter that Lucky had come from. Stefan immediately loved them, and with his grandfather's permission, he named them Duke and Duchess.

The Day of Horst celebration of 1849 was said to be the best anyone living had ever seen. The royal family was there in full, and a date was announced for Prince Erich to be married the following week. On that day, the duke did have a speech prepared, and in it he proclaimed that after seeing the peace and prosperity of his country, and the love and happiness evident in his own family, he knew that Horstberg had surely fulfilled its greatest quest.

Ⓔlizabeth D. Michaels began writing at the age of sixteen, immersing herself ever since in the lives created by her vivid imagination. Beyond her devotion to family and friends, writing has been her passion for nearly three decades. While she has more than fifty published novels under the name Anita Stansfield and is the recipient of many awards, she boldly declares *The Horstberg Saga* as the story she was born to write, with many volumes in the works. She is best known for her keen ability to explore the psychological depths of human nature, bringing her characters to life through the timeless struggles they face in the midst of exquisite dramas. *Through Castle Windows*, Volume Five of *The Horstberg Saga*, will be released May 4, 2015. For more information, please visit Elizabeth's author page on WhiteStarPress.com.